Praise for the Sabrina Vaughn Novels

Promises to Keep

"Edge-of-the-seat plotting will keep readers' attention late into the night."
—*Library Journal*

"Reads like the transcript of a breathlessly bloody computer game."
—*Publishers Weekly*

"Maegan Beaumont's third novel in the impeccable Sabrina Vaughn series delights the reader with more intricately developed plots, higher stakes, and unlikely criminals that astonish by executing twist after unforeseen twist."
—*Crimespree Magazine*

Carved in Darkness

Named a Best Debut of 2013 by *Suspense Magazine*

★ "Prepare to be overwhelmed by the tension and moodiness that permeates this edgy thriller. Beaumont's ability to keep the twists coming even when the answer seems obvious is quite potent."
—*Library Journal* (starred review)
and Debut of the Month

"Pulse-pounding terror, graphic violence, and a loathsome killer."
—*Kirkus Reviews*

"Beaumont knows how to keep you on the edge of your seat … Buckle up for the ride of a lifetime."
—*Suspense Magazine*

"Maegan Beaumont might be new to the thriller scene, but her debut thriller, *Carved in Darkness*, promises to be the first in a long line of novels. Be warned, however, this novel isn't for those who jump a mile every time they hear something go bump in the night. But for anyone who's ever dreamed about enacting a just revenge, this book is for you. Beaumont knows how to cook up and serve a dish called revenge, but she doesn't serve it cold. She serves it sizzling hot."

—Vincent Zandri, bestselling author of
The Remains and *Murder by Moonlight*

BLOOD

OF

SAINTS

A SABRINA VAUGHN NOVEL

MAEGAN
BEAUMONT

MIDNIGHT INK
WOODBURY, MINNESOTA

FIRST EDITION
First Printing, 2016

Cover design: Kevin R. Brown
Cover images: iStockphoto.com/71269937/©tobiasjo
        iStockphoto.com/23850124/©Daniel Barnes
        iStockphoto.com/2259285/©littleclie
Editing: Nicole Nugent

Midnight Ink, an imprint of Llewellyn Worldwide Ltd.

Library of Congress Cataloging-in-Publication Data
Names: Beaumont, Maegan, author.
Title: Blood of saints / Maegan Beaumont.
Description: First edition. | Woodbury, Minnesota : Midnight Ink, [2016] |
   Series: A Sabrina Vaughn novel ; 4
Identifiers: LCCN 2016008359 | ISBN 9780738748047 (softcover)
Subjects: LCSH: Policewomen—Fiction. | Murder—Investigation—Fiction. |
   GSAFD: Mystery fiction.
Classification: LCC PS3602.E2635 B58 2016 | DDC 813/.6—dc23 LC record
available at http://lccn.loc.gov/2016008359

Midnight Ink
Llewellyn Worldwide Ltd.
2143 Wooddale Drive
Woodbury, MN 55125-2989
www.midnightinkbooks.com

Printed in the United States of America

For my "other" Aunt Judy and
a magical place called Dos Cuervos.
Thanks for saving my bacon.

*"And in her was found the blood of prophets,
and of saints, and of all that were slain upon the earth."*
—Revelation 18:24

ONE

Yuma, Arizona
December 22, 1998

A MIRACLE.

The girl had been dead and then … she wasn't. It was a miracle. That was the only explanation for what he'd witnessed. A resurrection worthy of Christ Jesus himself.

Nulo watched, mesmerized, as her chest rose and fell in an uneven rhythm, exposed to the biting cold of the desert air. Quickening and stalling so those hovering about her became certain each breath she took would be her last. She'd been badly beaten. Her pale skin was awash with cuts and bruises, but beneath the damage he could see she was beautiful. So perfectly beautiful he found it impossible to look away from her. Looking at her bare breasts, his gaze trailed down her torso and a flush crept up his neck.

Father Francisco said something, a whispered plea offered up to Saint Rose, the patron saint to which they prayed. "*¿Qué clase de monstruo haría esto?*" He looked up, fixing his panicked gaze on the small knot of early-morning worshipers gathered around him as he knelt over the girl on the bench. "Call 911. She needs help—*rápidamente.*" The last of his words punctuated the thick air around them, a staccato jab meant to prod them into action. The young man nearest the priest managed to break the spell cast by the taboo before them, turning on his heel to run for the gate that guarded the entrance to the small prayer garden in which they stood. There was no phone inside the church—it didn't even have electricity. From the corner of his eye, Nulo could see the flapping white robe as it disappeared around the building, off to find help.

"Nulo, you found her?" The priest's dark eyes found him in the crowd, the voice seizing hold of him, jerking his head to the top of his neck.

Nulo nodded, keeping his gaze averted, the pulsing at his temple keeping time with his hammering heart. "Y-yes, Father. As soon as—as soon as I saw her...I-I came for you," he stammered out.

It had been early. So early, the coyotes still roamed the fields that surrounded the church, unchecked. The moon low and fat in the sky, the stars just beginning to fade. Officially, no one was allowed to sleep in the sanctuary, but Father Francisco was newly appointed and still soft to the poverty of his congregation. At ten o'clock the night before, he'd wandered around the small church, extinguishing lanterns and candles, completely ignoring the dark figures hunkered down on hard wooden pews. It was December and the desert's temperature often dipped below freezing. They had come in from the fields seeking warmth, and though the dark church had little to offer, it was better than sleeping outside.

The young priest had walked up the center aisle, stopping next to the pew he was curled up on. "Nulo..." He said his name quietly, not wanting to wake the others. "If I you don't see me by sunrise, come wake me."

"Yes, Father," he said, matching Father Francisco's hushed tone. "Goodnight ... and thank you."

"There is no need to thank me." The priest's face turned toward the back of the church, his gaze trained elsewhere. "I just wish there was something more I could do for you."

Nulo looked in the same direction to see a silhouette sitting in the dark a few rows back. His gut clenched. Perhaps it was his *tío*, waiting for Father to go to bed so he could drag Nulo back home. There would be a beating, its severity dependent on how much money his uncle been able to drink away. If he was very drunk, there would be more than just a beating ...

Father Francisco turned again to offer him a small smile. "You're a good boy, Nulo. Jesus loves you very much."

The priest's words jerked his attention back to his face. *Jesus loves you very much.* He didn't believe that. But he didn't want to make Father Francisco angry, so he didn't say anything in return.

After a few seconds, the priest gave him a final nod. "Sleep well, my son," he whispered before retreating.

Nulo listened to his footsteps, starting to drift even as they faded into the priest's small room behind the church's altar. As soon as he was gone, Nulo turned back in the direction he'd been looking, but the figure was no longer watching him. No longer waiting.

It was gone.

———

He didn't know what roused him. Maybe the soft creak of the garden gate. Maybe the shuffling of shoes treading through dirt. Whatever it was, he sat up, his breath escaping into the frigid sanctuary in visible huffs.

Someone was outside.

He moved with practiced stealth to the window of the church, stopping just short of the glass, staying in the shadows so he could look out without detection. One look told him hiding wouldn't be necessary; the man in front of him was nothing to worry about. He was young. White and clean. Good-looking. He'd seen him before.

The girl he carried was more than good-looking—she was as beautiful as an angel. She was also very much dead.

He could tell by the way her head flopped on the young man's shoulder. The way her arm dangled, soft and loose. Instead of fear, he felt a sort of fascinated anticipation as he watched the man kneel down to deposit her on the bench under a tree. He touched her face, his own drawn tight with emotions. Regret and pride. Lust and fear. He knew without being told that whatever had happened to the girl, the man who knelt beside her had been the one to do it.

He watched as the man drew something from the front pocket of his pants—something small and silver. He passed it over the girl's face, close to her eyes, before setting it aside. The man hovered there, looking at her when the blanket slipped down, exposing the girl's chest and stomach. He could see what had been done, even from inside the dark church. He could see it and it didn't frighten or disgust him. Not even a little bit.

The man reached out, cupping her breast while the other strayed to the front of his pants to caress himself. He looked as if he were teetering on the edge of something. Then his shoulders straightened, the hand at his crotch going still. No longer fondling her, the man pressed his gloved hand to the girl's chest and watched her as if he expected her to sit up and speak. He stared at her, rigid and unmoving, hand pressed to the young woman's breast until the low howl of a coyote cut through the night. Without warning, the man stood and, casting one last look at the girl, he left.

He waited. Counted to one hundred in both Spanish and English before he moved. He was not afraid of the man who left the girl, but something told him he would not be happy if he knew someone had seen him.

As soon as he was sure the man was gone, he exited the church, careful to ease the door shut just enough to stop the draft from entering the sanctuary and waking the others but not enough to lock himself out. Approaching the bench, he felt the sudden rush of fervor. The closer he drew, the heavier the sensation grew, until it was as if he were kneeling before Saint Rose herself.

As soon as he was close enough, he reached out to her, trailing his fingers along her opened palm. His hands were like ice but compared to hers, they felt as if they were on fire and he wondered at it for a moment—how cold she was. How purely empty. Her lids were held at half-mast, one slightly higher than the other. The eyes behind them were flat. Dull. Blood smeared across the delicate skin beneath them like tears. His gaze fell from her face to her breasts and he imagined touching them as the man had. How they would feel in his hands.

Suddenly, the lax palm beneath his jerked—fingers wrapping around his with a speed and strength that surprised him. A smile he didn't even know he wore was wiped from his face. The girl's eyes flew open, skewering him with a gaze so blue, so piercing—so *alive*—that for a moment he was certain she could see into the heart of him. That she knew what he had been thinking. What he'd been wanting.

"Nulo."

Father Francisco's voice was pinched, almost frantic. Nulo knew he shouldn't stare. That he was making the priest uncomfortable, but he couldn't stop himself. A grotesque collection of stab wounds littered the woman's stomach. They'd been grouped together—a warning to every other man who would ever look at her.

MINE

"*Nulo*," Father Francisco tried again. His voice reached out and rattled him from his stupor.

"Yes, Father?" a warm flush crept across his neck again, shame curling in his belly. He was looking and he shouldn't be.

"Was there anyone with her?" Father Francisco said. "Did you see who left her?"

"No, Father." He shook his head and looked away. It wasn't strictly true, but much better to tell a lie than the truth of what he saw. "When I found her, she was alone."

"Good," the priest said, sounding relieved. Nulo suddenly understood. Father Francisco was afraid one of them had done this. That one of his congregants had committed murder and left their victim on holy ground.

"Go wait with Manuel for the ambulance to arrive," Father Francisco said. "When it gets here, bring them around back, not through the church. Tell them to *hurry*."

Nulo turned away, starting to move even before the priest had finished speaking. Under normal circumstances, it would be considered a sign of disrespect, one he'd be admonished for, but no one noticed. There was nothing normal about this morning.

Sirens screeched in the distance, closer and closer with each re-volving wail. Help was coming. The girl would live. She would be taken to the hospital, healed by doctors. And they would confirm what he and the others at Saint Rose already knew.

She was a miracle.

TWO

THE McMILLAN TAC-50 FIT snuggly into the joint of her shoulder and she settled it in, leaning into the stock just enough to secure it. Michael had modified the assault rifle last week, shaving a few centimeters off to accommodate her slightly shorter arms. Thinking about it made her smile. It was the little things in their relationship that kept the romance alive.

Beside her, Avasa whined softly. "Shhh," she breathed, touching her cheek to the brace. The dog beside her went quiet, dropping her muzzle on top of her outstretched paws.

Her spotter lowered the field scope and looked at her, doubt plastered all over her face. "Are you sure about this?" she said, her voice thick with apprehension, giving the dog lying between them a commiserating look. "I mean ... is it *really* necessary?"

Sabrina took her eye from the scope and rolled from her belly to her side, lifting herself from where she'd been lying flat in the grass. The TAC stayed where it was, supported by the tripod that secured it.

"Christina, we've been over this," she said quietly, looking at the girl who lay in the grass, a few feet away. "This is *completely* necessary, and you know it. Remember what happened last winter? How much trouble he caused?"

It'd been their first winter here and while they'd made out okay, it could have been a lot worse if they hadn't been so well stocked.

The girl's shoulders slumped beneath the pale yellow T-shirt she wore, but she nodded. "Yes, I remember," she said, repositioning the field scope to her face. "It just makes me sad is all."

You and me both.

Refitting the TAC-50's stock into the groove of her shoulder, it took Sabrina a second to gain her bearings inside the scope. But then the terrain popped into focus in front of her and she found her target. A quarter mile away was a gray wolf—male, by the size of him—loping along the riverbank that snaked its way through the middle of the canyon they called home. This was the only spot in the river slow and shallow enough to make an easy crossing on foot. The only way to get at the cattle they relied on for food. The wolf stopped, dipping its head toward the water before stepping a tentative foot forward, into the river. "Do you trust me?" she said, resting her finger against the TAC's trigger.

"Yes," Christina said, sounding more resigned than trusting.

She didn't answer. Didn't try to reassure the girl. She just crooked her finger. The rifle rocked backward, gently nudging her shoulder like it was saying hi. Its high-powered report ricocheted around the canyon.

Almost as soon as she took the shot, the bullet found its mark fifteen hundred yards away, slamming into the water mere inches from where the wolf stood. Water rocketed upward into the wolf's face, startling him. He leapt back, front paws wet and in the air. He landed, sidestepping away from the riverbank even as he scanned the horizon for another assault.

Sabrina slid the bolt back on the TAC-50 to reload even as she prayed the wolf would take the hint. The cattle grazing on the other side of the river were off-limits.

Determined, he took a testing step toward the river, followed by another. She pulled the trigger again, this time delivering the bullet into the river's bank. A small explosion of dirt and rock rained down on the wolf and he jack-knifed, falling backward before rolling to find his feet and make good use of them. She slid the bolt back again, watching while the animal took off—unharmed—for safer territory. She didn't look away until all she could see through the scope was a bushy gray tail, flagging in the distance.

She rolled into a sitting position, taking the rifle with her. Christina was already up, sitting cross-legged in the grass across from her. "Thank you," she said, her small hand stroking over Avasa's flank, her face turned downward so Sabrina felt rather than heard the catch in her voice.

"For what?" she said, her tone casual as she laid the TAC across her lap to disengage the bolt. The .50-caliber bullet popped out and she caught it—something Michael had recently taught her how to do.

"You know what." Now the girl sounded irritated, not with her but with herself. Avasa chuffed softly at the sound. "It's childish of me," Christina said, looking up to fix wide brown eyes on her. "They kill our cattle—they'd run rampant if you and Michael let them."

"That's why we don't let them," she said evenly, scanning the canyon. *Their* canyon. Just under five hundred acres, surrounded on all sides by towering cliffs. They were slung low in the valley, dug in deep. The only way in or out was a narrow mountain trail, barely wide enough to squeeze a truck through. They were isolated. Alone. Completely cut off from anything even remotely resembling civilization. No phones. No Internet. Electricity provided by the sun and wind. Water fed to their house through a well. This was a different kind of life. One they were all still trying to get used to.

Sabrina detached the scope from the top of the TAC-50 and stored it in the weapon's case. "Michael and I will do whatever we need to make sure you're safe and taken care of, even if it means scaring the wits out of some poor wolf."

The girl smiled as she'd intended but the glint of it didn't reach her eyes. Thirteen years old, but her eyes often seemed much older. "I've seen killing before. I don't know why it should bother me so much."

Sabrina folded the legs of the tripod and secured it in its soft case before zipping it up. She stood, pocketing the bullet. Avasa followed suit, pressing her head into her knee, eager to head home. "I think we've all had our fill of death, Christina," she said, slinging the rifle's case onto her shoulder. She smiled down at the girl and held out her hand. "Come on; let's go see what the boys made for lunch."

─────

Lunch was grilled cheese and homemade tomato soup. Sabrina could smell the melted butter and rich tang of tomatoes and cream before they hit the porch steps. Christina shot her a grin, shoving the field scope into her hands before hustling up the stairs, Avasa hot on her heels. Grilled cheese was her latest favorite.

Catching the back door before it banged closed, Sabrina pushed her way through the doorway, stopping to kick the mud off her boots before entering the kitchen. There she found Michael standing over the stove, bare-footed, spatula in hand, tending a large cast iron skillet full of grilled bread and melting cheese. Avasa sat in front of him, waiting patiently. Christina was nowhere to be seen.

"Where'd she go?" she said, unslinging the TAC-50 from her shoulder and propping it against the wall.

"I sent her to wash up," he said without glancing up from the stove. From the corner of her eye, she watched him casually drop one of the finished sandwiches to the floor. It never made it. Avasa caught it, mid-fall, nearly swallowing it whole. She licked her chops and lifted a paw for more.

"I saw that," she said, face turned away so he couldn't see the smile on her face.

"No, you didn't," Michael said, tossing the dog another grilled cheese. "Hungry?"

"Starved." She reached into her shirt and pulled out the brass key she kept there on a chain. "Alex?" she said, fitting the key into an antique larder. She opened its door. Inside were enough weapons and ammo to take over a small country.

"Sent him too," Michael said, distracted. She looked over her shoulder, watching him flip the grilled cheese with the same delicate precision she suspected he'd use to defuse an IED. Avasa, knowing a third sandwich would be pushing it, found her bed near the fireplace to work on the beef bone she kept there. "He spent his morning in the woods—again. Walked off at eight, didn't see him again until about twenty minutes ago."

She put the TAC inside the cabinet and locked it back up before glancing at the clock. It was half past noon. "What do you think he's doing? Is it safe for him to be out there alone? He's only eleven."

"I wouldn't let him go if I thought he might hurt himself." Michael slid his spatula under the sandwich and lifted it from the skillet to deposit it on a platter with the dozen others he'd made. "I don't know what he's doing … but whatever it is, he doesn't want anyone to know about it."

Just then, Christina burst into the kitchen, Alex not far behind. He'd gained weight and color over the months. He looked healthy. Strong. Like a completely different kid than the one she'd found naked, cowering in the basement of an abandoned house—as long as you didn't look him in the eye. On the few occasions he'd allowed it, Sabrina could still see him, trapped in the dark. Sometimes it scared her. Mostly it just made her sad.

"Can Alex and I have a picnic?" Christina said, hopping from one foot to the other, a ball of pent-up excitement.

"Got your watch on?" Michael said, glancing over his shoulder to see her flash the fat black band and digital face at him. It was an unnecessary question. She never took it off. None of them did. Michael looked at her, his head tilted at a questioning angle.

She shrugged. "I don't see why not, do you?"

He shook his head. "Okay, just—"

Christina reached past him with an excited squeal, grabbing at the platter of grilled cheese. "Come on," she said to Alex around the sandwich in her mouth as she ran out the door with several others in her hands. Alex followed her, head down, hands stuffed into the pockets of his jeans. Avasa watched them go, floppy ears pricked forward in interest.

Sabrina caught the door before it banged closed. "*Beschermen,*" she said. The dog abandoned her bone and trotted out behind them to do her job. Protect.

"—be careful," Michael finished, lifting the platter off the counter and carrying it to the table while she went to the kitchen sink to wash up. "I made twelve sandwiches; she left us six."

"Hmm…" Sabrina said, not really paying attention. Through the window she watched Christina and Alex disappear into the woods, Avasa close behind. "Correction: whatever he's doing in the woods, he doesn't want *us* to know about it."

Behind her, Michael laughed. "He's not a Soviet sleeper agent, Sabrina. He's an orphan—just like the rest of us…" She heard him move in a moment before she felt the slide of well-muscled arms around her waist, bumping against the SIG strapped to her hip. "Besides, haven't you seen the way he looks at her?" he said close to her ear, the slight brush of his lips on her lobe enough to loosen the hinges in her knees.

She smiled, turning in his arms until she faced him. "How's that?" she said, lifting her hands to his hair. Standing on the toes of her boots she kissed him on the mouth, loving how it curved into an easy smile beneath her lips.

"Like he adores her." He nuzzled her neck, his hands gripped around her hips. "Like he'd do anything for her." Michael lifted her up, setting her down on the counter's edge, hands hooked into the crooks of her knees to pull her closer. "I suspect it's the same way I look at you," he whispered against her throat, fitting his hips into the cradle of her thighs.

Tilting her head back to give his mouth better access to her neck, Sabrina sighed. "Tell me more of this adoration you speak of," she said, locking her ankles around his waist, her arms around his neck. "How many grilled cheese sandwiches will it win me?"

He laughed, the breath of it skating across her collarbone. "Is that all you want me for?" Somehow, he'd worked the first five buttons of her shirt loose. "My grilled cheese?" His fingers skimmed along the cup of her bra, tangling her breath around her tongue.

"No …" She tightened the lock of her ankles around waist, pulling him even closer. "That would be unfair to your pancakes." She grinned against his mouth. "You make fantastic pancakes," she said and he laughed with her. She'd never get tired of it. The way they fit together. Perfectly …

She didn't hear it at first. She was too wrapped up in the words being whispered in her ear. His hands against her skin … but when his lips and hands went still, she caught the sound of it and by the way Michael suddenly fell silent, he heard it too.

A low-toned beep at three second intervals. She opened her eyes to see the strobes set above each doorway flashing in time with the beep. "Michael …"

He lifted his head from her neck and looked at her, his face set in grim angles. Tight and resigned. The man she loved was suddenly gone, the ruthless killer he usually kept locked away taking his place in the space of a breath.

"Get the kids back here." He stepped away from her and turned, lunch and everything in between forgotten. "We have approximately fifteen minutes to get you secured downstairs."

She slid off the counter, her boots hitting the floorboards so hard they rattled beneath her feet. Her shirt was open and she fumbled it closed, suddenly self-conscious.

"*Michael—*"

He barely spared her a glance as he moved across the room, reaching into the neck of the thermal shirt he wore to pull out his own brass key.

"No arguments, Sabrina. We don't have time—get them back here *now*." He punctuated the last of his words by jamming his key into the lock that secured the weapons cabinet. He reached in and pulled out his own TAC-50 before stacking boxes of ammo on the kitchen table next to the forgotten plate of sandwiches he'd made for lunch.

"Okay," she said, using the word to propel herself forward. "Okay ..." She nodded as she streaked across the kitchen, her steps so fast and heavy they rattled the dishes in the sink.

The alarm. The strobes. They were security measures. Meant to warn them. In the months the four so-called orphans been here, they'd never gone off. Not once. Three hundred fifty days of silence, suddenly shattered.

Someone was coming.

THREE

Sabrina stepped out onto the porch and looked at her watch. It was ten minutes to one o'clock. By 1:05, their canyon would be crawling with only God knew what. Pressing the blue button on the top of her watch, she watched the thick stand of trees to her left for movement.

They'd done so many drills. When they'd first gotten here, it was once a day. They'd let the kids scatter, encouraging them to go explore their new home only to sound the alarm and time how long it took them to make it back, each time pushing them to move faster and faster. They set a perimeter—an invisible barrier deciding how far they could wander from the house. The quicker they were, the farther they could go. As soon as Alex and Christina could cover a half mile in under five minutes, the drills were cut down to once a week.

Nearly a year later, with nothing but peace and solitude in between, the drills had tapered off into an occasional happening. Never more than once a month. They'd had their obligatory drill two days ago.

Christina burst through the trees with Alex in tow. She didn't look alarmed. She looked annoyed. That changed as soon as their eyes met across the yard. Reaching behind her, she said something to Alex and doubled her pace, pulling him along. Behind them both was Avasa, alert and focused on the pair in front of her.

The children stopped on the steps directly below, tapping the red buttons on the side of their watches to stop the vibrations they emitted. It'd taken them less than two minutes to respond.

"Inside," Sabrina said, and they moved without asking questions. Sabrina followed them through the door to find Michael had emptied nearly the entire contents of the weapons cabinet onto the kitchen table. The plate of grilled cheese lay broken on the floor, cold sandwiches scattered across the bare wood. Avasa didn't even look at them.

"If I'm not down in thirty minutes, close it up without me," he said, holding her TAC-50 in one hand and a stack of ammo boxes in the other. The alarm was still sounding, the strobes still flashing. "*Sabrina.*" His voice whipped out and grabbed her, shook her. She didn't answer—she just took the rifle and ammo he held out to her without looking him in the eye.

Sabrina slung the strap of the rifle over her shoulder. "Let's go," she said, moving across the room and through the doorway that led to the rest of the house, Christina and Alex following while Avasa stayed behind.

"You didn't say good-bye."

She kept moving. "What?" she said, crossing the living room toward the bedroom she shared with Michael.

"To him," Christina said, her tone crowded with panic. "To Michael—you didn't say good-bye."

18

She skirted the bed they shared, refusing to even look at it as she moved toward the closet. She pushed the door wide and ushered them in. It was the kind of closet most women dreamed about. One hundred fifty square feet of shelves, racks, and drawers, all stuffed with clothes and shoes she'd never wear. In its center was a storage island. Feeling along the wooden lip of the waist-high countertop, Sabrina dragged her fingertips until she hit a knot in the wood. She pushed it and the flat top popped open to reveal a motorized lift. "Let's go, we're out of time," she said, shooting a hurried glance at Christina. As if on cue, steel security barriers began to lower over the windows. They were connected—once the lift was activated, the barriers were deployed, leaving only a few vantage points unsecured. Soon the house would be on complete lockdown.

"*Christina.*"

The girl stuck her chin out, pretending the metallic screech of those barriers and what they meant didn't scare her. "You didn't say—"

"Because I'm not leaving him." She swiped a hand over her face. "I won't ... do you understand?" No time—there was no time left. "I can't. Now, *please*—"

The girl threw her leg over the side of the lift and boosted herself into its center before holding her hand out to Alex. "What do I do?"

Relief flooded her system. Fifty feet below was a fifteen-hundred-square-foot bomb-proof bunker equipped with enough water and supplies to carry eight people through nearly three months of hiding. "Do exactly what I showed you. As soon as the lift stops, get into the bunker and shut the door. Set the timer for thirty minutes—if Michael or I don't come back for you, it'll activate on its own." Without her or Michael to enter the deactivation code, it wouldn't open for six weeks, no matter what. "If the lift is activated by anyone but us before the door is secured, hit the green button on the right. It'll override the timer."

The lift began its descent, startling the girl in front of her. "I'm scared," she said, her dark eyes yanked wide, making her look years younger than she actually was. She clung to Alex, who stood beside her. Sabrina caught his gaze and he let her hold it, like he was showing her something. He didn't look scared or empty. He looked determined.

"Don't be," she said, peering over the side of the lift to watch as they disappeared down the shaft. "Michael and I won't let anything happen to either of you. I promise."

———

As soon as the lift hit the bottom, she lowered the lid to the storage island and set the lock before laying the TAC-50 across it. Tearing open the boxes of ammo Michael had handed her, she dumped them into her cargo pockets before heading back the way she'd come. Stopping in the doorway, she found Michael standing at the back door—feet still bare, his own TAC-50 positioned against his shoulder, its barrel aimed out the room's only unprotected window, toward the canyon's only road.

"Goddamn it, Sabrina." He said it without turning to look at her. His tone told her exactly how angry he was and that he was totally unsurprised she'd deviated from the plan he'd formulated months ago.

"I love you too," she said, watching his shoulders slump slightly at her answer. She couldn't help but smile a bit as she moved across the kitchen to stand beside him. "Any movement?"

He didn't answer so she pulled the rifle off her back and pressed it against her own shoulder before fitting her eye against the scope. In the distance she saw a truck, its dull green hood barely clearing the narrow canyon pass. It crawled along the dirt path leading to their house.

"Whoever it is, if they're here to kill us, they're sure takin' their sweet Jesus time about it," she said, lowering the rifle to wedge the stock under her arm. She popped the magazine from the bottom of the rifle. "Could be a diversion for an aerial assault," she said, reaching into her pocket for a handful of .50-cals and began feeding them into the magazine. "What do you think?"

"I think that if we live through this, I just might kill you," he said quietly, eye still pressed to the scope. "I think I love you so much it scares me." He finally looked at her, the gray of his eyes gone almost completely black with anger. "I think that if something happens to you, it'll probably be the end of me."

"Well, which is it?" She refit the magazine to the bottom of the rifle, clicking it in place. "Do you love me or want to kill me?"

"Both. Almost always, both." He shot her a smirk before refitting the scope to his eye. "Take high ground. If they decide to rappel in from the cliffs, pick off as many as you can before they hit the bottom of the canyon."

She leaned into him, kissing the hard line of his mouth. She pulled back, ready to go but he snagged onto her shirt and held her for a moment, looking her in the eye before letting her go. He opened his mouth to say something but she cut him off before he could get it out. She wasn't ready to say good-bye to him. She wasn't ready to hear it either.

"I want pancakes for dinner," she said, giving him a wink before turning to head upstairs to the loft.

"Wait."

When she looked back at him, his posture had changed, his spine less rigid. With a final glance through the scope, he dropped the TAC from his shoulder and reached for the door.

Her bravado left her, shoved aside by the kind of choking panic that could kill you if you let it. "Don't go—"

Her words fell on deaf ears as he stepped out onto the porch. She followed, moving to stand beside him just as the faded pickup truck rounded a bend in the river, crossing over a wood and stone bridge loaded with enough C-4 to punch a hole in the ground the size of Rhode Island. Instead of detonating the explosives, Michael let the truck pass over it.

Seeing them, the driver picked up speed. "Do you know who it is?" she said just as the driver of the truck pulled up less than ten yards from where they stood.

The driver's door popped open and a dusty boot stepped out, followed by two hands held aloft and a black cowboy hat. "I'm not armed," the driver said loudly, clearing the truck door to stand near the hood. "You remember me, boy?"

Beside her, Michael chuffed out a bark of laughter. "Kind of hard to forget you, Senator."

Senator. Sabrina looked hard at the man in front of her. Older, for sure, but almost unrecognizable behind the hat and sunglasses he wore. She'd only seen him on television but Michael had met him in person—the day he'd been asked to find and rescue the politician's grandson, Leo.

Senator Maddox laughed, "Playin' dead has a way of erasing a person's memory. Wasn't even sure I'd make it once I breached the pass."

Michael made a sound in the back of his throat, readjusting the rifle cradled in his arms. "Almost didn't," he said, shooting a hard look at the truck parked in front of their house. "Nice ride."

"She don't look like much but she gets the job done." Maddox slapped the pickup's dull green hood and grinned. "How'd the winter treat you?"

"We're still here," Michael said, his eyes scanning the cliffs that towered over them. "Speaking of *here*… what can I do for you, Senator?"

Maddox chuckled. "I forgot how much you love small talk," he said. "May I?" He tilted his hat toward the cab of his truck.

"Sure." Michael's tone was easy but between them she heard the distinct click of him flipping the safety off on the firearm he held.

The senator must've recognized how thin his welcome was being worn because he reached a slow hand into the cab of his truck, pulling out something bulky and black. A satellite phone. Wedged in between the phone and Maddox's fingers was a large manila envelope. Holding both out, he reached up with his free hand, peeling off his sunglasses to reveal a pair of dark eyes, razor sharp and aimed straight at her.

"Little lady, you have a phone call."

FOUR

"I still don't understand, Senator Maddox. Why would you drive over two hundred miles to play secretary? We've never even met." She could hear Michael in the kitchen, sweeping up the broken plate and smashed sandwiches off the floor. The kids were upstairs in the loft playing checkers. Avasa slept at her feet, relaxing in the afternoon sun. Everything was back to normal—and nothing would ever be the same again.

The satellite phone sat on the table between them, a living, breathing thing. Something that could hurt them. Something that could destroy everything they'd built over the last year. Beneath it was the folder, its flap secured shut by a bright red string wound around a circular tab. She didn't want to know what was inside. Sabrina refused to even look at it. Instead she focused on the old man on the other side of the table.

"First off, it's just Leon now. My civil servant days are behind me. I'm back to being what I was before I put on a suit and went to Washington." Maddox smiled at her, trying to reassure her everything was going to be okay. That his being here didn't mean everything had gone sideways.

"And what is that, exactly?" she said, allowing herself to be distracted from why he was here, even if it was for just a few moments.

"Cattle rancher, same as you," he said, his smile deepening into a grin. "Although, I'll admit, my operation is a tad bigger than yours." At less than five hundred head of cattle, she would hardly consider their motley household a ranch.

"So after nearly twenty years in the senate you just *quit*?" Sabrina could hear the skeptical edge in her tone but did nothing to temper it.

Maddox stopped grinning. "I've had my fill of politicking—left it to my son, not long after..." He didn't finish his sentence. He didn't have to. He'd announced his retirement the day after his grandson had been returned home, naming his son, Jon, as his successor to finish out his term. Retirement had been the easiest way to dodge the top-secret appointment he'd been about to receive. The one that would've had him heading a committee designated to decide how the country's $85 billion "black budget" would be spent. Which was the entire reason his grandson had been kidnapped in the first place.

Now he turned his gaze toward the yard, taking in the river. The towering cliffs in the distance. "As for why... well..." He looked at her again. "It took Leo a long time to talk about what happened. The kidnapping—he claims he doesn't remember much of it. Said he felt sleepy a lot."

She remembered dull green eyes watching her from across the dinner table. The way he plodded along beside the guard who moved him from room to room. "Reyes kept him drugged most of the time," she said quietly, not sure how the old man would react to information about how his grandson had been treated in captivity.

Maddox nodded, his mouth stretched thin and tight across his face. "Yeah. That's what I figured." He knocked his hat back on his head, lifting the shadow it cast across his eyes so she could see them when he looked at her. "One thing he remembers clear as day is you. You telling him you were there to rescue him. That you and your friend Michael would take him out of there." He swallowed hard, looking away from her. "And you did. The two of you saved him from …" He nodded once, a hard jerk of his neck, meant to rein in his emotions. "So, no—we've never met, Ms. Vaughn, but I know you." He smiled at her. "And after what you did for me and mine, the least I can do is play secretary."

Sabrina sat quietly for a moment, unsure of what to say. "Senator Maddox—"

He didn't let her finish. Obliviously, the subject of his grandson's abduction was closed. "You and that young man in there have made a nice home here. You deserve it—both of you. The last thing I want to do is disrupt that."

"Then why are you?" Her voice was small, edged in fear. From the corner of her eye she could see the thin red string. It blurred against the bright yellow of the envelope. The longer she looked, the more it looked like blood.

"He said you'd ask that." He chuckled softly. "He also said you'd want the opportunity to hear the facts and choose for yourself what happens next."

Ben. She didn't even have to ask. Benjamin Shaw was big on choices. The freedom to make them. A year ago he'd said as much to her before he'd told her she had to decide what she wanted more—her old life or a new one with Michael.

"I made my *choice*, sir." She pushed the words through clenched teeth. Ben had been smart to send the senator instead of coming himself. She'd been raised to respect her elders. If it'd been Ben sitting across from her, he'd have gotten a fat lip for his trouble. "I got on the plane that brought me here and I haven't looked back." Even as she said it, she knew it was a lie. She'd looked back plenty. Missed and longed for her old life. Her family.

In a perfect world, she would've been allowed to have both. She would have been able to find a way to be with Michael and still have Riley and Jason. Val and Nickels. Her old partner, Strickland. But the world wasn't perfect and she'd had to choose. She chose Michael and even though she missed them all, she'd never regretted her choice. Not ever.

"I'm here because I owe a debt. To both of you ... and to Benjamin," Maddox said, cocking his head toward the kitchen. The sweeping sounds had stopped but Michael was still in the kitchen. Probably listening. "By paying on one, I have a feeling I'm adding to another, but I agreed to deliver a *message*—not *you*. Once I've said my piece, I'll be on my way. What you do with this is up to you."

Sabrina finally let her gaze fall to the phone and the envelope, sitting on the table between them. "It won't work here, you know," she said. "Even if you could turn it on, which you *can't*, you wouldn't be able to get a signal. The canyon won't allow it."

"I know," Maddox sat back in his chair, watching her carefully. "I'm the one who suggested this place when Benjamin was looking for somewhere to stash the two of you." He looked around again, taking in the dull, dark gray of the canyon's walls. "This place seemed just as good as any"—his eyes sparkled with something that looked like mischief—"and better than most." The canyon walls were made almost entirely of iron, so densely packed with metals and minerals that drilling into them proved nearly impossible. They'd been abandoned over a century ago by miners for their impregnability. Sold to the government for pennies on the dollar and preserved as national forest under President Theodore Roosevelt. During the late nineties, a house had been built—one nearly as impregnable as the canyon that surrounded it—so that the president at the time, who'd fancied himself a frontiersman, could play homesteader in peace.

It was the Camp David no one knew about, abandoned as soon as the presidential frontiersman left office. Forgotten until Leon—who, as representative of the state that housed it, had been one of its only frequent visitors—remembered it and mentioned it and its unique properties to Ben.

Brokering the sale of a few hundred acres of inaccessible national forest on the US/Canadian border to an equally private buyer had hardly garnered notice. Requesting the sale of this land had been one of Leon Maddox's last acts as a US senator, and it'd gone off without a hitch.

"The message . . ." she said, her gaze drifting downward again. She let it settle on the envelope. "Is it about Val? Jason or Riley? Are they—" She couldn't even bring herself to think it, let alone say it.

The old man leaned across the table and took her hand. "Far as I know, everyone is okay." He gave it a squeeze. He understood where she was. He'd been there. Not knowing. Wondering if something you'd done or said had caused the hurt of someone you care for. He let go of her hand and sat back in his chair. "The message—he said it was for your ears only." Maddox raised his gaze to the back door that was cracked open behind her. The sound of the broom being dragged across the plank floor resumed.

A message from Ben. One that, for whatever reason, he didn't want Michael to hear. At least not right away.

"Well, Leon," she said as she stood, "let's take a walk by the river so you can give me this message and then you can be on your way. You've got a long drive home."

FIVE

Michael could hear them talking quietly on the porch, their voices barely above a whisper, but he didn't need to listen. He discerned everything he needed to know the moment he recognized Leon Maddox through that sun-beaten windshield.

Sabrina was leaving.

He'd known it would happen—that she'd leave him eventually. He'd known, even if she hadn't. He'd called them all orphans, but that was a lie. She had a family. People who loved and needed her. A life—a *real* life. One he never had a place in. One he couldn't compete with. He knew that. Understood it. Accepted it, even. But accepting it didn't make it any easier right at this moment.

He dragged the broom across the wood, carefully catching shards of glass and bits of congealed cheese sandwich in its bristles. He extended the handle, reaching underneath the converted larder to make sure he picked up everything he'd broke. Inside the cabinet, loose bullets rattled and rolled across its bottom. He'd have to reorganize it after the kids went to bed. He didn't like them to watch him handle guns unless it was absolutely necessary.

The creak of the porch steps brought his head up and he watched as Maddox and Sabrina stepped down into the yard, heading for the river. Most men would've fixed that step to stop its creaking by now, but not him. The back step leading to his home creaked on purpose. So he'd be able to hear someone approaching the back door. Someone who meant to kill them. It would give away their position so he could kill them first.

That's the kind of *life* he had to offer her.

He stooped, carefully sweeping the pile of debris on the floor into the waiting dustpan before dumping it in the trash. He stood there longer than he should've watching Sabrina and the old man stroll along the water. For a moment, he was able to convince himself the message he'd brought was a good one. That Val and her cop husband had had another baby. That Sabrina's old partner, Strickland, had gotten married. That her old Homicide captain, the one who hated her, had been hit by a bus.

"She's leaving us, isn't she?"

He turned to see Christina standing in the doorway. She looked the same way he felt. Powerless. Resigned.

He shrugged. "I don't know." He moved toward the pantry to store the broom and dustpan. "I hope not," he said, looking at her for a moment.

"You're lying." She cast her glance farther out the window to where Sabrina stood talking with Maddox near the hood of his truck.

"Have I ever lied to you?" he said, hanging the broom and dustpan from their respective hooks before closing the pantry door. Come to think of it, Christina was the only person in his life he *hadn't* lied to at some point or another.

31

"No," she said, her tone hard and quiet. "But there's a first time for everything."

"I promised you a long time ago that I would never lie to you. I don't plan on starting now." He closed the closet door and turned toward her. "How do you feel about pancakes for dinner?"

Instead of answering she rushed him, throwing her arms around his waist to bury her face in his shirt. "I don't want her to leave, Michael." She looked up at him, her chin digging into his sternum. "Don't let her."

He passed a hand over her dark hair and shook his head. She'd lost so much because of him. Her mother. Her father. And now this. Another loss he was powerless to stop.

He *wanted* to lie to her. Tell her he'd do as she asked. Make her believe he had the power to make Sabrina stay. Instead, he smoothed his palms over her shoulders, gripping them before setting her away.

"What if her family needs her?" he said, hunkering down to look her in the eye. It was his worst nightmare—that Sabrina's association with him could bring her family to harm. "Maybe her brother or her sister is in trouble. Maybe she's the only one who can help them."

"I don't care. She chose us." Christina set her jaw and glared up at him. "She doesn't get to take it back."

"I wish it were that easy ... but if we love her—*really* love her— then we should want her to do the right thing, even if that thing hurts us." He dropped his hands away from her shoulders and straightened his stance to look down at her. "That's who she is. She's the person who does the right thing, no matter what. It's one of the reasons we love her so much."

Behind him, he could hear the engine in Maddox's truck turn over and catch, rumbling to life under its worn hood. The porch step creaked a moment before the screen door wheezed on its hinges. "Go play with Alex," he said to Christina, his tone telling her there was no room for argument.

"I want chocolate chips in my pancakes," she said, a small act of defiance before she turned and stomped from the room, each footfall so heavy the dishes in the larder's matching hutch rattled with every step. Sabrina was a purist. She hated chocolate chips in her pancakes.

"I'm not going."

He turned to find Sabrina standing just inside the kitchen, her back pressed against the doorframe. The manila envelope was in her hand, unopened.

Behind her he could see Maddox's tailgate bumping across the bridge. He had the insane urge to blow it up. To kill the old man for what he'd done. For taking her away from him.

She took a step toward him, moving to the side so she could shut the door, blocking his view of the truck's retreat. Like she could read his mind. Like she could see murder on his face. She tossed the envelope onto the counter like it didn't matter.

"Did you hear me? I said I'm not—"

"Christina wants chocolate chips in her pancakes." He moved toward the refrigerator, pulling it open to retrieve eggs and butter. It was still too early to make dinner, but he needed to move. Needed to do something so he didn't grab her and lock her away to make her stay. "Any objections?"

Her mouth closed and she shook her head. "No. Chocolate chips are fine." She dug her hands into the front pockets of her cargos—a sure sign he was making her nervous. That she had more to say but was keeping it to herself because she knew he didn't want to hear it. Not yet anyway.

He watched her hands for a moment, the way they twisted in her pockets, before turning away from her. It's funny how people who love each other pick up one another's habits. He wondered how long it would take her to break his after she was gone.

SIX

As promised, Michael made pancakes for dinner.

The kids set the table, Christina plunking each plate down with a resounding *thud* while Alex followed her around the table with knives and forks. Neither of them would look at her. For Alex that was normal—he never looked at her—but Christina's unwillingness to acknowledge her spoke volumes. Somehow, she knew what was going on. Judging from her sullen glares and stubborn silence, Christina had already made up her mind Sabrina was leaving and she hated her for it.

Sabrina's gaze strayed from her plate, over Michael's shoulder to the manila envelope sitting on the counter by the back door. Maddox had handed it to her before he left. "I'm supposed to give these to you," he'd said grudgingly, slapping the thick packet into her hand. "For what it's worth, you and him"—he jerked his head toward the porch—"you earned the right to be selfish. You earned the right to want something for yourselves—a life, here, *together*."

She'd closed her hand around the envelope and pulled it from his grip. "Are you telling me not to open it?"

Sharp brown eyes peered at her from the shadow cast by the wide brim of his hat. "I'm telling you that if you took that envelope and tossed it into your fireplace the second I left," Maddox said before climbing into his truck and turning it over, "I'd be a happy man."

She hadn't tossed it in the fireplace. Hadn't opened it either. She had an idea of what was in it and didn't particularly want to see it, but she couldn't force herself to walk away from it either.

"May I be excused?"

Christina's stiff request—a throwback to her nightly formal dinners with her sociopathic, drug lord father—brought Sabrina back to the present. Michael nodded, wiping his mouth on his napkin, gaze locked onto her face. He knew her better than anyone. Sometimes it made her uncomfortable, the way he could read her. She dropped her gaze and focused on her pancakes.

"Yes," he said. Before she could even blink, Christina bolted, Alex on her heels. They finished their dinner in silence, Michael chewing each bite like he had a mouthful of nails. Her trying to find a way to convince him he was wrong. That she wasn't going anywhere. Finally finished, he lifted his plate from the table and carried it to the sink. He hadn't said a word to her the entire meal.

Sabrina stood, clearing the table of the remaining dishes and carrying them to the sink. She scraped them clean before filling the sink with hot water and adding soap. Washing dishes, she watched Michael in the reflection of the kitchen window as he reorganized the gun cabinet, stacking boxes of ammo and making sure each rifle and handgun was in its proper place as if their lives depended on it. From the living room, Alex's voice drifted in as he cautiously read *The Mouse and the Motorcycle* to Christina, his heavily accented words coming in stops and starts while she offered quiet words of encouragement.

"She's pretty amazing, isn't she?" she said, still watching Michael in the refection of the window. Behind her he stopped what he was doing for a moment and listened.

"She is," he answered quietly, his attention refocused on the task at hand.

"She must take after Lydia," she said. They'd never really talked about Christina's mother. What had happened to her. Sabrina knew Christina's father had killed her and that Michael blamed himself, but they'd never talked about *her*. The kind of person she was. How he'd felt about her.

"Not really," he said while he re-fit .50-caliber bullets into their carton. "Lydia was softer. Quicker to see and believe the best in people. Christina's been through too much to allow herself to be fooled." Carton filled, he stacked it on top of the others inside the larder and shut the door. In the black of the window, she saw him check his watch. "I'm going out to the barn."

It wasn't what he said—he went to the barn every night after dinner—it was his tone that bothered her. Removed. Controlled. Like her mind had already been made up. Like she was already gone.

Sabrina turned away from his reflection, toward him. "Michael—"

That was as far as she got before he passed through the door, pulling it shut behind him. She wanted to follow him. Force him to talk to her. To listen to her, make him believe her when she said she wasn't going to leave him.

Instead she finished the dishes, carefully washing each plate and fork before drying it and putting it away in the cupboard.

Next she wiped out the cast iron skillet with a paper towel before hanging it back on its hook above the stove.

In the living room, Alex finished reading and Christina praised him before asking if he wanted to watch a movie. It was their routine. Afterward, they'd go to bed and tomorrow, they'd do it all over again. The same, every day...

Sabrina looked at the envelope. Its tab and the string that wound it closed as red as blood. She'd been wiping the counter around it for a while now. Circling. Stalling.

Drying her hands on the seat of her cargos, she finally picked it up, carrying it to the table. She sat down, unwinding the string that closed it, and opened Pandora's Box.

SEVEN

THE BARN WASN'T REALLY a barn. Not anymore, anyway. Its fifteen hundred square feet had been converted into a multipurpose workspace long before they'd gotten here. Mechanic bays held the classic cars Michael had inherited from his father—the '71 Challenger and his dad's Roadster had been waiting for him when they'd arrived. Tinkering on them, even if he couldn't drive them, staved off the restlessness that crept in. He strode past the cars without sparing them a glance. Grabbing a tire iron as he went, he headed for the long workbench stretched along the back wall.

Right now, he wasn't thinking about spark plugs or oil changes. Right now he was thinking of one thing and one thing only.

Yanking the canvas drop cloth off the table, he stared at what was underneath. His fingers flexed around the hard length of metal in his hand, gripping it so tight he could feel the pull of it across his shoulders. He wanted to smash the thing, swing the iron into it again and again until it was nothing but a useless pile of plastic and wires.

Instead, he tossed the tire iron onto the table beside it and switched it on.

Like his cars, the ham radio had been here when they arrived. It was their contingency plan—his and Ben's. A low-tech way to communicate if things went bad. A way that wouldn't inadvertently trigger the microchip Ben's father had grafted to his spine and kill him.

Michael was to turn his radio on every night at seven o'clock sharp and leave it on for thirty minutes. That was the window—if there was a problem, Ben was supposed to use it to let him know. Warn him so he could get his family to safety in time. For a year, he'd tuned into the dedicated channel and listened to nothing but static.

Last week, everything changed.

"I'm sorry, man," Ben's voice reached through the speaker tonight, confirming Michael's suspicions: Maddox had been sent here by Benjamin Shaw.

"Only you would use a US Senator as an errand boy."

"I tried to do it the easy way but you ignored me ... and he's retired now."

A week ago, Ben's voice had come through the speaker of his radio: *Michael, I need to talk to Sabrina. It's important.* He'd listened for a few seconds, waiting for Ben to elaborate. To tell him what it was about. Why he needed to talk to her. When he didn't, Michael switched off the radio and went back into the house. He hadn't turned it on since.

"Retired or not, I almost killed him," he ground out. He could still see Maddox caught in the crosshairs of his scope. Feel the way his finger ached to squeeze the trigger when he realized who it was. What his being here meant.

"But you didn't—gold star for you," Ben said. "Playing house must suit you." Michael could tell from his tone he was only half joking. He was also right. Being here, filling his days with making grilled cheese sandwiches for dogs and rotating the tires on a car he hadn't driven in years had made him soft. A year ago, he would've pulled the trigger without a second thought.

"It was touch and go there for a minute."

"You wouldn't kill the messenger, Michael," Ben said, his tone confident. "It's not your style."

"Don't be so sure, kid. I've done a lot worse for a lot less."

"You haven't been that guy for a long time," Ben said, trying to convince himself he hadn't miscalculated.

Michael felt the weight of him—*El Cartero*, the man he used to be—settle across his shoulders. The heaviness of him, the things he'd done, seeped into his bones. He almost welcomed the feeling. "You'd be surprised how easy he is to find, given the right circumstances."

Ben made a sound, like he was suddenly uneasy with the turn the conversation had taken. "Like I said, I'm sorry, but—"

"I don't want an apology. Whatever it is, whatever you want her for …" His hands cranked tight, fisting themselves against his thighs. "I want you to make it go away."

Ben sighed into the static. "I can't do that. You know I would if I could, but—"

"Bullshit." Laughter, harsh and hoarse, barked out of him. "You're Benjamin Shaw. Making things go away is what you do."

"Under normal circumstances, you'd be right," Ben said. "But these circumstances are anything but normal."

"I don't believe you. I think you're bored without us to push around like chess pieces." Even as he said it, Michael knew he was being unfair—cruel even—to the one person besides Sabrina who'd ever been willing to risk his life for him.

Now it was Ben's turn to laugh. "You have no idea what pulling off your disappearance has cost me so don't—just *don't*." He didn't sound uneasy anymore. He sounded pissed.

"Like what? Did Daddy take your Lear away?"

"You know what? Fuck you, O'Shea." Silence charged with anger hissed between them and for a second, Michael was sure he'd killed the transmission. Ben cleared his throat. "Look, it doesn't matter. That's not what this is about," he said, sounding resigned. "I've got my father handled. What's going on has nothing to do with him."

Handled. No one *handled* Livingston Shaw—and if they did, it wasn't for long. Michael was suddenly sure whatever Ben had given to placate his father, it had been far more than his friend could afford to give.

"I still owe you one, you know."

"Bro, you owe me about *fifty*," Ben said and Michael was relieved to hear the smile in his voice. "I miss you guys."

Michael could hear the truth in his admission. The loneliness. The isolation. Ben was surrounded by people—people who would follow any order he gave without a moment's hesitation—and he didn't trust any of them. Didn't count a single one of them among his friends.

"Will you be there with her?" Michael said, suddenly realizing he had no idea where Sabrina was going. What was being asked of her or why. "Can I count on that, at least?" They both knew Sabrina was leaving, that she would allow herself to be drawn into whatever mess Ben had laid at her feet. That even if he could, he wouldn't try to stop her. It would be pointless to pretend otherwise.

More silence before Ben cleared his throat again. "No. My days of playing guardian angel are over. Been over for a while now ... but I'll do what I can for her. I promise."

Before Michael could ask what he meant, Ben switched off, leaving nothing but dead air in his place.

EIGHT

SHE'D KNOWN WHAT THEY were even before she'd reached inside but that didn't stop her fingers from jerking against the envelope. Instantly rejecting the cool, slick paper as soon as she touched it.

Photographs.

Sabrina forced herself to pull the stack free and spread them across the kitchen table. Forced herself to look at what Ben wanted her to see. Blood and death—so much of both that for a moment, she felt dizzy.

She closed her eyes, splayed her hand across the pictures in front of her. In the neighboring room, she could hear the movie Christina and Alex had chosen for the evening. *Pacific Rim,* one of her favorites. Under normal circumstances, she'd pop some popcorn on the stovetop and join them while waiting for Michael to come back in from the barn.

Her current circumstances were anything but normal. But they used to be. Once upon a time, what laid on the table had been as normal as breathing to her …

Just another case. Just another body.

Her old mantra came back to her. Pulled her in and calmed her. She opened her eyes and looked at the photos beneath her hand.

Three known victims in the space of twelve months. All showing signs of dehydration. Malnourishment. Rape. Torture. They'd been kept before they'd been killed. Ligature marks and antemortem injuries suggested for several days, one for as long as a month, before being executed.

Victimology was all over the place. The first victim, Danielle Watson, was forty years old. Another victim, Stephanie Adams, had been in her twenties. The latest victim, Isla Talbert—found two weeks ago—had been only twelve. She'd disappeared while on a bike ride to a convenience store, two blocks from her house. Found two weeks later inside a roadside shrine, naked, bound with bailing wire, and posed as if she were praying. Like the rest, cause of death had been a quarter-sized hole punched into the base of her skull.

Sabrina pushed the photos to the side, concentrating on the ME and investigation reports that accompanied them. Mixed in with official reports were full backgrounds on each of the victims. Scattered throughout the reports were highlighted portions that wove the victims together.

Still, she couldn't find a reason Ben would feel the need to drop this case in her lap. It took her nearly an hour of combing before she found it—to anyone else the notation would mean nothing. Less than nothing. A few sentences at the end of a lab report marked STEPHANIE ADAMS. An oddity chalked up to an almost crippling backlog at the lab and not enough manpower.

For Sabrina, it changed everything.

She'd gone to bed alone, though she'd waited for what felt like hours for Michael to come back inside. It'd been long enough for the movie to run its course and the kids to put themselves to bed before she finally gave up and closed her eyes, willing herself to sleep.

He'd come in sometime afterward, the weight of him sinking into the bed beside her. He reached for her, whispered her name against the nape of her neck and she'd turned toward him. Let him pull her under. His mouth and hands on her skin. Let herself believe, at least for a while, that none of it had happened. That the pictures and reports she'd been poring over just a few hours before had been nothing more than a bad dream.

She woke just before dawn to find him sitting in the chair he kept by the window, staring out into the dense gray beyond it. It was nothing new. More often than not, she'd wake to find him like this, half dressed, watching the night sky like he was waiting. Like he knew it was only a matter of time before someone came and took it all away.

The manila envelope Maddox brought her rested almost casually on his knee.

"Can we talk about it now?"

He'd known she was awake and he nodded at her like he'd been waiting for her to ask. "Yeah, we can talk about it." He swiped a hand over his face, nodding his head. "When are you leaving?"

The question, the finality in his voice scared her. Sent panic clawing up her spine. "That's what I've been trying to tell you. I'm *not* leaving. I'm staying right here."

"There's an active serial killer in Yuma, Sabrina," he said with a look that told her he thought she was being ridiculous and stubborn. "He's killed four women in the past year."

"So what?" she said. Sitting up, she fumbled for her tank, searching for it in the tangle of sheet and blankets. "It's got nothing to do with me."

"Okay, let's ignore the obvious—that the killing started less than a month after your very public and very tragic demise." He tossed the envelope onto the bed where it landed less than a foot from her hand. "We'll focus on the fact that the second victim was found with traces of Melissa Walker's DNA under her fingernails. That means it has *everything* to do with you."

Melissa Walker. The girl she used to be. The girl who'd fled to Yuma when she was just sixteen, her twin siblings in tow. She'd left Jessup, the small Texas town where she'd grown up, in a desperate attempt to start her life over. To protect her grandmother, protect Tommy, the boy she'd been in love with … In the end all she'd done was manage to get herself killed. She'd been abducted. Tortured and raped for eighty-three days before being left for dead in a churchyard. When she woke up, Melissa Walker was gone—the person she was now was all that was left of her.

That'd been nearly twenty years ago, when DNA evidence had been in its adolescence. And like most adolescents, it'd been unreliable and fickle. Most cops back then had been too old-school, too skeptical to trust it, relying rather on what they considered *real* police work. Will Santos, the detective assigned to her case, had not been one of them.

He'd insisted on collecting and cataloging every scraping and swab they'd taken from her and entering them into the system in hopes of someday finding the man who raped and tortured her. But not even Santos could have predicted that her DNA profile would somehow wind up in the results of a report generated almost twenty years later.

"Like you said, I'm dead." She found her tank and pulled it on. It'd been too much to hope for that he'd miss the notation buried in the stack of reports. Michael was too meticulous, too exact to miss something like that. "And thanks to Croft, everyone knows it." Jaxon Croft, the reporter who'd taken her whole sordid story public, had made her death national news. A few years ago, his constant hounding had been a nightmare, but when Ben had faked her death and Michael's, it had been a godsend. "Even if I wanted to, I couldn't—"

"Sure you could," he said, still watching her. Appraising her. "You've gained a good twenty pounds. You're softer. Fuller. You'd definitely need colored contacts. Different hair color. Maybe a cut. But with Ben clearing the way, you could slip back into the world without even a ripple."

He was right. She knew he was right. Instead of admitting it she just shook her head. "Why are you pushing this?"

"Because," he said, cutting his gaze back to the window, "I think you're staying here because you're afraid."

"Afraid?" Laughter scraped against her throat, erupting from her mouth, rusty and cold. "Afraid of what?"

"Not what," he said without looking at her, his hands fisted against his knees. "Who."

Wade.

Neither one of them had said his name out loud in what felt like forever. Not since she'd told him the truth—that after she'd killed him, Wade had started talking to her. That the only thing that made him go away was Michael. In the year they'd been to-gether, Wade had faded away into nothing more than a vague and unpleasant memory. Leaving Michael would change that. It would open a door. The panic that had clawed up her spine started chew-ing into her throat, making it hard to breathe.

"I'm not afraid of him and *fuck you* for thinking otherwise." Fishing her underwear from the foot of the bed, she swung her legs over the side, yanking them up before she stood. "And the only place I'm *going* is the bathroom."

"We both know how this ends, Sabrina," he said quietly. "We both know you were never meant to stay here forever."

The words nailed her feet to the floor. Stopped her in her tracks. Stole her breath, had her pressing her fist into her sternum, trying to find it.

We both know how this ends…

She turned toward the window to find him standing in front of it, arms loose, shoulders slumped. The manila folder was on the floor between them. "Marry me." The words tumbled out, rash and impulsive, but she meant them. As soon as she said them, she knew. Rushing forward, she closed the space between them. "Marry me."

Michael sighed, shaking his head. "Sabrina—"

"Do you want me to leave?" Even though saying it out loud made her voice shake, she had to know. "Are you trying to end it?"

"What?" He jerked back, looked at her as if she'd hit him. "No, I'm—" He shook his head, suddenly frustrated. "I'm just trying to do the right thing here," he said, swiping a rough hand over his face. "Why won't you ever let me just do the *right* goddamned thing by you?"

"Why do *you* always think you're the only one who knows what the right thing for me is?" she nearly shouted, tempering her voice at the last minute so she didn't wake the kids. "You? *This*— this is the only forever I want," she said, her tone sharp-edged and hot. He was frowning down at her and she lifted her hand to skim her fingers across his brow. She took a deep breath in an effort to cool the heat in her words. "Marry me."

Instead of answering her, he reached up and caught her hand. "You've never allowed fear to control you. Sooner or later, you'll remember that and you'll leave," he said, pressing her hand against his jaw. She could feel it, how hard he was fighting for control. "The right thing for me to do is to let you, maybe even encourage you … but I love you too much." His voice sounded tight, like he had to push the words out. "I don't want you to leave. I don't want to do the right thing—I want you to stay here with me … with us." His hand dropped away from hers. "But you'll end up hating me and yourself if you do."

"You're right about one thing." She said it quietly, letting her hand fall away from him face. "I am worried Wade will find his way inside my head again if I leave here." She backed away from him until the back of her knees hit the edge of the bed and she let herself sink onto it. "But what absolutely terrifies me is the possibility of leaving and not being able to find my way back … but if you marry me, that's a promise."

Michael sat on the bed next to her, lifting her hand from her lap to hold it between his own. "The kind we'd both have to keep," he said softly, understanding perfectly. It would be an assurance that in each other, no matter where they went or how long they were apart, they would always have a home to come back to.

"Exactly." She pressed her lips to his shoulder before perching her chin on top of it. "Will you marry me, Michael?"

His hand tightened around hers for a moment before he lifted it to his mouth, kissing each of her fingertips before pressing his lips to the center of her palm and whispering, "Yes."

NINE

Yuma, Arizona

THE WOMAN FINALLY STOPPED screaming. What had been left in place of the noise—a shrill, terrified keening—was a silence as deafening as the sound that preceded it.

Maggie leaned forward in the dark, toward the cracks of light that reached for her around the edges of the door. Listening. Waiting.

He would come for her next.

From down the hall another noise. Like a chair being dragged across a linoleum floor. Familiar. Almost comforting. She'd made that sound plenty of times. Like when she dragged a barstool from her countertop to the fridge to look for her car keys. She had a habit of tossing them on top of it and forgetting about them. Come to think of it, she had a history of thoughtless behavior. Keys tossed on top of the fridge. Wet laundry left in the washer for days. Driving off with her purse on the roof of her car.

Agreeing to meet a complete stranger for dinner.

She'd met him on one of those free dating websites. The kind most people used for casual hook-ups or harmless flirting. She'd been curious and, admittedly, lonely, so when he messaged her, she'd responded.

They'd private messaged for weeks before she'd felt comfortable enough to give him her number, and she hadn't agreed to meet him for dinner until they'd spoken several times over the phone. He'd been a perfect gentleman. Handsome. Well-spoken. A dream come true.

After dinner, she'd actually been disappointed when he'd insisted on walking her to her car. She hadn't wanted the evening to end.

"I've had a lovely time," he said to her back while she worked the car fob, unlocking the driver's door.

"Me too," she said, turning to find him standing so close it stole her breath.

He was going to kiss her . . . he was actually going to kiss her.

He lifted his hand, his fingertips grazing her neck, his thumb tracing the line of her jaw. "Can I ask you something, Margaret?" he said to her and she nodded stupidly even though she'd insisted, numerous times, that he call her Maggie.

He leaned into her, pressing his lips to her cheek before he whispered into her ear, each word, brushing his mouth against her lobe. "Do you believe in miracles?"

The question was followed by what felt like a bee sting, quick and sharp, which led to a feeling of warmth and melting. Like she was made of butter, left out in the sun . . .

The next thing she remembered was waking up to the sound of a woman screaming. It'd seemed to go on for hours. Days even. So long she ceased to register it as sound.

Another noise. This one softer. Almost a whisper. Growing louder and louder as it grew closer—*shhhhh*—its approach measured by footsteps. Long, confident strides she recognized immediately as belonging to the man who'd taken her to dinner. He'd told her his name was Gabriel but she was almost certain that was a lie.

Suddenly the light that reached for her was interrupted. The whispering *shhhhh* was as loud as a shout. Something was being dragged past her door. It sounded wet. Sloppy. Like a mop that hadn't been wrung out before being slapped against the floor.

Maggie jerked herself back, away from the sound, pressing her shoulders into the rough block wall she huddled against. She renewed her efforts, twisting and jerking at the wire that bound her wrists together.

She had to get out of here. She had to find a way. If she could just get her hands free, maybe she could—

A scraping sound. Metal on metal as a key was inserted into the lock and turned. The door swung open and he was suddenly *there*. Bright light from the hallway pinched into her eyes and she squinted up into the long, dark shadow he cast over her.

He held something in his hand. Something long and cylindrical. Heavy, like the kind of flashlight a police officer carried. He held it casually at his side while something dripped from the end of it, thick like syrup, splattering on the floor at his feet.

Whatever it was, it wasn't a flashlight. She jerked her eyes away from what he held in his hand, aiming them instead at his shoulder. His answering chuckle sounded both pleased and indulgent.

"Margaret, do you believe in miracles?"

The question pulled her gaze upward, from his shoulder to his face. He wasn't laughing anymore. "Why do you keep calling me that?" she said. "My name isn't Margaret. It's Maggie—Maggie

Travers. My name is Maggie... *Maggie.*" She shook her head, hysteria pushing her. Making her ramble. "Please let me go," she begged, each word caught on a hitching sob as she buried her face in bound hands. "Please let me go—I won't say anything to anyone. I swear, I just want to go—"

SNAPBANG!

For a moment she was sure he'd shot her. Her head wrenched up so fast her neck seized, eyes bulging from their sockets, aimed up at the man standing in the doorway. Her bladder loosened, a stream of urine leaking onto the cement floor she sat on.

"Hush, now," he said to her as he lifted the cylinder to pull at its top. Something inside it snapped loudly into place. "Answer the question, please. Do you believe in miracles?"

Did she believe in miracles?

It was what her mother had been calling her since she was a child.

Her little miracle.

She'd been four years old when it happened. Her older brother, their father, and she had been heading to Colorado to spend Christmas with her grandparents. A sudden winter storm and a slick patch of ice had sent them skidding through a guardrail and into the bottom of a ravine. She'd spent three days in the overturned car before they'd been found. Her brother and father had been killed instantly.

"Yes," she said, nodding her head. "Yes, I do."

He smiled at her, obviously pleased with her answer. "When was the last time you attended mass?"

The answer bobbled in her throat. The truth wouldn't please him but she forced it out. "Five weeks." Something told her that no matter how long she'd thought she'd known this man, he'd known her—watched her—infinitely longer. Lying would've been as pointless as it was dangerous. "I just started a new job and I'm scheduled to work Sundays." She was a vet tech at an animal clinic within walking distance of the apartment she shared with her mother.

He came toward her, crouching in front of her, and she fought the urge to shrink farther away. "Are you a virgin, Margaret?"

Ridiculously, the question stained her cheek. "No."

He nodded, if not pleased with her answer then at least satisfied with the truth. "Come with me," he said, holding out his free hand. "I want to show you something."

It came back to her—the wet, sloppy sound of something being dragged down the hall—and she started to cry again. Whatever it was he wanted to show her, she didn't want to see it.

"Are you him?" she whispered, her voice trembling, her hands cradled against her chest. "You're him, aren't you? The man on the news, the one who ..." She gagged, unable to finish the question, but he answered her anyway.

"Yes," he said, his hand still extended. "But I promise, I have no intention of hurting you. Not yet. Not as long as you do as I say." He could have forced her to come with him. Grabbed her by the wire that bound her hands and dragged her out of the room. But he didn't. It gave her a small measure of hope that he was telling her the truth. That he wouldn't hurt her as long as she did what he said.

She finally held out her hands, placing them in his. "There's my good girl," he said as he stood, pulling her up. Her dress clung against the backs of her thighs, wet and cold, and he looked down at the puddle they stood in. "You've made a mess." He didn't look pleased with her anymore.

"I'm sorry, I'm sorry, I'm sorry ..." She kept stuttering it out, again and again, hysteria crowding her.

"Shhh," he said, pulling her through the doorway into a corridor barely wide enough for them to stand shoulder to shoulder. Looking down at the floor, she forced herself to be quiet as they walked, his fingers gripping her elbow as if he were escorting her home from an evening stroll in the park. Between them a thick, red swath cut down the center of the floor. Bits of something, gelatinous and cool, squelched between her toes.

"Do you know how a saint is made, Margaret?" he said, looking down at her as if he expected an answer. Afraid to open her mouth, she shook her head. She was walking through brain matter. If she opened her mouth, she would start to scream and she wouldn't be able to stop.

"The canonization process is quite arduous, often painful," he said, stopping in front of another door. This one was cracked open, dim light peeking through. "Most saints aren't even recognized until after they're dead." He settled her hands on the knob before releasing her elbow. Because he seemed to want her to and because she wanted out of the hallway, she pushed the door open.

The room was twice as long as it was wide. At its farthest end was a hospital bed. On top of it lay a man. At least she thought it was a man. He was dangerously thin, nothing but skin stretched, gaunt and tight, over sharp, protruding bone. His chest rose and fell in an uneven rhythm, each breath shuddering in and out as if it could be his last.

Next to the bed was a folding partition. What she saw behind it sent her backward.

I promise I have no intention of hurting you. Not yet . . .

She wanted out of the room, back in to the hallway with the blood and the brains, but a hand at the small of her back stopped her retreat. Propelled her forward until they were standing at the man's bedside.

"Margaret, I'd like you to meet Robert Delashaw," he said to her as if he were making introductions at a cocktail party. "Robert, this is Margaret, the young woman I've been telling you about."

The man on the bed gave no indication he even knew they were there.

"What's wrong with him?" she heard herself ask. "He looks sick."

"He is, Margaret," he said. "Robert has stage-four renal cancer. The doctors sent him home to die."

"I don't understand," she shook her head, swallowing hard against the hard knot that seemed to be lodged in her throat.

"Robert is your second test, Margaret, just as Trudy Hayes was Rachel's. She failed, of course—they all did—but I have faith in you."

"I don't know what you want from me." She was a tech in a veterinary clinic. She gave vaccinations and took x-rays. Nothing she was capable of would help this man.

"I think you know exactly what I want, Margaret," he said to her, his tone taking on sharp edges. The kind of edges that promised pain if not heeded. "I want you to give to Robert what has been given to you. I want you to give him a miracle."

TEN

Kootenai Canyon, Montana

"Again."

Sabrina blew out an exaggerated sigh as she came out of the closet with an armload of clothes. "I don't want to go over it again," she said, aiming a sullen look in his direction. He was sitting on the edge of their bed, next to the carry-on suitcase she'd found in the ridiculously overprepared closet. Forty-eight hours ago she'd been sure she'd never wear or use any of this stuff. Now she was juggling sensible flats and trying to decide which of the two dozen pantsuits she should pack.

"Give it a rest, O'Shea." She half wadded, half folded a pair of navy dress pants and stuffed them in her suitcase. "You act like I've never faked my own death before."

"You're not funny."

She could hear the frustration creeping into his voice again. Now that it was settled that she'd leave, it was killing him to let her go. "I don't think you married me for my sense of humor," she gave him a cheeky wink, trying to keep the mood light, but it didn't work.

Michael retrieved the pair of pants from the bottom of the case and shook them out. "Humor me, Sabrina," he said, refolding the pants into a perfectly formed rectangle before holding them out to her. "Again, please."

She took the pants from him and tossed them over her shoulder. Turning toward him, she pulled her knees onto the bed to straddle his hips. "I'd rather do something else to you," she said, pressing him back onto the bed. He let her have her way for a few minutes. Let her distract them both from the reality of the situation.

She was leaving.

"Okay," he said pulling his mouth from under hers, groaning when she traced her tongue along the rigid line of his jaw. "Sabrina…" The groan deepened into a growl but he wasn't giving up. "I need you to go over it again. And after that, I need you to go over it *again*. Over and over until I'm convinced you've got it down."

She sat up. "Married less than thirty-six hours and you've lost all interest in me."

Yesterday morning, they'd sat the kids down after breakfast and told them a sanitized version of the truth. That she was leaving for a few weeks to take care of something that'd come up but that she was coming back.

"I need your help, Christina," she'd said to the girl, watching her trace her finger along the wood grains in the kitchen table. As soon as she said it, her hands went still but she didn't look up. Interested but still angry.

"Michael and I are getting married and I was wondering if you'd be my maid of honor."

That was all it took. Christina was out of her chair in a flash, dragging her back into her bedroom and into the closet where she'd wrangled her into a sundress and talked her into taking her boots off. She'd even let the girl braid flowers into her hair.

By lunchtime, Alex was walking her down the porch steps to where Michael waited for her under a tree by the river. It wasn't official—couldn't be—but they'd promised to love and protect each other for the rest of their lives.

As far as she was concerned, that was enough.

Now, Michael glowered at her, digging his fingers into her hips in an effort to keep her still. "Right now, I'm more interested in keeping you alive than getting you under me."

"No fun." She blew out an exaggerated sigh. "Fine … my name is Sinclaire Vance, but you can call me Claire. I'm thirty-six years old. I'm a Libra. I love long walks in the rain and horseback rides on the beach—"

"*Sabrina.*"

"I'm originally from Portland, Maine, but I grew up in Battle Creek, Michigan. I attended UNLV on a track scholarship, where I double majored in criminal justice and communications. From there I earned my master's in forensic psychology, after which I applied for and was accepted into the FBI training program." She smiled down at him. "Anything else I should know about myself?"

"Where were you stationed after graduating from Quantico?"

"Phoenix. I worked their field office for nearly seven years, and I aided in the apprehension of not one, but *three* serial murderers within a six-month period by providing psychological profiles of the suspects. I was offered a spot in the FBI's BAU task force in DC after all three arrests led to convictions." She gave him an exasperated smile and flopped on to the bed next to him. "Satisfied?"

He lifted the hand that rested in the narrow space between them, pressing his lips to her knuckles. "Not even close," he whispered against her hand before he closed his fingers around the thin platinum band he'd put there the day before. He started to pull it off and she stopped him by clenched her hand into a fist.

"Leave it," she said, shaking her head, pulling her hand from his. Claire Vance was married to her job. Her personal ties were limited. Sabrina knew she'd have to take the ring off sooner rather than later, but she wasn't ready. Not yet.

He didn't argue with her or tell her she was being unreasonable. He just threaded his fingers between her own and held on to her for a little while longer.

"I want you to call Phillip."

It came out of nowhere and it took her a few moments to realize who he was talking about. Phillip Song. Leader of Seven Dragons, the most powerful arm of San Francisco's Korean mob. The younger brother of David Song, the man who mutilated and murdered several young women in order to feed his own twisted delusion that her fate and his were intertwined.

"I can't just *call* Phillip Song. I'm supposed to be dead, remember?"

She could hear Christina and Alex in the bathroom they shared, brushing their teeth. Getting ready for bed. She glanced at the wind-up clock on her nightstand. It was after nine. Dinner had been grilled steaks and sautéed asparagus that grew wild in the sandy soil along the riverbank. Afterward, they'd played Uno and ate homemade brownies.

As far as last days go, it'd been perfect.

"Yes, you can," he said stubbornly. "He made his cousin help you once. He can make her help you again."

It had been Phillip's cousin Eun who'd told her that Wade's presence in her subconscious was more spiritual than psychological. Trained in Korea as a shaman, she'd called him a *Gae Dokkaebi*—an evil spirit—and given her a special tea that helped keep him at bay. Sabrina hadn't believed it at the time—she still didn't—but when she drank the tea Phillip's cousin made for her, Wade was quiet. Not *gone*, but silent. It had been the only thing that kept her sane before Michael came back into her life.

"That was a long time ago," she said. "Phillip helped me because he felt like he owed me and because it amused him. I'm sure both feelings have passed."

He laughed at her. "You're adorably clueless, you know that?"

"Adorable?" she said, glowering as she pulled her hand loose and attempted to sit up. "That's it, I want a divorce."

He kept laughing and rolled on to his side, anchoring her beneath him with an arm snaked around her waist. "If you think the only reason Phillip Song helped you is because he owed you"—he leaned down and dropped a kiss on the hard line of her mouth—"then you know nothing about men and their motivations."

"Phillip was a friend." Her breath caught at the feel of his fingers trailing across her belly, skimming along the waistband of her cargos. "Nothing more than that."

Michael pressed his lips to her collarbone. "Phillip was *your* friend," he whispered, nuzzling her neck. "What you were to him was much more than that."

"If that's true"—she arched up against the hand he slipped under her tank, pushing it up her rib cage—"why would you want me to call him?"

The mouth against her throat curved into a smile as his hand closed over her breast. "Because," he said, brushing his thumb across her nipple, teeth grazing along her jawline, "I'm not above exploiting some poor sap's feelings for you if it means keeping you sane and safe."

She laughed, even as her breath caught again. "Phillip Song is hardly a sap."

"Trust me," he said, angling himself up so he could press a kiss to her jawline before looking her in the eye, "for you, he is."

ELEVEN

THE CHOPPER ARRIVED BEFORE noon, its sudden appearance in the sky above their house sending Avasa into a wild flurry of alarmed barking.

Sabrina watched it touch down in the open grass on the other side of the river, its rotors slowing as whoever was piloting it powered down.

It was time to go.

Christina appeared in the doorway. Her jovial mood had dissolved overnight into the same angry silence she'd given them the day Maddox had arrived and changed everything. Behind her, Alex stood quietly, his face as impassive as always. Sabrina wondered if her departure even registered with him.

The faulty back porch step creaked moments before a sharp-knuckled rap sounded against the glass, the small figure beyond it vaguely familiar. Next to it, a larger, more imposing shadow. Moving across the kitchen, both children and the dog followed her, crowding around her as she opened the door.

"Miss Ettie." Sabrina felt her chest constrict a moment before she was enveloped in the elderly woman's arms. "What are you doing here?"

"Ben sent me," the old woman answered, pulling back until she could tip her chin to look up at her. "I'm Michael's consolation prize for letting you run off on whatever fool's errand he's got cooked up."

Miss Ettie was more than a consolation prize. She was a piece of home. That sharp longing she usually managed to fend off poked at her, causing her to catch her breath. The old woman ran a B&B the next street over from where she'd lived in San Francisco. They'd shared a fence line—it was what made staying there so convenient three years ago when Michael had come looking for her in hopes of catching his sister's murderer. The same man who'd abducted and tortured her.

Wade.

She pushed the thought of him from her head and focused on the here and now. Ben had sent Miss Ettie to them in hopes of making her absence easier for Michael and the children to handle, and in true Ben fashion, had absolutely ignored the potential dangers of it.

"Not to worry, dear," her old neighbor said as she patted her cheek. "Everyone is fine. They miss you of course but they're managing." There was something else. Something she wasn't telling her, but she knew from past experience that Miss Ettie said what she wanted and kept the rest to herself.

"You shouldn't be here, Miss Ettie." Sabrina shook her head while shooting Reese Harrison a disapproving glare. "It isn't safe." Reese was Ben's personal pilot. He knew better than anyone how dangerous it was to bring her here.

"Nonsense. At my age, getting out of bed practically runs the same risk as jumping out of an airplane." She gave her a grin, the depth of it folding into the soft, lined skin of her face. "Now, go on and say good-bye to that young man out there before he changes his mind about letting you leave."

Looking past the old woman, she saw him standing in the grass, next to the helo.

Michael was waiting for her.

"I think I'll get started on lunch," Miss Ettie said, bustling her way into the kitchen. "From what I've been told, someone around here has quite a fondness for grilled cheese sandwiches." She tied an apron around her middle and gave Christina a wink.

Sabrina looked at the man who'd brought her.

"I'm just following orders," Reese said, picking up Sabrina's suitcase and angling himself in the doorway so she could pass through. "It's what I'm good at."

Only a very select few knew Michael and Sabrina had survived the extraction of Leon Maddox's grandson from Alberto Reyes's island fortress. Reese Harrison was on the short list and had proved himself trustworthy countless times—both before and after their disappearance. It was his ability to follow Ben's lead without asking questions that not only saved him from disappearing off the face of the earth when Jaxon Croft started asking questions about Michael but made him an invaluable cog in a very dangerous wheel. Right now, it was not her most favorite thing about him.

They crossed the bridge single file, Reese leading the pack while the kids and Avasa trailing behind her, a silent trudge that made Sabrina feel as if she were marching toward her own funeral.

"Reese," Michael said as soon as they were close enough. The pilot reached out and the two of them shook hands. They'd flown together in the military, when Michael had been Special Forces and Reese had been a part of an elite pilot squad known as the Nightstalkers. He had also been the medevac pilot who'd flown her out of the woods the day she'd killed Wade. If there was anyone worth trusting, it was Reese Harrison.

As soon as pleasantries were dispensed, Reese stored her suitcase in the cargo hold of the helicopter and climbed into the pilot seat. "Whenever you're ready," he told her, shutting the door in order to give them a few minutes of privacy.

"I know better than to ask you to be careful," Michael said. He had something in his hand and he held it out to her. "You don't do careful... but you're coming back to us."

A zippered pouch. Heavy and thick, like a banker's bag. Whatever was inside was between them. Something he didn't even want Reese to know about.

She nodded, taking it from his grasp to tuck it into her tote. Looking up, she found Michael standing closer than he'd been. Close enough to touch her. "No matter what you have to do—or who you have to do it to." His hands caressed her neck, slipping around to her nape. She felt something thin and cool slide against her skin as he adjusted the collar of her button down. "Do you understand?" he said quietly, gazing down at her with eyes gone gunmetal gray.

"Yes." She pressed her mouth to his. "I understand perfectly." The key he'd hung from the chain around her neck lay flat against her chest, completely hidden. He also slipped something into her pocket. She could feel the cool of it through the thin lining of her pocket. His knife. Michael had given her his knife.

"I want you to look at them," she said quietly, very much aware of Christina and Alex standing behind her. His gaze drifted over her shoulder to settle on the pair. "Stay with them. No matter what happens."

He jerked his gaze back to her face, opening his mouth to protest. "Promise me," she said, cutting him off before he could argue. "*Promise.*"

He looked lost. Beaten. "Okay," he said softly. "I promise."

Beside her, Avasa let out a soft whine, lifting her paw to settle it against her knee. Sabrina dropped her shoulder bag in the grass to kneel beside her. "Not this time, girl," she said, giving the dog long, deep strokes along her neck and shoulders. "I need you to stay here and keep an eye on things."

Looking up, she caught Christina watching her, unshed tears glittering in her eyes. "I'm not your mother," Sabrina said to her bluntly. "But I love you like you're mine. When I chose Michael, I chose you too."

Her admission softened Christina for a moment and she swayed forward, her arms jerking like they wanted to fling themselves around her neck. But they didn't. Instead the girl turned on her heel to stalk several paces away.

Before Sabrina could stand, Alex came forward to settle a hand against her shoulder. He was eleven now, sturdy but still small. "*Do svidaniya,*" he said, his dark eyes pinning her in place. No longer flat, they snapped at her, reminded of the way he'd looked at her the day she'd put them in the lift.

Finally he leaned closer, pressing his lips to her ear. "I will protect them," he said in perfect English before allowing his hand to drop from her shoulder. Before she could react, he pulled away, stepping away to stand shoulder to shoulder with Christina, his gaze as unfocused and lifeless as it'd always been.

TWELVE

Helena, Montana

"ARE YOU SURE ABOUT this?" the stylist said, her fingers gripping the long, thick braid that hung down her back. She'd been waiting for them when they arrived. Just like the car had been waiting on the tarmac of the small private airstrip where Reese had set the helo down less than an hour after liftoff. Like Reese, Sabrina was sure the stylist had been chosen for her skill as much as her loyalty and discretion.

She'd been quickly and quietly sequestered in the penthouse suite of Helena's finest hotel, Reese carrying her suitcase as if he were her personal valet. Afterward, she'd expected him to leave her but he didn't. He was still here. Like he was waiting for something.

Or someone.

The stylist was still frowning at her hair, the scissors in her hand closed as if she couldn't bring herself to even open them, let alone use them to do what Sabrina had asked. With a small sigh, she shifted in her chair, lifting her hip so she could reach the side pocket of her cargos and the knife Michael had placed there before she left. She had it unsheathed and under the base of the braid before the stylist could blink. "Positive," she said, sliding the blade through her hair, cutting it loose. The auburn rope fell from her hand and onto the floor at the stylist's feet. The poor woman stared at it in abject horror.

Behind her, Reese let out a loud bark of laughter. "God, I've missed you."

She smiled at his reflection cast by the mirror in front of her. "I've missed you too. How've you been?"

"Oh, you know … living the dream," he said, his answer as vague as it was purposeful. Whatever Ben had him doing, he wasn't supposed to talk about it. Surprisingly, it stung that he'd instructed Reese to keep things from her.

She wasn't going to give up that easily. "How is he?" she said, careful to keep her head straight. Now that the hard part had been done for her, the stylist was more than willing to finish the job.

"Bored." Reese gave her a noncommittal shrug. "Ask me how many times I've been dragged to Vegas to see Britney Spears in concert," he said, lifting his hands, splaying his fingers wide. "Ten. Ten times."

She laughed. "Poor baby—"

His phone rang and he dug it out of his pocket. "Excuse me," he said, standing as soon as he glanced at the screen. He disappeared into one of the suite's two bedrooms to take the call in private.

———

Two hours later she was a strawberry blonde. The cut was short, even shorter on the sides, exposing her neck while longer layers on top swept across her head to angle across her brow. Michael had been right again. Coupled with the warm, hazel color of the contacts she wore, she looked like a completely different person.

The stylist packed up and left and Sabrina had expected Reese to follow suit. Instead of leaving he seemed to settle in deeper, stretching out on the couch watching old episodes of *Man vs. Food*. He looked relaxed, bored even, but she knew better. Reese wasn't bored. He was waiting.

"I'm gonna go take a shower," she said. Without waiting for an answer, she carried her tote into the same room Reese had taken her suitcase. As soon as the door was closed, she locked it, dropping the tote onto the bed. Reaching inside, she found the zippered pouch Michael had given her and carried it into the bathroom. There, she turned on the shower before lifting the lid on the toilet. Setting it on the counter, she opened it. Inside was a burner phone. She set it aside and reached in farther, pulling out a small white envelope. She pulled out the notecard and flipped it open.

The key opens a safety deposit box. Trust your instincts.
If something goes wrong, use it.
I love you.
M.

Below the message was the name and branch number to a bank in Yuma. She committed both to memory before dropping the card into the toilet. The paper dissolved the instant it hit the water. Sabrina reached into her shirt and pulled at the thin chain that hung around her neck. Suspended from it was the promised key. Tarnished brass, with the number 367 stamped into its back. Alongside it was her wedding ring.

A reminder of the promise she'd made him.

She knew the safety deposit box would hold everything she needed to make a fast getaway. Cash. A new set of identification. Passports. How Michael managed to put it all together so fast was something she didn't really want to think about. Neither was *why*.

She wasn't just hiding from her past. She was hiding from Livingston Shaw. If her resurfacing drew any attention, Shaw would be among the first to learn of it. Then everyone she cared about would pay for her mistakes.

———

When Sabrina exited her room an hour later, Reese was watching *Barefoot Contessa* and eating a burger he'd obviously ordered from room service.

He also wasn't alone.

"What the hell is she doing here?" Sabrina managed, cutting a look toward the person lounging in the chair directly across from her.

"*She* is eating tacos," Church answered her around a mouthful without bothering to look at her. "And watching my girl Ina make a kick-ass ceviche."

"Am I conscious right now?" she said to Reese, ignoring Church completely. "Did I slip in the shower and hit my head?"

Reese finally risked a glance in her direction. His burger stopped midway to his mouth. "No. It's really happening," he said, letting his double bacon with cheese hit the plate with a regretful sigh. "I *told* him this wasn't a good idea." Reese shook his head, slouching back into the couch. "Like I said before, Sabrina—I just follow orders."

Him. As in Ben.

"One of these days, Reese, that excuse is going to catch up with you." She cocked her head slightly, her jaw tight. "He sent her here? *Her*. His father's pet sociopath."

"Ah—well … yeah." He looked at Church, hoping for some help but she seemed content to eat her tacos and let him languish.

"Where is Ben?" She should have asked sooner. Should have asked why he wasn't here. Why he hadn't come for her himself after sending Leon Maddox on a potential suicide mission to retrieve her in the first place. "Where is he? When is he—"

"Ben isn't coming, Kitten," Church finally chimed in, muting the television with a disgruntled scowl. "And for the record—I'm nobody's pet."

THIRTEEN

ALL THINGS CONSIDERED, SABRINA slept well. The fact she slept at all was a small miracle. It might have had something to do with the .45 she tucked under her pillow before closing her eyes.

She lay in bed for a few moments listening to the silence until she was able to pull small noises from the void. The low murmur of the television. The quiet scrape of utensils against glass. It was barely five a.m. and Church was already up for the day.

Sitting up, she pulled her hotel room robe on over her boy shorts and tank, knotting the belt with a quick jerk. Reaching under her pillow, she retrieved the gun and dropped it into the robe's wide, deep pocket.

Exiting her room, Sabrina caught the mingled aromas of coffee and bacon. Church was seated at the suite's dining room table, pouring a stream of hot water from a pot over a tea bag and into a waiting cup. Reese was nowhere in sight. "Hey, sleepyhead," she said. "I was beginning to wonder if I was going to have to drag you out of bed. Our flight leaves in a few hours."

Our flight. Sabrina clamped her jaw around the useless string of protests that bubbled up. Church was under the notion she'd be accompanying Sabrina to Yuma.

Church was wrong.

"I didn't know what you were eating these days so ..." she said, drowning her tea bag before giving it a light squeeze. "I ordered all of it."

"Eating?" she said, as she slipped into the empty chair across from her companion. The table between them was covered with platters and serving dishes.

"Yeah, you know—you're off sugar. You're vegetarian. You're carb-cycling. You only eat foods that start with the letter *K*. I was trying to be thoughtful." Church shrugged. "People do that, right?"

Sabrina turned her cup over in its saucer and reached for the coffeepot. "Do what?" she said, pouring herself a cup. "Care about other people?"

"Yeah. Orange juice?" Church poured her a glass without waiting for a response.

Sabrina looked at the orange liquid in front of her and wondered if it was poisoned. Maybe Livingston Shaw sent Church here to torture her for information on Michael's whereabouts. Maybe Ben didn't even know she was here.

"If I wanted to kill you, you'd know." Church grinned at her before leveling her gaze on the glass of untouched juice. "Mostly because you'd already be dead."

Because it felt like a dare and because Church was looking at her like she'd just bested her somehow, Sabrina picked up the glass of juice and took a drink, gulping it down like she was dying of thirst.

"I know you're dying to ask ..." Church lifted her teacup and blew across its rim. "So ask."

"Why would Ben send you?" Sabrina said, setting her empty glass aside before reaching for a dish of scrambled eggs. "You work for his father." She piled it high before trading it for a platter of bacon. Food was fuel and she'd need it if she was going to have to deal with Korkiva "Courtney" Tserkov', more famously known as the assassin Church.

"First off, I don't work for Livingston Shaw anymore. I don't work for *anyone* anymore," Church said. "Thanks to my brief and decidedly distasteful crisis of conscience over killing your bestie and that baby of hers, I'm a free agent."

"So what? You got fired?" It sounded ridiculous, Livingston Shaw firing someone.

Church must've thought it sounded ridiculous too because she was suddenly laughing so hard she snorted tea through her nose. "Fired?" She shook her head, still recovering while using the side of her fork to cut into her biscuits and gravy. "Not hardly. Mr. Shaw's idea of *corporate downsizing* doesn't usually involve severance packages and exit interviews."

"So, how'd you manage to—"

"How'd I manage to get out of Colombia without a hole in my head?" Church waved the strip of bacon in her hand like a magic wand. "I just walked off into the jungle and didn't look back."

Disappearing is the easy part. It was staying gone that proved to be impossible.

"Fascinating, really," Sabrina said before lifting her cup of coffee to her mouth. "But none of it really answers my question, does it? Why would Ben send *you* to help *me*?"

"No one *sent* me," Church said, managing to sound both proud and sad at the same time. "Ben mentioned you'd need some back-up so I volunteered."

Which meant despite her hasty retreat, Church hadn't completely cut ties with FSS. "Why? Why would you offer to help me?"

"People do that too, don't they?" Church said. "Help other people."

"People?" Sabrina said, stabbing at her eggs. "Sure, people help other people all the time." She shook her head. "But you're not a person. Not really."

"*Ouch.*" Church cut her a grin that didn't quite reach her eyes. "Is that any way to talk to the person who had orders to kill a good portion of your family and didn't?"

"Yeah. I don't really understand that either." Val and Lucy should have been dead. The only reason they weren't was because Church had decided to incapacitate her best friend rather than kill her as she'd been instructed. Knowing that did little to settle the unease that tied Sabrina's stomach into knots.

"*Why, why, why* ... honestly, Sabrina, you sound like a two-year-old," Church said while she smeared a thick layer of cream cheese onto the top of a bagel. "I let them live for the same reason I offered to help you: *because I wanted to.*"

"If you're trying to convince me you're not a sociopath, I gotta tell you"—Sabrina shrugged—"it's not working."

"You might not believe it, but I'm here to help."

"I don't want your help," Sabrina said. Reaching into the pocket of her robe, she pulled out the .45 and set it on the table next to her plate, her hand resting on top.

"I'm sure you don't, Kitten." Church gave her the kind of exasperated smile a mother gives a toddler in obvious need of a nap.

"But you need it," she said, flicking a glance over the gun under her hand. "I'm it. I'm all there is. There is no Ben. There is no cavalry. You want to find out how and why your DNA got mixed up in some weirdo murder. That means slipping back into the world, right under Satan's nose." Church ran a finger over the surface of her bagel, spreading the cream cheese a bit more evenly. "The problem is, if he gets a whiff of you, you'll never see him coming."

"And you will?" It irked her that Church was right. That she needed her. While she'd technically been an FSS asset herself, she'd never been in the field—not until Church had scooped her up on Shaw's orders and dropped her on Alberto Reyes's doorstep. Knowing the inner workings of Livingston Shaw's private militaristic firm was not her forte.

"Of course," Church said, sounding slightly insulted. "It's what I do."

"And if Shaw does find out I'm still alive and sends someone after me? Then what?"

Church sighed. "Then I'll do that other thing I do," she said taking a bite of her bagel. "I'll kill each and every one of them."

FOURTEEN

Yuma, Arizona

THE LAST TIME SABRINA had flown commercial was with Michael. They'd been on their way to Jessup to find the man who'd abducted her when she was a young woman. The same man who'd brutally murdered his sister and her grandmother.

Wade Bauer—her brother.

Half-brother, she instantly corrected herself. Not that it made it any better. Not really. Shooting him the face hadn't even done that. If anything, it'd made it worse.

She hadn't thought of Wade or what he'd done to her—*not once*—since she'd made up her mind and boarded Leon Maddox's private plane in Colombia. Right now, she couldn't get it out of her mind.

Maybe it was the plane ride. Maybe it was where they were going. Maybe it was the fact that without Michael beside her to keep him at bay, it was only a matter time before Wade slinked his way back into her brain and made himself at home by driving her completely insane.

She could hardly wait.

They retrieved their bags from the carousel, Sabrina wheeling her stupid designer luggage that probably cost more than a mid-sized car, while Church lugged her appropriately travel-battered suitcase and mismatched carry-on.

She missed her duffle bag.

Letting Church lead the way, Sabrina followed her through the solitary terminal. Beyond the mirror-tinted glass she saw the dark, tri-level parking garage. Even from where she was, she could see the lot wasn't even close to full. No one comes to Yuma in August. Not without good reason.

Stepping outside was like stepping into a blast kiln. Hot, dry air blistered against her face and seared her newly exposed nape. Sweat blossomed between her skin and her tank, soaking it instantly, making her want to strip it off and wring it out. She thought of the clothes she'd packed—pantsuits and silk shirts—and suddenly wanted to kill herself.

Church lifted the key fob in her hand and pressed the button, an audible sigh escaping her lips at the answering beep from the dark sedan a few cars ahead.

As soon as Church popped the trunk, Sabrina spotted the requisite metal case stowed inside. Lifting it out, Church spun the dials and the lid clicked open. Inside, on top of the standard FSS fare of cash, prepaid cells, and maps, was another manila envelope. Reaching for it, the woman beside her shut the case. "Here you go, Agent Vance," she said, handing her the package along with a familiarly weighted box—a gun.

She opened it. Inside was a Kimber .45, standard issues for FSS operatives. She clipped its holster to her waistband before nesting the gun. The heft of it pressing on her hip was a comfort.

Next Sabrina opened the envelope, pulling out a fully stocked wallet, a cell phone, and a set of FBI credentials. It took her a few moments to realize it was real. The badge and the identification that accompanied it. Her picture, as she'd looked yesterday afternoon, was embossed into the ID, along with a raised, official-looking seal that looked authentic. Looking at the image, Sabrina barely recognized herself.

"It's fully backed. Ironclad. Transcripts. Commendations. Evaluations." Church tossed the case back into the trunk, along with their suitcases. "For all intents and purposes, you're the real deal," she said, slamming the trunk closed. "We both are."

They drove away from the airport, the AC on full blast. "Is it as hot as you remember?" Church said it like she didn't know how awkward and strangely vulnerable the question made her sound. She was making an honest-to-God effort at conversation.

Sabrina could hear Val hissing in her ear, *Be nice.*

"It's the same," she said to the tinted window, watching the steady whip of patchy brown dirt and faded green scrub brush pass by them. "Most of it."

She experienced exactly one Arizona summer before Wade had kidnapped her. One seemingly endless stretch of days that broke triple digits well before noon and didn't let up until the sun had been down for hours. Kids with parents too poor to own swimming pools ran through sprinklers or played in the hose. If they were really lucky, they got dropped off at the public pool. She'd bought Jason and Riley one of those sprinkler attachments you hooked up to a hose. It looked like a ladybug with spaghetti hair. As soon as she turned it on, the water pressure sent the bug's mop of mini hoses squiggling and spraying water in every direction. The two-year-olds had loved it, squealing and running through the water in the little patch of grass in front of their apartment.

Happy. They'd been happy here. Safe before he'd found her and taken it all away. Before he'd killed her ... and just like that, her memories of this place, of that summer, turned sour.

She felt it. She felt *him*—Wade—a sudden, heavy weight in her head. A niggling itch inside her skull, like fingers digging into the bone of it, trying to touch her. To find his way out.

It was only a matter of time before he did.

FIFTEEN

Berlin, Germany

As far as days go, this one had been for shit.

Usually, his days were just boring. He woke up in his opulent penthouse suite and ate an exquisite gourmet breakfast prepared for him by a Michelin-starred chef. Then he showered before donning a suit that cost more than some people made in a year and riding his private elevator to his corner office. There he'd greet his agonizingly proficient assistant and pretend to listen while she gave him the rundown of the day's appointments, nodding appropriately when she handed him a stack of papers that needed his signature.

Most days, he managed to extricate himself from her grip without too much fuss before holing up in his office until she buzzed him to tell him he was late for a meeting or that he'd missed a video conference.

In other words, Benjamin Shaw was living in hell.

He had no illusions that what he did every day held any sort of importance. No way his control-freak father put him in charge of anything *real*. No meeting he attended or paper he signed held any significance. It only mattered in the respect that it kept him busy. Out of the way.

Trapped.

It should have been Mason. He was the heir, the one who mattered. The one their father had hung all his hopes on. If not for his older brother's death, Ben would have been allowed to fade into oblivion. This was not the life he'd chosen, but it was the only one he had.

No use bitching about it now.

"Mr. Shaw," his secretary's voice said, filling his office via the state-of-the-art intercom system, "your father would like to see you."

Ben instantly shot a glance at his desk clock and did a quick calculation. It was just after nine a.m. in Arizona. Sabrina and Church would have landed by now. When Reese left them last night, they'd been getting reacquainted. Hopefully that didn't involve shooting each other.

"Mr. Shaw?" His receptionist sounded nervous, like she was afraid he'd taken a header out his window rather than spend one nanosecond in his father's company and she'd have to be the one to break the news.

"Okay, Gail," he said, kicking his feet up onto his desk. "Tell *Mein Führer* I'm on my way."

———

Despite the late hour, his father's receptionist manned her desk, watching him with pale blue eyes as he cut across the expanse of blood-red carpet. "Good evening, Mr. Shaw," she said in slightly accented English. Unlike his own assistant, who looked like Mrs.

Doubtfire, this woman was gorgeous and, he knew from personal experience, more than accommodating.

"Good evening, Celine," he said without glancing in her direction. "This shouldn't take long. Why don't you get naked and meet me in my suite in, say …" He rolled his wrist to take a look at the face of his Jaeger-LeCoultre. It was well after seven o'clock. He'd purposely kept his father waiting for nearly an hour. "Fifteen minutes."

The door directly in front of him popped open. "You presume too much, Mr. Shaw," she said in an icy, dismissive tone that never failed to make him smile. They'd been sleeping together casually for a few weeks now. He liked her well enough and she was an invaluable source of information where his father was concerned.

"I presume nothing." He shot her a smirk over his shoulder before passing through the open door and shutting it with barely a whisper.

Livingston Shaw was where he always was, sitting behind his large, imposing desk. He had an unopened file in his hand. As soon as Ben walked in, his father's head came up and he pinned him with an irritated glare. Then he lowered the file, flashing the red band of tape that sealed it shut. Whatever was in it was important and he'd just interrupted his father's reading of it.

Maybe today hadn't been a total bust after all.

He took a seat and waited while his father placed the unopened file on the desk between them. "Where is Reese Harrison?"

The question was meant to rattle him. If he'd been anyone else, it probably would have. Instead of making him sweat, the question made him smile, gave him a hint of what was inside the file. "Reese?" He shrugged, leaning back in his chair. "Fuck if I know. Haven't needed him since I flew to Georgia for that meeting with—"

"Dispense with the theatrics, Benjamin." His father placed a hand on the file. "I know he's in the US and that he's doing something for you, so why don't you save us both a lot of time and trouble and tell me what it is."

The file could be anything. It could be an alphabetized list of his father's favorite animals. It could be the wine list from his favorite restaurant. It could also be a detailed report on everything Reese had been doing for the past seventy-two hours. Where he'd been. Who he'd been with. If that was the case, Sabrina was finished before she even had a chance to get started.

"Doing something for me?" He quirked his brow, giving his father a *WTF-are-you-talking-about-now?* look. One that never failed to get under his skin. "Like what, exactly?"

Instead of answering, his father picked up the file and opened one of the drawers in his desk. "I had hope, Benjamin," he said, dropping the sealed file inside. "Hope that with you finally agreeing to a leadership role here, that you and I would, at long last, find a common ground." He fit a small brass key into the drawer's lock and gave it a twist, securing the file inside. "That we would begin to heal as a family."

Ben leaned forward in his seat, every ounce of humor drying in an instant. "Hope? Healing? Are you for real?" The sound that followed could have been a laugh if it hadn't tasted so bitter. "Let's get a few things straight. I didn't *agree* to be your little sock puppet because I wanted to. I agreed because if I hadn't, you would've killed an innocent woman and her baby." He could still see Val, Sabrina's best friend, and her infant daughter. Lucy was nearly two years old now. He remembered that whenever he began to regret his decision. "And the only common ground between us is the three-by-eight plot where I buried Mason. There is no hope and there sure as fuck won't be any healing."

"Still blaming me for your brother's death," he murmured. "There was nothing I could do for him, Benjamin." His father sighed. "What they were asking of me would have compromised—"

"He was your son." The words sounded flat. Heavy.

"Yes, he was … and then he became a liability." His father blew out an exasperated breath. "Mason would have understood and accepted that. He would not have wanted me to do what they were asking me to do, merely to save him. Unlike you, he saw the bigger picture."

"Maybe, but he would've wanted you to save Em." Ben shook his head. Emily had been his brother's wife for exactly twenty-two days. She'd been Ben's friend considerably longer. "You could've let me go."

Now his father laughed. The sounds he made were no longer ones of annoyance. Now he sounded amused. "Benjamin …" He looked at him like he was a kid who'd insisted wearing a red cape instantly made him Superman. "What could you have done?"

He gripped the edge of the desk in front of him to keep himself from launching across it. "I could have *tried*."

"And you would have failed." His father waved a hand at him, his tone as dismissive as Celine's had been only minutes ago.

He thought of the pair of Desert Eagle .40s he used to carry. He hadn't worn them in months. Hadn't had a reason to. If he'd had them right now, his father would be dead. "I really, *really* need you to stop talking now."

Incredibly, his father fell silent for a few moments before changing tactics. "Is that why you've developed such an affection for Michael O'Shea? Why you insist on hiding him from me? Because he reminds you of your brother?"

"I'm not hiding anything," he lied smoothly. "O'Shea was just a guy. Now he's a *dead* guy at the bottom of the ocean."

"And Sabrina Vaughn? Is she just some woman?"

Not *was*. *Is*.

He stood. Being the son of Livingston Shaw, he'd learned very early to recognize when he was being played with. Usually it amused him to play back, but not tonight. There was too much at stake to keep engaging in his father's games.

"Sabrina who?" he said, feigning puzzlement for a moment before shooting the cuffs on his hand-tailored shirt. "Now, if you'll excuse me ..." He glanced at his watch. It was ten minutes after seven. Celine should be settled in and naked by now. "I have other, *better* things, to do."

"You're forcing my hand, Benjamin," his father said, tipping his head slightly so he could look him in the eye. "Michael and Sabrina may not be within my grasp, but there are others. Expendable others that—"

Panic slammed around inside his chest, knocking against the rage that always nested there, shaking it loose, and he nearly choked on its bulk. Valerie. Her husband, Devon Nickels. Their baby. Jason and Riley, Sabrina's brother and sister. Her partner, Strickland ... Mandy Black, the medical examiner who'd been her friend. Incredibly, Ben had assumed responsibility for them over the past year. He—the guy who didn't give a fuck about anything or anyone—suddenly found himself at the helm of a lifeboat filled to capacity.

"We have an agreement," he ground out. "I've kept my end of it."

"Barely." His father tented his manicured fingers under his chin, giving him a sympathetic smile. "Which is why I'm renegotiating the terms of our *agreement*."

"No, you're not." He shook his head. "You won't touch them— *any* of them." Ben leaned over his father's desk, slamming clenched fists into hardwood, glaring down at him. "Not. One. Hair. Not if you want me to keep playing show pony." He straightened himself, still looking down at his father because he knew how much he hated to be looked down at. "You even *think* about them and I'll blow it all. It'll be over before it even gets started."

"Think about what you're saying, Benjamin," his father said quietly. "And who you're saying it to."

"I know exactly what I'm saying, Dad—dead or alive, Michael and Sabrina are *gone*. You lost. Get used to it. Stop trying to punish other people in their place."

"It should have been you instead of Mason." It was the closest his father had ever come to admitting he regretted his decision to let his brother die. It didn't even hurt, knowing he felt that way. Hearing his father tell him he wished he was dead.

He didn't feel anything at all.

Ben smiled, the frost of it turning his lake blue eyes to ice. "Finally, something we agree on."

SIXTEEN

Yuma, Arizona

THE POLICE STATION HADN'T changed much. Two-story brown stucco with long, narrow windows. The sections of glass were wide enough to offer a slight view of the barren landscape that surrounded the building without being wide enough to allow the oppressive heat outside to seep its way in. She'd come here once with Valerie and her mother to pick up her younger sister, Ellie. Ellie had been fourteen at the time, caught with a bunch of other kids who'd been out in the fields busting watermelons. Senseless, petty vandalism, but to Val's mother, who'd spent nearly forty years in those fields alongside her husband, it'd been much more than that.

Sabrina could still see her standing over a surprisingly sullen Ellie, hands planted on her hips, mouth a hard, bloodless slash cut across her dark brown face. "What were you thinking, Elena? How could you be so cruel?"

"They're just watermelons," Ellie said, shrugging to cover the wavering in her tone. "You act like we were caught strangling puppies or something."

Before her mother could react, Val stepped in, pulling Ellie out of the chair she'd been sitting in. "You ungrateful little snot," she said, giving her little sister a brief shake. "How many of those watermelons do you think *Mamá* had to pick to feed you? Buy those ridiculous designer jeans you begged her for, huh?" Val was tiny. In that moment, glaring at her sister, she'd looked like a giant.

Ellie scoffed, jerking her arm out of Val's grip. "I don't know—how many do you think it took *Papi* to pick before it killed him? A thousand? Ten thousand?"

It was the first and last time any of them mentioned Val's father or what had happened to him. Until then, Sabrina had suspected he'd left them, gone back to Mexico to start a new life. One that didn't involve the responsibility of a wife and children. It probably would've been easier if he had.

It'd turned out to be an isolated incident. Ellie hadn't been in trouble, before or since. She'd left Yuma directly after high school, earning a partial academic scholarship to ASU to study forensic science.

"You ready for this?"

Sabrina looked at Church, still seated behind the wheel. She hadn't killed the engine yet, unwilling to give up the cold blast of air from the AC unless it was absolutely necessary. Was she ready for this? No. She wasn't. A week ago, the only thing she had to worry about hunting was a solitary wolf stalking a few head of cattle. What she was hunting now was far more cunning and infinitely more dangerous. She didn't want this. She didn't want any of it.

She wanted to go home.

"Let's just get it over with," she said, kicking her door open and stepping out into the blazing heat.

———

Their reception wasn't a warm one. The uniform behind the information desk took one look at their credentials and barely managed to stifle the sneer that teased at his mouth. "Major Crimes is on the second floor. I'll phone it up and let Santos know you're here."

"Santos? Will Santos?" she said, struggling to keep her tone light and curious. Santos had been the lead detective on her case nearly twenty years ago. In his early thirties then, he'd be in his fifties now.

"Yeah," the uniform said, cradling the desk phone against his shoulder, his gaze focused on her face. "You from around here?"

She shook her head, silently thanking Michael for insisting she memorize her cover story so thoroughly. "I was plugged into the Phoenix field office straight out of Quantico," she said, the lie so effortless for a moment, it felt like the truth. "A couple of cases led me down here. Must be why I recognize the name."

"Yeah, Detective Santos is a minor legend around here. He's the one who—" he said before he was cut off. "Hey, detective—the suits you ordered are here." He laughed at his own joke before giving them both a look. "Yes, sir," he said before dropping the handset back into its cradle. "He's on his way down."

"Is there something I should know?" Church said under her breath, shooting the uniform a brief look.

"Probably," she said in a matching tone. She remembered sharp eyes and a ruthless calculation barely hidden behind a smile that was a little too harsh to be genuine.

The last time Will Santos had seen her, her face had been obliterated. It'd taken nearly a dozen surgeries to put her back together after Wade had finished with her. Still, thanks to the countless articles written about her the last few years, there was a chance he'd recognize her.

Before she could say anything else, the elevator across the lobby dinged, its door sliding open to release its passenger. He hadn't changed much. Same dark, assessing gaze. Same crooked nose. Same cauliflower ear. Short stature but powerfully built, with wide shoulders and muscular arms. The only thing that gave away Santos's advance in years was the silver threaded through his hair and a slight softening around his belly.

He headed straight for her and for a moment, Sabrina was sure she'd been made. "I'm Detective Santos," he said, extending his hand while giving her one of those smiles that said he was carefully weighing her. "Thanks for coming so quickly."

His words made it sound like he'd been the one to request the FBI's involvement, and she wondered how true that was. While not all locals hated federal intervention, most of them resented the perceived loss of power when the FBI showed up. "Not at all," she said, forcing herself to look him in the eye. "I'm Agent Vance and this is my partner, Agent Aimes."

Santos shook Church's hand before turning his attention toward her. "Your timing is impeccable, agents. We've got another victim—care to join me?"

94

SEVENTEEN

"You know him."

It wasn't a question and Church didn't phrase it like one. Instead of denying it, Sabrina just nodded. "Yeah. I know him."

She and Church had decided to follow Santos to the crime scene rather than ride along. They'd been driving for about twenty minutes, heading away from the city into the flat, dusty desert that surrounded it.

"From before—when you lived here?" Church said, choosing her words carefully. It made her wonder just how much Ben had told her about what had happened to Melissa Walker. If she had to, Sabrina would guess he'd told her everything.

"He was the lead investigator on my case," she said. "But that's not where I met him." She stared out the window, waiting for Church to pepper her with questions. She didn't, which only confirmed that Ben was the king of the overshare. Finally she continued. "A few weeks before he took me, Wade killed a kid in a gas station bathroom." The corner of her mouth lifted in a humorless smile. "He and a bunch of his friends had come into the restaurant where I worked and he tried to hit on me." Outside her window, brown gave way to green as they made their way through farmland. Beyond the grass she could see workers in the fields, men and women, walking alongside a slow-moving truck, relaying melons into its bed. "Wade stabbed him to death and cut off his hand."

"He killed a guy for hitting on you?" Church gave a low whistle. "Let me guess, Santos caught that case too?"

Sabrina nodded. "Yeah. I was sure it'd been because of me, but then Santos came back into the restaurant a week later to tell me the clerk at the gas station had confessed." She'd thought she was safe. She wasn't. Wade took her a few days later and she was pretty sure it was something Santos never really got over. "He's a good cop. Sharp. Careful."

"That's not really going to work in our favor here, is it, Kitten?" Church said.

"You think he'll recognize me?" It worried her. The last time she saw Santos she'd just gone through another surgery to repair the damage done to her face. She'd worn a compression mask for nearly three months while it healed. When she finally took it off, her own grandmother hadn't recognized her. But that was before Jaxon Croft had come along and dragged her story—and her real identity—into the public eye.

Despite the very real possibility, Church shook her head. "I'm not worried about him recognizing you. You don't look like you. The real you *or* the fake you."

"Yeah," she said, running a quick hand over her short hair. "The stylist did a good job."

"It has nothing to do with your hair, Kitten," Church said. "Everything about you is different. You seem lighter somehow. Less … *occupied*."

The assessment reminded her of Wade. Made her wonder how long she had before he pushed his way in. Instead of voicing her fears, Sabrina slipped a pair of mirrored Aviators from her breast pocket and put them on. "Stop calling me *kitten*."

———

Up ahead Sabrina could see what looked like a roadside circus. Tents and protective screens had been erected, forming a barrier between the crime scene and the cluster of news vans across the street. Squad cars and unmarked SUVs formed a haphazard circle around the tents, bright yellow caution tape looped around side mirrors and door handles. Uniformed officers were stationed at intervals to ward off bystanders.

The car ahead of them swayed onto the soft shoulder, kicking up a plume of dust, and Church followed. Pulling up alongside Santos, she killed the engine. Before she could ask Sabrina if she was ready or if she needed a minute or any of a thousand inane questions Church would see as *normal* or *thoughtful*, Sabrina opened her door and stepped out of the car. The heat of the day pushed back at her, the sun instantly scorching the back of her neck, gluing the ridiculous silk of her blouse to her damp skin.

Without waiting for Church to join her, she circled the hood to stand in the space between their car and Santos's. It wasn't long before he joined her. "Hear you worked down in Phoenix for a few years, out of the academy," he said to her. Whether it was small talk while they waited for Church to join them or if he was vetting her story, she didn't know—but the Santos she remembered hadn't been one for small talk.

"Seven years." She cut him a look behind the reflective lenses of her sunglasses, grateful for the coverage they offered.

"Yeah . . ." He wagged a finger at her like he'd just remembered something. "It was your profile that busted the Russel case," he said, letting her know he read her jacket. "Pretty impressive."

"Not really." She shook her head, refusing to take the bait. That Ben had managed to plant her alias into the FBI database so quickly and back it up wasn't even surprising anymore.

"Don't sell yourself short," Santos said. "Russel was a sick son of a bitch who hurt a lot of women." Roger Lee Russel had been dubbed The South Mountain Killer by the media. He'd stalked and strangled seven female joggers in the state park on the south side of Phoenix, taking their engagement rings as trophies before he was caught.

"Phoenix PD did the heavy lifting. All I did was provide some insight."

"I read the profile," he said. "You did a hell of a lot more than that. You were the one who figured out he was targeting women who were engaged to be married and led the police to focus on wedding venue cancellations around the same time the murders started up." Santos nodded his head. "You're a helluva profiler."

Because she'd done none of those things and pretending to made her uncomfortable, she changed the subject. "I read about you too," she said, flashing him a cool smile. She remembered this game. It was a cop's equivalent to measuring dicks in the locker room. She hadn't enjoyed it when she was on the job and she didn't enjoy it now. "You were the lead investigator on the Melissa Walker case, weren't you?"

His jaw flexed, clamping down tight, letting her know they weren't just playing anymore. That jab had drawn blood.

Before he could say anything more, Church joined them. She'd been smart enough to shed her jacket. "Whoever said *it's a dry heat* is a complete liar," she said, softening her complaint with a good-natured grin.

"It'll cool off as soon as the rain starts," Santos said, pointing a thick, blunt finger upward. Dark, heavy clouds were starting to accumulate in the distance. "We're in the middle of our monsoon season, which means we're racing the clock." He angled his body toward the tents and started walking, forcing them to follow. "Once it starts coming down, CSU will be finished."

Stooping below the tape, the three of them walked in silence, heads down and necks stiff against the shouts and calls of the reporters across the street. So far they'd all minded their manners and stayed on the far side of the narrow strip of blacktop that served as a road, but that wouldn't last long. Sooner or later, one of them would get tired of waiting. "Suppose you'll want to hold a press conference," Santos said, reading her mind.

"That's your call, detective," Church said, leaving the media behind as they neared another cordoned-off area, this one surrounded by CSU techs in shirtsleeves. "My partner and I are here to help catch a killer. The operative word is *help*. Any and all decisions pertaining to the case and how it's handled are entirely up to local law enforcement."

From inside the dark interior of the stucco sanctuary, someone coughed, "*Bullshit.*" The word was followed by another cough.

A look of pure exasperation passed over Santos's face. "Agents Aimes and Vance, I'd like you to meet Detective Mark Alvarez, my partner."

In the open doorway stood a man in a limp-looking polo shirt and a pair of lightweight khakis, his short dark hair plastered to his scalp by sweat and humidity. Instead of offering to shake their hands, he looked at his partner. "You were right," he said, his tone holding an odd mixture of awe and anger. "It's her. She's dead."

EIGHTEEN

"Old lady found the body," Alvarez said, rummaging through the pages of his pocket notebook until he found the one he was looking for. "Mrs. Graciella Lopez." He read the name off the page before tucking it back in his pocket. "Said she's a housekeeper at the Vega place." Alvarez jerked his chin in the direction of a private drive about a hundred yards away. "As soon as she made the discovery, she high-tailed it back to the house, called 911, and promptly fainted."

The name was familiar. Twenty years ago, Vega Farms accounted for nearly a fourth of the crop production in Yuma. It had been Vega watermelons Ellie had been caught smashing as a girl. Sabrina nodded, surveying the land around her as if for the first time. "Is this all privately owned land?"

"Yup," Santos said, his jaw going tight again. "If it grows out of the ground and you're eating it within a hundred miles of here, chances are you peeled a *Vega Farms* sticker off it before you took a bite. This is all Vega land." He made an encompassing gesture. "Last count, nearly fifteen thousand acres."

"Mrs. Lopez stopped in on her way home to light a candle for her grandson—we've got him locked up on drug charges," Alvarez said. "She took one look at what's going on in there and forgot all about her grandson's legal troubles."

While Alvarez filled them in, Santos stood to the side to allow her into the sanctuary while Church hung back. It was dark inside the small, windowless room, forcing her to take off her sunglasses. Once her eyes adjusted to the gloom, it took everything Sabrina had in her to stay put.

Just another case. Just another body.

"You said, *it's her,*" she said to Alvarez. Reaching into the front pocket of her pants, Sabrina pulled out a pair of gloves. "You were able to identify the victim?"

Another look passed between Santos and his partner. "We can't say with one hundred percent certainty until we get her back to the morgue and call her family down to make a formal ID," Alvarez said, digging his hands into his pockets. "But it's Rachel Meeks."

"Rachel Meeks?" Church spoke up from the doorway. The structure was too small for all of them to fit at once. Along the back wall was a deep cement ledge littered with tall glass votives and flowers wilted by the oppressive heat. In front of the ledge was an altar. That's where he left her.

"Rachel Meeks, a local girl. Went missing a few weeks ago from the mall parking lot," Santos said, filling them both in but Sabrina was barely listening, his voice nothing more than a faint drone as she circled around the front of the altar.

There were obvious signs of torture. Cuts and abrasions—some deep, some more like scratches—littered her body. Bruises, in shades varying from yellow to black, scattered across her back and belly. Her fingernails were missing while the fingers themselves appeared to be broken. She'd been posed, her body forced into a kneeling position and secured with what looked like baling wire. Wrapped around tight enough to cut into her skin, it bound her thighs to her calves, holding her in place. Her legs, bent behind her, were crossed at the ankle. A large nail was driven through the sole of each foot.

Her hands had been posed also, flat and clasped together as if she were praying, pinned against each other at the wrist with another large metal spike, then held aloft with more baling wire. Sabrina's gaze followed the length of wire upward, seeing the way it was secured to the braided steel cable that ran down the center of the roof. Her eyes had not been taken, but they'd been gouged. Dried blood ran down her face like tears, the color of rust. The wounds at her wrists and feet were reminiscent of religious stigmata. Their significance was obvious. The eyes brought back memories she'd rather not harbor.

"A miracle," she said to herself, but Santos and his partner fell silent instantly.

"What?" Santos said while Alvarez puffed out his cheeks and rattled the keys in his pocket.

"She was a miracle," she said distractedly, circling her way to the rear of the body. "They all were. Your victims—they were chosen because they'd survived some sort of disaster or had a near-death experience." She looked up to find both Santos and Alvarez watching her. "Danielle Watson was shot in the head by her boyfriend during an argument and dumped at a rest stop on the way to Los Angeles when she was twenty-three. About the same time her boyfriend was pulling the trigger, a long-haul trucker spilled about a gallon of soda in his lap and pulled off to clean up. He found her in the parking lot, later reporting that he usually never stopped on a haul. Under normal circumstances, he would've blown by that rest stop like his truck was on fire."

"But he didn't," Santos said, rubbing a hand over his chin. "And that's what saved her."

"Everyone involved—doctors, police, EMS—they all said it was a miracle she survived." Sabrina shrugged. "Isla Talbert's mother took her to the doctor after weeks of complaining of joint pain. She thought it was just growing pains but Isla's CT scan lit up like the fourth of July. Her entire body was riddled with tumors. Bone cancer. Doctor told her mom it was too late, treatments would be a waste of time, and sent her home to die. Only she didn't. A few weeks later she told her mother she felt fine and wanted to go back to school so, her mother took her back to the doctor. Her next CT scan was clear. Not one tumor."

"A miracle," Alvarez said, nodding his head, aiming a look at the back of Santos's head. "It jibes with the religious theme he's got going. What else you got?"

"Stephanie Adams drowned on a trip to Rocky Point when she was in high school. She died in the water but was inexplicably revived while they were transporting her body back to the States forty-five minutes later." She looked at the girl they'd identified as Rachel Meeks. "She's a miracle too, and that makes our guy very angry."

"What makes you say that?"

"Because he's using what makes them special to punish them." She wasn't sure who asked the question but she answered anyway. "No matter what lies he's telling himself about why he's doing this, it's because he hates them for what they are."

Suddenly Sabrina wasn't standing in a small roadside sanctuary. She was crouched in the dark, weak and defenseless. Battered knees drawn to her heaving chest, the smell of infection and old blood—the smell of *him*—filled her nostrils. Her breath ragged, terror stabbing at her lungs, making it impossible to hold on.

And she wasn't alone.

Wade was standing over her. She could hear him, his breathing quick and shallow—thrilled by the sight of her, cowering and bleeding beneath him. The quiet *snick* of the knife he used as he flicked out the blade. There was a shuffling sound as if he'd stepped forward and suddenly, she could feel him. His breath on her cheek, hot and fast. Anticipation and excitement rolling off of him in waves as he crouched directly in front of her. Eager to get started.

The cool of the blade pressed against her skin, its keen edge biting into her, bringing with it a pain so sharp, so clean she almost didn't feel it as it sliced across her flesh.

Hey there, darlin'. Did you miss me?

NINETEEN

Kootenai Canyon, Montana

AVASA WOULDN'T MOVE. No matter how many times he tried to entice her away from the back door, the dog wouldn't budge. She sat with her nose practically pressed against the wood, tensing at every sound on the other side, waiting for Sabrina to walk through it. Michael knew exactly how the dog felt.

He looked at his watch for what was probably the tenth time in as many minutes. He did the math, running the numbers in his head and not liking what he came up with. She'd been gone for a full day now—nearly two—and he hadn't heard a peep. Not one word.

From the living room he caught snippets of conversation. Miss Ettie and Christina getting acquainted. The murmur of the movie they'd put on after dinner. He'd gone out to the barn as soon as the table was cleared, heading straight for the radio. He turned it on and listened to it spit static at him for nearly two hours—far past the communication window he and Ben had set up. Long enough for him to be certain that as far as Sabrina was concerned, he was being kept in the dark.

He tried to convince himself no news was good news. That if something had happened to her, Ben would have told him. If something was wrong he'd *know*.

The only thing he knew for sure was he was about to lose his fucking mind.

"*Terug,*" he said, commanding the dog away from the front of the door as he dropped his hand on its knob. For a second he thought she'd ignore him but then she complied with a soft whine, looking up at him with soulful brown eyes. Behind her, her tail gave a hopeful swish.

Pulling the door open, he stepped out on the porch, letting the dog precede him. Watching her race down the steps, Michael sat down in the same chair Sabrina sat in a few days ago when Leon Maddox had showed up.

He wasn't worried about Livingston Shaw dropping down from the sky and he wasn't worried he'd somehow work his way around the numerous precautions his former partner Lark and Ben had devised to keep him out of Shaw's reach. If Shaw found them, Ben would warn him. As for the chip in his back … Michael had resigned himself to a sudden and inevitable death a long time ago. He reached around, pressing his fingers into his lower back. Feeling its smooth edges. The way the pressure he put on it dug into his spine. It was a physical manifestation of every mistake he'd ever made, every fucked-up choice, every wrong move—and it was going to kill him. The past year had been a gift. A stay of execution. He'd made Sabrina promise to come back to him but the truth was he knew he couldn't stay with her.

Not forever. No matter how much he wanted to.

Avasa whined from the stretch of black that blanketed the yard. He could see the shape of her, pacing back and forth along the edge of the water. "I know, girl. I miss her too," he whispered. He didn't want to say the rest. That he was powerless. Stuck here with no way to help her. No way of knowing what was happening. If she was okay.

My days of playing guardian angel are over. Been over for a while now ... but I'll do what I can for her.

Ben hadn't been able to go with her but he hadn't sent her alone. That worried him more than anything. Reese was a pilot, not an operator. Ben would see sending him in to be Sabrina's back-up as the same as sending an electrician to fix a leaky faucet. Things like loyalty wouldn't enter into the equation. People were tools. Like his father, Ben manipulated them ruthlessly and applied them appropriately.

That's where he and Ben differed. To him, loyalty was all that mattered. Blind devotion was all he required. He had his own short list of people he knew he could trust to help her. People who would give their life for her if necessary. No hesitation. No questions. Her former Homicide partner, Strickland. Her former SWAT teammate, Nickels. Both of them would take a bullet for her without even thinking twice ... but if anything happened to either of them, Sabrina would never forgive him. If it meant the difference between her living and dying, he didn't care.

Standing, he walked to the edge of the porch. Beyond the eaves, the sky opened wide, showering him in the light of a million stars. It wasn't the stars he cared about right now.

He could make out the stark, black outlines of the sheer cliff walls that surrounded their valley. Three days ago, it'd been his sanctuary. Everything he'd ever wanted or needed had been held within it.

A place he'd been able to build a home.

Now it was a prison.

Something warm and soft pressed into his knee. He looked down to see Avasa looking up at him, those mournful brown eyes of hers aimed at his face. "I know, girl…" he sighed, dropping a hand to the top of her head to comfort them both. Shifting his gaze from the dog back to the cliffs, he reoriented himself to the black that surrounded them both. Turning his head, he found the hard ribbon of road that cut its way through the valley.

The only way in. The only way out.

He ruffled the dog's ears and the abrupt movement seemed to make up his mind. Decision made, he smiled. "Come on, girl— let's go for a ride."

TWENTY

Yuma, Arizona

"Where did you go?"

Sabrina turned toward the woman pretending to be her partner and studied her. Church wasn't looking at her, concentrating her attention on the road she was driving down. It was just the two of them again. They'd left Santos and his partner at the crime scene, volunteering to question the witness rather than stand around and twiddle their thumbs. Surprisingly, it'd been Church's idea—now she knew why.

"I don't know what you're talking about," she said dismissively, aiming her gaze out her window. Large flatbed trucks were scattered through the fields, carrying people in from a day's work.

Liar, liar, pants on fire...

"Sure you do, Kitten," Church said, taking a soft right onto a long gravel drive. "You've been on autopilot for the past twenty minutes."

Tell her you and me are just getting reacquainted, darlin'. Tell her all about how busy you've been remembering all the nasty things we got up to together in the dark...

"It's my first murder case in over a year," she snapped, jerking her head toward the woman sitting next to her. "Cut me some friggin' slack."

Church didn't answer her, at least not right away, nor did she seem stung by her harsh words. She simply drove on, choosing not to speak until they pulled into a circular drive in front of the posh ranch house surrounded by tall cottonwoods and sprawling palo verdes. Parked under one of the trees was a bright red Ford F-350 King Ranch. The truck easily cost more than what she'd gotten for an annual salary at SFPD.

"Look, you don't like me—I get that," Church finally said, killing the engine. "But I deserve to know if you're going to have some kind of PTSD freak-out. It's just common courtesy, especially considering I'm being expected to keep your ass alive."

PTSD. She'd been diagnosed with the disorder after her kidnapping and then promptly ignored her condition for over a decade. It always got worse around the anniversary of her abduction, but for the most part it'd been manageable. She'd foolishly believed finding and killing the man responsible for hurting her would lay things to rest but she'd been wrong. Finding out the person who'd held her, tortured and raped her for eighty-three days had been her own half-brother had nearly destroyed her... and Wade had taken the opportunity to squirm his way into her brain and set up shop.

He started talking to her. Taunting her. Reminding her she hadn't really killed him. That she'd only set him free. What was happening to her went far beyond PTSD. A psychologist would call it a psychotic break. Phillip Song had called it something else.

He'd called it a haunting.

This ain't no haunting, darlin', and I'm no ghost. I'm as real as you are. A part of you. Inside you... right where I belong.

"*Sabrina,*" Church snapped at her, all playfulness aside. She sounded worried. Sabrina couldn't blame her.

"I'm fine," she said in answer, forcing herself to look Church in the eye before aiming her gaze past her, out the windshield, at the deep wraparound porch that wound around the perimeter of the house, a pair of uniforms planted on either side of the front door. "Let's just get this over with."

She popped her door open and Church followed, muttering something under her breath. Church could talk shit all she wanted. No matter what she said to the contrary, confiding in her would be a mistake. Sabrina couldn't trust her.

That's right, darlin'. You don't need her... not when you have me.

"Did you say something?" Church said, looking at her over her shoulder as they mounted the porch steps.

"Nope." Sabrina stepped forward and in a gesture that already felt practiced, flashed her badge at the uniforms posted on the porch. "We're here to question the witness," she said, suddenly sounding and feeling like her old self.

"Santos radioed ahead," the uniform to her left said, reaching for the doorknob. "She's in with CSU now," he said, leading them into a spacious foyer. Saltillo tile, interspersed with hand-painted tiles, imported from Mexico. The walls, covered in framed family photos, were painted a creamy off-white. The officer led them through a set of double French doors and into what looked like the main living area. Settled into a large leather armchair was a woman who looked to be Miss Ettie's age, her shock of thick white hair twisted into a braid that fell to the middle of her back.

Crouched in front of her was the crime scene tech, dark head bent as she gently removed the old woman's shoes, placing them in a heavy plastic bag. Her shoulders were held tight. Stiff. She either shared everyone else's sentiment about the FBI or there was something about her assignment she objected to. Maybe she didn't appreciate being taken off an active crime scene to gather shoes and take fingerprints.

As soon as they entered the room, a man stood to greet them. The uniform spoke up. "Mr. Vega, these are agents with the FBI. They'd like to ask Mrs. Lopez some questions." Sabrina would've had to have been deaf to miss the tone the words had been delivered in. Respect bordering on reverence, as if the officer was asking for permission rather than simply explaining their presence.

If he'd noticed the officer's deference, Vega gave it no notice. "Of course," he said, reaching out to shake her hand and then Church's. "I think she's in shock..." Vega cast a concerned glance over his shoulder at the elderly woman behind him. "She hasn't said a word since the police arrived."

Behind him the crime tech stood, evidence bag in her hand. "I'm finished," she said, gaining the attention of everyone in the room. She no longer looked stiff; now she looked downright hostile and suddenly, Sabrina understood why.

It was Ellie Hernandez. Valerie's little sister. She was here and she was looking right at her.

TWENTY-ONE

HE'D PROMISED NOT TO hurt her if she did what he asked.

He lied.

Maggie lay in the dark, battered cheek pressed against the rough concrete floor, long gone warm under her feverish skin. She was bleeding. She could feel the sluggish weep of it drying against her face. Her back. Her arms. Between her legs.

Thinking of it—of what he'd done to her—made her want to curl into a ball, but she couldn't. She couldn't move. Couldn't protect herself. Couldn't fight back. Couldn't run.

She'd tried and she'd failed.

What he'd asked her to do was impossible. How could she give someone a miracle? She wasn't God. She wasn't anyone. But she'd done as he asked anyway because he'd promised ...

I want you to give to Robert what has been given to you. I want you to give him a miracle. Save his life.

Feeling foolish, Maggie had lifted her bound hands, dropping them onto Robert's chest. The man standing beside her watched, his gaze riveted to the place where her fingers pressed against the sick man's sternum. She'd been about to ask if she was doing it right. To tell him she didn't know what she was doing but then her gaze traveled the length of his arm, giving her a good look at what he held. As a vet tech, she'd seen something like it before. Knew what it was used for. It was a snap-action bolt gun, used by ranchers to kill cattle and horses. Pressed against the base of the skull, once triggered, it would shoot a bolt, as long and as thick as a man's finger, through bone and soft tissue and into the brain.

Maggie looked away, fixing her eyes on the wire wrapped around her wrists. The raw red rings left from where she'd fought against her restraints. She thought of the woman she'd heard earlier—her terrified screams, the keening wail of them suddenly cut short—and knew how she'd died.

Maggie had bowed her head and began to pray. Out of practice, she fumbled the words before she found their familiar rhythm. Her palms flat against the man's chest, she could feel the shallow rise and fall of it. How close he was to dying.

Hail, Holy Queen, Mother of Mercy, our life, our sweetness and our hope, to thee do we cry, poor banished children of Eve...

She didn't know how long she prayed but when she finally raised her head, she looked up to find that the man beside her was watching her. As soon as she made eye contact with him, she tried to look away. She didn't like what she saw there.

"You please me, Margaret," he said to her, reaching for her hands before she had a chance to pull away. He led her across the room, toward the door. Relief sapped the strength from her bones, causing her knees to buckle slightly, and she stumbled to keep pace with him.

He'd take her back to the room he kept her in. She'd sit in the dark and wait quietly. She'd be good. Do as he said and he'd keep his promise. She'd get to go home soon.

But he didn't take her back and he didn't keep his promise.

Instead he reached for the screen that stood across from the door. The one she'd seen when she came in. Thinking of what she saw behind it, she jolted back, yanking on the grip he had on her. Ignoring her protests, he simply jerked her forward before folding the screen back to prop it against the wall, giving her a full view of what she'd only caught a glimpse of before. It looked like a saw-horse, the kind you'd find on a construction site. Harmless—until you noticed the leather straps.

Like the bolt gun, she'd seen this thing before too. It was a breeding stand. Dog fighting was prevalent in the area and so was the brutal, disgusting practice of forced breeding. She knew without asking what he intended to do with it.

She pulled against the hold he had on her. The wire bit deeper, chewing at the sensitive flesh of her wrist. "You promised," she said, digging her bloodstained heels in to the cement floor, even as she started to shake her head. "You said if I did what you wanted, you wouldn't hurt me." Her voice climbed an octave, taking on the same hysterical edge she'd heard in the other woman's screams. "*Please, you promised.* You can't—"

He hit her, his closed fist slamming into the side of her head. Stars exploded across her field of vision. She crumpled to the ground, stunned, a high-pitched peal sounding between her ears, making her nauseated.

"I did no such thing, Margaret," he said, bending at the waist to lift her to her feet. The sudden shift knocked her off balance and she tilted forward, gagging on the oily roll of her stomach as she pitched forward again, her shoulder hitting the floor with another dull thud. "I said I wouldn't hurt you—*yet.*" He sighed as if exasperated and gave up on trying to stand her up. He settled for dragging her to the stand instead. "Unfortunately, suffering is a part of the process," he said, lifting her again but only far enough to sling her over the back of the bench, looping her bound hands around the hook set at its top. "I hope you understand this gives me no pleasure, Margaret."

He lied about that too.

———

She could hear him through the stout metal door, his voice penetrating the dark cocoon she'd wrapped herself in. He was talking. The rise and fall of his tone said he was speaking to someone else, but there had been no one. She'd screamed for help and no one came. Strained and tore against the leather straps he'd used to keep her in place. The only person she'd seen had been the man who lay dying in the corner of the room where he'd hurt her. Listening to him talk now, she slipped away. A final thought came before the dark pulled her under.

He isn't alone.

TWENTY-TWO

WHAT THE HELL WAS Ellie Hernandez doing here? Not only in Yuma, but *here*—at her crime scene?

It took Sabrina a moment to realize that while there was plenty of hostility in Ellie's sharp gaze, there wasn't an ounce of recognition. She was plenty angry but it wasn't at Sabrina. Ellie had no idea who she was.

"Thank you," she said, shoving aside the shock of seeing Val's little sister. "Find anything interesting?"

"She has blood on her hands—I think she might have touched the body." Ellie shot Vega a quick look, the angle of her shoulders making it obvious she was not including him in the conversation. "I took swabs and I took her shoes to do a comparative analysis against the shoe prints we cast at the scene." Ellie held up the bag. Through the heavy plastic she could see a pair of sturdy, expensive-looking leather shoes.

Beside her, Church reached into her pocket and pulled out a card. "We'd like everything run through our lab," she said, handing Ellie the card. "Just call the number on the back and our guys will get you set up." The lie was so smooth, for a second, Sabrina actually believed they had access to the FBI forensics lab. Then she remembered Ben had things like that—Lear jets that flew him around the world at the drop of a hat and secure, anonymous labs that processed evidence in hours, not weeks. For all she knew it actually *was* an FBI forensics lab he had access to.

Ellie nodded, aiming another look at Vega over her shoulder. "I'll do that as soon as I get back to the office," she said, tucking the card into the front pocket of her pants. If she didn't know any better, Sabrina would swear she looked relieved. She thought of the way the officer had addressed Vega. Like he was the only one who deserved respect and deference. It was obvious Ellie saw it too and she didn't share the sentiment.

"Did you know the victim?" Sabrina blurted it out, following instincts that felt rusty at best. Ellie would have seen the body at the crime scene. If she knew Rachel Meeks, she would have recognized her.

Ellie shifted in her boots. She didn't look hostile anymore; now she just looked sad. "We went to high school together," she answered vaguely, shooting another quick glance over her shoulder. "I should go," she said, making her way toward the door. Before she could say another word Ellie was gone, the front door slamming behind her.

"What about you, Mr. Vega?" she said as soon as Ellie was gone. "Did you know the victim?" Something was going on between Vega and Ellie, she just couldn't figure out *what*.

"Me?" Vega leaned away from her as he said it. Guilty people did that. Tried to physically distance themselves from the truth.

Reading the situation perfectly, Church stepped forward. "Mrs. Lopez, I'd like to ask you a few questions if you don't mind," she said, her tone easy and nonthreatening. Even though the old woman didn't respond, Church took a seat on the ottoman in front of her, flicking Sabrina a glance before bouncing it to the man standing in front of her. She'd caught it too—Vega was hiding something.

"Mr. Vega, would you mind stepping into the foyer with me for a few minutes," she said, gesturing toward the open doorway Ellie had just disappeared through. Despite her words, it was clear she wasn't making a request. She was giving him an order.

Vega hesitated like he was going to refuse but thought better of it. "Of course," he said, following her into the foyer. "But, to be honest, I'm afraid I won't be much help. There isn't a whole lot I can tell you."

"You can start with answering my question: did you know the victim?" She nailed him with a glare she hadn't used in well over a year. One that said lying was useless.

"How can I answer that?" he said, running a hand over his short dark hair. "I don't even know *who* the victim is."

"Preliminary ID says she's a missing person by the name of Rachel Meeks," she told him while watching him closely and she wasn't disappointed. Whether he knew it or not, he'd just answered her question. Not only had he known Rachel Meeks, he'd had some sort of relationship with her.

Best watch yourself now, darlin'. This one wouldn't know the truth if it walked up and slapped him the face.

"Like Ellie said, we all went to high school together," he said, shaking his head, suddenly looking uncomfortable. "And I don't think—"

"Where were you when Mrs. Lopez discovered the victim?" She cut him off before he could say it. He was about to ask for a lawyer. Once he did that, she was done asking questions. While it was perfectly legal for her to question a witness without legal counsel present, she was walking a thin line and they both knew it.

"I—" He hesitated again before giving her a defeated shrug. "I was in my study, answering e-mails. Graciella poked her head in to tell me she was going home and I offered to drive her but she declined. She said she'd rather walk—I'm assuming so she could stop at the shrine and light a candle for Hector." Hector must be the jammed-up grandson. He shrugged. "Anyway, she left. Next thing I know, she's back ... and screaming."

Sabrina listened to his story, trying to find an angle. "Do you always do that? Give your maids rides home?"

"Graciella isn't just my maid," he said, his tone suddenly going defensive. "She was my nanny. She raised me." Whether she'd meant to or not, she'd hit a sore spot. "And I'm through talking." He reached into the snap pocket on the front of his shirt and pulled out a card of his own. "If you want to talk to me again, you'll have to set it up through my attorney." No sooner did she have the business card in her hand than he moved toward the front door. "I'll see you out."

Before she knew it, she was turned out like a stray cat, left to wait for Church to finish her interview with the witness on her own. She glanced down at the thick, satiny piece of cardstock in her hand, running her thumb over rich, raised letters.

Arturo Bautista, Esquire
Attorney at Law

"Agent Vance?" There was only one uniform attending the door—the other would have left with Ellie to transport the evidence back to the crime scene. The skies had finally opened up, letting a loose a torrent of desperately needed water. Whatever evidence the CSU techs hadn't managed to lift before now was being washed away.

"Yes," she said, raising her voice slightly to be heard over the din of falling rain.

The uniform looked over his shoulder, like he felt guilty for what he was about to do.

"There was someone here to see you," he said, his tone telling her that whoever it was, he didn't approve. "He asked me to give this to you." He thrust a piece of paper at her. "Said he needed to talk to you."

It was a phone number, scrawled on the back of a fast food receipt—one she didn't recognize. She was about to stuff it into her pocket when she caught the short message and name that accompanied it.

We need to talk.
—Croft

TWENTY-THREE

First Val's little sister and now Jaxon Croft. In the space of a few seconds, it became abundantly clear to Sabrina that as far as the case went, she wasn't going to be catching many breaks. The only difference between Croft and Ellie was Croft had recognized her right away. And judging from the note in her hand, he hadn't changed much in the two years since she'd last seen him.

As usual, he wanted something from her. Something she would more than likely be hard-pressed to give.

"Thanks," she said stuffing the scrap into her pocket before turning and making a mad dash through the downpour, heading for the car. There was no doubt the officer who'd talked to Croft would tell his superior a reporter had come sniffing around, looking to talk to the FBI. That wasn't going to sit well with the locals, especially after Church had made it clear that handling the media would be left to them.

Not trusting herself to remain calm, Sabrina used the cell Michael had given her to send a text to the number Croft left for her.

What are you doing here, Croft?

She waited less than thirty seconds for a reply.

Meet me at Luck's. 10 o'clock and I'll explain.

Luck's. Of course Croft would want to meet her at Luck's. It was the restaurant she'd worked at when she lived here as a young woman. Where she'd met Val. It was the place Wade had found her. She'd been heading home from Luck's when he'd abducted her. Dragged her into the dark and kept her there.

Before she had a chance to respond, another text came through.

It's important.

She laughed, unable to hold it in anymore. Important? Yeah, extortion and blackmail usually were. It was nearly six in the evening now. Four hours would give her plenty of time to figure out how she was going to shake Church.

As if a mere thought could conjure her into being, Church appeared. Darting off the porch, she made a run for the car, calling over her shoulder to someone standing in the open doorway of the house. She caught a glimpse of Vega, silhouetted against the lights inside the house. She couldn't see his face but Sabrina was sure he was looking at her.

"Holy shit," Church squealed as she flung the door open and dove into the driver's seat. "It's like the end of the world out there."

"No," she answered vaguely, attention still trained on the cell screen. "Just Arizona monsoon season." Another text came through.

It's about Wade.

"You get anything useful out of Old McDonald?" Church said, running a hand over her face, trying to squeegee the rain off her skin. Sabrina didn't have to look up to know she was trying to get a glimpse of the phone's screen.

"Just that he knew the victim," she said, stabbing her thumbs against the cell's touchscreen, punching out a text before she could change her mind. "And the number for his attorney." Beyond the window, the darkening sky continued to pour. Rain and thunder so close it shook the car she sat in. Before she could change her mind, she hit send.

I'll be there.

TWENTY-FOUR

You sure about this, darlin'?

The voice inside her head had been trying to talk her out of her meeting with Croft for hours now. Logic told her it was just her subconscious warning her Croft couldn't be trusted. That the last time she'd trusted him she'd regretted it, but now, as then, she ignored the warning. Meeting Croft was risky but so was refusing him. He'd recognized her. If he wanted to make trouble for her, he could ... and it would be the last thing he ever did.

In the end, she'd decided to try honesty for a change and tell Church what was going on. She'd been less than pleased to find out they hadn't even made it a full twenty-four hours into their investigation before she'd been recognized. "Let me go instead, I'll find out what he wants," she'd said in the same easy tone she'd use to describe garroting someone. "Report back before you know it."

Now there's an idea. Let your new partner do your dirty work.

"Yeah—would that be before or after you killed him?" she said while she pulled on the only t-shirt she'd packed, along with a pair of worn jeans.

Church shrugged. "Probably after."

Sabrina shook her head. "Working with you is like working with a psychotic toddler, you know that right?"

"Thanks," she said, sounding genuinely pleased by the comparison. "What does he want, anyway?"

It's about Wade.

Suddenly, her new honesty policy began to chafe. "He didn't really say—just that it was important."

"So, he wants to meet you but won't say *why*?" Church shook her head, skeptical. Whether it was because she didn't trust Croft or because she could sense the lie, Sabrina couldn't tell. "Smells fishy, Kitten. Just stay here, let me take care of it."

Sabrina laughed. She couldn't help it. The truly insane part of it all was that for a few seconds, she actually considered it. "This is where I'll be," she said, bending over to write Luck's address across the hotel notepad tossed on the nightstand. "If I'm not back by midnight, you can kill him—deal?"

Suddenly all business, Church glared at her. "I'm being serious, Sabrina. I was sent here to do a job and despite my recent lackluster performance concerning your family, I *do* my fucking job."

"Your job is to make sure that the fact I'm alive remains a secret," she said, applying logic to the situation. "Croft isn't going to sell me out without at least telling me what he wants . . . besides, he played it smart. He approached a local officer and asked him to deliver a message to *me*." She shook her head while she shoved her foot into first one boot and then the other. "Croft isn't stupid. Someone knows he's here," she said, jerking hard on her boot laces, pulling them tight. "If he disappears or turns up dead, that little note he passed to me is gonna pop up. That uniform will remember and he'll say something and then I'll be questioned. If that happens, it'll only be a matter of time before everyone knows who I really am."

Church glared at her for a few seconds before flopping back on the bed. "*Fine*, if you're gonna be all logical about it." She sighed. "Midnight—and not one minute past."

———

Exiting the car, Sabrina could see nothing about the place had changed. Large, rumbling tractor-trailers waited in line at the weigh station while others filled up on gas for the next leg of their trip. She could see lot lizards—what truckers called prostitutes who frequented truck stops—moving from parked vehicle to parked vehicle, looking for someone to buy what they were selling.

Someone ought to warn them about how dangerous it is out here for a woman, all by herself…

She walked across the expansive parking lot, dodging raindrops on her way to the brightly lit brick and glass building. Sabrina yanked open the door, setting off the automated chime. Out of nowhere, a perky hostess appeared. She was young, almost as young as she'd been when she worked here. Her starched, white uniform looked brand-new and the bright green four-leaf clover on her breast pocket had the name *Lauren* stitched across the front of it. Twenty years and the uniforms hadn't changed.

Behind her, a man in a pair of dress slacks and a white button-down wiped down the lunch counter. The badge clipped to his shirt was engraved with the name *Manny*. It took only a few seconds to recognize him as the busboy she used to work the late shift with.

He stood taller than she remembered, thicker around the middle. Softer. Gray threaded through the dark hair he'd always kept short, but he essentially looked the same. He turned toward her just a bit, still wiping at the counter. She could see his badge had the word *manager* under his name.

"Can I get you a booth, sweetie?"

The hostess was talking to her, calling her *sweetie,* even though she was practically old enough to be her mother. "Yes," she said, glancing at the large shamrock-shaped clock that still hung over the counter area. It was a quarter to ten. "I'm meeting someone—"

"Oh," the hostess said brightly, tucking the menus back into their holder. "Is it a gentleman? Dark hair? Dreamy brown eyes?"

Dreamy? As far as she was concerned, Croft was about as dreamy as a bout of dysentery, but she nodded. "That's him."

Of course Croft beat her here. He had an annoying habit of always being two steps ahead of everyone else. He was like Ben that way.

"He's waiting for you in back," the hostess cocked her head to the side, jerking it toward the back of the restaurant. Croft was sitting in a corner booth, watching her. "Can I get you something to drink?"

Ain't too late, darlin'. You can still leave. Let that crazy gal kill 'im before he mucks everything up.

She thought about the last text Croft sent her. *It's about Wade.* Croft was reckless but he didn't have a death wish. No way he'd play that card unless it was true.

"Coffee would be great," she said, moving in the direction the hostess had indicated. The closer she got, the more uncomfortable Croft seemed to get. Whether it was from the hostile glare she was giving him or if he was having second thoughts about asking her to meet, it was hard to tell.

"What?" she said, sliding across the worn vinyl bench. Sitting on the seat next to him was a cardboard banker's box. The kind you used to store paperwork.

"Hello to you too," he said, a wry smile lifting the corner of his mouth, his dark gaze folding over her, appraising her. "You look good for a dead woman."

"I don't really qualify my appearance as important, Croft." She sat forward a bit and dropped her voice. "So maybe you should just tell me what this is about before I lose my patience."

"Huh," he said, giving her a one-note chuckle. "It's been awhile —I forgot how patently unpleasant you can be."

This was a mistake. She moved to stand but he stopped her, one of his arms shooting across the table to wrap a hand around her forearm. "Wait—"

The look she gave him caused him to yank his hand back before he could blink.

"I'm sorry—I forgot. No touching." He flattened his hands against the table and leaned away from her. "It's just…" He let his words die out, giving the hostess a flat, polite smile as she deposited her coffee onto the table between them. As soon as she was gone, he continued. "I was surprised to see you, although I don't know why—this isn't exactly the first time you've faked your own death."

"Don't *ever* say that out loud again," she said, dropping her voice low as she leaned across the table. "Not unless you're tired of living."

Croft opened his mouth like was going to say something but then thought better of it. He let it snap shut before giving her a curt nod. Like she'd told Church, he wasn't stupid. He knew there was no way she could've pulled off her disappearance alone. Not again. Not with Michael involved.

130

"Now," she said, lifting her coffee cup to her mouth to take a sip, "what are you doing here?" She lowered her cup. "No, wait— let me guess. You're following a story."

Croft shifted in his seat, lacing and relacing his fingers on the tabletop. "I'm not a reporter anymore." His elbow bumped against the box sitting next to him. "It's—I…" He looked away from her, catching his bottom lip between his teeth. "I'm writing a book. True crime. About Wade Bauer."

Well, look at me. I'm gonna be famous.

Sabrina felt her gut clench, instantly rebelling against the coffee she'd just drank. "Of course you are," she said, setting the cup down with a sharp click. Her gaze fell to the box, imagining what was inside. She suddenly didn't want to know. "What does that have to do with me?"

"Aside from the obvious?" Croft shrugged. "Nothing." He sighed, letting his gaze find hers again before he continued. "But I've been doing a lot of research. Interviewed friends and family. Trying to get a handle on it. What he did. Why he did it."

Now it was her turn to laugh. "Is that all? I can answer both questions in short order. Wade abducted, raped, and tortured nineteen women. He played with them. Chased them down like animals and then, when he couldn't control himself anymore, he stabbed them to death before leaving them in the woods to rot. As for why—"

I did it—all of it—because of you. Because you ran from me. All those girls are dead because of you. Their pain. Their suffering… that's on you, Melissa—every single second of it.

She swallowed hard, forcing down the surge of rage that suddenly gripped her. "He did it because he could. Because he wanted to. Because no one stopped him."

"I contacted his wife. Shelly Bauer." The words sounded like an apology. Like it was something he regretted.

"I knew Shelly." She'd been Shelly Keene back then—and Jed Carson's girlfriend. How she'd gone from one best friend to the other was a mystery. One Sabrina hadn't given much consideration. Things like that happened in small towns like Jessup. "She hated me back then. I can't imagine that's changed, seeing how I shot her husband in the face."

Croft blanched slightly, letting her know exactly how right she was. "She didn't want to talk to me about you or Wade … didn't want to talk to me about anything, actually." His hands went still again. "But she sold me the key to a storage locker in Marshall for two thousand dollars."

His admission brought her gaze to the banker's box beside him. The hair on her arms stood up and she suddenly realized Wade had gone quiet inside her head. Like he was waiting. "What's in the box, Croft?"

Realizing he had the upper hand, he took the opportunity to ask a question of his own. "He's the reason you're here, isn't he? Wade—he's connected to the murders. The crime scene I saw you at today." He pushed his shoulder off the back of the booth, his tone hushed and eager. "It's got something to do with him."

"You may not be a reporter anymore, Croft, but you still get this excited gleam in your eye when you smell a juicy story." She sat back, forcing her jaw to loosen as she folded her arms across her chest. "It's kinda disgusting."

He jerked back in his seat, rubbing his hand across his mouth like she'd punched him in it. "People have a right to know the truth. To be able to find a way to move past it." He leaned forward again, having the sense to drop his voice before he continued. "Not everyone has the luxury of just disappearing from their lives without a trace when shit goes south."

Fuck this. "I hope you die in a fire," she said, moving to leave.

"Letters," he blurted out, grabbing at her with his words, nailing her in place. "They're letters. Newspaper clippings. Sent from someone here in Yuma, to a PO box in Marshall. Wade's PO box."

"You're lying." She said it plainly, sounding more certain than she actually felt. "No one here knew Wade or what he did to me. No one."

Croft shook his head, his jaw set at a tight angle. "Not no one. Someone *knew*. They're tons of them. Whoever wrote them claims to have seen him the night he left you at the church. Describes it to a tee. What he wore. *Where* he left you . . . right down to the description of the blanket he covered you up with."

Each word sucked more and more oxygen out of her lungs. Spun it away from her, made it impossible to reclaim. She recalled none of it. The caustic sting of bleach when Wade washed traces of himself off her skin. The darkness of the trunk he'd put her in. The frigid bite of the cement bench he'd left her on. But someone else did. She'd filled in those blanks on her own, but . . .

Someone else saw it all.

"Is everything okay here?"

She looked up to find Manny standing over them, coffeepot in hand. She forced herself to smile and nod. Looking past him she could see several diners glancing nervously in their direction. "Everything's great, thank you." She shot a look at Croft across the table and he nodded in agreement.

Manny wasn't buying it. "Just try to keep it down, okay?" he said, tipping more coffee into her mug. "I don't want to have to ask you to leave."

She nodded, not really trusting herself to speak. As soon as Manny was gone, she leveled a look at Croft.

"He idolized Wade," he told her, confirming her worst fears. "They wrote back and forth. Talked about … things."

Something cold did a slow crawl under her skin and she fought the urge to brush it away. "What sort of things?"

"You," Croft said, that excited gleam in his eye replaced by something that looked almost like regret. Like he wished he'd never started down this path. The one that led him to her and the story of what Wade had done to her. For a moment, he looked like he wished he'd never heard her name. "They mostly talked about you." He didn't have to tell her anymore than that. She understood what that meant.

"None of that explains why you asked me to meet you here," she said, her voice so flat and calm, the sound of it terrified her.

"Really?" Croft gave her an exasperated shake of his head. "Okay, let me spell it out for you: the guy who wrote to Wade is the same guy who's been killing people here for the past year. He's picking up where your brother left off."

TWENTY-FIVE

"Half. Brother." She bit each word in half, spitting them at him from across the table. "Wade was my—"

"If splitting hairs makes it easier for you to deal, *fine*," Croft said, leaning into her, batting her anger away like it was nothing. "Personally, I think it's a waste of goddamned time. This freak is killing people."

"*People*," Sabrina said. "Not just girls. Not just blue-eyed waitresses. Women. Children. All shapes and sizes." But even as she said it, she knew she was grasping at straws.

"There're those hairs again." Croft shook his head, jaw clenched in what looked like disgust.

The silence inside her head was deafening. It was how she knew Croft was right. That he was telling her the truth. Whatever he had in that box could be the key to finding this killer. Or at the very least, the key to figuring out how her twenty-year-old DNA could have ended up under the fingernails of a woman who'd been abducted and murdered only a few months ago.

"Is that why you're here?" Sabrina said, turning in her seat to look at him, doing her best to keep her gaze from landing on the box sitting beside him. It was all about power with Croft; if he thought he had any, he'd exploit it shamelessly. "You found a few pieces of paper in a storage locker so you hauled ass to Arizona?"

"I could ask you the same thing," he said, gaze roving over her face, looking for a crack in the smooth surface she was showing him. "What could possibly have happened that'd force you to leave whatever tropical island you and your contract-killer boyfriend have been sunning yourselves on for the past year? Had to have been pretty big."

"I don't have a boyfriend. Never have."

"Okay." Croft snorted in disbelief. "Whatever Michael O'Shea is to you then."

"What Michael *is,* is dead," she said, forcing her voice flat. "He died in a helicopter crash off the coast of Colombia a year ago."

"Dead…" Croft let out a short bark of laughter. "Sure he is— just like you were until about six hours ago."

Instead of arguing with him, she just smiled. The last time they did this, there'd been nothing smooth about her. Wade had been chipping away at her sanity, tearing her apart from the inside out and it'd showed. She'd been vulnerable and desperate.

This time she was neither.

"You want something from me—that much is obvious," she said, carefully folding her hands on the tabletop between them. "So, why don't you just nut up and ask."

"A few years ago, you promised me interviews." He looked at her hands. Probably making sure they weren't about to reach out and throttle him. "I want them."

"I didn't *promise* you anything, Croft." She shook her head slowly. "You blackmailed me—don't get it twisted."

"And I could do it again." His expression hardened under the glare she gave him. "Wouldn't it just be easier to give me what I want?"

"Easier?" The corner of her mouth quirked up in the kind of exasperated half smile you gave an over-indulged child. "No ... what would be easier would be for me to have you killed." The half smile bloomed into a full-fledged grin. "Seriously. It would take less than five minutes."

The color drained from Croft's face but he stood firm. "I thought you said he was dead."

"I'm swimming in shark-infested waters these days, Croft ..." She smiled softly. "Michael isn't the only killer I know."

He must have heard the truth in her voice because he visibly blanched. "You wouldn't do that," he said, not sounding at all confident.

"Are you sure?" she said, bluffing him flawlessly. "I'm not the person I used to be."

"Look, I didn't come here to blackmail you," Croft said, losing his nerve. "I came here to propose a trade—I'll give you the box and everything in it if you agree to give me my interviews."

She eyed him for a moment, shifting her gaze between Croft and the box. "It's all in there?"

He sighed, suddenly sounding tired. "Yes."

"Then you know everything," she said. "You don't need me."

"I know what *he* knew—Wade." He swiped a rough hand over his face. "I know what he felt ... *his* reasons for doing what he did," he said, looking sick. "I want your side of things."

She studied the box. What Croft was proposing made her want to throw up, but she didn't have much of a choice and he knew it. Still, she didn't have to make it too easy. "I'm dead, remember? How can I talk to you and stay that way?"

"I'll backdate them—make it clear you granted me interviews before your death. I won't tell anyone about … *this*. I swear," he said, reminding her he might be a lot of things but he'd never been a liar.

"Okay." She stood from her seat and this time he didn't try to stop her.

He looked up at her, relieved she'd agreed. "How—"

"Meet me here, day after tomorrow. Same time." She held out her arms, gesturing for the box.

Croft hesitated, but only for a moment, before he lifted the box and gave it to her. "There's other stuff in here too," he said, averting his gaze while setting the box into her arms. "Journals."

Journals. Wade had kept journals.

She almost dropped the box. The way he couldn't look at her told her more than a direct answer from him ever could. Croft had read them. He knew everything.

Sabrina balanced the box in one arm while she dug a few crumpled bills from her pocket. "See you later," she said before she dropped the cash on the table and left, a box full of secrets tucked against her hip.

TWENTY-SIX

THE BOX SAT ON the seat beside her, lid crammed tightly in place. She couldn't stop looking at it. Sabrina drove, making turns and stopping at traffic lights without having a clear idea of where she was headed. Within minutes, she was miles from her truck stop meeting with Croft. Heading as far away as she could from what he'd told her.

Wade had kept journals.

We both know you're dyin' to, darlin', so why don't you just ask?

He'd been heckling her for a while now. Pushing her. Poking at her. Reminding her she'd never be rid of him—not really—and she'd been a fool to think otherwise.

She needed to talk to Ellie. It was obvious she knew more than she was letting on. If she could just talk to her, ask her—

You want to know if I told him about all the things I did to you in the dark . . .

Before she knew was she was doing, she jerked the wheel to the right, piloting the car into a deserted dirt lot. She barely had the car slammed into park before she was grappling with the door handle, getting it open only seconds before she threw up, coffee and stomach acid splattering against the hard-packed earth beneath her.

It was something she never talked about—*couldn't* talk about. Twenty years later and she'd never told a soul. What he'd done to her. How badly he'd hurt her. How she hadn't been able to stop him. The shame of it stung. Tears prickled at the corners of her eyes and she squeezed them shut, forcing them back.

Come on now, darlin'... be a brave little toaster and ask. Isn't that why you came here? To figure it all out? To finally understand why?

Knowing that Wade had written it all down, pored over the pages, carefully choosing each word, using them to describe what he did to her so he could relive it. So he could share her shame with someone else...

The truth. She was here for the truth.

She pressed her forehead against the armrest attached to the car door and squeezed her eyes shut. "Did you?" she whispered, ignoring the loosening sensation in her gut that saying the words out loud caused. Like her fingers were peeling back from the edge she always seemed to be dangling over. "Did you..."

Did I what? Laughter rang inside her head. *Did I tell him all about it? Every time I chased you. Every time I cut you. Every time I forced my way inside you...*

"Stop." The word ground against her throat, harsh and angry, like a threat. She wiped her mouth against the back of her hand before pulling the door shut. Sitting in the dark she wrapped her hands around the steering wheel, tightening their grip until she could pretend they weren't shaking.

Ohhh… The voice went velvety soft within her head. *You wanna know if I told him how much you liked it.*

Her hands cranked around the steering wheel, lip curled in a snarl, lifted by the guttural sound that ripped its way from her mouth. "You disgusting piece of—"

Something thumped against the glass, the hard, fast knock of it jolting her in her seat. She wrenched around in her seat, aiming her gaze out the window, at the source of the sound.

There was a man standing on the other side.

As soon as she turned to look at him, his knuckles fell away from the window, leaving dark, bloody smudges in their place.

TWENTY-SEVEN

"Miss, are you okay?"

The voice on the other side of the window sounded concerned, the question it conveyed at odds with the blood his hand left behind on the glass between them. Shrouded in shadow, the man was nothing more than a towering figure, his features lost in the dark.

Behind him Sabrina could see the squat outline of a low-slung building sprawled in the dirt. From the gentle peak of its roof rose a plain wooden cross.

Looking at the blood he'd left smudged on the window, the man took a step back. She caught a flash of white at his collar. Relief washed through her as she reached down to open the door.

Ain't this how things went down between you and me? I coaxed you out of the car and then I shot you ... good times.

Her hand stalled on the handle for a moment, her gazed fixed on the blood streaked across her window. A priest. He was a priest.

She could trust a priest.

And I was a cop. You trusted me and look what happened.

She yanked on the handle, pushing the door open to step out, driving him back even farther. "What church is this?"

"Saint Rose of Lima," he said, looking around like he wasn't sure himself. He glanced hopefully at his watch. "Are you here for mass?"

Saint Rose.

Somehow she'd ended up at the same church where Wade had left her for dead. How was a mystery. She didn't remember this place. Had never been here that she could recall. "Why is there blood on your hands?" she demanded, her words hard and fast, gaze falling to his hands. They were stained dark, clasped in front of him. Her hand found the grip of her Kimber, wrapping around it. "I'm not going to ask again."

"I—" He looked down at them, his expression going blank for a moment before he reached into one of his front pockets.

She pulled the gun off her hip and waited.

"There's a stray cat in the prayer garden," he said, pulling out a handkerchief. He was frowning, too busy rubbing at his blood-coated hands to realize she'd drawn her weapon. "I think a coyote got hold of it. I was trying to—"

"Show me," she said, reaching into the car to pull the keys from the ignition. Turning back around, she caught him shaking his head no.

"It's dead. There is nothing you can—"

She reached into the car again and pulled out the credentials Church had given her. "Show me," she said again, flashing the badge before using the key fob to lock the car.

He finally noticed the gun, his gaze falling to it for a moment before finding her face again. This time, instead of refusing the priest merely nodded. "This way," he said, tipping his head to indicate the direction. If he thought it was strange that a semi-deranged FBI agent wanted to investigate a dead cat, he didn't say so—just led the way around the side of the church toward a wrought iron gate. "I think she must have climbed the wall, trying to get away from the coyote," the priest said, angling his body away from the gate so she could pass through it ahead of him.

The prayer garden was small, a nearly perfect square surrounded by a stucco wall easily twice as tall as she was. Cobblestone pavers cut down the middle of it, lined on either side with rain-battered rose bushes. Under the garden's tree stood a bench—black marble stretched between two squat cement pillars.

Sure you don't remember this place? I sure do.

Splayed across the bench was a cat. At least she thought it was a cat. It looked like a lump of dark fur, tattered and matted with blood. Without even thinking about it, Sabrina reached into the pocket of her jeans for a pair of gloves but came up empty. It'd been a long time since she'd broken the habit of carrying gloves with her wherever she went.

Old habits die hard, huh, darlin'?

Scanning the cobblestone for footprints, she hunkered down to examine the cat, hands hovering at her sides. She didn't need to touch it to know whatever killed it hadn't been a coyote. Looking up, she found the priest watching her, standing a few feet away. "Poor thing," she said, not having to fake the remorse in her tone. "I'll take care of this for you." She forced her mouth into a small smile. "Do you have a paper bag or a box to put her in?"

He nodded, seemingly relieved she'd given him something to do. "Yes, I'll go get it," he said, ducking back into the church.

As soon as he was gone she pulled her cell out and started to take pictures. Snapping off several, she caught the glint of something with the flash. Circling around the bench, she reached into her pocket. Pulling out the knife Michael had given her, she used the tip of it to lift at the collar. An ID tag, the name *Cuervo* engraved across its front. The cat was no stray. It belonged to someone.

Snapping a picture of the tag, she moved on. There were footprints in the dirt surrounding the bench but their impressions were obscured. Whoever had left them had worn shoe covers. She took pictures anyway, hoping there would be something similar in the file Maddox had given her.

"Here you go."

Sabrina looked up to find the priest standing over her again, a cardboard box in his hand. "I got new shoes last week," he said, a regretful smile on his face. "The first time in ten years."

That's when she realized how young he was. His hair was dark. His olive skin smooth. He looked to be only in his mid to late forties. "I'm Claire Vance," she said, hoping manners would force him to tell him her name.

"Father Francisco." He held out his hand as if to shake hers for a moment before he remembered the blood. "I'm the parish priest here at Saint Rose," he said, his hand flopping back to his side, untouched. "Thank you for your help, Agent Vance, but now if you'll excuse me"—he looked at his watch—"I have a service to prepare for."

"You usually have mass this late, Father?" she said, standing quickly, her question stopping his retreat. It was nearly midnight.

"No," he said, shaking his head, more regret showing on his face. "The majority of my congregation work the fields that surround this church and their hours are long. Midnight mass is a luxury most of them can't afford."

"Then what is so special about tonight?" she said.

"It is the feast of Saint Rose, our patron saint," he said, reaching for the door. "Tonight everyone will be here to pay tribute to her."

For some reason Sabrina looked down at the cat sprawled across the bench. Something about his tone told her that no matter what he said, he knew that it hadn't been killed by a coyote.

"Father—" She started to ask him why, even if a coyote *could* get over a wall nearly twelve feet tall, why would it leave a cat, mutilated but not devoured, on the garden's only bench... but she couldn't.

Because he was gone.

TWENTY-EIGHT

Kootenai Canyon, Montana

THE CHALLENGER STARTED ON the first try. Those hours spent changing its oil and spark plugs paid off. On the seat beside him, Avasa wagged her tail, excited to go.

He'd rolled the barn door opened to find Miss Ettie standing on the other side of it with a thermos of coffee in her hand.

"I've got to go," he said shaking his head against what he was sure was about to be a lengthy lecture. "I've got to try to help her as much as I can—"

Instead of arguing with him, Miss Ettie laughed. "Well, of course you do," she said, holding the thermos out. "How long will you be gone?"

He thought about it. Thought about leaving the valley, driving until he'd traded Ponderosas and black bears for palo verdes and rattlesnakes. That's what he wanted to do. He wanted to go to her. It was what he'd always wanted. From the first moment he saw her. For as long as he could remember.

Protect her. Keep her safe.

To be the kind of man who could do those things for her.

But that's not what she needed from him. Sabrina had never needed him to protect her. She saved herself. Always had.

What she needed was something he couldn't give her. But he could make sure she got it.

"I'll be back before sunrise," he told her, taking the thermos from Miss Ettie, trading it for a quick kiss dropped onto her soft, wrinkled cheek.

"You better be in that kitchen making me pancakes when I wake up." She gave him a quick pat on his cheek, catching him before he could fully pull away. "Be careful, Michael," she said to him, her sharp, dark eyes meeting his, making him wonder just how much she knew about his predicament.

"Before sunrise," he said again, making her an unspoken promise. "I'll even make bacon."

———

Two hours later he pulled over, the Challenger's tires grabbing onto the soft shoulder of the highway. Shifting into park, he killed the lights and then the engine, plunging himself into total darkness and a silence that was so loud it seemed to scream.

Avasa shifted on the seat next to him, whining softly. "Shhh, it's okay," he said to her, not even really sure what he was waiting for. The bright, blinding lights of a fleet of black SUVs speeding in to surround him. A platoon of Pips to drop out of the sky. A sudden, violently painful death.

Whatever it was, it never came.

One minute turned into ten and nothing happened. No one came for him. He kept breathing. He had no idea what kind of safety nets Ben had Lark devise to block the signal that would set off his chip, but whatever they were, they seemed to be holding.

He reached up and clicked on the dome light on the roof of the Challenger and the dog sitting beside him woofed softly. "Okay, okay," he said to her, reaching across the bench seat to open her door. She gave him a swift swipe with her tongue before darting out into the dark. "Stay out of the road," he called out to her flagging tail, but he needn't worry. She only went a few yards before she sat in the dirt to keep watch.

The dog took her job seriously.

Unlatching the glovebox, he found what he was looking for. Closing his hand over it he pulled it out. An old analog cell phone. It was his contingency plan. His escape hatch. He had identical phones stashed in the bunker and buried in the woods where the kids liked to play.

He turned it on, waiting for the small green screen to power up before he searched the short list of contacts. Finding the number he was looking for, he hit send.

As he suspected, his call was dumped into voicemail—an automated message that did nothing more than recite the number back to him and beep. "This is Michael O'Shea," he said into the phone. "We need to talk." He hung up, clicking off the dome light to wait.

Two minutes later, the phone rang.

"Is she alive?" No greeting. No surprise or disbelief. Just the question. The only thing that mattered to him.

Michael leaned his head against the Challenger's headrest and closed his eyes, his jaw suddenly tight. "Yes." He forced the word out, fighting the urge to hang up the phone. To run it over. To drive to San Francisco and commit murder.

He listened to breathing on the other end of phone, the silence waiting for him to elaborate. To explain. He didn't.

"I don't think you called me a year later, at two a.m., to tell me that, Michael."

"She needs your help."

"My help?" Phillip Song chuckled softly but there was a smug, satisfied edge to the sound that made Michael want to cut his tongue out. "What could I possibly—"

"You *know* what, asshole," he said through gritted teeth. "You helped her once before. I need you to do it again."

"Wade." It wasn't a question. Hearing Phillip say the name told Michael all he needed to know about how close Sabrina and Phillip had become. Close enough for her to confide in him. Close enough that when he said Wade's name out loud, it sounded like a curse.

"Yes."

"If she's in need of my help, why wouldn't she call me herself?" Phillip said, sounding both wary and concerned. "She knows I'd do anything for her."

"Because of me." He'd known, as soon as he asked her to call Phillip and ask for help, exactly what she'd do. She'd agree in order to placate him and then stubbornly refuse to do what they both knew was best for her. "Because you're in love with her—or at least you *were*."

More silence. For a second, Michael was sure he'd hung up the phone. Finally, he spoke. "Where is she?" Phillip said quietly, not even trying to deny it. "Tell me where she is and I'll—"

"I don't want it to be you," he said, matching Phillip's tone perfectly. "Because I know what you'll do. You'll play knight in shining armor with your fucking tea and your expensive suits that cover up the tattoos that spell out just what kind of man you really are. You'll call her sweetheart and you'll do for her what I can't."

"And what is that?" Phillip said, sound equal parts pissed and amused. "What can I do for her that *El Cartero* can't?"

"You can be there." Michael caught his reflection in the rearview mirror and looked away. "Got a pen?" He rattled off the number to the cell phone he'd given Sabrina and listened to Phillip write it down.

"I can protect her. Give her her family back. Her friends," Phillip said, warning him he was right: he could do more for her than Michael ever could. "With me, she could even be a police officer again if that's what she wanted."

"Pretty lofty proclamations for a simple businessman," he said, but he knew Phillip wasn't overstating his abilities. With him, Sabrina would be what she could never be with him.

Free.

"I'm not bragging," Phillip said. "I'm telling you how it will be. What I'll offer her."

Michael turned his head to look out the open car door. Avasa sat in the wedge of it, watching him with what looked like pity. "Do what you gotta do, Song," he said before ending the call. He patted the seat next to him and she jumped onto it.

She was ready to go home.

TWENTY-NINE

Yuma, Arizona

HER PHONE WAS RINGING in the front seat. She could see it through the passenger-side window, next to the box Croft had given her. She put the shoebox with the cat inside it on the roof of the car and popped the lock, reaching for it just as the sound of it was cut off. Six missed calls and eight text messages.

Five of the calls were from Church. One of them was from a number she didn't recognize, save for the area code.

San Francisco.

Before she could even figure out how to deal with that one, the phone buzzed again, signaling another text. A picture of Croft's dark green Jetta, parked in a slot in front of a cheap motel. Room 122.

Hitting redial, Sabrina wedged the phone between her ear and shoulder, bending over to grab the box. Church let it ring. She hung up and looked at her watch. It was 12:05 a.m.

Shit.

Using the key fob to pop the trunk, Sabrina tucked the box Croft gave her inside. On impulse, she added the box with the cat carcass before punching out a quick, one-word text.

DON'T

Shutting the lid, she noticed that the parking lot was nearly full. Parked across the lot, along the shoulder of the road, was the same King Ranch she had seen outside Vega's house.

He was here.

Her phone rang and she breathed a sigh of relief, answering it quickly before Church changed her mind and hung up in favor of following through on her threat and slitting Croft's throat.

"I stopped by Saint Rose on my way back to the hotel—Vega is here for midnight mass. I'm going to slip in and—"

"You have no idea how relieved I am to hear your voice, *yeonin*." Phillip Song's voice wrapped around her, deep and smooth, as playful as always. "Almost as relieved as I am irritated that you disappeared without telling me."

She squeezed her eyes shut for a second, trying to make sense of what he was saying. "How did you—" She stopped short, panic squeezing at her throat. "Michael. Michael called you."

He'd left their valley. Used a cell phone. Risked his life and everything they'd built. For her. She didn't know if she wanted to kill him or kiss him.

"He did," Phillip said, his tone going flat. "He also told me he'd asked you to do it but that you'd refused. Why would you do that, Sabrina?"

The parking lot was emptying, the last few people filing into the small sanctuary. Men in shirts that looked clean and pressed. Women, their heads covered with shawls and scarves. Children in what looked to be their very best clothes. Within moments, she was alone.

"A secret only stays a secret if you keep your mouth shut, Phillip." She told him the truth. At least part of it. The rest—that some part of her knew Michael was right, that Phillip's feelings for her had grown far beyond his perceived debt to her—was something she didn't want to get into.

"You don't trust me." There was no question in his tone, only something that sounded like hurt, mixed with disbelief.

She really didn't have time for this. "It's not that." She sighed. "I trust you but there's a lot at risk here—not just me. Not just Michael." She thought of Christina and Alex, the children they'd rescued. Loved. "We're a family. That's not something I'm willing to jeopardize. Not for anyone or anything."

"It seems to me," Phillip said quietly, "that when it comes to your well-being, you and your Michael are willing to risk very different things. He says you need my help and for once I am inclined to agree with him."

For a second, she tried to imagine introducing a powerful Korean mobster to the former pet psychopath of Livingston Shaw. The mental picture made for a spectacular shit show. She needed to keep Phillip and Church far apart. "I don't need your help, Phillip. I'm—"

She watched a lone figure materialize from the shadowed fields surrounding the church. It was Will Santos. She watched him walk across the dirt lot, pausing for a moment in front of the King Ranch she'd tagged as Vega's before continuing on. He hesitated for a moment before he pulled open the door to the church and stepped inside.

Phillip was still talking and she had to force herself to focus on what he was saying.

"… I care for you, Sabrina," he said, his voice hardening around the words. "But you have always been a poor judge of what and who you need. I'll see you soon."

She looked down at the closed trunk lid, weighing her options.

The box can wait, darlin'. Better hurry inside now—the show's about to start.

"Okay." She didn't have time to fight a battle she'd already lost. "Whatever," she said, without bothering to tell Phillip where she was. If he wanted to put his nose where it didn't belong, he was going to have to work for it. She killed the call without waiting for a response, then she followed Detective Santos into the sanctuary.

THIRTY

SHE WAS ALONE.

There was a silence to the place she'd never heard before. An emptiness that made her sure that wherever he'd gone, the man who took her was not here. She didn't know how long she'd lain there listening to the empty black that surrounded her, but somewhere between realizing there was no one to stop her and remembering where she was, Maggie made a choice.

Pushing herself against the wall, she planted her bound hands on the floor, levering herself up until she was sitting. She'd pissed herself again. The cold sting of it rubbed into the chafed skin of her thighs, mixing with the tacky blood and the …

That's when she started to remember.

What he did. How much it hurt. How long it went on. What he said to her. The lash of a whip, the brutal thrust of his hips. Over and over until each unbearable pain bled into the next. Until she screamed and cried. Begged for him to stop.

Until she wanted to die.

She started to shake. Her arms and legs trembling so hard she had to wrap herself into a ball and press her face into the top of her thighs to keep herself from coming apart. "Stop it," she said out loud. "*Stop it right now.*"

She didn't have time to fall apart. She was alone, but for how long? Ten minutes? An hour? Unwrapping herself, she planted her bound hands on the floor and pushed again, pulling her legs beneath herself slowly, finding her balance, until she was standing.

The room was pitch black. When he'd dragged her back down the hall and toss her into it, she'd hit the floor, her knees buckling before she scrambled across the cracked concrete until she hit a wall. Wedging herself into its corner, she'd cowered and waited.

He'd stood in the doorway for a few minutes, watching her—his fingers flexing around the handle of the knife he'd used on her. "Do you still believe in miracles, Margaret?" he said to her in the same calm, reasonable tone he'd used while systematically raping and beating her.

"Yes." She whispered it, worried that if she raised her voice he'd be able to hear the lie. She knew instinctively that the moment she told him the truth—that she didn't believe in anything anymore—he'd kill her.

Instead of answering her, he just laughed and shut the door.

Now, hands outstretched, she shuffled forward, shoulder scraping the rough block wall. The dark had a way of disorienting you. Turning you upside down. Growing and shrinking until you didn't know where you were. Making it impossible to find your way to the other side.

The more she stared at it, the more the crack of light beneath the door seemed to stretch and wane, growing farther and farther away with each step she took. She kept going. One step in front of the other. Eyes fixed on the crack of light that would show her the way out.

When her hands closed over the door handle, her breath caught in her chest. *Please. Please let it be open. Please God, help me find my way out. Please, please, please . . .* She levered the handle downward. Felt the latch that held it closed give way.

The door swung open.

It was a test. Some sort of trap. The certainty of it had her shrinking away from the open doorway. She'd try to escape and she'd be caught. He'd punish her. Drag her back into that room and do things . . .

She leaned heavily against the doorframe and waited. Listened. There was nothing. No sound. No movement. Trap or not, this was her chance. She wouldn't waste it. Pushing herself away from the door, Maggie took a tentative step into the hallway.

The space was deserted. There were other doors. Other rooms. Trying them, she found some locked, some not. The ones that opened were empty. There were no windows. Not anywhere. No way out that she could find. Looking down, she saw the blood trail that cut down the center of the floor.

Maggie followed it. Not toward the room he'd taken her to, but in the opposite direction. Around a corner and down another corridor. The blood trail grew fainter and fainter until it was nothing more than indistinct brown streaks soaked into the concrete, disappearing under a closed door.

If this is where he'd taken the body of the other woman, maybe it led to the outside. Maybe it was a way out. Again, she stopped and waited for the trap to snap shut.

After a few seconds of more nothing, she yanked on the handle. The latch released and the door swung open. Her chest went tight, constricted with hope. She would find her way out. She would escape. She would run.

She would live.

It took her a moment to realize what she was seeing. What she was smelling. Bodies. So many of them, heaped on top of each other in a gruesome tangle of mottled skin and rotting flesh. She gagged, the smell of it—spoiled meat and spent fluids—pushing her back into the hallway.

"Did you get lost, Margaret?"

She was spun around by the heavy hand that landed on her shoulder and she swung out with her hands and missed, throwing herself off balance. He grabbed for her but she lunged out of the way, slamming into the wall. She almost went down but kept her feet. Kept running. Kept moving.

Back the way she'd come. Past the room she'd been kept in. Past the room she'd been raped in. She could hear him behind her, shouting at her to stop. That he would kill her if she didn't.

She didn't stop. She ran until she found stairs.

She climbed them faster than she thought she could, slamming into the door that topped them. Pushing it open, she launched herself through it.

More dark. The howl of a coyote.

Below her, she could still hear him. He wasn't shouting anymore but he was coming. He'd warned her what would happen if she didn't stop. He was coming and if he caught her, he would kill her.

Maggie had made her choice the second she opened the door and stepped into the hallway. She didn't want to die. So she ran.

THIRTY-ONE

SABRINA FOUND SANTOS IN the chapel's small atrium, standing at the stoup just beyond the entrance. She watched him dip his fingers into the basin before making the sign of the cross. Easing the door closed as quietly as possible, she watched the detective continue up the sanctuary's only aisle to the front of the church.

He sat directly behind Vega.

Vega seemed to know he was there, stiffening in his seat the second Santos slid in behind him, cutting a quick look over his shoulder before he settled back against the hard wood of the pew. The man sitting beside Vega dropped a hand on his forearm and leaned in, whispering something in his ear before giving Santos another, decidedly nastier look.

Slipping into the last pew, Sabrina took a look around. The place was lit by what had to be hundreds of candles, the heat of them warm against her face. Father Francisco stood at the altar, a bright white robe over the dark pants and shirt he'd been wearing in the courtyard. He bowed his head and began to pray in Spanish.

There was a slight rustle to her left and she turned to see the last thing she needed. An old woman sliding across the hard wooden bench, coming right at her. Behind her was Val's little sister, Ellie. She'd changed her clothes, trading her pants and YPD rain jacket for a modest summer dress, her long hair caught at the nape of her neck in a low bun.

Turning her face away, Sabrina focused on Father Francisco, pretending to listen to what he was saying. Ellie was here, sitting less than three feet away from her—and she'd brought her mother.

Years ago, Amelia Hernandez had been a mother to her in a way her own had never been. Had patted her cheek and called her *mija*. Fed her warm tortillas and watched Jason and Riley for her while she waited tables, refusing to take a dime for any of it, even though her own need was obvious. If not for this woman, she would have lost hope long before Wade found her and locked her in the dark.

She pushed the memories aside, forcing herself to focus on the service Father Francisco was giving. The way Vega kept sneaking looks at Santos over his shoulder. The altar boys clustered on the front pew, perched on its edge in their white robes like a dole of doves, waiting anxiously for communion. Anything to distract her from the fact that Valerie's mother sat inches away from her, staring at her like she recognized her.

Like she knew her.

Which was impossible. When she'd been found, no one but the doctors who treated her, her grandmother, and Val even knew she'd survived. As much as it killed her, Sabrina had demanded that Val keep it from her mother. As far as Amelia Hernandez was concerned, Melissa Walker died nearly twenty years ago.

That ain't entirely true, now is it? Thanks to that reporter of yours the whole damn world knows you survived, darlin'.

As if to prove Wade right, the woman reached over, pressing her softly lined palm to Sabrina's cheek, turning her face so that the two of them were practically nose-to-nose. "*Mija*," Amelia whispered, tears glittering in her sharp brown eyes. "You came back."

Before she could react, Ellie leaned over, pulling her mother's hand back. "No, *Mamá*—" She stalled out when she realized who it was her mother had put her hands on. "My apologies, Agent Vance. My mother suffers from mid-stage Alzheimer's," she said quietly, patting her mother's hands into her lap. "She thinks you're my sister."

Amelia frowned at her, her eyes suddenly dry and dull, any hint of recognition lost in a sea of confusion. "It's okay," Sabrina said, smiling first at the woman sitting next to her and then at her daughter. "It's okay," she said again, nodding at Ellie who returned the nod with a relieved smile.

The rest of mass passed in silence. Around them, people stood and sat, knelt and prayed. Through it all, Ellie never moved, her hand anchored in her mother's, staring straight ahead while Amelia hummed softly to herself. Sabrina recognized the tune as one she used to sing to Jason and Riley when they were babies.

> *A la roro niño*
> *A lo roro ya*
> *Duérmete mi niño*
> *Duérmete mi amor.*

When Father Francisco finally called for communion, Amelia stood, reaching down to take her hand. "*Ven conmigo, mija,*" she said, pulling her out of her seat, and Sabrina followed because it was easier than trying to extricate herself from her grip.

Standing in the church's center aisle, with Amelia's arm looped through hers, Sabrina listened to her jabber on in Spanish about her garden and how much she enjoyed riding her horse, Chula. As far as she knew, Amelia never had a horse—or a garden, for that matter. Casting a look behind her, she caught sight of Ellie. She was standing near the stoup, talking on her cell phone and looking right at her.

"*Ni si quiera sé por qué vino aquí. Padre Francisco no le dará la comunión. No después de loque le hizo esa chica.*"

Amelia's sing-song voice snagged at her, pulling at her attention. "What girl?" She looked down at the older woman standing beside her. "Amelia, *¿qué chica?*" she said, switching to Spanish in hopes that it might trigger an answer.

"She was Ellie's friend." Amelia frowned like she wasn't sure of what she was saying. "I never liked her much—I guess I should feel bad about that now."

Rachel Meeks. Amelia had to be talking about Rachel Meeks. "Who hurt her?" she said, drawing more than a few looks. "What was his name?" She finished in a whispered rush, hoping to beat the clouds she could see rolling across Amelia's mind. "Who hurt Rachel?"

"Who's Rachel?" Amelia asked in broken English, confusion and something that looked very close to fear casting shadows across her face. "Where's Ellie?"

Sabrina forced herself to smile, feeling grief and disappointment in equal measure. "Ellie's here—she had to take a phone call, Mrs. Hernandez."

"Okay." Amelia visibly relaxed, returning her smile. "Are we waiting for communion?"

"Yes," she said, the word getting stuck in her throat. Looking behind her, she could see Ellie, still standing by the stoup. She was still talking on the phone but she was staring at them. Giving her a small smile, Sabrina redirected her attention to the line in front of her.

Ahead of them, people received their communion wafers and Father Francisco's blessing before exiting the chapel through the door that led out into the prayer garden. Suddenly there was a commotion, people murmuring to themselves as they moved aside for someone pushing their way up the aisle.

It was Paul Vega and the man who'd been sitting beside him, Santos following in their wake. None of them looked happy. Vega looked right at her as he passed by before averting his gaze completely.

"I'm glad you came home, *mija*." Amelia patted her arm and smiled, oblivious to the commotion. "I've missed you."

As distracted as she was, Sabrina felt the words tug at her. Even if they were nothing more than confused nonsense. "I've missed you too," she said, playing along because she wanted to keep Amelia calm and because it was true.

"Do you remember how I'd make fresh tortillas every morning?" Amelia chuckled before she released the rest of the memory. "Valerie would never eat them because she was afraid of getting fat, so you ate her share as well. One of the thousand things I loved about you."

The tumble of emotion nearly turned her upside down. Panic. Joy. A sadness so keen it choked her into the sort of stunned silence that turned the edges of her vision gray. Amelia wasn't confused. She wasn't lost inside her own mind.

Somehow, Amelia knew exactly who she was.

THIRTY-TWO

MARGARET WAS GONE.

She'd disappeared into the desert. More afraid of what lay behind her then what lay in wait for her in the dark. She charged into the open, stumbling across loose dirt and rocks. Her breath escaping her lungs in panicked little bleats. Crying and flailing into the desert, bound hands outstretched in front of her, she disappeared.

He let her go. Let her run. Instead of chasing blindly, he followed patiently. There was no need to hurry. No need to worry. Where could she go? There was nowhere to hide. Not out here.

He stopped for a moment and listened, remembering what his mentor had told him once about why he liked to chase his prey. Why he turned them loose and ran them down.

It gives 'em hope. It ain't fun if they don't have hope.

He hadn't understood what Wade had meant at the time, but he did now. He could feel it—exhilaration. Anticipation coupled with an almost crippling sense of inevitability. He would find her and he would kill her. Nothing she did would stop that now. The power of it was intoxicating. A drug he could quickly come to crave if every step he took didn't cause him pain.

Fun, ain't it, boy?

"Margaret?" he called out to her, his voice calm and steady while he clipped the bolt gun he carried to the belt on his pants. "I know you're out here," he said loudly, dangling hope and then ripping it away. "There's nowhere for you to go. No one out here to help you."

He fell quiet. Listening. Waiting.

Around him, the desert was a living thing. Moving and breathing. Skittering and crawling. The flap of wings. A rustling burrow. But that was it. The frantic bleat had gone silent. The desperate scramble of bare feet across sharp rocks had stopped.

She'd gone to ground. Margaret was listening and waiting too.

Visualizing the wide, flat expanse of land that surrounded him, he could see it—a shallow ravine about fifty yards to the west. Carved into the desert by flash floods, lined by palo verde and brittlebush. To someone who didn't know better, it would seem like the perfect place to hide.

He stooped, running his hand over the ground, sifting dirt between his fingers, quickly finding what he was looking for. A rock—roughly the size of an orange. Standing, he walked toward the ravine, making no attempt to hide his approach. Each footfall sent smaller desert creatures scurrying for safety.

Fight or flight. All animals possessed it. The instinct to either run or stand their ground. It was in their nature—who they were. A preprogrammed response they were unable to deny. Uncontrollable. Unstoppable. Marking them as predator or prey from the moment they were born.

He'd known what Margaret would do—what she was—even before she did.

Stopping a few feet from the edge of the ravine, he scuffed his shoes in the dirt, sending loose rocks and clumps of dead grass tumbling into the chasm. It had been a raging torrent of water only hours ago, a flash flood, fed by the storm cell that'd ripped across the desert. A few inches of water slowly soaking into the bottom of the ravine was all that was left of it, but the rain left the earth soft and unpredictable beneath his feet.

There she is. In the bush, right in front of you.

"I see you," he whispered loudly and like he'd fired a starting pistol, she popped up from the bush she'd been crouching behind, no more than six feet below him. She tumbled down the slope of the ravine, terror knotting her feet together, making it impossible for her to find them until she reached the bottom. Rolling herself up onto her hands and knees she forced them beneath her, those panicked bleats pumping out of her lungs with every scrambling footstep. He was close enough to hear the words they formed, over and over.

"Please, God, please…"

He let her run. Let her think she was going to get away. Let her believe that her prayers would be answered. That miracles were real.

He gave her hope. Then he took it away.

Lifting the rock to chest level, he held it tight, splitting his fingers around it while he curved his thumb around its base. Taking aim, he lifted his knee, letting it kiss his elbow for just a moment before he lowered it, planting it firmly in the dirt. His shoulder snapped forward, turning his arm into a rocket as it exploded away from his chest. The rock left his grip, missiling toward its target in a blur of speed and accuracy.

It struck her just where he knew it would, where he meant it to: in the space where her ear joined her head. She fell instantly. Face down in the mud, hands still bound and pinned awkwardly beneath her.

He waited. Watched her crumpled frame from the edge of the ravine. She didn't move. Didn't try to get up. He wanted to leave her there. It could be days—possibly *weeks*—before someone found her and that would be after the coyotes made a meal of her corpse. They were at least two miles from where they'd started. He could leave her here without fear of leading the authorities to their secret place.

Don't get sloppy now, boy. That ain't how I taught you.

The voice in his head came through loud and clear. He ground his teeth together to keep from arguing. "Yes, sir," he said instead, even though the mere thought of it made his knee ache. He stepped off the lip of the ravine to pick his way down its crumbling side. The moon was high and bright. Full enough to show him the dark splotch of blood matted against her hair, its glossy fingers sliding along her cheek, the rock he'd thrown now at his feet like it was waiting for him. He bent and picked it up, jamming it into his front pocket. A few inches from his shoe, Margaret's hands clenched in the mud, her fingers digging in it like she was trying to push herself up.

You ain't got all night, boy. Get to work.

Unclipping the bolt gun from his belt he crouched down, brushing his hand over the back of her head, moving her tangled hair to the side, exposing the base of her skull. She turned her head under his hand, trying to shake him loose. Knotting his fingers in her hair, he yanked, forcing her face into the mud. Her hands were no longer scrambling in the mud; they were shoving against it. Trying to push herself up. He stepped on them, flattening them until they sunk into the sodden dirt beneath them.

"Robert is dead." He pulled back on the bolt, pressing the barrel of it to the back of her head. "You failed to save him, Margaret," he whispered, his voice carried on the warm desert air that surrounded them. "You aren't at all what I'd hoped."

She was trying to talk, her mouth open and full of mud. Eyes squeezed shut against the sight of him. He used his free hand to grip her chin and turn her head to the side. "I tried." The words were muddled and sluggish, her brain clearly not fully present. "I did what you said. I did everything…"

"Shhh." The hand on her face went gentle, stroking her cheek softly. "Yes, you did. That's why I'm willing to make you a deal. Tell me the truth and I'll let you live." He pushed the barrel of the bolt gun against the base of her skull. "Can you do that, Margaret? Can you tell me the truth?"

She nodded blindly, the blood from where he'd struck her with the rock skating around his fingers, pulled by gravity along the curve of her jaw. "Yes."

"Do you still believe in miracles?" He brushed his fingertips against her mouth, staining it red. "Do you think you're worthy of what He gave you?"

Margaret shook her head. "No." Her tongue peeked out, brushing against her lower lip, and she recoiled slightly at the taste of her own blood.

"Do you still think God saved you for a reason?"

She shook her head again, too frightened to say the word out loud.

"Good," he told her, fisting the hand he'd used to soothe her in the bloody thatch of hair at her crown so he could reposition the bolt gun he still held against her skull.

Forcing her face back into the mud, he cut off the cry she let loose at his word. He pulled the trigger, releasing the bolt. The force of it made a loud snapping sound, punching a quarter-sized hole in the base of her skull.

Beneath his shoe, her hands stopped digging in the mud.

"Now what?" he said, watching blood and tissue ooze from the hole in Margaret's head. The heat of the hunt and the kill that followed had cooled in his veins. He knew Wade was right. His DNA was all over her. He couldn't just leave her here.

The voice inside his head chuckled softly.

Don't worry, just trust me, boy. I'll take care of everything.

THIRTY-THREE

AFTER STANDING BY WHILE Amelia received communion, Sabrina piloted her through the doors leading to the prayer garden. It was nearly deserted, most people hurrying off for a quick meal and to change clothes for their early shift in the fields. All that was left were a few old women chatting quietly by the gate and Ellie, sitting on the bench, the angel statue looming over her.

When she saw her daughter, Amelia frowned. "There you are, Elena," she said, clucking her tongue while she held out her hand like she was a child. "I've been looking everywhere for you. Come on, let's get home so I can get dinner started. Your father will be home soon."

At the mention of her father, Ellie's face went still, her gaze landing on Sabrina face before finding her mother again. "I'm sorry, *Mamá*," she said, standing as she took the hand her mother offered her.

Sabrina followed behind, worried that Amelia would turn toward her again, like she had in the church. Expose her for who and what she really was, but her worry went unrealized. Amelia did nothing but ramble on in Spanish about what she was going to make her husband for dinner and how Valerie had a history test in the morning.

Ellie played along, nodding and answering while she opened the passenger door of her late-model compact and settling the old woman inside. "Wait here, *Mamá*," she said, adjusting her mother's seat belt before shutting the door. "I'm sorry about that," she said, turning away from the car to look at Sabrina. "She's gotten worse recently. It used to be she couldn't remember what day it was or where she put her purse but now..." Ellie shrugged. "I'm not sure how long I have until she's gone completely."

The thought of Amelia, lost, broke Sabrina's heart. "You mentioned a sister—what about her? Can't she help?"

"She keeps threatening to come out here, but..." Ellie shrugged, shaking her head. "Val's pregnant, with a cop husband and a toddler. The last thing she needs is to deal with this mess."

Val was pregnant. Something sharp and sweet lanced through her—happiness mixed with sadness and regret. Lucy, Val's daughter, would be nearly two years old by now. Jason and Riley—her own brother and sister—were close to twenty. Strickland, her old partner, would have a new workmate.

Life had moved on without her.

She nodded like she understood even though she didn't. "If she's offering to help—"

"This is *my* responsibility, Agent Vance." Ellie rounded the front of the car. "And my business," she said, reminding her that she'd overstepped her bounds. "Good night."

Sabrina watched her leave, pulling out of the deserted dirt lot, her taillights disappearing into the dark. Ellie was right; it wasn't her business. She got busy convincing herself of that fact while she walked to her car on the other side of the church. She had enough to worry about—finding out how and why her DNA ended up on a dead girl and hopefully catching a killer, for starters.

"Hey, Kitten."

Sabrina's head turned so fast her neck cramped up. Church was sitting cross-legged on the trunk of a car parked a few spots down from their rental, a sugary smile on her face. She recognized the car. It was Croft's dark green Jetta.

Shit.

"How'd you find me?" she said, stopping in front of Church.

Church waggled her phone at her. "Cloned your cell." She said it like she was admitting to eating the last doughnut from the office breakroom. "Was that the tech that took Graciella Lopez's shoes today?"

"Where is he, Church?" Sabrina said, ignoring her question completely. Hernandez was a fairly common last name. There was no reason to tell her psycho sidekick that the crime tech assigned to their case was actually Valerie's little sister.

"Where's who?" Church answered, drumming her fingers on the lid of the trunk.

Walking the perimeter of the car, she half expected to find Croft hog-tied in the back seat. Save for a pile of fast food wrappers and a few books, it was empty. "Quit dicking around, you know *who*," she said, yanking the driver's door open. She reached down, finding the trunk lever. "Get up."

Church reluctantly slid off the trunk to stand next to the car, hip cocked against the fender, arms crossed over her chest. "You're a ruiner."

"So I've been told." She popped the trunk before slamming the driver's door and making her way to the back of the car. "Is he alive?" she said, her hand on the lid. As many times as she'd threatened to kill him, Sabrina wasn't sure she was prepared to see a dead Jaxon Croft.

Church gave her a sullen shrug. "I don't know—open the trunk and find out."

Sabrina's fingers tightened for a few seconds before she lifted the lid, suddenly sure he wasn't alive. That she'd been the cause of yet another death. That Church had killed Croft simply because she'd been late.

He was blindfolded and trussed up with a set of what looked like police issue cuffs and chains. There was a ball gag strapped around his face and a pair of earbuds stuffed into his ears.

Other than a cluster of Taser burns on his neck, he looked unharmed. And alive.

"Jesus," she said. Reaching into the trunk, she grabbed onto the blindfold. "How many times did you tase him?" He jerked away from her but she snagged the blindfold anyway and pulled it down. As soon as he saw her his whole body relaxed and he started yelling, his words a muffled mess behind the red rubber ball stuffed in his mouth.

Church gave her a disinterested shrug. "It's not like I counted," she said before rolling her eyes at Sabrina's expression. "Relax, Kitten. I had the juice dialed down ... most of the time."

"You're a true humanitarian," she said, reaching behind Croft to unbuckle the strap that secured the ball gag to his face. As soon as it was loose, he kicked his yelling into high gear. She held it gingerly, fingers pinched lightly around the strap. She didn't even want to know how many people Church had used it on. "You own a ball gag?"

"You don't?" Church said, leaning into the trunk to press a finger to her lips. "*Shhh*." She aimed her finger at Croft and his mouth clamped shut like it was on a timer. Holding up her hands, she wiggled her fingers before reaching into the trunk to pop the buds out of his ears. "Clark Kent and I have been getting to know each other, isn't that right, Clark?"

"Fuck you, you crazy bitch."

Church sighed. "Name calling isn't nice," she said, winding the earbud cord around the iPod it was plugged into. "He told me everything. Eventually."

Everything was a relative term when dealing with Croft, but the word worried her. Especially since she had no idea what *everything* was. "Great," she said, feigning disinterest. "Uncuff him so we can get out of here."

"Don't you want to know *what* he told me?" Church said, sliding along the length of the fender until she was standing next to her in front of the trunk. "I'm pretty sure you do, Kitten."

"Now, please." Sabrina spit the words out, still pretending to be disinterested.

"Suit yourself." Church shrugged as she dug into the front pocket of her jeans. She produced a key and held it up, twirling it in the air like a magic wand. "Roll over, doggie."

Croft did what she told him. She was sure he'd make a grab for Church as soon as the cuffs were unlocked, but he didn't. He lay there for a few moments, rubbing the feeling back into his wrists while he glared up at them.

"Come on, Clark, be a sport," Church said, totally unaffected by the fact that he obviously wanted to kill her. "Tell her what you told me."

"You tase me, kidnap me, and torture me with Yanni and *now* you want to act like we're friends?" Croft swung his legs over the lip of the compartment and dropped them onto the dirt so that he was sitting on the edge of the trunk. "I liked your old partner better, Sabrina," he said, aiming a look her way.

"Me too," she said, looking at Church. "Yanni?"

"My patented playlist." She smiled and held up the iPod. "Yanni. Michael Bolton. Kenny G., a little Hasselhoff. Very effective." She tucked it into her back pocket before rounding on Croft. "So, tell her what you told me or you, me, and The Hoff are gonna go for another ride."

He folded instantly, the fight going out of him before she could blink. Whatever Church had done to him, it'd involved a bit more than a Taser and an iPod full of crap music. "Okay, okay." Croft nodded and looked at Sabrina, swallowing hard against the words that welled up in his throat. "He was here. Wade."

"What do you mean?"

"I *mean*," Croft said, each word scraping along the inside of his mouth like he had to force them out, "he was here—in Arizona."

She split a confused look between the two of them. "I know that. I was here too, remember?"

"No," Croft shook his head. "He was here *after* you … died," he said, struggling to find the right words to describe what'd happened to her all those years ago. "He flew into Sky Harbor under the name Wayne Conway at least three times between 2000 and 2008." He sighed, rubbing a hand over his mouth like the words inside it tasted bad. Like he wanted to spit them out but couldn't.

"The guy he was writing to—he wasn't just some sick pen pal he exchanged torture fantasies with. He was teaching him. Showing him how to hunt. To kill." Croft looked away from her for a moment, his jaw flexing with what looked like anger and more than a little self-disgust. "He was Wade's apprentice."

THIRTY-FOUR

Berlin, Germany

"Mr. Shaw ... Mr. Shaw."

The words were delivered on an exasperated tone, followed by a sigh, the kind usually reserved for unruly toddlers and carpet-pissing puppies. He knew it well—his babysitter couldn't go five minutes without using it on him.

Ben burrowed his head under his pillow and pretended not to hear her.

"Mr. *Shaw*." This time Gail said it through clenched teeth, emphasizing the last word with a sharp smack to his bare ass with what felt like her day planner wrapped in barbed wire. "You've missed your morning meeting. Again."

"*Oww* ... so?" he mumbled, taking a swipe at her, his eyes still screwed shut. "Do your job and reschedule it."

"I did. *Again*." She sounded angrier than usual so he lifted his face from the mattress and took a peek. She glared down at him

179

with equal parts anger and affection, the hiss of the shower running in the next room filling the silence between them. "She's still here."

He burrowed his head under his pillow again to hide the fact that he was just as surprised as she was. "Again, I say, *so?*" He turned his head to the side so she'd hear him. All he could see were her no-nonsense navy slacks and plump hands wrapped around the planner she used to try to dictate his life. Sometimes it worked. Most times it didn't.

"*So* have you given any thought to what will happen to that poor girl when your father finds out the two of you are carrying on?"

The running shower meant Celine had spent the night. She was usually gone before he woke up. Overnights were an unspoken no-no. That she felt confident enough to spend the night meant she thought she could count on him to protect her if his father found out about them.

She was wrong. He'd already picked his team and she wasn't on it.

On the upside, it also meant that after weeks of fucking her silly, his father's personal assistant finally trusted him. Oxytocin was a wonderful thing.

He pulled his head out from under his pillow and looked up at Gail. "*Carrying on?*" He laughed a little, the sound of it sharpening her glare. "Is that what the kids are calling it these days?"

"I don't know about *the kids*," she said, disapproval dripping from every word, "but I call it stupid and selfish."

Instead of answering her, Ben rolled over, stacking his hands under his head, and gave her the Full Monty. "Gail, Gail, Gail ..." he said, giving her a lewd grin even though she was old enough to be his mother. "Always the Grumpy Gus."

Gail narrowed her eyes at him, completely unfazed by his behavior. "I'm being serious, Mr. Shaw," she said, the worry in her voice overriding the disapproval. "Your father will—"

"Never find out," he finished the sentence for her even though he was pretty sure he was lying. "Look—it's not a big deal. I'm just blowing off steam," he said, gingerly setting a discarded pillow over his morning wood. "God knows I can't have any real fun with you hanging around my neck all the time."

Gail wasn't buying it. "Fun?" she said, shaking her head. "There are a dozen women working for FSS who are under the age of fifty and relatively attractive—eleven of them are not your father's personal assistant."

He shrugged. "I have a thing for blondes."

"What you have is a *thing* for is driving your father crazy," she said, taking a step away from the bed. "It's as immature as it is dangerous."

"Why, Gail," he said, shooting her a lopsided grin, "are you worried about me?"

"You?" She huffed the word while reaching over and lifting his robe off the chair to toss it at him. It was a game they played. She tried to get him to wear it and he refused. "Hardly," she said, marching toward the door. "Who do you think is next after your father kills the two of you? *Me*, that's who." Even though she denied it, he knew she was concerned and not just for herself. That for some reason, she cared about what happened to him. It made him feel bad—mainly because she was right. Gail's job was to make sure he kept his dick in his pants and his tie on straight. One task was proving infinitely more difficult than the other.

"Am I still on for that thing today?" he called after her, trying to make up for the fact that he made her job categorically impossible, just by being himself.

Gail stopped in the doorway. "Yes, Mr. Shaw, you're still on for *that thing*," she said, her back still turned, shoulders squared. "Your plane leaves in three hours."

"I'll be there in two."

She mumbled something as she walked out the door that sounded like *bullshit*.

As soon as he heard the door click closed, he tossed the pillow off his johnson and stood up, scanning the room, hoping Celine hadn't taken it into the bathroom with her.

Nope, it was exactly where she'd left it. Pausing for a moment to make sure the shower was still running, he reached for her purse, rifling through its contents until he found what he was looking for.

Celine's keycard.

As his father's personal assistant, Celine went where he went. Her keycard wasn't just good for his Berlin office—her card was the equivalent to keys to the kingdom. A master card that opened every door and private elevator in every office his father kept across the world. Aside from his father, no one had that kind of unrestricted access to FSS. Not even him.

Using the scanning app on his phone, Ben scanned the coded strip on the back of it before punching out a quick text.

Thirty minutes or less.

He attached the scan to the message and hit send, receiving an answer in less than a minute.

Seriously? Do I look like the pizza guy?

Ben smirked at the screen, tapping out a response before tossing Celine's purse back on the chair where she'd dropped it.

No. You look like my bitch. Get it done.

In the next room, the shower shut off. He imagined Celine, wet and naked, drying herself off with one of his ridiculously huge towels. Without bothering to wait for a text back, he locked his phone down and tossed it onto the bed on his way into the bathroom. He wasn't worried.

It didn't matter who or what it was. He was his father's son and that meant he always got what he wanted.

THIRTY-FIVE

Yuma, Arizona

January 17th, 1998

I SAW YOU.

You carried her into the churchyard, wrapped in a blanket, and placed her on the bench just before dawn. You knelt over her and did something to her eyes.

You touched her. You touched yourself.

I knew she was dead and that you'd killed her.

I could have gone to Father Francisco, woken him, and called the police, but I didn't. Instead I watched you. I waited until you left before I went outside. I saw what you did to her. The word you carved into her stomach.

Mine.

It didn't scare me or make me angry. It made me feel understood. Like there is someone in the world who wants and feels the same things I do.

You don't have to worry. I'm not going to tell anyone what you did or who you are. No one else came out until you were gone. I just wanted you to know that your secret is safe with me.

Nulo

Sabrina dropped the piece of paper into her lap. She'd been sitting here for hours, reading the letters and journals that Croft had given her. He'd organized them all in chronological order. The letters according to the date they were written, the journals according to victim. She glanced at the stack of composition books on the nightstand next to the bed. Each of them had the date OCT 1ST printed across the front, followed by the year. Under the date was a name. VICKI. SUSAN. TAYLOR. OLIVIA . . .

Hers was not the first in the pile.

Jealous that you weren't my first, darlin'? Don't worry, I thought about you the whole time.

There'd been a girl, a waitress, in Oklahoma. Wade had met her by chance and taken her to Big Thicket National Preserve. He'd chased her through the woods. Terrorized and tortured her for hours before stabbing her to death. Afterward, he carved the word LIAR into her stomach and set her body on fire.

Because she was *a liar. They all were.*

185

Afterward, he'd gone home and calmly written down every detail of it. The way the blade of his knife slid into her soft folds of flesh. The sweet, meaty stink of that flesh when it burned. The murder had never been linked to him. She'd been an accident. An impulse brought on by unspent rage and frustration. Twenty years ago, Jenny Parsons had been brutally murdered and no one knew why or who. Until now.

She sat, surrounded by answers to the hundreds of questions that haunted her. But for all her searching, she couldn't find the answer to the one question that needed answering now.

Who was Nulo?

He's ours, darlin'. Yours and mine—born the moment he watched me stretch you out on that bench and saw what I'd done to you.

Sabrina imagined him, standing in the shadows, watching Wade through the cold glass of the window. Waiting until Wade left before allowing his curiosity to get the best of him and lead him outside. Had this Nulo touched her? Had he known she was still alive? That she'd been alive, at least long enough for someone to call 911? If so, why hadn't he told Wade?

"What's a Nulo?"

Sabrina looked up to find Church sitting in the armchair not more than five feet away, ceramic mug balanced on her knee, flipping through one of Wade's journals. She hadn't even heard her come in.

"What?" she said, leaning into the space between them to snatch the book from Church's hand.

Church set her mug of tea on the nightstand. "Nulo. You keep saying it," she said, grinning as she snatched another book from the stack. "So, what is it?"

Nulo meant nothing. Zero. What kind of person accepted that word as their name? What had to be done to you before you believed it? Instead of answering Church's question, she asked one of her own. "What did you do to Croft?"

Church slouched back in the chair and rolled her eyes. "Nothing a few sessions with a therapist won't cure," she said, irritable fingers picking at the seat's worn upholstery. "Which makes him the luckiest man alive, considering he should be rotting in some hole in the desert right about now. *You're welcome.* Speaking of our fearless reporter, why is there a dead cat in the trunk of our car?"

She was right. Maybe Croft was unaware of how close he'd come to a bullet, but Sabrina wasn't. Church had orders to kill anyone who could expose her for who she really was. Instead of thanking her, she answered her question.

"It's not a what, it's a *he*." She said it reluctantly, her eyes glued to the journal in Church's hand. "And I found the cat in the prayer garden at the church last night. The priest said it was mauled by a coyote."

Church fanned herself with the journal. "I took a peek—that was no coyote. Want me to take care of it? I can have someone take a look, tell us what's up."

Sabrina nodded. "Sure," she said, tracking the journal's movements, the name printed across the front of it flickering in front of her. FRANKIE. Michael's sister. She hadn't been able to bring herself to read it yet. Every time she tried, she envisioned the Frankie she remembered—the little girl with bouncy black curls and Kerry blue eyes. She tried to reconcile her with the young woman Wade had stolen and mutilated. The body left propped against a tree alongside the highway.

She tried and couldn't.

You ever wonder why, darlin'? How Frankie ended up on the side of the road? Why I didn't drag her out into the woods and leave her with the rest of them?

"So that's him?" Church said, glancing down at the journal in her hand. When she saw the name printed across the front of it, she tossed it back on the table where she'd found it. Either she'd gotten tired of the snatch and grab game they were playing or she realized whose rape and torture it chronicled. "This Nulo is the guy we're looking for?"

"Yes." She tucked the letter into its envelope before studying the front. The handwriting was neat. The careful, well-spaced cursive of a young man who took pride in his penmanship. There was no return address. Probably because he was afraid that Wade would use it to find him and kill him.

He was right. If he'd given me a way to find him back then, I'd have gutted him. He must've written me a hundred times before he finally found the balls to get a PO box...

"Holy shit." She lunged at the box, digging through it until she found an envelope with the box number and zip code written in its corner. "He had a PO box. Maybe it's still active," she said, holding it up to show Church. Enlisting Santos's help would mean turning over the box full of evidence Croft had given her. It also meant things she didn't have time for—judges and warrants to name a few. "Call Ben. Have him—"

Church cut her off with a sharp look. "Remember the part where I told you that calling Ben wasn't an option? That all you have is me?" She shook her head. "I didn't say it to be an asshole. It happens to be true. Ben has done for you everything he can."

"Which is what, exactly?" she nearly shouted, the letter crumpling in her hand as she cranked it into a fist. "Dropped this giant steaming pile of shit in my lap before disappearing into thin air?"

Church cocked her head and shrugged. "Pretty much." She studied her for a few seconds before standing. "We don't need Ben," she said, making an impatient motion with her hands. "Give it."

Sabrina hesitated before holding the letter out. "I can't just go around tasing people and stuffing them in the trunk of my car until they answer my questions."

Church snatched it with a smile, folding it in half before slipping it into her back pocket.

"Of course you can't, Kitten. That's why you have me."

THIRTY-SIX

SABRINA WOKE THE NEXT morning to find Church gone and a quick note scribbled on a hotel notepad.

The cowardly lion and I are off to see the wizard.
P.S. Took your dead cat to the lab

She twitched the curtain away from the window and looked out into the parking lot. Their car was still there. Which meant Church had hijacked Croft to play chauffeur/hostage. Hopefully, between the two of them, they'd be able to come up with some answers. Like the legal name of the person attached to the post office box used to exchange letters with Wade.

It was late August in Arizona. The sun was barely peeking over the horizon, but with it came the kind of heat you have to experience to truly appreciate. She could feel it even through the heavily lined hotel curtains. The cooler temperatures brought by yesterday's rain were gone, leaving the air thick enough to cut and hot enough to burn. Reluctantly, she traded boy shorts and a tank for another pair of smothering dress slacks and an equally oppressive button-down before slamming a cup of bad hotel room coffee. She looped the beaded chain attached to her badge around her neck. She'd forgotten over the last year how it felt to wear one. How heavy they were. Feeling the weight of it against her chest, she realized how much she missed it.

Stepping into the corridor of their hotel, Sabrina turned to pull the door shut, jiggling the handle to make sure it was locked. It was an unnecessary precaution—the door locked automatically—but she did it anyway. Satisfied, she turned toward the stairwell just a few steps away. Pulling open the door, she collided with a broad, sturdy chest covered by a damp T-shirt. She jolted backward, instantly forcing distance between them. Her sensible shoes tangled beneath her and she pitched back, her legs giving up the fight.

A hand shot out and gripped her, keeping her upright. "*Shit-sorry,*" he said smashing the words together as he hauled her toward him to keep her from falling.

"It's okay," she said, pressing a hand to his chest, pushing him away while she mentally cataloged his appearance. Gray T-shirt. Navy basketball shorts. Sandy blond hair darkened by sweat. Blue eyes. Nearly a head taller than her and built—muscular but not a total meathead. Good-looking but not too pretty. The kind of guy you'd notice but then forget about as soon as you passed him on the street. "It's okay," she said again, forcing herself to smile. "I've only had one cup of coffee this morning. That means I'm only half awake."

"I hate to tell you," he said, smiling back, the curve of his mouth upping his pretty points by about a hundred, "but if you're referring to that stuff they offer for free in the room, you *still* haven't had any coffee this morning." His eyes trailed downward, from her face to

191

her chest before settling on the badge that lay against it. His demeanor changed instantly. "My apologies," he mumbled, squeezing against the frame of the open door while he edged around her like she had some sort of contagious disease.

She laughed, moving past him to jog down the stairs. The badge was either a total turn-on or worked as a repellent. There was rarely an in between. "Have a good day," she called up, just to twist the knife a bit. The only sound that answered her was the sound of the door above her slamming closed.

———

The hotel was close to the I-10, situated in a bustling pocket of fast food restaurants and strip malls. This Yuma was very different than the one she remembered. She started the car and headed east, toward Yuma's only police station. After a year spent surrounded by nothing but silence and trees, it was disorienting—the speeding cars and tall stucco buildings slammed too close together. The noise and the heat. She welcomed the feeling. It helped her pretend she was a stranger. That the girl she'd been when she lived here all those years ago had been someone else. Like she never really existed.

When she got to the station, she parked in the employee lot, noting that it was nearly empty. None of the cars looked like any she'd seen in the dirt lot in front of Saint Rose last night. Hopefully Detective Santos wouldn't be here yet. His absence would make what she came to do a lot smoother.

Striding across the lobby with a confidence she didn't feel, she flashed the badge around her neck at the uniform manning the information desk on her way to Major Crimes. He was on the phone, calling her arrival up before she even hit the stairs. They'd set up a temporary office for her and "Agent Aimes" in a conference room. In it was a computer that would give her access to old case files. Tasers and ball gags might not be something she'd use to get information, but unauthorized digging through police records was right up her alley.

Her plan was derailed the moment she made the third-floor landing. Detective Mark Alvarez, Santos's partner, was there to greet her. Looking freshly showered and pressed despite the early hour, in his office casual short-sleeved polo and breathable cotton Dockers, he stood at the top of the stairs like he'd been waiting for her, a thin stack of case files in his hand. "Morning, Agent Vance—" He looked at his watch before offering her a quick smile. "Will had a late night so he's not in yet. Coffee? I just made a fresh pot."

It was barely six a.m. She hadn't expected either of them to be here yet. Santos had disappeared directly after mass was over, following Paul Vega down the aisle in the wake of whispers and stares, and she hadn't seen Alvarez since she'd left the primary scene yesterday afternoon. "Sure," she said returning the smile Alvarez gave her. "Coffee'd be great."

He led her to a small, windowless breakroom that held a soda and snack machine. Seeing them made her smile, a small chuckle escaping her. Strickland used to call the bags of potato chips and canned soft drinks they gave to suspects and witnesses *snitch bait*. He'd dig into that landfill he called a desk, coming up with loose bills to feed into vending machines, giving her a shit-eating grin that told her just how much he enjoyed the delicate dance between cop and suspect.

She was good at her job, but Strickland was a thing to watch. Underneath those stained ties and neglected haircuts was an interrogator so slick, so cunning, he'd have you confessing every sin you ever committed before you even thought of asking for a lawyer. When Strick was in the room, there was always an audience behind the two-way—more than a few of them taking notes.

Alvarez tossed the files onto the table as he passed it. "Something funny?" he said, aiming a look over his shoulder on his way to the coffeepot.

"No," she said, watching as he pulled a couple of paper cups off the stack and filled them with coffee from an industrial-sized urn. "It's just been a while since I've been in a police station." She leaned across the table to read the tabs of the files he'd tossed there. TRUDY HAYES. EDWARD SHERMAN. ROBERT DELASHAW. SARA PIKE.

"Missing persons cases."

She looked up to see him standing over her, a cup of coffee in each hand. He offered her one along with a lopsided smile. "Unfortunately, being a border town, we get more than our share."

Sabrina had a feeling there was more to the cases than that, but she didn't press him. Instead, she took the offered cup, returning the smile with one of her own. "I remember that about Yuma."

"That's right—you got your start in the Phoenix field office before making the jump to Quantico." He gestured with his cup at a chair before sitting. "You do a lot of work with PPD before the move?"

"I helped with a few cases," she said, evasively. The last thing she had time for was to sit and chat over a cup of coffee with Santos's rookie partner, but she smiled, accepting the cup while she slid into an empty chair. If partnering with Strickland had taught her anything it was that when it came to answers, there was more than one way to get them.

Alvarez laughed a little, shaking his head at what he must have thought was modesty. "One of those was The South Mountain Killer, wasn't it?" he asked, even though he obviously knew that, according to her file, it was the case that made her career. "Will says you pretty much solved the case single-handedly."

"There's no such thing as *single-handedly* in investigative work," she said. "All I did was give PPD a few ideas on what to look for. They did the heavy lifting."

Alvarez gave her a smile, this one telling her that evading his compliment while giving props to the locals had earned his respect. "Well, my partner isn't usually free with the *attaboys* so when he hands one out, I tend to believe him."

"Tell me your story," she said, changing the subject. If he noticed, he didn't seem to mind. "How'd you end up a cop? You don't really seem the type."

Alvarez shrugged. "I lost my scholarship. Dropped out of college and after a short *What the hell am I gonna do now?* crisis, applied to Tucson PD. Rode patrol for a few years before I made detective and transferred here."

She nodded. His story wasn't much different than most she'd heard. "You and Santos haven't been partners long."

"About a year now." He laughed. "Is it that obvious?"

Sabrina shrugged, thinking of Strickland. Wondering who had his back now that she was gone. "How's it going?"

"Actually, Will is the first partner I've ever had. I rode patrol solo …" He trailed off. "We've got different styles but he's a great cop. I'm lucky to partner with him." He said it like he was reading off a cue card. "How about you and Aimes? Been together long?"

Too long. "Believe it or not, this is our first case together," she said, tipping her cup in his direction before taking a sip. "The Bureau is all about *sink or swim* when it comes to field work."

"Ahh …" He laughed, nodding his head slowly. "That's it then."

"That's what?" she said carefully.

"The tension I caught between the two of you." Alvarez lifted a shoulder before taking a sip of his coffee. "You know, the awkward honeymoon phase—months of forced politeness and feeling each other out until one of you finally snaps."

"You and Santos seemed to get through it okay," she said, steering the conversation back in his direction.

"We've had our growing pains." Alvarez gave her a sheepish grin. "Neither of us like to take orders, but he's got the experience so I don't mind playing the sidekick."

She grinned back, silently thanking him for finally opening the door. "Yeah, from what I hear, he's worked a few high-profile cases."

Alvarez tilted his half-empty cup toward himself, pretending to gauge if he needed a refill. What he was really doing was deciding whether or not he wanted to slam the door he'd just opened in her face. "He had his fingers in the Vega case for a few minutes, back in 2000, but that didn't last long." His tone was flat, tinged with disgust, like just thinking about it pissed him off. "They closed ranks—surprise, surprise. Shut the whole thing down before Will could even take a formal statement."

She remembered Santos, the look on his face as he passed her by, following Paul Vega out of the chapel. It hadn't been anger she'd seen; it'd been the look a predator gets when it catches the scent of wounded prey. And it hadn't been about old wounds. It was the scent of fresh blood that brought Santos to the chapel last night.

Santos believed Vega had something to do with what'd happened to Rachel Meeks, she was sure of it. Instead of pursuing it, she filed it away for later, giving Alvarez a small smile like she knew what he was talking about.

"He was also the lead detective on the Melissa Walker case, wasn't he?" Santos had stonewalled her yesterday when she'd asked. Alvarez was the back door and she kicked it in with a smile.

The easy-going attitude he was throwing her went stiff around the edges. "Yeah, but that was way before my time," he said, trying to keep it casual with a disinterested shrug "Will isn't really the *share your feelings* type, you know?"

She nodded like she understood and she guessed she did. That particular case wasn't something *she* liked to think about. "So he doesn't like to talk about it?"

"Girl gets kidnapped, raped, tortured for months, and then murdered by her sicko brother on *your* watch ..." he said, staring into his half-empty cup. "Would you want to talk about it?"

"I suppose not," she said, giving him a smirky half smile even though his casual summary of the hell she'd lived through made her want to throw up. She felt something inside her break away, burrowing deep inside her brain. She let it go, didn't try to dig it out. It was an old habit, allowing herself to detach, and she clung to it now, grabbing at it with the desperate hands of a junkie. It was how she survived. The only way she could have this conversation without completely losing her shit.

"Way Will figures it"—Alvarez stood up, making his way to the coffeepot to top off his cup; he didn't ask her if she wanted a refill—"he could have stopped that freak before he even got started," he said, sliding back into his seat. "He blames himself."

"So, your partner fancies himself a clairvoyant?" She smiled, felt the cold slide of it across her mouth followed by a numbness that wasn't entirely unpleasant. "I read the reports. Wade Bauer tracked her across two states. Nearly fifteen hundred miles. Santos couldn't have known that. He couldn't have stopped him." She believed that. No one could have stopped Wade. What happened. What he did to her.

Alvarez let out a long breath, shaking his head at her perceived ignorance. "Maybe you feel that way because you don't know the whole story."

THIRTY-SEVEN

BINGO.

Sabrina's eyes went wide, hands turned palms up. "So," she said, throwing in a challenging smile for good measure, "enlighten me."

"Look," he said, aiming a glance over her shoulder to make sure they were alone. She was suddenly sure he knew more than he'd originally let on, and that what he knew wasn't necessarily something he was supposed to. "Melissa Walker was involved in a murder case a few weeks before she was abducted," he said, picking at the pressed seam that ran the length of his paper cup. "Some jock kid from Gila Bend was here for a high school football game. Ended up stabbed to death in a gas station bathroom."

Andy Shepard. She remembered him. His arrogant smile and careless hands. The way he'd touched her like he had the right. "Did she kill him?" She remembered wanting to. He'd reminded her of Jed Carson, the boy back home who never gave her a moment's peace. She'd hated them both, the way they thought that anything they wanted was theirs for the taking.

"No." Alvarez shook his head at her. "She was his waitress that night. He made a pass at her, grabbed her ass. She put him down pretty quick. According to Shepard's friends, she was so angry about it she was sent home. Another waitress had to finish her shift."

She remembered that too. Val dragging her away from the table, the drunken chatter that'd surrounded her fading away. Her glare nailed to the back of Shepard's head while he played the victim. That same night one of the bus boys told her that someone had been in the restaurant asking about her.

Alvarez spoke again and she forced herself to listen, to hear him instead of what was happening in her head. "A few hours later, a car full of them stopped on the way home so Shepard could take a leak," he said. "Five minutes stretched into ten … fifteen … twenty."

"Twenty minutes and no one went after him?" she said incredulously. "No teenager is that patient."

"Yeah, well … none of them were really watching the clock on account of the girl who was with them giving out blow jobs in the back seat to pass the time," he said, shrugging. "The driver, who got his happy ending first, finally got tired of waiting. He goes after Shepard to tell him to hurry the hell up. He sees the blood leaking under the door and starts screaming his head off. Shepard was stabbed once—clean, between the ribs and through the lung. Bled out while his buddies were lined up for free hummers in the parking lot." He shook his head at the ridiculousness of it. "Perp took his hand as a souvenir. No one saw him and if they did, they were too drunk or too busy getting their dick sucked to remember or care."

"I still don't understand what this has to do with Melissa Walker," she said, allowing irritation to creep into her tone. "Or why your partner blames himself from what happened to her."

"Will was part of the interdepartmental murder investigation—his first lead case. He questioned her, only he didn't know it was *her*. She was living and working under a fake name. He *knew* she had something to do with it. He knew Shepard's murder was connected to her somehow..." Alvarez sighed, sliding down in his chair until his slumped shoulders hit the back of it, leaving his cup behind. "But then out of the blue, the night clerk at the gas station confessed. Said he'd killed Shepard because he and his buddies had done a beer run there the weekend before and cost him his job. Took his hand for stealing. Evidence found in his possession supported his confession."

She remembered. Sitting in a back booth at Luck's with Santos while he laid it out for her. He told her that the case was closed and thanked her for her time while she'd pretended to be relieved. Pretended to believe it was over. That she was safe.

But it had been a lie. All of it.

Wade took her two days later. Snatched her off the street while she walked home from work, leaving nothing behind but a box of leftover birthday cake dumped in the gutter.

The store clerk who confessed was named James Toliver. He'd been convicted and sentenced to life in prison within months of his arrest. Because of his work on the Shepard case, Santos was made lead detective on her disappearance. He was a good cop; he must've seen the connection right away. He must've at least suspected that the confession was bogus, that he'd gotten the wrong guy. That maybe if he'd pursued it instead of swallowing the hook and allowing himself to get reeled in by the rush of solving his first lead case, he'd have been able to see the truth. A thing like that would eat at a cop like Will Santos. Keep him up at night. Haunt him like a ghost.

"Will never got over it," Alvarez told her, confirming what she'd just been thinking. "When that thing with Vega happened, he took it personal." He must've finally realized that he'd said too much because his eyes narrowed into slits. "Why are you asking about her anyway?" he said, aiming a suspicious look her way. "Melissa Walker? It's been twenty years—you're a little late to the party."

"Am I?" she said, setting her own cup aside. "Because the report I read said there was DNA found on Stephanie Adams. She had Melissa Walker's blood under her fingernails. Seems to me, I'm right on time."

Something close to embarrassment passed over his face. "How do you know about that?" he said, the words falling tight and clipped against her ears. "Those results were struck from the original report."

She smiled again, tapping a finger against the badge Church had given her. "FBI," she said, relying on the initials to explain everything.

"It was a mistake," he said, his affable expression slammed shut. "Samples got contaminated. The tech responsible was reprimanded, corrective action was taken, and the tests were regenerated." He fed her the party line before he stood, draining his cup. "If you'll excuse me, I have some paperwork to catch up on."

"Who was it?" she said, looking up at him, unwilling to let him go until she got at least one of the answers she'd come for. The tech who'd taken the samples and run the test might know things that had been stricken from the report that even Ben hadn't been able to get his hands on. "The tech who screwed up?"

Alvarez bared his teeth at her in something that most people would mistake for a smile. "Does it really matter?"

"I know you don't know me very well, Detective Alvarez, but I can assure you"—she returned his smile—"I'm not in the business of asking unnecessary questions."

Alvarez crushed the cup in his fist before tossing it in the trash can on his way to the door. She was sure he'd ignore the question. That he'd leave without answering her, forcing her to go after him, but then he told her. "Elena Hernandez," he said, forcing the name between clenched teeth just before he disappeared down the hall.

As soon as Alvarez walked out, Sabrina tossed her own cup and followed him. By the time she reached the bullpen he was at his desk, head buried in a stack of files. He didn't look up when she passed by on her way to the conference room she and Church had been assigned. Santos was still nowhere to be found.

Installing herself behind the computer, she turned it on, waiting for it to power up before she typed the first in a short list of names into the search bar.

PAUL VEGA

Barely a second after she hit enter, a message flashed across the screen.

no matches to your search inquiry found

Santos was a Major Crimes detective. Anything he'd been called to investigate would have carried with it a felony charge. The four majors were rape, murder, armed robbery, and kidnapping. Whatever happened, it'd been bad. What had Alvarez said? *They closed ranks.* Stopped a felony investigation in its tracks. That meant nothing about a felony crime involving Paul Vega would be in the system. But erasing Vega's involvement didn't mean they could turn back time. Whatever it was he'd been suspected of doing still happened. There'd still be a paper trail. She thought about it and tried again.

MAJOR CRIMES, UNSOLVED, 2000

A few seconds later, a row of file numbers tumbled down the screen. Nearly a dozen of them. Scrolling the mouse over the first number she clicked it, opening the file. Reports and case notes filled the screen. A drive-by shooting in her old neighborhood. She opened the next in line. An armed robbery at a Circle K. She opened the next one. A burned body found in the desert. The next one. A hooker strangled to death in Luck's parking lot. That one looked promising, even though she had a hard time imagining Vega trolling for prostitutes. She closed it and moved on.

The next file on the screen was an unsolved rape case. According to the case notes, it'd been brutal. The victim was a seventeen-year-old girl—a senior at Yuma High School. Cheerleader. Photographer for the school newspaper. Yearbook editor. Solid B student. She'd left home late Friday night, sneaking out of the house after her parents went to sleep. When they woke the next morning, she was gone, something both of them swore was against her character, despite the fact that they'd waited until after noon to call the police.

A field foreman name Tomas Olivero found her in a pump house four days later, chained to the waterwheel, naked and badly beaten. Severely dehydrated. She'd been raped and beaten repeatedly. Sodomized. Forced to perform sex acts on her assailants before being left to die. The pump house she'd been found in was one of twenty-two belonging to Vega Farms.

The victim's name had been Rachel Meeks.

THIRTY-EIGHT

Kootenai Canyon, Montana

"I don't think this is a good idea."

Christina looked up and over at him from the driver's seat of the Challenger. She looked terrified and exhilarated all at once and he tried not to laugh, he really did.

"Are you laughing at me?" She narrowed her eyes before aiming them out the windshield, delicate fingers wrapped around the steering wheel.

"What?" Michael cleared his throat. "No, I would never—"

"Because I'm only thirteen," she sniffed at him. "I shouldn't be driving."

He swallowed another burst of laughter, angling his head a bit lower so she couldn't see it. "Christina, I'm asking you to pull the car into the grass, not jump it over a dozen flaming school buses. You've done it a hundred times."

"Yeah, with you *in* the car with me." She glared at him for a moment before dropping one of her hands to the gearshift while she pressed the clutch into the floorboard. She gave him a long-suffering sigh. "Whatever. Move or I'm going to run you over." She slipped it into first and eased off the clutch, exchanging it smoothly with the gas pedal. The Challenger inched forward, carried through the open barn door by the rumbling engine.

Like he'd been told, Michael stood straight, backing away from the car so she could guide it from the barn onto the grass in front of the house. She did perfectly, moving slowly, like he'd taught her. As soon as the Challenger was where he'd told her to put it, Christina shifted into neutral and cut the engine. She even set the emergency brake. But she didn't get out of the car. She just sat there, staring straight ahead.

Michael closed the distance between the barn and the car. "You gonna pout all day or are you gonna pop the hood so we can—"

"There're bug guts on the windshield." She finally looked at him, her tone careful and even. "Why are there bug guts on the windshield?"

Shit.

"You left," she said, dark brown gaze narrowed on him accusingly. "You left me. You left *us*."

"Christina, I—"

"You said you wouldn't do that," she said, lunging out of the car to push past him.

"Just let me explain," he said, voice raised louder than it should have been.

"Explain?" She turned on him, jabbing an accusatory finger in his face. "You said you wouldn't leave." He reached out to catch her arm but she yanked back before he could make contact. "You *promised*."

"What was I supposed to do, Christina?" He finally caught her arm and she went still, turning on him, waiting for him to let her go. "She's out there *alone*, and I—"

"Is that why Miss Ettie is here?" Christina said, her arm tense and heavy in his grip. "Just in case you decided that sticking around was too much of an imposition?"

"What?" He jerked back, his hand dropping away from her. "No." He shook his head, sagging against the fender of the car. "You're a kid, Christina. You don't understand."

"Then explain it to me," she said, crossing her arms over her chest. "Because the way I see it, *Sabrina* left *us*."

"It's not that simple," he said, shoving his hands into the front pockets of his jeans while glaring at the toes of his boots. "All of this is my fault. All of it—the last four years of her life have been a waking nightmare and that's because of me. I'm the one who brought her brother to her doorstep. I'm the one who brought it all to her doorstep. If I'd have left her alone, she'd still be in San Francisco. She'd still have her family. She'd be—"

"Bullshit."

The curse jerked his head up and had him swinging his gaze toward her. She didn't look like Christina anymore. Her jaw was set in silent challenge, her dark eyes wise and older than they had a right to be. She looked like Lydia. She looked like her mother. Seeing his lost friend in her daughter was suddenly too much.

"What?"

"You heard me," she said, losing some of that hard-won nerve but still refusing to back down. "You act like she's not capable of making her own choices. She knew what she was doing when she came here. And she understood what would happen if she left."

No matter what she thought, there was still a lot Christina didn't understand. A lot they'd chosen not to tell her. "Like I said, you're a kid." He pulled his hands from his pockets and straightened himself off the hood of the car. "You don't understand."

"I understand that you're going to have to choose, Michael," she said, her arms tightening against her frame, like she was afraid of what came next. "Her or me. You can't keep your promises to both of us."

"That's where you're wrong, kiddo," he told her with a sad smile. "Because when she left she made me promise not to go after her. She made me promise to stay here, no matter what. I broke my promise to both of you."

Her arms dropped away from her chest, her eyes filled with tears. "Then why—"

"Because I love her. Because I can't just leave her. She's in danger, every moment of every day—" Michael swiped a hand over his mouth. "And that *is* my fault. At least when she's here, I can protect her …" He sighed. "I just made a phone call. That's it. That's all I did." It was all he could do. The uselessness he felt chewed at his gut, making him want to throw up.

"A phone call?" She looked at him like he'd lost his mind, eyes wide with disbelief over his recklessness. "*You used a phone?*"

"It's an old analog—practically untraceable. I was almost three hundred miles away before I turned it on and the call lasted less than two minutes. After I was finished, I wiped it down, destroyed it and tossed the pieces into a lumber truck headed for Idaho." He forced a reassured smile onto his face. "And the person I called is just as careful, I promise."

"Who?" she said quietly. "Who did you call?"

He thought of Phillip Song, struggling to find a way to describe him that wouldn't make him sound like what he was—an alleged gangster. Possible drug lord. Probable murderer.

"Someone who can help her."

She didn't push it; instead she nodded, chewing on her lower lip. "She said the same thing, you know," she said, fixing him with a look that said she finally understood. "That day the senator came, she put Alex and me in the lift by ourselves and I freaked out. She told me she loved you and couldn't leave you. I was relieved that you wouldn't be alone but I was scared too." Tears stood out in her eyes and she gave them an irritated brush with her fingertips. "I know you and Sabrina would die for each other..."

"It's not just me she's willing to die for, Christina." He reached out, pulling her into a hug. This time she let him. "Sabrina will do whatever it takes to keep you and Alex safe. She's a fighter. Hiding isn't in her nature."

"It not in yours, either." She said it against his chest, her hands gripped tightly against the thin cotton of his T-shirt. "That's what scares me."

"I'm sorry," he said, running a gentle hand over her sun-warmed hair. "I'm not going anywhere—not again. I'm keeping my promise to the both of you."

She didn't answer him. Didn't say she believed him. Probably because she didn't.

THIRTY-NINE

Yuma, Arizona

Sixteen years ago, Rachel Meeks survived four days of rape and torture. No food. No water. Just ninety-six hours of relentless abuse. That was her miracle, and what had drawn her killer to her.

Sabrina didn't wait for Detective Santos to show up. Closing the file, she hit PRINT ALL. If someone searched her computer history, it would look like she was interested in all unsolved cases, rather than focused on one in particular. She had no idea if Vega still had someone in the department mopping up after him, but until she could hang him, Sabrina planned on making herself as small as possible.

Stopping at Santos's desk, she wrote a quick note telling him she'd be out in the field, following it up with her cell number. Alvarez sat a few feet away, head still buried in a stack of files. Still ignoring her. She decided she didn't care and left without saying good-bye.

As soon as she hit the stairs, she pulled her cell from her pocket, stopping long enough to punch out the number Ellie had given her yesterday.

Whaddya think you're doin', darlin'?

She listened to the phone ring, ignoring the voice in her head, while she jogged down the stairs.

Calling that girl ain't the smartest thing you've ever done. The more time you spend with her, the more chance there is she'll recognize you.

"This is Hernandez," Ellie said.

"Hi, this is Agent Vance," Sabrina said, walking across the lobby toward the parking lot. "Any chance I can get you to meet me?"

Maybe that's what you want. Maybe you want Ellie to see you for who you really are. Maybe you want her to know. Maybe you want them all to know …

A soft sigh accompanied the sound of shuffling papers. "Uh … sure," she said, even though she didn't sound sure at all. She actually sounded like she'd been sleeping. "I guess I can cut out for a bit. Where?"

Using the key fob in her hand to unlock the car, Sabrina tossed the files she'd printed into the passenger seat before sliding behind the wheel. "Saint Rose," she said, stabbing the key into the ignition.

The other end of the phone went so quiet that for a second, she thought Ellie had hung up on her. "Okay," she said, finally answering her. "I'll be there in an hour."

———

The lot was empty when Sabrina pulled in. Not surprising—Saint Rose's congregants were in the fields that surrounded it, bending and tossing in sweat-soaked shirts and wide-brimmed hats.

The chapel was comparatively dark and cool, empty save for an old woman who knelt in front of the altar, covered head bent over a lit candle. Feeling intrusive, Sabrina gave her little more than a glance before surveying the rest of the sanctuary. She spotted Father Francisco in the prayer garden, sitting on the bench, an open book in his lap.

Not just any ol' bench is it? That's our *bench, darlin'.*

Father Francisco wasn't alone. The man who'd attended last night's mass with Paul Vega was with him, standing over him, hands dug into the pants pockets of his expensive suit, an affable smile on his familiar face. Despite the man's relaxed posture and smile, Sabrina got the impression that the two of them weren't having a friendly chat. Father Francisco looked almost angry. He sat as still as stone, his gaze aimed at the other man's tie, a grim expression on his face, listening to what was being said to him.

As soon as the door leading to the sanctuary opened, the priest's head popped up. The other man stopped talking, his gaze following the priest's. He gave her a look that said her intrusion wasn't a welcome one but it was fleeting, covered up with another pleasant smile. "See you on Sunday, Father," he said, leaving out the garden gate without another word.

Father Francisco smiled like he was glad to see her. "Agent Vance," he said, closing his book before setting it aside. "What brings you back?"

"I'm meeting someone." Sabrina smiled back. She had a few minutes to kill before Ellie showed up. She might as well put them to use. "Who was that? He looks familiar."

The relieved look bled away. "Arturo Bautista."

"Paul Vega's attorney?" she said, her tone sharp and hard against her ears. Why would Vega's lawyer be here, giving what looked like a stern lecture to his client's priest?

He looked startled that she'd know who Bautista was. "Yes, he represents Vega Farms," he said evasively before offering her another small smile when she didn't retreat back into the sanctuary. "Was there something I can do for you, Agent Vance?"

"I have a few questions that need answering."

His smile folded in at the corners, getting smaller as he looked at his watch. "I have confession in a few minutes," he said, retrieving his book before standing. "Perhaps—"

"I won't take too much of your time." The smile on her face remained firmly intact while she waited for his manners to force him to concede. "I promise."

As predicted, he caved after a few seconds. "Okay," he said, giving in with a small nod. "What can I do for you?"

"Who is Nulo?" she said, going for the jugular. She wasn't disappointed. The welcoming look he'd given her was completely blown away, replaced by something that looked like fear.

Father Francisco shook his head, nervously transferring the book from one hand to another "I don't understand."

"Oh, I think you do." She cocked her head and gave a short, quick nod. "You *are* the same Father Francisco who ran this place in 1998." It wasn't a question and she didn't phrase it like one. "The same Father Francisco who found Melissa Walker, half dead, on that bench you're sitting on."

He visibly blanched, his face draining of blood so fast it was a miracle he didn't pass out. "I am, but I don't know who you're asking me about."

He's lying. He knows exactly who Nulo is. Probably even knows what he is . . .

"I've never arrested a priest before," she said quietly, nailing him with a look perfected over the course of nearly fifteen years and hundreds of interrogations. "Please don't make me do it now." When he did nothing but stare, she continued. "It was Nulo. He was the one who found Melissa Walker the night Wade Bauer left her here. Not you. He was here . . . with you. A young, handsome priest, alone in a church with an even younger, presumably impressionable boy. I understand why you lied."

The nerve it'd taken him to lie to her abandoned him, leaving him weak and he sunk slowly, as if the heat of her glare was melting him into the bench. "If you think I hurt that boy or that I took advantage of him in some way—"

"What *I* think is irrelevant." She could feel it welling up inside her, the shame and humiliation. "You told the paramedics you found Melissa Walker because the truth would put you in the very awkward position of having to explain why he was here." They must've known, the moment they saw her, what'd happened to her. How long did Nulo stand over her, watching her, before Father Francisco found him? Had he touched her? Had he felt the same sick excitement that Wade had over what had been done to her? Is that why he wrote to him? Because he'd stood over her and felt a kinship to the monster who destroyed her?

"Do you know what *Nulo* means, Agent Vance?" Father Francisco shook his head sadly. "It means nothing. Void. No one was looking for that boy. No one cared where he was. What happened to him."

"What did happen, Father?" She said it quietly, tempering the hard edge of her tone. "What was he doing here?"

"He was just a boy, Agent Vance—" He looked up at her helplessly. "He was frightened. Unsure of what he'd witnessed."

"He knew *exactly* what he was witnessing." She took a step forward, closing the gap between them until she was almost standing over him. "Why would you lie to me about him? Why are you protecting him?"

Father Francisco shook his head. "I ..." He glanced up at her for a moment before he looked away. "I was newly ordained when I came to Saint Rose. Barely twenty-five—too young and inexperienced to be given my own church, but the head priest here died not weeks after my appointment and there was no one else."

"Regardless," she said, even though impatience gnawed at her, "you must've made an impression if they were willing to give you your own church so quickly."

He scoffed at her. "The only impression made was by my last name. I was soft, eager to win over my flock." His mouth flattened into a grimace. "I allowed things that I shouldn't."

"Like?"

"Nulo was young, just a boy ... I didn't know how to stop what was happening to him so, I allowed him to sleep here. Him and others like him who had nowhere to go. He'd sneak into the church at night and hide from his uncle." His eyes found hers again, showing her a lifetime of regret and sadness. "He did things to Nulo that should never be done."

"Who is he?" She didn't ask what kind of things—she didn't have to. "What's his real name?"

"I don't know. I never knew." The priest shook his head sadly. "His parents died when he was little more than a baby. I don't think he even knew what his given name was."

"What do you mean *was*?" she said, picking up on the word.

"I mean *was*, Agent Vance," he said, looking up at her. "A few years after he found that poor girl, Nulo disappeared."

"*Disappeared?*" She said it quietly, the hairs on the back of her neck standing on edge.

"He showed up one night, late. I thought he wasn't coming so I locked the doors and put out the candles..." Father Francisco sighed, his hands tightening around the book in his lap. "He woke me, broke that window," he said, pointing at the pane of glass set into the heavy wooden door that led to the chapel. "He was covered in blood. At first I thought he'd cut himself trying to get in. When I dragged him into the bathroom to clean him up I realized that he wasn't hurt. The blood wasn't his. I didn't ask what'd happened. I already knew."

So did she. "He killed his uncle."

"He was hysterical." The man nodded his head. "Rambling on and on about that night—"

"When?" The word slipped between them, as thin and sharp as a blade. "When did he kill his uncle?"

One of his hands fell away to rest on the bench he was sitting on. The bench Wade had left her on. "When..." he said, shaking his head. "It was spring 2001." The hand on the bench curled into a fist. "He'd just turned eighteen."

"You didn't call the police, did you?" she said, even though she already knew the answer.

"Do you know what that man did to Nulo?" The priest shook his head like he was disappointed in her. "I do. *Horrible* things, from the time he was barely old enough to walk. He would have been arrested. Surely convicted. At eighteen he would've been sentenced to life in prison, and that was the best-case scenario. No, Agent Vance,

I didn't call the police. I cleaned him up and gave him clean clothes. Then I took every last dime out of my collection box and gave it to him," he said, his jaw set at a self-righteous angle. "Afterward, I drove him to the bus station and I never saw him again."

FORTY

Sabrina sat in the back pew, watching people file in for confession while she waited for Ellie to show up. Nothing Father Francisco had told her made any sense—and none of it connected to Paul Vega or what'd happened to Rachel Meeks.

Pulling her phone from her pocket, she checked it for what felt like the hundredth time. No messages, which meant either Church and Croft hadn't turned up anything or her new partner had decided to let her sweat. Checking the time, she noted that Ellie was nearly twenty minutes late. Dropping her phone into her lap, she settled in to wait.

She'd managed to get one more question in before Father Francisco cut her off completely. "Who was his uncle?" she'd said, blocking the door with her hand so he couldn't open it. "What was his name?"

The priest's grip tightened around the handle of the door she was barring him from using. "What does it matter?" he said, stubbornly yanking on the handle. "He is dead and Nulo is gone."

"You do know *why* I'm here, don't you?" She slammed the door shut and glared at him. "That people are being murdered, violently tortured. Raped and—"

"*Enough.*" He barked the word at her, no longer the soft-spoken priest. "And you think that Nulo did it?" he said, shaking his head at her. "Did you not hear me when I told you that he left? That he hasn't been back?"

"Why? Because you haven't seen him?" she said, eyes locked on his face. Instinct told her he was telling her the truth—that he hadn't seen Nulo since the night he'd dropped him off at the bus station—but she'd been fooled before. "Yuma holds over one hundred thousand people, Father. Do you know every single one of them?"

His hand fell away from the handle, his arm suddenly slack at his side. He opened his mouth but nothing came out so he closed it again, averting his gaze to stare at her shoulder. "I don't remember." He shifted his gaze again, looking her in the eye. "I'm an old man and it was a long time ago" he said, reaching for the handle again. This time when he pulled the door open, she let him go.

"Sorry I'm late."

Sabrina looked up to see Ellie standing in the row in front of her. She sat, turning on the bench to drape her arm over the back of it so that they were face to face. She looked nervous. Like she didn't want to be there. "It's okay," Sabrina said, offering her a small smile, trying to put her at ease. "How's your mom?"

"She's okay," Ellie said, wincing a bit. "I wanted to apologize and thank you for being such a good sport last night."

"There's no need to do either," she said. "Your mother is a lovely woman."

Ellie nodded, looking at her lap for a moment before raising her gaze again. "I don't think you wanted me to meet you here to ask about my mom, Agent Vance," she said quietly, worrying something flat and silver between her fingers. "Mark called me. He told me you asked him about the corrupted sample I took off Stephanie Adams."

Sabrina didn't know which surprised her more—that Alvarez would call Ellie to warn her that the big, bad FBI agent was sniffing around her mistake or that he and Ellie were on a first-name basis. "I'm not here to drag you through the mud," she said, shaking her head. "I just want to know what happened, Ellie."

Ellie sighed. "I noticed particulates under Stephanie Adams's fingernails so I bagged her hands at the scene, according to department procedure. Back at the lab, I processed the sample and ran it through CODIS against possible matches … and I got two hits."

"Stephanie Adams and Melissa Walker," Sabrina said, carefully gauging Ellie's reaction to the name. She flinched slightly, like the name carried a current of electricity that shocked and stung every time it was uttered.

"Yes. I thought it must've been some sort of mistake so I … I ran it again." Ellie nodded, finally looking up at her, fingers still working and worrying. "The whole procedure—from start to finish—with a new sample. I even changed my gloves … and I got the same results," she said firmly.

Separate samples meant that the department's official story of contamination was unlikely but, for a small department with limited resources, not impossible. "Then what's your explanation for your results?"

"I don't know." Ellie dropped her gaze again. "All I know is I didn't mess up."

"I believe you."

Her words jerked Ellie's head up on her neck, and she pinned her with a look that was half hopeful, half wary. "You believe me," she said, shaking her head. "Just like that, you believe me."

"Yes, just like that," she said, giving the woman in front of her a small smile.

Ellie let out the breath she'd been holding in a relieved gust. "Now what?"

The smile on her face went sharp, stinging the corners of her mouth. "Now we figure out what DNA from a twenty-year-old murder case was doing under Stephanie Adams's fingernails."

"I think I might already know," Ellie said quietly. "I tried to explain it, to tell them it wasn't a mistake, but no one would listen to me."

"Explain what?" she said, leaning forward to close the gap between them.

"After the second round of tests came back with the same results, I ran a full composite analysis on the scraping I took from Stephanie Adams." Ellie lowered her voice even more, looking around the chapel before continuing. "The particulates were comprised of dirt, calcium, aluminum, and limestone."

Sabrina thought about it for a moment. "What is that? Concrete?"

Ellie nodded. "Melissa Walker's blood was adhered to what turned out to be pieces of cement block," she said, her tone carrying the words carefully, like they meant something. "The kind used in buildings."

Sabrina could feel them. The stinging scrape of them against her shoulder as she walked. Pushing herself forward, propped against the wall, moving as fast as her drug-tangled legs would carry her.

She thought of Nulo again. Wade's student. His progeny. The one he passed it all down to. The sickness. The rage. Wade would tell him where he'd kept her. A safe place that would never be found. A place where a person could scream and never be heard.

You got it, darlin'. Our boy's been keepin' the home fires burnin'.

"The same place," she said slowly, like she was trying to shake herself from the nightmare she was suddenly convinced she'd been plunged into. "He's keeping them in the same place."

FORTY-ONE

ELLIE STARED AT HER for a few moments, waiting for her to elaborate. Sabrina leaned forward, adopting the same hushed tone Ellie had used earlier. "That's why Melissa Walker's blood was stuck to those cement particles under Stephanie Adams's nails." The words were coming fast now, carried on the wave of excitement that coursed through her. "He's keeping his victims in the same place Wade Bauer kept Melissa. Stephanie Adams must've dug her nails into—"

Ellie shook her head, stopping her cold. "No," she said firmly. "That's the thing—there *was* no digging. No ripped nailbeds. No torn cuticles. No signs she fought back or tried to escape."

She imagined Stephanie Adams, crouched in the dark, totally accepting of what was happening to her. Resigned to her own death. Patiently waiting for it like someone waits for a bus. "That can't be. How else could particulates get under her nails? It's not like he put it there."

"That's exactly what he did. You might be right about where it came from but that blood evidence was placed under Stephanie Adams's fingernails on purpose," Ellie said, her tone hard and determined. "All victims were meticulously bound and posed. Intricately positioned … and washed with bleach."

I taught our boy well, darlin'. He don't make mistakes.

The hand in her lap curled into a fist so tight her knuckles nearly punched through her skin. Ellie was talking. She dug her nails into the palm of her hand to clear the fog that floated around her brain.

"… she'd been scrubbed clean just like the others, inside and out. No way someone who pays *that* much attention to detail forgets the nails. No way." Ellie shook her head again. "The only thing I can't explain is *why*. Why would he purposely place Melissa Walker's blood under one of his victim's nails?"

The way she said it cleared the rest of Sabrina's cobwebs. Like she knew why but was afraid to say it. "Well, what's your theory?" Sabrina said, forcing her hand flat against her thigh. "You must have one."

Ellie hesitated, looking away again, her eyes trailing over the wooden confession booths against the far wall of the church. "I knew Melissa Walker," she said, her gaze trained elsewhere. "She and my sister worked together at a restaurant. She lived in our apartment complex …" Her voice grew as thin and brittle as blown glass. "I babysat for her. Loved her like a sister."

Sabrina pretended to be thinking in order to buy some time. So she could force the hurricane of emotion that swirled and raged within her into a chokehold. "You're Valerie Hernandez's sister," she said, like she'd just put the pieces together. "You think the killer was reaching out to you somehow?"

"I don't know," Ellie said, her voice losing that confident edge. "It sounds crazy, right? I mean, why would he reach out to *me*?"

Sabrina didn't have an answer for that. But this Nulo guy obviously didn't know Sabrina had actually survived after being brought to the hospital, or he would have told Wade. So he can't have been trying to reach her. "I don't know," she said, tilting her head slightly. "Maybe Melissa Walker is just a piece of the puzzle. Can I ask you something else?"

Ellie's hands went still for a moment. "Sure," she finally said, giving her a curt nod.

"What was your relationship with Rachel Meeks?" she said quickly, watching Ellie stiffen up the second the words left her mouth. "And please don't tell me that the two of you just went to high school together."

"Rachel was my best friend for a while." Ellie gave her a sad smile. "We were inseparable. Where one was, the other was right beside her." She laughed, shaking her head. "It used to drive my mother crazy. She thought Rachel was a bad influence."

She remembered what Amelia had told her last night—that she'd never liked Rachel Meeks. That she felt bad about it now that she was dead. "I've had a few friends like that. Usually that's what makes them so great."

"She was fearless. Exciting…" Ellie's smile widened, even as tears gathered in the corners of her eyes. "Talked me into some pretty crazy stuff when we were kids."

"When did the two of you stop being friends?" She could hear it in Ellie's tone, a wistful sort of sadness that told her that whatever they'd been to each other as kids, it'd changed a long time ago. "Was it after she was raped?"

"How…" Ellie's eyes widened for a moment before she slumped in her seat. "Oh, right… FBI." She let her gaze rest on the badge around Sabrina's neck for a moment before she forced it up to her face. "Yeah. Afterward, she acted like nothing was wrong. Like those four days never happened. I tried," she said, the tears in her eyes finally falling. "I stayed. I tried to help her. I *tried*."

"It wasn't you." She let the words slip out before she could catch them. Sabrina fought to remember that this was Ellie talking about Rachel, not Val talking about her. Guilt pressed in anyway. "It wasn't your fault."

"If I'd just kept my mouth shut and played along…" Ellie shook her head. "She didn't want to press charges. She wouldn't even say his name to the police. He chained her up like an animal and let his friend do whatever he wanted to her for *four days*."

"*He*." Sabrina sat forward, her hands wrapping around the back of Ellie's pew. "She knew the man who raped her?"

"She knew and so did I." Ellie's tone went flat, her wide, dark eyes suddenly dry. "It was Paul Vega."

Something cool brushed against her nape before tumbling down her spine. The irrigation shed Rachel Meeks had been found in was on Vega Farms property. Still… "I read the report, Ellie. Nothing in it points—"

"You don't understand," Ellie said, the words a sharp bark of frustration. "I *know* it was Paul Vega. Because I was there."

FORTY-TWO

HIS HANDS REEKED OF gasoline. It wasn't wholly unpleasant, the smell of it. The scent drifted up to him, sharp and heavy, from where his fingers gripped the steering wheel, and every breath he took reminded him of his Margaret and what he'd done to her.

You mean what we *did to her, don't you, boy?*

The voice inside his head sounded petulant, like a complaining child who'd been told he couldn't go outside to play. It annoyed him. Still, he owed Wade Bauer his freedom. Without him, the night he'd watched him drape a very dead Melissa Walker across that bench, he never would've understood the urgent need that had gripped him since he was a young boy. Never would've had the guts to act on it.

He would have been alone.

His father long gone. His mother dead. There'd been no one else to guide him, to tell him it was okay. To show him how to be who and what he was.

A killer.

"Of course I mean *we*," he murmured out loud, the ghost of a grin sliding across his face. He'd been sitting in his car for a while now, watching the steady trickle of people flow in and out of Saint Rose for confession. Thinking about all those sins, confessed in hushed, shame-filled tones. All the bad things people did that needed forgiving. Aside from the killing, it was his favorite part of what he did. Saying it out loud. Listening to the soft, labored breathing of the old priest behind the screen while he shared his sins. The difference was, he never asked for forgiveness. He didn't want it. Didn't need it.

She was inside. Nosing around. Asking questions about him. It was only a matter of time before the priest told her everything.

You're gonna have to make sure that doesn't happen.

"I know," he muttered, distracted by the slam of a car door. He watched Elena Hernandez cross the lot, heading into the sanctuary.

What's little sister doing here?

He knew she was an observing Catholic but he suspected that her attending mass and giving regular confession was more for her mother's benefit than because she actually believed. He could see it, her doubt. Her loss of faith. She knelt and prayed. Accepted communion and the blessings of the old priest, but it was all for show.

Elena stopped believing in miracles a long time ago.

He wondered if she'd change her mind if she knew the truth. That she *was* a miracle. That every breath she'd taken since that night had been a gift from God.

God don't want no part of what we're doing here, boy.

For some reason, knowing that made him smile.

FORTY-THREE

THE ADMISSION HUNG BETWEEN them while Ellie watched her, as if she were waiting for her to call her a liar. Her claim was unfounded. Nowhere in the case file did it mention Ellie Hernandez or the fact she'd been there with Rachel the night she was taken. But looking at her, Sabrina believed her.

I was there.

"Who else knows you were there?" she said, purposely softening her tone. She knew a secret when she heard one. She'd be willing to bet that the answer to her question amounted to less than a handful of people.

"Now that Rachel's dead?" Ellie said, bitterness clinging to every word. "Me, Paul, a few of his friends."

A handful of people.

"Take me through it," she said, resorting back to what she did best: investigating and finding answers. "Tell me what happened that night, starting from the beginning."

"Okay." Ellie nodded, tucking whatever it was she'd had in her hand into her pocket. "Rachel and Paul were off and on. They'd date for a few weeks, one of them would get jealous or pissed off at the other and break it off. Then a few days later, they'd be back at it."

"Who knew about their relationship?"

"No one, really. They kept it pretty quiet..." Ellie shook her head, rubbing the palms of her hands on the legs of her pants. "Not her parents, that's for sure," she said. "As far as they were concerned, Rachel was perfect. Paul was way older—they wouldn't have approved."

"So that night, the two of you agreed to meet up with Paul and a few of his friends?" she said, filling in the blanks.

"Yeah." Ellie nodded while chewing on her bottom lip. "We waited for her parents to fall asleep and snuck out through her bedroom window. They were waiting for us at the end of her block in Paul's truck. It wasn't the first time we'd done it."

She remembered the incident with the watermelons when Ellie was fourteen. Had Rachel and Paul been involved then? Had she been out partying in the fields and things got out of hand? Regardless, the remembered episode lent credence to what Ellie was telling her now.

"Okay," Sabrina said, going over it in her mind, "what happens after you get to the irrigation shed?"

"Paul had the key. He'd brought a case of beer and everyone starts drinking, partying," Ellie says quietly. "About an hour after we got there, Rachel and Paul started to fight, which was totally normal. She tells Paul we're leaving and we started walking."

"Did you guys make it home?" Sabrina said, remembering her own walk home the night Wade abducted her. She'd almost made it. She could still remember the lights above the row of apartment mailboxes, the dull shine of them bringing on a starburst of hope in her chest as she hurried home. She'd almost made it before Wade's hand fell against her mouth.

Almost.

"She was pretty drunk so after we left, her fight with Paul became her fight with me. It was a long walk home and we didn't even make it to the main road before she wanted to go back, but I refused," Ellie said. "When we finally got to her house, we were fighting so bad, I decided to walk the rest of the way home. When I left she was standing on her front porch, looking for her keys."

The fast skim she'd given Rachel's rape file at the station didn't say anything about Ellie or that she'd been with her. It also didn't say anything about Rachel sneaking out of the house to party with Paul Vega either, but that didn't mean it wasn't true. All it meant was that the Vega family had a long reach and deep pockets. Long and deep enough to erase witnesses and suspects as if they never existed.

"The report doesn't mention any of this." She had to say it, even if she believed her. "The party. The relationship between Rachel and Paul. You being there. His friends. None of it's documented. Why is that?"

"I'd caused my mother so much grief already..." Ellie said, looking miserable. "I knew right away that it was Paul. It had to be, but... he had a temper. I'd seen him lose it on Rachel more than once. I was afraid of what he would do—what his *family* would do—if I said anything. After a few days, I made up my mind that I was going to the police but then..."

"But then they found Rachel."

Ellie nodded. "When they found her, I was sure she'd say something. That she'd tell them it was Paul and his friends who'd raped her, but she didn't. She lied for him."

"Did you know everyone there that night, Ellie?" Sabrina said. "Had you met Paul's friends before?"

Ellie's brow furrowed for a moment while she rifled through memories, her eyes widening just a bit when she landed on the one she was looking for. "Kids from school. I think his cousin was there. A few of his friends … one guy I'd never seen before."

"What did he look like?"

"White guy. Around Paul's age. Kinda cute …" she said slowly. "I think his name was Wayne."

Wayne Conway was the name Wade had used to fly to and from Arizona to meet Nulo. To teach him how to kill. If Paul Vega had been the one to abduct and rape Rachel Meeks, he hadn't done it alone. He'd had a partner.

Wade.

"Did Paul have a nickname in high school?"

Ellie looked confused for a moment. "Not that I know of, why?"

Sabrina shook her head. "Did anyone ever call him Nulo?"

"Nulo?" Ellie said, her face crumpling again. "No. What's this about?"

Before she could answer, the main door to the sanctuary opened, letting in a bright burst of sunlight. She opened her mouth to share her theory as if shafted across the chapel, but the words dried on her tongue as she caught movement from the corner of her eye.

It was the guy from the hotel stairwell. Different clothes. Mirrored aviators to obscure his features, but it was him. He moved down the center aisle toward the front of the church without so much as a glance in her direction, but she knew his being here wasn't an accident. He didn't look like a Pip—one of Livingston Shaw's personal watchdogs—but she'd learned the hard way that that didn't mean anything. Church didn't look like a Pip either and she'd been one of Shaw's most vicious operatives before she defied him by letting Sabrina's family live.

She watched him over Ellie's shoulder as he knelt in front of the altar, moving his hand in the sign of the cross before bowing his head. As it fell, he turned it slightly, casting a quick look over his shoulder that landed right on her. She shifted in her seat, planting her feet to push herself up to go after him. To ask him what he was doing here. Why he was following her.

"Agent Vance."

She turned, looking up to find Mark Alvarez standing over her. He didn't so much as look at Ellie, but there was no other way he could've known where Sabrina was.

"Yes?" she said, dividing a look between him and the man at the front of the church. He was no longer looking at her. Crossing himself again quickly, he stood before moving toward the door that led to the prayer garden. She needed to follow him. Find out—

"I tried calling you," Alvarez said, finally flicking a glance in Ellie's direction. "But you didn't answer ... we need to go." Santos stood at the back of the aisle, nearly lost in the shadows of the chapel's atrium.

"Go where?" She stood, aiming a quick glance at Santos over Alvarez's shoulder. He looked tired. "What happened?" she said, even though she *knew*.

"There's another body. And this one is different."

FORTY-FOUR

Berlin, Germany

BEN STEPPED OFF THE elevator on the sixtieth floor, moving quickly across the reception area of his father's office suite, cloned keycard in his hand.

When he'd gotten out of the shower, the card had been in an envelope slid under his door and Celine was long gone. His father had meetings in London before heading to South Korea. That meant she would be scuttling along behind him, juggling his schedule like a perfectly coiffured circus clown. It also meant his father's office was empty.

Empty or not, security remained tight. Aside from the Pips—the less-than-flattering nickname Michael had given to lower-level FSS operatives—and surveillance cameras, each of his father's office suites was equipped with added measures. Like its original, the keycard he'd scanned and cloned was embedded with a microchip. Once that chip was scanned it would send a signal, alerting the small army his father called a security detail that his office had been breached. Since he and Celine were currently somewhere between Berlin and London, that presented a problem.

As soon as Ben swiped the card, the clock would start ticking. He figured he had less than three minutes before he was surrounded by Pips. That meant he had less than that to get into his father's desk and get what he came for. Taking a deep breath, he let it out slowly while he settled the tip of the card into the reader, sliding it downward swiftly.

The door let out a soft *click*.

Ben pushed it open. Not bothering to close it behind him, he crossed the sea of blood-red carpet, heading straight for the desk. Angled in front of the vast bank of floor-to-ceiling windows, he took a seat behind it before reaching into his breast pocket, producing a large folding knife. While he had no doubt Michael had the skills to pick the lock in the time it would take him to sneeze, he wasn't that good. His B&E skills were more *angry looter* than *international art thief*. Before he could go to work on the lock, his cell rang.

"What?" he said, in lieu of hello, putting the call on speaker before tossing it on the desk.

"You got company," Lark said, his tone stuck somewhere between amusement and panic. "About eight of them. Four in the stairwell, the other four in the elevator. You've got less than a minute."

Fuck. They were faster than he'd thought.

"So…" He worked the flat of his knife between the collar of the lock and the hard wood of the drawer. "Stop 'em," he said through clenched teeth, giving the blade a vicious jerk. The following metallic *twang* of the lock falling apart inside the desk drawer was music to his ears.

"I hate this shit, you know that, right?" Lark griped, but in the background Ben could hear his fingers clacking across his computer keyboard.

He laughed, couldn't help it. "Bullshit. You love it."

"What's to love, motherfucker?" Lark bitched while he worked. "You and Mikey keepin' me buried in shit? Knowing that when I start doing you assholes favors, a messy, painful death is all I'm probably gonna get out of it? A brother can't even catch ... *there*." One final *clack* followed by a sigh of relief. "Got the group in the stairwell jammed up on fifty-eight and the elevator is stuck between fifty-nine and sixty. Now hurry your cracker ass up because it won't hold them for long."

"Keep your panties on, Green Mile, I'm in," Ben said, yanking the drawer open, sending the scrapped lock bouncing and flying across the carpet. "Give it another twenty and then let them out." He hung up on a string of Lark's protests.

Snagging the file, Ben slipped it into the zippered lining of his suit jacket. There was no time to open it now. He'd have to take it with him. He'd been about to shut the drawer when he caught sight of it. Beneath the file was a key. Not a plastic card but an actual key. The two-pronged metal piece was as long and thick as his finger. Deep, jagged cuts on each side, the head of it nearly as wide as his fist. He'd never seen it before.

But that didn't mean he didn't know what it opened.

He could scan it, have Lark make him a copy like he had with Celine's card, but there was no time. A quick glance at the clock told him he had less than ten seconds and both escape routes were clogged with his father's goons.

On impulse he swiped the key and dropped it into his pocket along with his cell phone. Lifting the lid on the humidor his father kept on his desk, he pulled out an Opus X, cut the tip, and stood, taking a stroll to the sleek, polished sideboard his father kept stocked with liquor.

Down the hall, he heard the elevator let out a discreet chime, followed almost immediately by the loud bang of the stairwell door being thrown open. Within seconds his father's office was flooded with Pips, guns drawn and pointed straight at him.

Showtime.

"Afternoon, fellas," he said, cigar still clamped between his teeth, turning slightly to cast a dismissive glance at them over his shoulder. There were nearly twice as many as the eight Lark had counted. He lifted the stopper from the mouth of a cut crystal decanter before bringing it to his nose. Scotch. He hated scotch. He poured himself a couple of fingers anyway and turned to face them. He scissored the Opus between his fingers to pull it out of his mouth. "Something wrong?"

Guns were immediately dropped but they weren't reholstered. A few of them had been there the day his father had ordered his head of security to put a bullet through Ben's hand to stop him from saving his brother. Most had heard the story about what Ben had done to the man afterward. All of them knew what he was capable of.

Which meant none of them wanted to be the first one to approach him.

He sipped his scotch and watched them. Fifteen of them now, all displaying varying degrees of apprehension. Waiting for him to make a move. Finally one of them found his balls and spoke up.

"What are you doing in here, sir?" Mr. Ballsy said, the FSS-issued Kimber twitching in his hand as his flat brown eyes slid across the room, over the surface of the desk before landing on the pilfered drawer. "Mr. Shaw left for London an hour ago."

"I wanted a cigar." He moved to the front of the desk, still grinning. "You guys want one?" he said, spinning the humidor around to face them. A few of them flinched like he'd just pulled the pin on a grenade.

"No, sir," Mr. Ballsy said, shaking his head, trying like hell to put some bass in his tone. "You really shouldn't be in here."

"Yeah, well …" He slammed the rest of his drink before gently setting the glass on the edge of the desk with a pronounced *click*. "What are you prepared to do about it?"

"I, uh … I …" Mr. Ballsy looked around, hoping to find someone to back his play. Unfortunately for him, players were in short supply. "I'm gonna have to ask you to come with me, sir," he finally managed, his eyes widening just a touch, like even he couldn't believe what he was saying.

"I'll leave when I'm ready." Leaning across the desk, he reached into the drawer and fished around while all fifteen of them tensed up, hands flexing around the grips of their guns. He pulled out the large desktop lighter his father kept there. "And I can guaran-*fuckin'*-tee that when I do leave, it won't be with you, sweet cheeks," he said before sticking the cigar back into his mouth. Lifting the lighter, he clicked it, turning his head to the side so he could catch the short burst of flame, puffing on it until the blunt end of the cigar glowed red.

He stood there for a moment, puffing on a two-hundred-dollar cigar he didn't want, letting the room fill with smoke, making sure every single one of them knew he was *here* and there wasn't a fucking thing any of them could do about it. The file he'd taken pressed against his ribs. The key weighed heavy in his pocket. The fact that he took them wouldn't stay hidden for long. As soon as he left, this chump would call his father and fill him in on his latest episode. Hopefully the show he was putting on would buy him a few hours—*just another one of Ben's tantrums*—before his father realized what he'd really been up to.

He pulled the Opus from between his teeth, flicking a considerable amount of ash onto his father's desk blotter, the movement of it putting the mass of gnarled scar tissue in the center of his hand on display. He smiled, reaching into the humidor to scoop up a few thousand dollars' worth of cigars. "Now," he said, "I'm ready to leave."

He strolled across the room, Pips parting like the Red Sea. As he passed, he tucked a cigar into each of their breast pockets, smiling. Not one of them was willing to make eye contact with him, much less actually try to detain him. Stopping in front of Mr. Ballsy, he slipped a cigar into the guy's pocket before pressing his fingertips against his chest. His heart hammered wildly beneath the pressure of Ben's hand. Ben's smile widened. "Don't worry," he said in mock whisper, the thick, cloying smoke of the Opus X in his hand curling around his nose. "When my father and I have a conversation about this, I'll make sure to tell him how forceful you were." He winked before fitting the cigar between his teeth and walking out the door.

In the outer office, he passed by Celine's empty desk and felt a twinge, remembering what Gloria had said earlier about her. About how his father would kill her if he found out they were sleeping together. Once his father figured out what he'd really been up to and how he gained access to his office ...

"Sorry, sweetheart, my boat is full," he muttered under his breath, swiping the keycard through the reader for his father's private elevator. He waited less than a half a second before its door slid open.

Stepping inside, he turned to find them all where he'd left them, standing there, clustered in the doorway of his father's office, cigars sticking out of their pockets like party favors, staring at him like he was some sort of rabid dog who'd slipped its chain. Like he was unpredictable. Indiscriminately dangerous. Someone you didn't want in your blind spot. Not ever.

They had no idea.

As the elevator door slipped closed, Ben gave them one last grin. Lifting his scarred hand, he waved good-bye.

FORTY-FIVE

Yuma, Arizona

SABRINA TURNED THE KEY in the ignition, switching the car off but she didn't get out. Not yet. A few yards away, she watched Ellie climb out of her late-model compact while Alvarez and Santos slammed the door closed on their unmarked. None of them looked in her direction but she knew they were all waiting for her, the FBI agent, to get out and take charge of the situation. She yanked on the door handle, throwing it open before stepping her foot onto the rain-softened ground.

She could see bright yellow tape fluttering in the breeze, wound around bushes and sharp outcroppings of rocks—but that's all she could see. At first glance, the crime scene looked deserted.

"Where's your partner?" Santos said, meeting her at the hood of her car while Alvarez and Ellie walked ahead, heads bent while they talked quietly, shoulder to shoulder.

"She pulled the short straw—eight a.m. debrief with our SO," she said, the lie delivered so smoothly that for a moment, even she believed it. "She's going to meet me at the station later."

Sabrina thought about where Church really was: running down the legal name attached to the PO box used to exchange letters with Wade. There was a definite link between what happened to her nearly twenty years ago and what was happening now. She didn't want to say anything until she'd untangled the truth.

You sure you're ready for the truth, darlin'? You sure you even know what it looks like anymore?

"You ready for this?" he said as they started walking toward the crime scene, hands dug into his pockets like they were out for an evening stroll.

"What's that supposed to mean?" The question echoed Wade's. Hearing it out loud sharpened her tone. "Why wouldn't I be?"

Santos pulled his hands from his pockets and held them up in surrender. "I just meant that chasing after these serial killer freaks probably gets old after a while, is all."

"You could say that." The corner of her mouth lifted in a wry smile "Sorry—I'm running on two cups of coffee and about three hours sleep." She'd been up well into the small hours of the morning, reading Wade's journals and the letters he'd received from Nulo during their correspondence. Croft had been right—the two of them had been partners in at least three kills, possibly more.

There's more. There's always more, darlin'. How's that for truth?

Santos nodded. "No worries," he said as he started to walk in the direction Alvarez and Ellie had taken. "Body was found in a ravine by a couple of border militiamen this morning. Crime scene is a mess. Assholes damn near ran her over before they realized what she was. They figured it for a smuggling operations gone wrong and called border patrol. BP called us."

"In a ravine?" she said while she walked, keeping pace beside him. "That *is* different. You sure it's our guy?"

Santos jammed his hands into his pockets. "That's not the half of it, and yeah," he said, lifting the tape for her to step under, "I'm sure."

About five yards from the tape was a steeply sloped drop-off, shrubs desperately clinging to its face, a path trampled through the middle of them, like someone had slipped and slid their way down the side of it. "We think she came in here," Santos said, confirming what she'd been thinking, pointing to a place where the mud and rock had crumbled away from the ledge. "No tire tracks, aside from those militia fucks, so we're thinking she came on foot."

"On foot?" Sabrina turned, surveying the vast stretch of desert behind her. It was flat and brown, splashed liberally with varying shades of green. "From where?" she said, her skeptical gaze finally landing on his face. "There's nothing out here."

Santos gave her a grim nod. "Yeah. But unless she was dropped from the sky, there's no other explanation for how she got out here. I've got uniforms walking the desert, trying to pick up her trail, but I'm not holding my breath."

Neither was Sabrina. It'd rained again, the second wave of monsoon moving through at about four a.m. It'd come down pretty hard. Any foot trail their victim might have left had more than likely washed away. But if their victim came in on foot, she couldn't have come more than a few miles.

That meant that wherever she'd come from had to be close by.

About twenty yards away, a couple of men in ball caps and long sleeves despite the warm weather stood next to a pair of all-terrain vehicles. They had rifles slung over their shoulders, too busy answering questions from a pair of Yuma County deputies to pay her much attention. They must've been the militiamen Santos had referred to earlier.

"We're about a mile from the city limits so Yuma PD is outside its jurisdiction here," Santos told her while they picked their way down the slope. "YCSO called us in anyway."

It made sense since Yuma PD caught the initial case. They landed on the bottom of the ravine, a few feet from where Alvarez and Ellie stood, faces aimed at the form stretched out on the ground, face down. It had been burned beyond recognition, hair and skin seared away, leaving nothing but charred bone covered by patches of scorched muscle.

Sabrina moved closer to the body, hunkering down beside it so she could get a better look. As soon as she did, she understood Santos's certainty that despite the difference in MO and signature, they were dealing with the same killer. At the base of the victim's skull was a quarter-sized hole. "She?" Sabrina said, looking for something that would identify the victim as a human, let alone a woman. "You've identified the victim as female?"

Instead of answering her, Alvarez sank down across from her and reached over, placing a gloved hand on the charred shoulder of the body between them. Gently rolling her, he exposed the face. It was intact. Completely preserved from the damage done by the fire that had consumed the rest of the body. Sabrina looked up at Ellie, trying to catch a glimpse of recognition like she had with Rachel Meeks, but there wasn't one.

"You have any missing persons that fit her description?" she said, noting there wasn't any clothing debris mixed in or melted to the victim. Whoever she was, she'd been out here naked, which lent to Santos's working theory of her being on foot. It also told her that the escape attempt had been an impulse born of opportunity and panic. If she was running for her life, she wouldn't have stopped to put on clothes.

"We're a border town, Agent Vance. Plenty of missing persons—unfortunately, more than a few of them young females," Santos said, rubbing a gloved hand along his jaw. "Maybe the Bureau can run facial recognition. See if we can get a match."

Sabrina nodded. "I'll have Aimes do it as soon as we get back to the office."

"What I don't get is, why the deviation?" Santos said, crouching down next to the burned, human-shaped ruins. "Four victims left exactly the same way and then this? I don't get it."

Whoever she was, she'd been left face down in the mud, killed, and then cast aside like a broken toy. No theatrics. No feigned remorse. This is what their killer really thought of the people he killed.

Our boy got some anger issues he's workin' on, darlin'. Running from someone who's got 'em ain't such a good idea . . . but you already know that, don't you?

"She ran," Sabrina heard herself say without bothering to raise her head. "Ruined his fun, and that made him very angry."

"*His fun?*"

It'd been Alvarez who'd said it. When she looked up, she found him standing where she'd left him. He was watching her, his expression decidedly hostile.

"Yeah, his fun." She stood up, the movement bringing them nearly nose-to-nose. "The posing, the praying, the shrines—it's all a game to him. None of it means anything."

That's where you're wrong, darlin'. Our Nulo is a complicated guy. It means something, you just gotta figure out what.

"What makes you say that?" Alvarez scoffed at her. "Your FBI-issued Magic 8 Ball?"

She smirked at him. "I left that at home—thought I'd rely on my training and experience for a change."

Alvarez opened his mouth to the fire off a comeback, but Santos rose from his crouch to drill a finger into his partner's chest. "You need to—"

"Uhhh, guys?"

She looked over at Ellie and found herself gazing at the top of her dark head. Instead of watching her and Alvarez go toe-to-toe, Ellie was looking down at the body they were all standing around. "You find something, Ellie?"

"Yeah …" Ellie looked up, a deep frown creased into her brow. "This isn't the crime scene. Wherever this woman was killed, it wasn't here."

FORTY-SIX

THEY ALL STARED AT Ellie for a moment, letting it sink it. When it finally did, Sabrina felt the hope she'd been harboring slip loose, cut free by the certainty in Ellie's tone. It was the same tone she'd used earlier when she'd told her she was certain that the blood evidence found under Stephanie Adams's fingernails hadn't been a mistake.

Santos didn't give up so easily. "Sure it is," he said, pointing at the obvious trail that tumbled down the face of the ravine. "She came in here—"

"Probably a mule deer or cattle coming down for a drink of runoff left in the ravine." Ellie shook her head firmly. "Whatever it was, it wasn't the victim."

"How can you be so sure?" Santos said, stubbornly holding on to the illusion that they'd finally caught a break.

"The sky opened up at about four this morning and poured buckets out here for a good forty-five minutes." Now it was Ellie's turn to crouch down, angling her gaze upward so she could see them standing over her. "This ravine would have been full of fast-moving water—I'd guess four to five feet deep. Water that deep and fast would've carried her down the ravine, no problem."

"Maybe he weighed her down?" Alvarez said, shooting his partner a nervous glance. "Or maybe she—"

"Why would he do that? He'd *want* her carried away from the crime scene." Ellie shook her head impatiently. "And he got what he wanted. This isn't where she was killed. This is where the current left her."

"You've made mistakes before," Santos said, ignoring his partner in favor of leveling a caustic glare in Ellie's direction. "Been dead wrong before too." Sabrina was suddenly sure that Santos didn't share his partner's protective instinct when it came to the crime tech.

"I wasn't wrong then," Ellie said, aiming a pleading look at her before continuing. "And I'm not wrong now." Doing as Alvarez had done earlier, she wrapped a careful hand around the victim's shoulder and rolled her, exposing her face and torso again. It was littered with debris. Leaves and a few pieces of trash that'd been left in the desert and swept into the ravine by the torrent of rain speckled her blackened belly. None of them were burnt but Sabrina had a feeling that wasn't what she was showing them. "Her face is completely preserved. My guess, he was chasing her and managed to incapacitate her somehow and she fell face down in the mud," she said, pointing to the hole that'd been punched into the victim's skull. "That's when he did this. Instead of taking her back to wherever he chased her from and risk getting caught, he set her on fire and let Mother Nature handle the rest. All her fluids settled to her front, making her heavier there. That's why she re-settled in the same position."

Sabrina looked at the ground. It was stony, covered in rocks washed there by the flood, stuck to the floor of the ravine with the thick, clay-like mud that it was carved from, creating a surface nearly as smooth as a mortared walkway.

"*Goddamnit*," Santos bellowed, snapping his gloves off with a frustrated yank that ripped the latex, causing uniforms and crime techs to cast wary glances in their direction. Seemingly oblivious to the concern his outburst caused, he turned away from all of them, walking farther down the ravine.

Sabrina followed him. Removed her own gloves slowly before tucking them into the pocket of her slacks. Standing shoulder to shoulder with Santos, she aimed her gaze in the same direction as his, up the wide swath of the ravine, in the same direction the body would have come from. "We need to talk," she said, her tone low and even. From the corner of her eye, she could see Santos nod.

"I was wondering when we'd get around to it," he said, the corner of his mouth lifting in a sardonic half smile. "To be honest, I'm surprised my CO hasn't called us in for a sit-down to discuss my *limitations* yet."

His admission made her think of her old captain and his love of verbal abuse. Mathews had hated her—blamed her for everything from a colleague's gruesome murder to the sour milk in his refrigerator. She imagined that attending her funeral had made his year. "I don't consider your prior experiences to be limitations." She smiled when he looked at her. "I see them more like insider information. The only reason I didn't push it before now is because when I brought it up, you seemed a bit … tender about it."

"A young woman was tortured for nearly three months and then killed because of my sloppy police work," Santos said, the line of his jaw drawing tighter and tighter with each word. "And then, to top it off, the sick asshole who does it slips through my fingers and skips on home … and keeps up with the raping and killing for another decade and a half." He looked away, casting his gaze up the ravine again. "*Tender* isn't the word I would use to describe how I feel about what happened to Melissa Walker."

"Is that why you have such a hard-on for Paul Vega?" she said plainly. "Because you think the same thing is happening now?"

"Christ," Santos muttered, shaking his head and shooting daggers at his partner over his shoulder before turning his gaze on her. "That punk needs to learn how to keep his mouth shut."

Sabrina turned, looking in the same direction. Behind them, Ellie and Alvarez stood close together, talking to each other in hushed tones. Neither of them looked happy. In fact, it looked like they were in the middle of a pretty bitter argument. Deciding to give them their privacy, she turned toward Santos. "Alvarez was less than forthcoming when it came to answering my questions," she said, failing to mention that his partner's helpfulness only ended when her questions about Ellie started. "All he did was mention that Vega was briefly involved in a particularly nasty case you worked a while back and that his family made it disappear. I put the rest together on my own."

Santos nodded, tipping his head slightly. "You sure you didn't pack your Magic 8 Ball?"

She cut him a slight smirk. "Trust me, if I had my Magic 8 Ball, finding this guy would be a hell of a lot—"

Her phone let out a chirp and she gave Santos an apologetic smile while she unclipped it from her belt. It was a text from Church. Two words.

Graciella Lopez

FORTY-SEVEN

"You want to explain what we're doing here, Agent Vance?" Santos said from where he stood beside her, hand settled on the grip of his service weapon. Instead of answering, Sabrina knocked again, her knuckles stinging as she rapped them against the beveled glass set inside the door. She did want to explain. She wanted to tell Santos everything, to explain what was happening, but there wasn't time.

Shadows shifted along the glass and she took a step back, her hand finding the grip of her Kimber, wrapping around it, squeezing it like she was saying hello to an old friend.

Admit it. You miss this. The hunt. The capture. The kill. We're the same, you and me. Two rotten peas in a fucked-up pod.

"I'll explain later. For now, just follow my lead," she said a fraction of a second before the door opened. She hadn't expected Graciella Lopez to be the one on the other side of it but she felt the disappointment anyway when a woman she'd never seen before opened the door. "Good afternoon, we're here to see Paul

251

Vega." She tapped the badge strung around her neck, causing the woman's eyes to bug slightly. She hesitated for a moment before moving away from the doorway to let them in.

"Please wait," she said aiming her request at Santos before she hurried down the hallway that fed into the foyer.

"Now can you tell me what the hell is going on?" Santos hissed at her as soon as the woman disappeared.

"Have you ever had dealings with someone called Nulo?" she said instead of answering his question. "It would have been close to twenty years ago." From somewhere inside the house, she heard a soft knock followed by the softer murmur of voices. "He would have been a teenager around the time Melissa Walker disappeared, used to hang around Saint Rose."

"Nulo?" Santos shook his head, looking confused. "No. Who is he?"

That is the question, ain't it, darlin'?

"What about Tomas Olivero?" she said, remembering the foreman who'd found Rachel. If she could find him, maybe he'd admit to knowing more than what she'd read in the report.

Now recognition flickered across his face. "What does he have to do with this?"

"So you've heard of him?" she said, even though it was obvious who he was.

Santos nodded. "He was a foreman for Vega Farms."

"I think we should bring him in—he might know more than he told police."

"Olivero is dead," Santos said, his expression soured. "And even if he wasn't, he wouldn't tell us shit. He was old man Vega's right-hand man. No way he'd—"

"I thought I made myself clear, Agent Vance," Vega said as he appeared at the mouth of the hallway. "I told you that I won't be answering any of your questions without my lawyer present."

Sabrina nodded. "So you did," she said, reaching into her pocket to pull out her cell phone and the card he'd given her yesterday. She dialed the number on the front of card and listened to it ring.

"This is Arturo Bautista," a smooth, deep voice came at her across the line, sounding almost as if he'd been expecting her call.

"Mr. Vega, this is Agent Sinclaire Vance with the FBI. I'm calling on behalf of your client, Paul Vega," she said. Vega opened his mouth and she held up a finger to keep him from talking. "He's being taken in for questioning for the rape and murder of Rachel Meeks and he'd like very much for you meet him at the station."

FORTY-EIGHT

AFTER DEPOSITING VEGA IN one of Yuma PD's interrogation rooms, Sabrina took herself back to the conference room she and Church had been given as a base of operations to wait for his lawyer to make an appearance. It'd been over an hour since she called him to let him know that they had his client in custody and still no sign of him. She'd spent the time learning everything she could about Paul Vega.

Through the open blinds that covered the window, she could see Santos and Alvarez. The young detective sat on the edge of his desk, arms crossed, head bowed while his partner stood over him, hands wadded into fists, jaw clenched so tight it barely moved while he spoke.

As soon as they had Paul Vega stowed in the back seat of her car, she'd sent Church a text.

Bring her to the station for questioning

After a few seconds of thought she sent another one.

Bring the box too

She had no idea how Santos would react to finding out that not only had Wade returned to Arizona and committed multiple murders, but that there was evidence to support the theory that he'd also been involved in what had happened to Rachel Meeks in 2000. She knew how she'd reacted when she found out that what Wade'd done to her had been the beginning of a fifteen-year killing spree. If her experience was any indication, it wasn't going to be pretty.

She could still see Michael standing at the foot of her porch, glaring up at her, watching her fall apart after he told her that the man who'd spent eighty-three days raping and torturing her had continued hunting and killing even after she'd been presumed dead. That the monster had taken his little sister, Frankie.

You think he still hates you for it, darlin'? You think maybe, sometimes when he looks at you and smiles, he's thinking about killing you for what you did to poor little Frankie?

"Shut up," she said quietly, closing her eyes for a moment, hands fisted in her lap. "Just shut the fuck up."

Truth hurts, don't it? He's probably glad you're gone. I bet he sleeps better at night knowing you're out here with me, getting what you deserve—

"Hey."

Sabrina opened her eyes and turned to find Church wedged into the space between the door and its jamb, watching her. How long she'd been there was anyone's guess.

Long enough to know you're shithouse crazy.

"Where have you been?" she said, each word laced with barely contained frustration.

Church flashed her a sugary smile. "Aw, did my Kitten miss me?"

255

"I'm not your *kitten*," she ground out, careful to keep her tone from spiking. "I texted you almost two hours ago."

"You gave me quite the honey-do list, *partner*." The smile on Church's face faded slightly. "I've been busy."

"I'm sorry—you're right." She forced herself to relax, to pretend she wasn't scrambling to keep herself together. "Did you bring Graciella Lopez in for questioning?"

"Yeah, about that . . ." Church said, slipping fully into the room before shutting the door with a sharp *click*. Snugged against her hip was the box Croft had given her the night before. "She's gone."

You sure you want to open that thing again? Play show-and-tell with what's inside? Let everyone know exactly what I did to you?

"Gone?" She tore her gaze from the box and focused her attention on Church. "What does that mean—*gone*?"

"It means I was already at her house when you texted me," Church said, sliding the box onto the table in front of her. "The place was completely empty. Neighbor said a truck pulled into her driveway around three a.m. and a bunch of men piled out, loaded her up—along with everything she owned—and left."

Always one step behind, aren't you, darlin'?

Sabrina was out of her seat before she had time to think, Wade's laughter bouncing around her skull, pushing her past Church to fling the door open. She strode down the hall, aware that the heated conversation between Santos and Alvarez had dried up and they were both watching her, mouths hanging open.

"Agent Vance?" Santos called out to her a moment before she ground to a halt outside the interview room they'd put Vega in. "Agent—"

Her hand closed over the door handle, she jerked it upward, and the door flew open to reveal Paul Vega, pacing the short length of the room, thumbnail anchored in his mouth while he tried to chew it off. The second the door opened, he stopped pacing and dropped his hand to look at her.

"Is he here?" Vega said, aiming his gaze past her, trying to glimpse salvation. "Did my attorney—"

She jabbed a finger at the chair he'd probably vacated the moment they closed him in. "Sit down."

"No." Vega shook his head. "You can't do this. I invoked my right to an attorney," he said, a slight tremor in his voice. "I'm not going to say a word until he gets here."

"That's fine." Sabrina smiled, aware of the small crowd that had gathered in the hallway behind her. "As a matter of fact, I don't want you to say a word. I just want you to listen." She jabbed her finger at the chair again. "You should really take a seat, Mr. Vega. You're gonna want to be sitting once you hear what I have to say."

Vega clamped his mouth shut and circled the table to do as he was told, glaring at her the entire time. They stared at each other for what felt like forever before he finally cracked. "I don't—"

"Shhh ..." she said, pressing the finger she'd used to point him into his seat to her lips. "You don't get to talk. You get to listen." She leaned against the doorframe, listening to the mumble and whispers of the small clutch of uniforms and detectives standing behind her. The majority thought she'd lost it. Santos included.

"While you've been pacing around like a caged animal," she said, crossing her arms over her chest. "I've been doing my homework on you. You're a very interesting man, Paul."

Vega opened his mouth but she wagged her finger at him. "Hush now," she said, and he closed it with an angry snap. "Says in your file that your mother died giving birth to you. After that, your biological father just walked out of the hospital and never came back."

Vega peeled his glare from her, sticking it to the wall in front of him instead. "Fuck you, lady," he snarled at her. "You don't know shit about me or my father."

"I know he blamed you for your mother's death. I know he took one look at you and decided that living a life in third-world squalor was preferable to being your father." She pushed herself off the doorjamb, letting her arms fall to her sides as she moved toward the table he sat at. "I know you were adopted by Jorge and Isabel Bautista. Lucky break for you since Isabel Bautista was Isabel Vega before she married. I guess ol' Jorge didn't want to share the family name with a boy who wasn't his flesh and blood, huh? Had to take your adopted mother's maiden name? But then Arturo had no interest in the family business, so it was given to you."

He shook his head, jaw clenched. "*Graciella* raised me," he ground out. "And no one *gave* me anything. I earned every square inch of it."

"Funny you should mention her," she said, giving him a brief half smile. "Mrs. Lopez is gone. Let me guess ... Mexico?"

Vega's head whipped in her direction, mouth opened again but this time he clamped it shut before saying a word.

"How'd it go down, Paul? You sent her there, set her up real nice and pretty in appreciation of all those years of keeping your sick, twisted behavior a secret?" She shook her head, the half smile planted on her mouth at odds with the frigid glare she was icing him with. "Gotta hand it to you, I figured you'd just cut her up and dump her like you did the rest of them."

He looked like she'd just spit on him. "I'd never hurt Graciella," he said to the table between them. "And she knows that."

"I bet Rachel Meeks thought she knew the same thing," she said evenly, jerking his gaze upward.

His head came up. "This is about Rachel?" he said, aiming a look out the door and into the hallway. He was looking for Ellie, she'd bet her life on it. "I don't know what you've—"

"It's about all of them, Paul." She sharpened her glare, let it dig under his skin until he was fighting to keep himself in his chair. "All the women you've killed."

Vega shook his head, palms pushed flat on the tabletop between them. "I didn't kill anybody," he said, tearing his gaze away to look at his hands.

"Maybe you didn't." Sabrina shrugged. "Maybe Nulo did the killing." She said the name casually, watching Vega carefully for his reaction. "Is that how it goes, Paul? Is Nulo the one who has the guts to do what you can't?"

The name had his head rocking back on his neck, eyes narrowed. "Where did you—"

"Please tell me that you haven't been questioning my client outside my presence, Agent Vance."

Sabrina looked up to find the man she'd seen standing over Father Francisco in the garden at Saint Rose earlier that morning. He stood in the open doorway, a gaggle of cops behind him, watching the exchange with an odd mix of awe and apprehension.

She smiled as she stood. "I asked your *brother* several times to be quiet," she said with a shrug. "He's not very good at following directions."

Bautista flashed a set of bright white teeth, suit crisp despite the wet, oppressive heat outside. "Apparently, neither are you," he said, motioning for Vega to stand up. "Come on, Paul, we're leaving."

She watched as Vega pushed himself away from the table and stood. "What were you doing at Saint Rose this morning?" she said it on impulse, not really expecting an answer.

Surprisingly, Bautista smiled. "I suppose I go to church for the same reasons most practicing Catholics do," he said, his tone telling her that the question was ridiculous. "Good afternoon, Agent Vance."

"I'm going to find her, Vega," she said, all pretense at humor stripped away. "I'm going to find Graciella and when I do, she's going to tell me everything."

Vega stopped in the doorway, despite the protesting jerk Bautista gave his arm. He gave her a quick, cold smile before he let his lawyer pull him down the hall.

FORTY-NINE

Berlin, Germany

As soon as the elevator door slid closed, Ben reached into his pants pocket and retrieved the strange-looking key he'd taken from his father's desk. It'd been little more than childish impulse that'd pushed him to do it. Curiosity over what kind of things his father kept hidden behind locked doors.

He opened the access panel next to the rows of lit buttons and lifted the key, fitting the blades into an oblong opening in the panel as wide as his finger. Giving it a turn, he watched the illuminated buttons go dim. A second later, the elevator car began to move. It traveled downward, passing the ground floor and underground parking levels.

"Okaaay…" he said, hand moving to his waistband out of habit. There was nothing there. He'd stopped carrying when he agreed to his father's insane plan.

People have to trust you, Benjamin. They have to see you and feel safe. How can they do that if you're armed all the time?

Thinking about the conversation now, he almost laughed. Instead, he reached into his pocket again and pulled out the folding knife he'd used to break into his father's desk. Flipping it open, he pressed it close to his thigh, concealing it from view while the elevator descended farther and farther.

"Curiosity kills more than cats, Bennie-boy," he said out loud, and this time he *did* laugh. Mason used to say that to him when they were kids. The hand he had wrapped around the hilt of the knife started to ache, responding to the memory. His fingers had started to stiffen from lack of use, the pad of scar tissue in the middle of his palm thickening and hardening as months of inactivity floated by.

Golf games and fundraisers were making him soft.

He flexed his fingers, felt the crackle and pop under his skin before he tightened them around the knife until his knuckles screamed and the back of his hand felt as if it wanted to split wide open.

The elevator stopped moving a moment before its doors slid open. He reached up with his free hand to pull the key from the access panel, exiting the car seconds before the doors crept closed.

The room was large and stark white. Walls, floor, and ceiling insulated in a slick, shiny material. He recognized it for what it was almost instantly. Lifting his arm, he moved the sleeve of his suit jacket to get a look at his watch. It had stopped.

Created by FSS's R&D department, the material was embedded with fiber-optics half as thin as a hair. Trillions of them webbed together, they emitted a signal that killed all things electrical. EMP in a wallpaper, it could be painted over or woven into the fabric of a suit. Disguised in a thousand different ways. You'd never even know it was there, until you tried to call for backup and realized that you'd been absolutely cut off from the outside world.

He'd been trying to get his hands on it for months now.

Dropping his arm, Ben took a look around, his gaze instantly landing on the box. It looked to be five feet square, about eight feet tall, made of thick, molded glass that was set into the floor and anchored in place from the outside. The box was also a creation of FSS, built to his father's specifications. The glass was four inches thick and bulletproof. The bolts that locked it into the floor were as big around as his forearm, and they rested on top of pressure plates buried in six feet of solid concrete. Tampering with them would result in … well, Ben wasn't sure what, but he was sure it would be pretty fucking horrible. The bottom line was that the box was escape-proof.

He knew because he'd spent six months of his life trying to find his way out of one exactly like it.

In the center of the box stood a man. Hands cuffed behind him, naked as the day he was born save for the black hood on his head.

Here, kitty, kitty.

Strolling across the room, Ben noted the absolute absence of sound. Nothing made noise. Not his shoes as he walked, not the knife in his hand as he worked it closed.

Up close he could see them. More fibers were buried in the glass. Still, he half expected to be rendered mute as he raised his hand and used the hilt of his knife to knock on the glass. The deep, muffled sound raised the head of the man inside the box, but that was about it. There was no panic. No fear. Just an air of impatience that made Ben smile.

Using the hilt again, Ben pressed a button set flush into the glass of the box. "Can you hear me?" Ben said, leaning against the thick glass.

The man inside the box nodded. The feeling of impatience thickened, making Ben wonder how long it'd been since someone had been in to tend him. His answer lay in a puddle at the man's feet.

Trading his knife for the key, he inserted it into the lock just below the intercom. "Fantastic," he said, giving it a turn. "You wanna get out of here?"

FIFTY

Yuma, Arizona

"I want you to follow him."

Sabrina stood at the second-floor window of their conference room watching Vega climb into the passenger seat of his lawyer's Audi R8 Spyder. Reverse lights flashed a second before the convertible sped off, blowing the stop sign without even so much as a cursory brake tap.

Douche bag.

As soon as the car disappeared, she turned away from the window to find Church sitting at the long, heavy table, feet kicked up, a pile of papers in her lap. "Did you hear me, Church? I said—"

"I've been following him since yesterday afternoon, Kitten," Church said without so much as a glance in her direction. A slight smirk brushed across her mouth. "Or at least I've been following his cell phone."

Of course she had. "And?"

"And…" Church shuffled through the papers on her lap, exchanging them for the journal that was buried underneath. "Nothing. No incriminating phone calls. No trips to his cozy, out-of-the-way, serial-killer lair," she said, finally looking up. "Maybe he's not the guy."

Sabrina was beginning to wonder the same thing but she shook her head. "Or maybe he's just smart enough to leave his phone at home."

Church shrugged. "Sorry," she said, flipping the journal open. "It's the best I can do."

"I've seen your best," she said, annoyance sharpening her tone. She needed to catch Vega in the act, and as much as it pained her to admit it, she'd need Church's help to do it. "This isn't it."

"Okay," Church said, flipping through the journal's pages. "It's all I'm *willing* to do."

"What's that supposed to mean?"

"It means, I'm not here to catch a killer," Church said, running her finger down the length of the page before turning it. "*You're* here to catch a killer. I'm here to make sure Livingston Shaw doesn't send his T-1000s to Sarah Connor your ass."

Hearing Shaw's name reminded her of the man in the stairwell. The same one in the church this morning. He'd been following her, she was sure of it. She opened her mouth to tell Church but quickly changed her mind. If she told Church, she'd do her job—which, according to her, was kill half of Yuma and haul Sabrina back to Montana. As much as she wanted to go home, she couldn't. Not until she nailed Vega to the wall. As for her newly acquired shadow—she'd take care of him on her own.

You sure you want to go home, darlin'? What's there, anyway? A man who resents you for getting his sister killed? A couple of kids who hardly talk to you? Hell, even the dog would be better off without you.

"Without Graciella Lopez, I'm not sure how I'm going to do that," she said carefully.

Church looked up and smiled. "I'm not going to Mexico." She glanced back down at the page she was reading, running her finger down the length of it. "And neither are you."

"You let me meet Croft on my own," she said in a complaining tone so irritating it made her want to kick her own ass. "And nothing happened."

"Did I?" Church said, a *you're adorable* smirk on her downturned face, telling her what she already suspected. Church had been following her last night. Probably snatched Croft the second she left him at the truck stop.

"She needs to be found, Courtney."

Church laughed, her finger stopping midpage. "Using my first name to capitalize on our perceived relationship—you *must* be serious."

"This *is* serious, you sociopath." Sabrina's gaze swept across the table, settling on the box next to Church's feet. "He killed another girl last night, only this one must've really pissed him off because he set her on fire after he punched a hole in her skull."

"We'll find him, Sabrina," Church said to her, her tone suddenly serious. "We just have to keep digging."

"All the digging in the world isn't going to give us what we need, which, just in case you missed it, is Nulo's real name," she said, her frustration spiking. "Right now, I don't have anything but a bunch of half-baked speculations. That means all we can do is wait for this asshole to kill again and hope we get lucky. That's not something I'm willing to do."

"I can't help you," Church said.

"You *won't* help me," she said quietly. "Big difference."

"I operate within the parameters I'm given, Kitten." Church shook her head. "Ben understands that about me … which is why he left me very little wiggle room."

"Then call him." Ben wouldn't drop this case in her lap and then tie her hands completely. He wouldn't do that.

You sure about that? That kid's as slick as a greased pig. Maybe he didn't send you here. Maybe he lured *you here …*

Church sighed. "I told you—"

"*You're lying.*" Now she did shout, and the sound of her voice picked up a few heads beyond the conference room window—curious detectives inside the bullpen, aiming their attention straight at her. She took a deep breath, walking toward the window. "He wouldn't push you out of the plane without a parachute," she said, her tone level as she twirled the wand attached to the blinds until they closed. "Someone with your skill, your lack of morality—you're too valuable to a person like Ben." She turned, nailing Church with an icy glare. "He'd give you a back door. And you're going to use it."

FIFTY-ONE

International Airspace, North Atlantic Ocean

"What the fuck kinda game you playin', bro?"

Irritated by the interruption, Ben looked up. Lark stood over him, his own glare not so much annoyed as it was angry and terrified. "I'm not playing a game." Ben held up the book in his lap, his tone laced with annoyance. "I'm reading." When Lark didn't answer, move, or change facial expressions, Ben lowered his book back to his lap. "Oh. You mean with him," he said, turning the page. The movement sent pain spiraling from the center of his palm all the way to his elbow. "Not really sure. It was one of those impulsive *my daddy has it so now I want it* kinda things." He shrugged, not even bothering to glance at the man in the suit sitting a few rows ahead of them. "I'll probably just cut him loose as soon as we land."

"Cut him loose?" Lark threw a cautious look over his shoulder before sliding into the seat facing him. "Look, I know you got daddy issues," he said quietly, "but that would be a decidedly bad idea."

"Okay, I'll play." Ben sighed loudly, closing his book. "Why is that, Lark?"

Lark looked at him for a moment before reaching up to rub the smooth brown skin at his crown. "You really don't know who that is, do you?"

"Nope," he said, tossing his book onto the seat next to him. When he'd opened the glass box, he'd been prepared for a fight. He didn't get one. Instead, the naked man had followed him quietly to his father's private elevator.

When they'd gotten to his apartment, Ben led him inside. "I'm gonna take the hood off," he announced a half second before he yanked the black sack off the guy's head. A dark blond head matted with sweat and a pair of brown eyes so dark they looked almost black came up, aimed straight at him. If he recognized Benjamin Shaw or had any idea who he was, he didn't show it. Given the fact that it was his father who'd been keeping the guy in a 5x5 box, Ben hadn't been inclined to announce his parentage.

The guy drank seven bottles of water, draining them faster than Ben could pull them out of the fridge. He wanted to know who the man was. What he'd done to get The Box. The *who* was likely easier to answer than the *what*. He was either an FSS operative who'd displeased his father but still held value, or he was someone his father had been paid to make disappear but was too valuable to kill. The common denominator in both scenarios was value.

This guy had it ... so, of course, Ben wanted it.

"I've been calling him Naked Guy for the past three hours," Ben said to cover up his curiosity. He wasn't naked anymore. After the water, Ben gave him a shower and a suit. The shower put him behind schedule and the suit, while long enough, was a bit loose

270

across the chest. Not a lot of opportunity to hit the weights when you're being kept like a bug under a water glass.

When they boarded the Lear, Gail looked up from her day planner, her mouth about to run a mile a minute. "Fifteen minutes late," he said as he passed her, hustling Naked Guy down the aisle. "For me that's like two days early."

Gail's mouth slammed closed on a scowl while she eyed his companion in the ill-fitting suit. Naked Guy never said a word.

"That's Noah Dunn," Lark said to Ben now, his tone held low in the hopes that they wouldn't be overheard.

"*That's* Noah Dunn?" Ben craned his neck to see over Lark's shoulder, catching a look at the back of Naked Guy's head. He was staring straight ahead—hadn't moved an inch since he sat down nearly two hours ago—but that hardly mattered. He was listening to every word they said. Ben would bet his life on it. "You sure? He doesn't look like much."

"How the hell is he supposed to look?" Lark shot him a look that called him ten kinds of stupid. "You father's had him stuffed in a box for the past four years and I'm *positive*," Lark said hitching his thumb over his shoulder. "That soggy piece of white bread is Noah *fucking* Dunn."

"How do you know?" he said, watching the back of Dunn's head for a reaction.

Lark's eyes narrowed. "Bringing him in was the first assignment Michael and I ever worked together."

He'd heard the stories. Dunn had been his father's golden boy. King of the Pips. His right-hand man. The second son he'd always wanted ... until shit went sideways. No one knew what really happened, although there were some pretty wild speculations. All anyone knew for sure was that one minute Daddy Dearest and Dunn were holding hands and making doe eyes at each other, and the next, his father was issuing a kill order with Dunn's name on it. Why Michael brought him in alive was anyone's guess. Maybe he'd already gotten tired of his father jerking his chain. Maybe, after years of being *El Cartero*, he'd just been tired of all the killing. Ben's guess was it was a bit of both.

Dunn went stiff at the mention of Michael. It was brief. Nothing more than a transitory tensing of the shoulders, but it was there. It told Ben in an instant that Lark was right. The guy he'd sprung from The Box *was* Noah Dunn, and good or bad, he knew exactly who Michael O'Shea was. Before he could decide whether to snap the guy's neck or offer him a job, the phone in his pocket let out a chirp.

Since letting it ring really wasn't an option, he reached in and quickly silenced it. It rang again three seconds later. He silenced it. It rang again.

"I don't think whoever it is can take a hint," Lark said, eyebrow arched, elbows braced on his knees. The look on his face said he knew exactly who it was.

It wasn't his regular phone that was ringing. Only one person had this number, and no, taking a hint had never been one of Church's strong suits. He yanked the cell out of his pocket and silenced it mid-ring. "This isn't a good—"

"What was it you used to say to me? Oh, yeah—I don't give a shit."

Sabrina. He had to fight the urge to smile. To give in to the relief that hearing her voice brought him. "I'm in the middle of a meeting. Can I call you back?"

"No," she said, slightly out of breath. "I had to stick my gun in Church's ear just to get the phone from her. I don't think I'll have another chance."

He could imagine it—Sabrina besting his father's super-spy. The mental picture made him smile. "I wish I was there with you." The words slipped out on a sigh, full of regret.

"I wish you were here too," she told him quietly. "You're an unreasonable prick most of the time but at least you have a conscience."

He thought about the things he'd done for his father over the past year. "That's debatable," he said turning toward the window so he wouldn't have to stomach Lark watching him. "What do you need?"

"I need to find a witness…"

"Okay," he said, choosing his words carefully. "Tell your associate to—"

She sighed. "In Mexico."

"Absolutely not." He thought of the information he'd taken from his father's desk, still unopened inside his jacket. It was very possible that sending Sabrina to Yuma had been a huge mistake. Allowing Church to take off on a wild-goose chase would be like killing her himself.

"I need to find her, Ben." She bit each word in half. "All I need is a location."

Goddamnit. "Text me the information and I'll see what I can do." He looked at Lark. "Just … don't do anything stupid, okay?"

As soon as he hung up, Lark arched another eyebrow at him. "Lemme guess. *I'll see what I can do* means *Let me make Lark my bitch*—again."

"We all have our places, Lark. And we're all somebody's bitch." Ben looked out the window and shrugged, thought about where he was going and why. "Crying about it just makes you pathetic."

FIFTY-TWO

Yuma, Arizona

SABRINA ENDED THE CALL and switched to text mode. Beside her, Church shifted in her chair. Sabrina thumbed the hammer back on her Kimber.

"You're such a bitch," Church griped at her while she thumbed out a few short texts.

Graciella Lopez

Look for any houses or properties owned by Vega Farms or their associates.

Just find her, I'll take care of the rest.

Thanks

She hit send and smiled. "See, that wasn't so hard, was it, *Kitten*?"

Church batted the gun out of her face and grabbed at the phone. "When this is over, I'm going to kill you," she said without any real heat, jamming the phone back into her pocket.

"There's too much at stake—"

"*I* understand the stakes," Church said hotly. "Pretty sure it's you who keeps playing fast and loose with everyone's lives."

It reminded her that this wasn't just about her or Michael. If she was found, the people she left behind—Val, Strickland, the twins—wouldn't last a week. "Shit." She pulled out a chair and sank into it. "You're right...I just..."

Church sighed. "You take it personally," she said like she understood. "People die and you can't help but feel like it's your fault."

She nodded. "I don't know what to think. On one hand, we have Vega. Given his relationship with Rachel Meeks, his apparent relationship with Wade, and his established relationship with Graciella Lopez, he's our prime suspect."

"But then we have this Nulo character who keeps popping up," Church chime in. "You think he and Vega are the same person? Maybe he used the name to keep his identity a secret in case Wade turned on him?"

"Maybe. What I've learned about Vega so far jibes with what Father Francisco told me about Nulo. Dead mother. No father. Asshole uncle... But I don't know." Sabrina shrugged. "What I *do* know is the only person who can tell me has been hijacked and I can't get to her."

"You're wrong you, know." Church stood. "I might not be able to tell you *who* Nulo is, but I've got a pretty good idea of *what* we're looking for."

Sabrina studied the box. "How much of this stuff did you read?" The thought of anyone having access to what was in that box made her want to throw up.

Afraid they'll see the real you, darlin'?

276

"Most of it. All of the letters. A few of the journals." Church said without so much as a hint of an apology. "I'm reading by chronological order so … I'm working my way through 2001 now."

Which means she knows all about you and me. All those nasty things we got up to in the dark.

"And?" she said, barely able to choke the word out.

If Church noticed her reaction to the admission, she didn't let on. Probably didn't care. "He's not much younger than Bauer was then—I'd say mid to late thirties—which puts him in Vega's age bracket now." She reached into the box to pull out the pile of letters. "Despite the closeness in age, Bauer was definitely a father figure to this guy. My guess is he never had one of his own—or if he did, he was a bad one."

Sabrina remembered what Father Francisco told her. That Nulo had been raised by his uncle, Tomas Olivero. That he'd been abused so severely that he ran away constantly, seeking sanctuary in the church. While those factors certainly won't turn you into a sadistic serial killer, they didn't exactly help either. She remembered the way Vega reacted to her questions about his childhood. Had his adopted father given him the family business in order to buy his silence about being abused by the Vega Farms foreman?

"Another thing: the letters stop in 2001." She flipped to the last page in the file. "No explanation. No *see you later.* The last one is dated April twenty-sixth. He talks about committing a murder but just waxes poetic about it. No real detail other than referring to the victim as a *she,*" Church said, laying the letters on the table.

"*She?*" Father Francisco assumed that the murder Nulo committed in the spring of 2001 had been his uncle's. What if he'd been wrong? "Any mention of killing his uncle?"

"No." Church shook her head. "Not that I saw."

"So why the sudden stop?" Sabrina said.

"Something happened." Church shook her head again, a slight frown crinkling her brow. "Something big—big enough to knock him off course. Or at least point him in a different direction."

"So ... by 2001, he'd already killed," Sabrina said, picking up the thread. "And according to his letter to Wade, he liked it ..."

Like *ain't the word. Our boy* loved *it. He's good. A born killer— just like you and me.*

"He wouldn't have been able to just stop." She glanced at the journal Church set aside to dig through the box. "Which one is that?"

Church held up a journal. Across the front of it was a name.

RACHEL

FIFTY-THREE

5/6/2000

The plan had been to take both of them.

He wanted Rachel. He was angry with her, hated her for the way she treated him and he wanted to teach her a lesson. He wanted her to be his first.

I wanted Elena. I wanted her to know it was me who'd taken Melissa away from them. I wanted her to know who I was and what I'd done. I wanted to tell her the story of how I'd come so close to doing the same things to her sister a few years ago. She'd slipped through my fingers and gotten away, by some miracle. But miracles have a price and little Elena was going to pay it.

So we compromised.

Dizzy, Sabrina closed the journal for a moment, pressing her hand against the cover as if trying to keep it shut. Val. Oh God. How close had Wade come to taking her? To taking the one person in her life who'd known her. The *real* her.

Close, darlin'—real close. And if it hadn't been for more pressing matters, I'd have done it too.

The memory came to her in a flash. The night Wade killed Andy Shepard for harassing her. *"Almost as cute and twice as sweet,"* Val had said, laying on a lazy southern drawl. *"If he tips more than fifteen percent, I might offer to have his baby."*

He'd been there. In the diner.

Like fishin' with dynamite, it was. She was just like the rest of them—practically jumped right into my boat. A few smiles and she'd been ready and willing to follow me anywhere ...

Sabrina shook her head and reopened the journal.

We let them leave, deciding to follow them home because it was easier and it'd kill some time. We gave them a head start so by the time we made it to Rachel's house they'd already be there but when we got there, Ellie was gone. They'd had a fight and Ellie decided she wanted to go home. I was angry but decided not to ruin Nulo's fun. It was his first time, after all.

Talking Rachel into the car was easy. She wasn't the good girl she pretended to be. She got into the back seat and we drove around for a while, drinking beer while we decided where to take her. Nulo wanted me to show him where I'd taken Melissa but I said no. It was a special place. Sacred. Hers and mine and I wasn't going to share it, no matter how special the occasion was for him.

We finally settled on taking her back to the irrigation shed. It was secluded. In the middle of nowhere. Not perfect but it would do. No one would hear her screaming while I showed Nulo how it was done.

Her hands started to shake so she closed them around the journal in her lap, clamping down so hard on it her knuckles turned white. Everyone. Wade had planned on taking everyone away from her. Knowing that made her angrier than she'd ever thought possible.

"I've got a question for you."

Sabrina looked up to find Santos standing in the conference room doorway, glaring down at her. He looked confused and angry as hell about it. She caught a glimpse of Alvarez, standing in the hallway, arms crossed over his chest, head tipped down. He looked uncomfortable. Like he didn't want to be there. That made two of them.

"Okay, hopefully I have an answer," she said, setting the journal aside before motioning for him to take a seat. He refused, obviously preferring to stand over her and glare. His use of classic interrogation techniques would have been amusing if she wasn't so pissed off.

Who you so mad at, darlin'? It ain't him and it ain't me ... not really. Could be you're mad at yourself for letting our boy jerk you around by your nose?

"Yesterday, you and your partner show up and give us the standard *we're just here to help* speech, and not more than twenty-four hours later"—Santos swiped a rough hand over his face before letting it fall to his side—"you hijack our interrogation without so much as a *here, hold my jacket*."

Twenty years ago, he'd reminded her of a boxer and she saw it now, in his calculating gaze and tightly clenched jaw. "Well?" he barked at her when she didn't offer an explanation or an apology.

"Well what?" she said, rocking back in her chair. "I'm still waiting for the question."

His hands tightened into fists. "Okay. Here's my question: what the fuck is going on?"

She didn't answer him. Instead, she sighed, lifting the lid off the box before tipping it over, spilling out its contents. Journals. File folders. Discs housed in paper sleeves. 8x10 glossies. It all scattered and slid across the table and he watched it go with a look of confusion. "What's all that?"

"It's Wade Bauer's murder box," she said, her gaze drifting across the avalanche of filth that stretched in front of her. "He was active for nearly two decades and is thought to be responsible for the deaths of nineteen women. The evidence in this box raises that number considerably."

Santos crossed the room, Alvarez trailing behind him, arms finally unlocked and hanging loose. He was carrying files. The same four files he'd been carrying yesterday—she could see the names across their tabs.

Santos pulled a pen out of his coat pocket to poke through the pile. "None of this is cataloged." He turned to look at her. "Where did you get this?"

"A reporter bought it off Bauer's wife for two thousand dollars," she said, skirting dangerously close to the truth. "After an uncharacteristic crisis of conscience, he turned it over to me . . . and before you ask, I've had it for less than twenty-four hours, so, no—I wasn't hiding it from you."

"Has any of it been dusted for prints?" Alvarez said, leaning across the table to read the name off the front of one of the paper-sleeved discs. "Run through forensics?"

"What's the point?" She shook her head. "We know who it belonged to. It was kept in a storage locker for the better part of two decades—a storage locker no one but Bauer knew about until his wife got notice that it was going to auction for nonpayment."

"I appreciate the share, Agent Vance," Santos said, lifting one of the journals with his pen to get a look at the one under it. "But I don't understand what any of this has to do with our case."

She stood, circling the table to lift a file folder off the table. It was thick, secured with a sturdy binder clip. She slapped it down on the table in front of him. "Love letters from our current whack-job to Bauer. Bauer wrote back. A lot."

The confusion deepened, mingling with an odd sort of understanding. "You think—"

She shook her head. "I *know*. Wade Bauer was here," she said, reaching over to lift the journal she'd been reading from where she'd dropped it. "And he taught our killer everything he knew." She put the journal on top of the pile and watched Santos's face drain of color when he read the name written across the front of it.

RACHEL

"Is he in here?" he said, snatching it up to rifle through its pages. "Does Bauer mention Vega by name? If he does we can—"

"No." She shook her head. "Wade's careful. He never uses his partner's given name. He probably didn't even know it. His partner called himself Nulo."

"Nulo?" Santos shook his head. "Not familiar. Alvarez?"

Alvarez stared at the table's contents in disbelief. "No. Sounds like a street name."

Sabrina cleared her throat before continuing. "As far as I can find, there's no record of who this kid really is. The closest I got was the PO box used to send and receive the letters between him and Bauer, and that was leased and paid for by Graciella Lopez."

"That's why you went so hard at Vega." Understanding bloomed across Santos's face. "You think she took out the box for him."

She let Santos recover from the evidence bomb she'd just dropped, turning her gaze toward Alvarez. "You've been carrying the same four files all day," she said, her eyes drifting down to the collection of files clutched in his hand. "Why is that?"

"Well …" Alvarez gave her a sheepish look. "What you said the other day at Rachel Meeks's crime scene got me thinking," he said, smacking the stack of files against his fist. "Every victim was alive because they'd received some sort of miracle. That's the—are you Catholic?"

She shook her head.

"I didn't think so," he said, that sheepish look intensifying into full-fledged embarrassment, tinged with excitement. He was on to something. "Well, we're big on saints. We've got one for just about everything. And they aren't born. They're made."

She looked down at the stack of files in his hand. Tried to grasp the string he was dangling. "You think this guy is making saints." It wasn't a question and she didn't phrase it like one. "What does that have to do with *them*?" she said, jabbing a finger in his direction.

"Everyone in these files was in dire need of a miracle." He tossed the first folder onto the table between them. "Sara Pike was born barren. She couldn't have kids, no matter how many fertility experts she saw. Ed Sherman was paralyzed from the chest down in Iraq. Trudy Hayes was blinded in a boating accident. All of them disappeared a day or two before our victims but, unlike our vics, they've never been found."

Before she had a chance to digest what Alvarez just said, Church popped her head through the doorway. "I've been going through missing persons. I think I found something."

FIFTY-FOUR

"Her name was Maggie Travers," Church said, holding up the missing person's report she'd dug out from the backlog. "Twenty-three-year old vet tech from El Centro, California."

Thirsty for new information, Sabrina lunged for the file, pulling it from her partner's hand. "El Centro?" she said, thumbing it open. On top was what must've been a recent photo of Travers. She was pretty—what her grandmother would have called *handsome.* Dishwater blond hair, dark hazel eyes. A smile that somehow managed to be both confident and unassuming. Church was right. The young woman in the picture was the same woman found in the ravine.

"Yeah." Church reached into the file and pulled out the typed report. "Her mom reported her missing yesterday when she didn't come home from a dinner date on the nineteenth."

"That was five days ago," Alvarez said, raising his head from a journal he'd been combing through. He closed it and traded it for a nearby manila folder, this one holding what looked like lab reports. The insignia on the front of it wasn't one she recognized. "Why'd her mother wait so long to report her missing?"

"She didn't," Church said, her mouth flattening into grim line. "She called El Centro PD the morning of the twentieth when she woke up and found her daughter's bed not slept in."

Sounds familiar, don't it, darlin'?

"That's the same thing that happened with Rachel Meeks back in 2000," she said, staring at the picture in her hand. "He lures them in. Makes them think he's Prince Charming. A Good Samaritan. Whatever it is they're looking for. He becomes what they need most. A savior."

You should see our boy operate. He's a natural. Taught him everything I know.

"Yeah, but if Vega *is* our killer," Santos said, shaking his head, "there was no way he charmed Rachel Meeks in order to kidnap her this time. She already knew what kind of monster he was."

He was right. Vega was suspected of raping and torturing Meeks for days before she'd been found in 2000. There was no way she'd put herself in the position to have that repeated.

"What I don't get is *why*," Church said. "I mean, was his targeting her a simple case of unfinished business or did she threaten to finally expose him?"

"Maybe both," Sabrina said, placing the photograph of Maggie Travers back in the file. "Assuming our guy is Vega, he would've had a lot to lose if she finally spoke out." She thought about the circumstances surrounding Rachel's disappearance. What she endured. "Or maybe, to him, her survival was a miracle."

"I need some coffee if I'm gonna keep looking through this shit." Alvarez closed the folder before tossing it on to the table. "Anyone else need anything?" he said as he stood.

"Chamomile tea, if you have it," Church said, glancing up from the journal in her lap. Alvarez flashed her the *okay* sign on his way out the door.

"So now what?" Santos said, his eyes tired and shoulders slumped.

Sabrina could feel him looking at her. Waiting for her to tell him what to do. To find who they were looking for. She was the supposed hot-shot profiler. She was supposed to know what she was doing.

Think he knows what a fraud you are, darlin'?

"All right," she said standing up. "We know this Nulo was busy in 2000. Murdered a prostitute in April. Raped and kidnapped Rachel Meeks in June. That's our starting point." She looked at Church. "You and Alvarez are going to go over backlogged cases. Look for any that fit our guy's MO. Since we now know that he's not afraid to stray outside his immediate kill zone, I want you to stretch your search parameters from San Diego to El Paso. The more potential victims, the more potential witnesses. Check to see if any of it links up to Paul Vega's movements."

She got halfway to the door before Church stopped her. "Where are you going?"

Sabrina smiled, knowing her partner couldn't stop her while Santos was within earshot. "Confession," she said, on her way out the door.

FIFTY-FIVE

International Airspace, Northern Atlantic Ocean

As SOON AS HE got Lark set up with his latest assignment, Ben moved to the back of the plane. In the rows ahead he could see Gail nodding off in her seat, that blasted planner opened and about ready to slide off her lap.

Ben unzipped the large pocket in the lining of his jacket and pulled out the file he'd liberated from his father's desk.

Using his knife, he slit the seal. Inside were copies of Reese's flight plans. Surveillance photos of Sabrina's family. Her friends. There was one of her brother, Jason, out with a group of friends. Her sister, Riley, jogging in the park. Valerie and her daughter, Lucy, playing in the park. Sabrina's old partner, Strickland, standing outside a crime scene. Mandy Black in the parking lot of the Marin County morgue. They were recent, taken within the last few days. Attached to each were detailed reports. Their schedules. Their habits. Everything someone tasked with killing them would need to get the job done.

Something peeked out at him from the back of the file. Something that dropped his gut to the tops of his hand-stitched Italian leather shoes.

Topographical maps of Oregon. Washington. Idaho ... and Montana. Each of them were marked with fat red circles. A few of the circles had been Xed out. His father didn't just believe that Michael was alive; he was actively searching for him. And if the maps were any indication, he had a pretty good idea of where to find him.

Ben looked up from the file in his lap, toward the front of the plane. He could see his latest acquisition, the top of his dark golden head peeking up over the back of his seat. He was still, like he'd been when he'd found him. Like he was sleeping. But Ben knew he wasn't sleeping.

He was waiting.

Closing the file, he slipped it back into the hidden pocket in his jacket and stood, making his way forward.

"Hey, Naked Guy," he said, sliding into the seat across from Dunn. "Mind if I call you Noah?"

A slow smile spread across Dunn's face and he shrugged. "Truthfully, *Naked Guy* was sort of growing on me," he said in a voice full of gravel, making Ben wonder how long it'd been since he'd actually spoken out loud.

Ben let out a short bark of laughter. Across the aisle, Gail stirred, the planner slipping down her lap. He stood, bent over, and caught it before it hit the floor. On its open pages he could see his life, captured in thin-lined squares. Every minute of it planned out, used up before he'd even had a chance to live it.

Closing the book, Ben slipped it under Gail's seat before settling back into his own. As he did, he caught Dunn openly studying him, a slight smile on his face. "You're different than I thought you'd be. Not how Mason described you at all."

The hair on the back of his neck stood straight up. "What did you just say?"

"Mason—your brother. He always talked about how ..." Dunn cleared the dust from his throat. "Normal you were. Removed from all this shit. I think he'd be pretty disappointed to know you finally let your dad get hold of you."

"Mason can't be disappointed," he heard himself say. "Because he's dead."

Something close to sadness slipped across Dunn's face before he was able to brush it off. "I know. I'm sorry," he said to the empty seat in front of him.

"Why?" he said, his tone a bit too harsh. "Are you the one who killed him?"

Now Dunn's head snapped around, aimed in his direction, pinning him with a hard look. "No."

Ben forced himself to relax, slumping his shoulders into the seat. "Then you have nothing to be sorry for," he said, smiling. "How did you know him?"

Dunn looked away again. "We were friends."

There was more to it than that, but Ben didn't press. There were more important matters at hand than his dead brother. "What about Michael O'Shea? Were you friends with him too? Is that why he ignored my father's kill order and brought you in alive?"

"What does it matter?" Like before, the mention of Michael's name stiffened Dunn's spine. "From what I've heard, O'Shea is as dead as your brother."

"You've been in a box for four years. Where would you've heard that?" he said, even though he had a fairly good idea. His father was the only one with access to Dunn. Ben could imagine him standing on the other side of Dunn's box, telling him all about the things he was powerless to change or stop from happening.

Dunn grinned at him like he'd read his mind but he didn't answer.

"Do you hate my father?"

"Yes." Dunn didn't hesitate, delivering the one-word answer with enough force that he could physically feel it.

"Is that why he stuck you in a box?"

"Your father stuck me in a box because he knew it was the only thing outside of a bullet that would keep me from killing him."

"So, why didn't he just kill you?" he said, pushing in, question by question. "Michael brought you in against orders, but it's not like there's a shortage of people willing to do what he wouldn't."

"I don't know." Dunn shrugged. "Next time you see him, maybe you should ask him yourself."

"You used to be one of them—all wagging tail and lolling tongue when my father snapped his fingers," Ben said, giving as good as he got. "The way I hear it, you were his number-one Fido. What happened?"

The question hardened Dunn's jaw, clouding his eyes. "Your father took things from me I can never get back."

Ben knew that look. Understood the kind of loss that shaped it. "Your family."

Dunn smiled again, a quick baring of teeth that looked more predatory than amused. "Enough questions for today, Little Brother," he said before settling into the seat. He closed his eyes and went still again, his face smoothing out into an emotionless mask.

"I've got one more," Ben said quietly, watching Dunn's expression. As far as he could tell, the guy couldn't even hear him. "If I asked you to, would you kill my father?"

The corner of Dunn's mouth twitched a fraction of an inch. "Little Brother, I *am* going to kill your father," he said without even bothering to open his eyes. "Whether you ask me to or not."

FIFTY-SIX

Yuma, Arizona

RATHER THAN WALK THROUGH the lobby, Sabrina took the back stairs that fed directly into the department's employee parking garage. A quick Google search told her that Saint Rose's confession hours were from 10 a.m. to 5 p.m. It struck her as slightly ridiculous that a church that didn't even have electricity would have a website but she wasn't about to complain.

You think you're gonna get that old fool to tell you the truth? Think again, darlin'. He's just as guilty of killin' as the rest of us.

Entering the parking structure, she looked at her watch. It was almost four thirty. By the time she got to the church, confession would be wrapped up and Father Francisco would be preparing for evening mass. That meant she'd have about an hour to get some answers. Looking up, she saw the sleek, dark outline of a limousine parked next to the car she and Church shared.

Her first thought was Livingston Shaw. She should have listened to Church. Believed her when she warned her about the danger of being out in the world, unprotected. The realization reminded her of the man she'd seen at the hotel and later, at Saint Rose.

She took a step back, ready to retreat into the stairwell but she didn't get far. Colliding with a broad, solid chest, strong hands bracketed her biceps. She took a step back, planting her foot between his, hands cranked into fists. Before she could make her move, the limo door swung open.

"I wouldn't do that if I were you." He stepped through the open door and stood, an amused smile on his face. "She doesn't take kindly to being manhandled."

The man behind her suddenly released her. She wanted to believe it was because of the warning that had been issued, but she knew better. It had everything to do with who issued it.

"Hello, Phillip," she said, relief sapping the steel from her bones. "I told you not to come."

"I believe," he said with a shadowy half smile, turning toward the open car door, gesturing her inside, "your exact words were, *whatever*." The man behind her stepped to the side and she caught an imposing glimpse. Wide shoulders. Expensive suit. Tattoos peeking out from under his collar and cuffs. Phillip Song's underlings were as easy to spot as Livingston Shaw's.

She complied without protest. Even if he was the last person she wanted to see right now, Phillip Song was her friend. Sliding across the soft leather seat of the car, he followed her inside, closing them in with a soft *click*. "You look well, Sabrina," he said, angling himself on the seat toward her while studying her. "Different. Not like yourself at all. Your hair. Your eyes. The shape of your face, even. I almost didn't recognize you."

"How did you then?" she said, forcing herself to submit to his appraisal. "Recognize me."

"*Nan naega jangnim hadeolado, dangsin eul bol geos-ibnida,*" he said quietly. For some reason, the words made her uncomfortable.

"No fair," she said playfully, resorting to what worked between them. "You know I don't speak Korean."

"My apologies, *yeon-in,* I tend to forget there are actual limits to what you're capable of." The corner of his mouth lifted in a wicked half smile. "It was your walk—it's always been full of purpose. Like you're perpetually charging into battle. I'd know it anywhere." He reached over and powered up the glass partition that separated the front seat of the limo from the back. As soon as it was closed, he continued. "Eun is worried about you," he said, reaching into the breast pocket of his suit. The movement pulled the crisp cotton collar of his shirt away from his neck to reveal the flat, sinewy scales of a dragon inked into his skin.

"Just Eun?" she said, falling effortlessly into their old rhythms, and he smiled.

"There is no point in worrying about what you can't control, is there?" He removed the red silk pouch and the gap fell closed, hiding the tattoo completely. "With this comes a warning." He held it out to her. "My poor cousin still holds onto hope that you'll actually listen to her."

She reached for the pouch, frowning. "I listen."

"Yes, you listen—but rarely heed," he said, his hands reclosing over the pouch before she could take it from him. "His prolonged banishment will have angered your *Gae Dokkaebi.* Made him dangerous."

"Tell Eun I said thank you," she said, forcing her mouth into a reassuring smile. "And not to worry about me so much. I'll be okay as soon as this is all over and I can go home."

Song nodded once before placing the pouch of tea into her outstretched hand. "There is another solution, *yeon-in*," he said softly, his fingers closing around hers while his other hand reached out to skim fingers along her jawline. "Let me take you home … your *real* home."

She closed her eyes for a moment and imagined it. Returning to San Francisco under Song's protection. He was head of Seven Dragons, the Korean mob's most powerful family. Even a man as connected as Livingston Shaw would think twice before crossing him. She could go back. To Val. To Riley and Jason. Strickland. It would almost be like she never left.

Almost.

She reached up, closing her hand around Song's to pull it down, holding it in her lap. "Michael *is* my home."

"Eun says he is your *senteo*." Song rocked back in his seat, pulling his hand from hers. "Your center—that he holds you still. Keeps you balanced," he said, that wicked smile going sad around its corners. "Fills the empty places inside you."

She smiled. "As usual, Eun is right."

His dark eyes glittered, something unreadable passing quickly across his face. "All I see is someone who has stolen you from the people who love you and places you in harm's way, time after time."

"He can't steal something that already belongs to him, Phillip." She shook her head, holding her hand up to stop him when he started to speak. "And no one *places* me anywhere. You of all people should know that."

He chuckled softly. "I care deeply for you, *yeon-in*," he said, leaning toward her. "And I know you care for me. You know I can protect you. Come back. Not only to me but to everyone who—"

"Michael and I are married," she said quietly. Reaching into her shirt, she pulled out the length of chain Michael gave her before she left. Dangling from it was the platinum band.

As soon as he saw it, Song slumped back against the seat. He was a lot of things and she'd wager he'd done a lot of horrible shit, but if she knew anything about Phillip Song it was that he lived by a strict code of honor. Being another man's wife made her untouchable. She tucked the chain away before reaching for the door handle to let herself out. "Thank you for coming all this way to bring me tea," she said, giving him one last look.

"*Naneun dangsin-eul dasi bol su jiog eul geol-eossda geos-ida,*" he said, watching her go.

"Still don't speak Korean," she said bending over to look at him through the open car door.

Phillip inclined his head, giving her another slight smile. "I know," he said, before closing the door between them.

FIFTY-SEVEN

THE CHURCH PARKING LOT was empty. Even though he'd switched cars, he drove past the lot. A single car would be noticed. Remembered. He'd made it this far by being careful. By listening. Paying attention. Following the path that had been laid for him.

Just keep doing what I tell you, boy, and we'll both get what we want.

He parked about a hundred yards away, on the soft shoulder of the road, leaving the car where it mingled with the trucks and hatchbacks belonging to the fieldworkers that dotted the landscape. He hurried toward the church, hands jammed into the pockets of the jacket he wore despite the oppressive heat, head ducked to keep his face hidden beneath the bill of a faded U of A ball cap he found in his back seat. To a passerby, he'd look like one of those fieldworkers, hoping to make confession.

Is that why we're here? Wade laughed, the sound of it ringing in his head, grating against his nerves. *Are you here to confess your sins, boy?*

"No," he said, answering the question only he could hear. "I'm here to punish him." He yanked the door open, standing in the slice of bright light he'd created for no more than a moment before he stepped inside, letting the dark church swallow him whole.

Standing still, he gave his eyes a few moments to adjust. Shapes and figures pulled themselves from the dim. The silhouette of Saint Rose herself, face turned upward, crown of roses settled on her head. The pew where he'd used to sit while he watched the Father attend his flock.

Listening to their troubles. Giving them counsel. A shoulder to lean on ... to everyone but you. Almost like he couldn't stand the sight of you. Like he knew what you were, even back then.

He gritted his teeth to keep himself from answering out loud.

It only hurts because it's the truth, boy.

Finally adjusted, his gaze found the confessional. The door to the booth was still closed, the tall pillar candle beside it lit. Father Francisco was still inside, waiting out the last few minutes of confession in silence.

He approached quietly, slipping inside the neighboring booth before locking the door. Respecting the collar while hating the man who wore it kicked up a whirlwind of conflicting emotion inside him. Giving in, he took off the hat that hid his face, setting it on the bench beside him. The partition covering the window that joined the booths slid open almost instantly, the soft *clack* of it making him smile. "Forgive me, Father, for I have sinned ... again." The smile widened into a grin. "We both know how long it's been since my last confession."

There was a quiet intake of breath behind the screen that separated them, the only indication that the priest had heard him. That he knew who he was and what he'd done.

300

"Her name was Margaret. She was a veterinary assistant from El Centro. Young this time. Pretty, in an awkward sort of way," he said, relishing each word. The wounds they inflicted. "When she was a little girl, she was in a car accident with her father and older brother—"

"Please," the priest said sadly. "Please, stop."

"They both died but she survived. Three days in the snow before she was found. Three days trapped in a car with her dead brother and dead father before she was saved." He looked down at his hands, rubbing his fingertips together. Still feeling the warm slip of her blood between them. "That made her a miracle, didn't it, Father?"

"Please." The word was croaked at him now, harsh and low. "Please, I'm begging you, stop this—"

"I can't." He raised his gaze, settling it on the shadow that sat beside him behind the screen. "I won't. Margaret was chosen. Given a gift," he said, his hands tightening into fists. "I submitted her to the canon and she was proved unworthy—just like the rest of them."

"You have to stop this madness," the priest demanded. "There's a woman, an FBI agent. She was here today. She knows who you are."

"She knows who *I* am?" Laughter bubbled in his throat. "That's funny. But I didn't come here to talk about her. I want to tell you about Margaret."

"You're insane," the priest said, sounding broken.

"Maybe … but let's stay on track, shall we?" he said, peering hard at the priest's shadowy profile. "Our Margaret wasn't a virgin but I think I can safely say the things I did to her—"

He watched as the silhouette in the neighboring booth jolted in its seat, lunging for its door a second before it was flung open.

He listened as the priest tumbled through the doorway, the candelabra clattering to the floor.

Go after him.

He kicked the door to his own booth open to see Father Francisco stumbling into the front pew, the toe of his shoe snagging against its corner. He fell, sprawling across the floor a few yards away. He was stunned, his mumbling mouth pressed against the cool tile floor.

"—forgiveness, Lord. Please forgive me."

"Forgive *you*?" he said, using the toe of his own boot to turn the priest over. "That's a little selfish, don't you think?" He crouched down, reaching out to finger the thin trickle of blood that painted the corner of the man's mouth. "Aren't you going to offer *me* forgiveness, Father? Don't I deserve absolution?"

The priest's eyes widened in surprise before they narrowed into a glare, defiant and terrified. "*You* are worthy of neither."

The words angered him, but only for a moment.

You don't need his forgiveness, boy. You've got me.

"You're right." His mouth twitched upward when the priest shrank away from him as he stood. "I don't need him," he said, a moment before he lifted his foot and brought the sole of his boot down onto the priest's face.

FIFTY-EIGHT

WHEN SABRINA DROVE AWAY from the station, she half expected Phillip to follow her. He didn't. Instead, his chauffeured car peeled away almost instantly, turning left while she turned right. The red silk pouch he'd given her sat in the center console, the delicate scent of the tea Eun hand-blended for her drifted upward. Tempting her.

Who do you think you're foolin'? We both know you aren't gonna drink it, darlin'. You need me.

As soon as the words came, she rejected them. "Like I need a fucking hole in my head," she muttered, her remark greeted by laughter.

I'm the only person who knows him. I'm the only person who can show you the way.

"You're not a person." Sabrina pulled off the pavement and into the dirt parking lot that surrounded Saint Rose of Lima church. "You're not here. You can't tell me anything I don't already know."

We both know that ain't entirely true. I might be dead but I'm not gone, and I'm as real as you are.

She slammed the car into park and cut the engine. "If you don't shut the fuck up—"

Alright, alright . . . just calm down, darlin'. You don't want to go in there all riled.

The words were a warning—either from her subconscious or the dead man inside her head—that experience told her she should heed. Looking around, she didn't see anything out of the ordinary. The squat stucco building in front of her looked quiet. Almost deserted. The main door was cracked open—a slice of black against the bright heat of the afternoon. By modern standards, the chapel was primitive. No electricity meant no heating or cooling. Father Francisco and his patrons would be careful to keep it closed against the oppressive heat of the late Arizona summer.

Apprehension prickled against her scalp. She got out of the car and looked around again, casting her gaze past the empty lot that surrounded her. In the distance, cars and trucks lined the shoulder of the road, waiting while their owners worked the fields. Scanning the fields, she watched the men and women as they stooped and crouched, moving with almost surgical precision as they cut, pulled, and tossed their bounty into baskets and bags. None of them seemed out of place and none of them paid her even the slightest bit of attention.

Whatever waited for her was waiting inside.

Careful, now . . .

The words echoed softly, so close she could almost feel the mouth that delivered them brush against her ear, cautioning her to move slowly. She closed the distance to the church, approaching the cracked door until she stood on the other side of it. Sounds drifted through it. Dull thuds, coupled with a soft squelching. Harsh breathing punctured with muttering.

Sounds like someone's havin' themselves some fun.

Her hand found the grip of the Kimber .45 that rode her hip as she turned sideways to ease through the opening, her body's width forcing it to open wider, the wedge of light doubling as it shot through the dark chapel. The sounds were suddenly cut off. Whoever was inside knew they were no longer alone.

Better shake a leg, darlin'.

She yanked the Kimber clear of its holster, bringing it up as she charged forward, leaving the sun behind. Spots danced in front of her eyes while they tried to adjust to the sudden lack of light. "Stop," she bellowed as she ran though the atrium and down the center aisle of the church. A dark figure shot across her vision, streaking from one side of the room to the other, followed by a sudden burst of bright light as he pushed his way through the side door that led to the prayer garden.

She started after him, lengthening her stride as she rushed blindly up the center aisle of the church. That's when she found him, nearly tripping on the outstretched arm splayed across her path.

It was Father Francisco—or at least she thought it was him. The blood-splattered clerical collar was his only recognizable feature.

"Oh God…" She dropped to her knees, one hand gripped around the Kimber while the other fumbled into her jacket pocket to find her phone. "Hang on, okay? Jesus, just hang on," she said, eliciting a groan from the figure beside her. She stabbed her thumb against the keypad while she listened to the labored breathing of the man on the floor, blood bubbling and whistling through his ruined nose, his mouth nothing more than a jagged maw, teeth broken and scattered on the blood-smeared ground around them.

Takes a lot of rage to stomp someone's face in. I'd know, wouldn't I?

"What's up?" Church's tone reached out and grabbed her, shaking her back to reality.

"He was here. He was here—" She took a deep breath, casting her gaze toward the man she knelt over. His face wasn't just flat, it was *caved in*, flesh torn and split from repeated blunt force blows. "Send an ambulance. He—Father Francisco." She squeezed her eyes shut, forcing herself to remain calm. "Hurry."

Sabrina ended the call on a tidal wave of questions, letting her phone clatter to the floor beside her. "Stay with me, Father," she said, her free hand reached out to find the priest's. "Help is coming."

FIFTY-NINE

Within minutes, she heard the frantic wail of the approaching ambulance. Five minutes after that, paramedics burst in, carrying what looked like toolboxes, shouting at her to get up. To get away and give them room to work.

Sabrina did as she was told, sitting heavily on the front pew a few yards away, face tipped toward her shoes. There was no use going after the attacker. He was long gone by now. Preserving the crime scene rated a distant second to saving a life. Once it was all said and done, she'd have nothing more to go on than a half-formed impression of the perpetrator and no real way of proving that the attack had any connection to their case.

You're battin' a thousand, darlin'. I knew you were a bit rusty coming into this but, Jesus—

"Agent Vance?"

She looked up to find Detective Santos standing over her, notebook held in his hand. She wasn't a cop right now. She was a witness and he wanted her statement. "I arrived at approximately five o'clock. The parking lot was empty but the front door to the church was ajar. I found it odd so I approached with caution." The palms of her hands felt like they'd suddenly sprung a leak. "I heard ... sounds coming from inside the church," she said, rubbing the flat of her hands against her pant legs.

"Sounds?"

She looked up to find Santos watching her closely. The squelching sounds came back to her. Soft and wet, followed up with the sound of heavy footfalls. "Stomping. Cursing. It was obvious that someone was in distress, so I drew my weapon and took the door."

"Without calling for backup." Santos glanced up from the mini-pad he was scribbling on. Instead of looking angry, he looked like he understood.

"There was no time," she said, shaking her head. It was a necessary question. One that had to be asked in order to cover all their bases, but it still grated. "When I entered the church, the assailant ran through the side door and into the prayer garden. I started to pursue but ..."

"Is that when you discovered—" The words seemed to stick in his throat and he cleared it before continuing. "Father Francisco?"

"Yes. He'd been badly beaten and I feared that without immediate medical attention, he'd die. I terminated the pursuit in favor of staying with the victim and calling for assistance."

Beaten? Our boy stomped 'im near to death. I think I saw boot tracks on the ol' padre's forehead.

Santos nodded. "Can you describe the suspect you saw fleeing?"

"Five-ten. Medium build. Dark clothing ..." It was a bullshit description, one that fit two-thirds of the population, and giving it made her angry. In other words, she didn't see shit. "Where's Vega?" she said.

"I have a car sitting on his house." Santos shook his head and sighed. "Far as I know, he hasn't left since that stunt you pulled at the station."

Stunt. Like her questioning him had somehow pushed Vega over the edge. Like this was somehow her fault.

Well, ain't it, darlin'? Ain't it always?

She looked around, her gaze landing on Church. She stood near the confessional with a couple of crime scene techs, talking quietly while the grim-faced paramedics secured the priest on a gurney. They'd been working for nearly thirty minutes now, trying to stabilize him for transport. She didn't have to ask to know that they didn't think he had much chance for survival.

The number I did on you was a hell of a lot worse, remember? You had no business living, but you did it anyway.

She watched as they wheeled him up the center aisle, one of them rushing ahead so she could hold the door open for the rest.

Miracles happen every day. You're proof of that.

Santos cleared his throat, the sound of it pulling her back to the here and now. "Did you see his face?"

"No. My eyes were still adjusting to the light change." She shook her head. "It happened too fast."

"Okay." Santos flipped his notebook closed and tucked it into the breast pocket of his shirt. "I'm gonna head across the street and see if anyone working the fields caught a look at him as he was fleeing the area."

She nodded, not bothering to offer to help. He had Alvarez. He didn't need her. As soon as he was gone Church closed in on her while the techs descended on the crime scene. "You're making it difficult for me to do the job I was hired for," she said, keeping her voice low so the techs couldn't hear her.

Sabrina shook her head. "I should've asked you to come with me. If you'd been here, you could have stayed behind while I went after him."

"You're right," Church said bluntly.

"Whatever Ben is paying you, he needs to double it," she said.

"It's not like I haven't earned it," Church said, deftly ignoring her ham-handed attempt at an apology. It probably made her as uncomfortable hearing it as it made Sabrina to say it. "I've drank about a thousand gallons of chamomile tea since hitching myself to your wagon."

Sabrina laughed, rubbing her knuckles across her cheekbone. "Is it helping?" she said, her gaze drifting from the pair of techs to the confessional. There was something on the bench. Throwing long, candlelit shadows against the wall of the booth. She stood up and walked toward it.

"Hell no." Church laughed with her. "I've assassinated world leaders with less stress than being your pretend partner causes me."

"Just tell me it was worth it," she said over her shoulder as she slipped inside the booth. "Tell me you guys found something while I was out here messing things up."

"Actually, I did," Church said, her tone going heavy. "I found three murders that fit. College-age girls. Disappeared from local bars. All dumped within a few miles of the abduction site. Torture. Rape. Eyes gouged out. Sound familiar?"

Familiar, yes. But not exact.

It was fun, watching him come into his own. Showin' him how. Makes me proud to know a part of me is still out in the world, killing…

"—first victim turned up a week after he sent Wade his last letter, but they didn't happen here. You were smart to widen the search window."

She was only half listening, most of her attention focused on the object left behind in the confessional. It was a hat. Sabrina crouched in front of the bench, tilting her head so she could catch sight of its front without touching it. "Tucson," she said as she studied the patch stitched to the cap. "They happened in Tucson."

Arizona was home to a few major universities. U of A was one of them. The university's mascot, a white and red wildcat, stood out in sharp contrast to the cap's bright blue bill.

"How'd you guess?" Church said. Sabrina could feel her standing behind her and she turned, aiming her gaze upward.

I lost my scholarship. Dropped out of college and after a short What the hell am I gonna do now? *crisis, applied to Tucson PD. Rode patrol for a few years before I made detective and transferred here…*

The conversation she'd had with Mark Alvarez over coffee came back to her like it'd happened only moments ago. It suddenly made perfect sense. The way he'd been able to stay ahead of the investigation. Mislead and redirect them. Plant her DNA under Stephanie Adams's fingernails. Lure her here. He was a cop.

Just like Wade.

"Where is he?" She stood quickly, giving the sanctuary a quick survey. It was illuminated brightly by the portable klieg lights brought by the crime techs. For the first time she realized that while

311

Santos had been questioning her, his partner was absent. Her gaze landed on the techs again. Something about them bothered her.

Confusion skimmed over Church's features, wrinkling her brow. She followed her gaze, bouncing it around the chapel before resettling it on her face. "Where's who?"

"Where's Alvarez?"

SIXTY

Kootenai Canyon, Montana

Four days.

Michael slid his spatula under the pancake and gave it a flip. She'd been gone for four days. No update. No word. Nothing. It was like she'd dropped off the face of the planet. He wasn't sure what he'd expected after his ill-advised call to Phillip Song. Armageddon? Livingston Shaw himself, delivered to his doorstep, surrounded by Pips? If he were completely honest, a part of him had wanted that. For it to be over, one way or another. A confrontation would finally free him. Instead, he'd gotten more of the same. Silence. Nothing. Waiting.

"Your flapjacks are burning."

Miss Ettie's voice snapped him back. She was right. Smoke was beginning to curl up from the skillet in front of him, carrying the smell of charred batter and chocolate. "Shit," he muttered as he jerked the skillet off the burner. He shot an apologetic smile over his shoulder at the pair sitting at the kitchen table. "Sorry, guys."

Christina gave him an indifferent shrug while Alex stared out the window like he was waiting for something. He'd been doing that a lot lately. Most days his behavior was puzzling at best, leaving Michael to wonder if he even knew what was going on, but every once in a while he caught a sharpness in the boy's gaze that told him Alex Koto saw and understood more than he pretended to.

"Why don't you let me take over," Miss Ettie said as she gently pried the spatula from his grip. "Besides, I think everyone's about finished with breakfast." Some unseen signal passed between the old woman and the kids at the table and they stood to carry their plates to the sink. He moved away from the stove, leaning against the counter with a small nod. He'd made enough pancakes to feed the four of them for a week.

"Okay." He peeled one without chocolate chips off the stack and handed it down to the dog at his side. She craned her neck slightly before nipping it softly from his hand. She licked her chops and whined, pressing her head against his knee. Without Sabrina, Avasa was as lost as he was, but at least she wasn't sitting at the back door anymore, waiting for her to come back.

"You're done moping," Miss Ettie said sternly as soon as the children left the room to wash up. "I want you out of this house."

He almost laughed. Not many people in his life saw fit to boss him around like that. "Yes, ma'am."

"I'm serious, Michael," she said, using her tiny frame to shoulder herself in farther between him and the mess he'd made. "And I don't mean go out to the barn and listen to that damnable radio hiss static at you for hours on end. I want you to get your boots on and go for a walk." She picked up the spatula and started to scrape burnt chocolate from the bottom of the skillet. "A long one."

His gaze found its way to the antique larder that'd been converted into gun storage. It'd been a few days since anyone had walked their fence line. Not since Sabrina had taken Christina out with her the day Maddox showed up. It seemed like a lifetime ago.

"Okay, you win." He looked down at the dog again before nodding. "Whaddya say, girl, feel like a walk?"

Avasa chuffed at him softly before ambling over to the back door to sit down and wait.

———

Thirty minutes later, Michael carried his boots outside and sat down to pull them on, loosening the laces just enough to slip his foot inside before pulling them tight again. He glanced at the barn. Aside from his little field trip, he'd been within sprinting distance of it—and the radio inside—since Sabrina left. He'd fallen asleep last night on the hood of his car, listening to dead air, just like Miss Ettie had accused him of.

"*Mogu li ya poyti s toboy?*" Can I go with you?

Michael glanced up from the boot he was lacing to find Alex standing beside him. He'd traded his sneakers for sturdy boots and added a lightweight jacket. A .22 rifle was slung over his bony shoulder.

It was the first time the boy had spoken directly to him in days and the first time he'd ever shown interest in spending time with him. "*Da,*" he said to the boy, nodding his head before standing. Avasa was already waiting for him, sitting at the lip of the bridge, her tail swishing impatiently in the dirt. "*Ty gotov idti?*" Are you ready to go? Instead of answering, the boy nodded on his way down the stairs. Michael chuckled softly as he shouldered his TAC-50 before following suit.

They walked for a while in silence, the dog jogging a few paces ahead, nose to the ground, before circling back to wedge herself between them. Every few minutes, she'd catch scent of something up ahead and trot off to investigate before coming back.

The grass along the fence line had grown thick and high. It shuttered and hissed, rattled by a low-sweeping wind. The sound of it caught Avasa's attention and she shot forward before banking left to dive into the waving sea of green. They both stopped walking, Alex watching the dog while Michael watched him. Something was going on with the boy. Something beyond his carefully blank stares and firmly held secrets.

"*Pochemu ty zdes', Aleks?*" Why are you here, Alex? The question came out of nowhere. If anyone had asked him the same thing, he'd have told them that Alex was here because he was like the rest of them. Lost and alone. Despite the truth of it, Michael was suddenly sure that his orphan status had nothing to do with why Alex was here.

The boy turned toward him, dark gaze sharp. "*Potomu chto vy menya nuzhno.*" Because you need me.

Michael opened his mouth to tell him that he knew. He knew the boy could speak English. That he could probably speak it all along. He knew he was hiding something. Or that he was hiding *from* something. "Look—"

Alex held up a hand, palm flat and pressed against the air between them. "Shhh," he said without even bothering to look at Michael, the sound blending perfectly with the wind as it whispered through the grass. "*Sushchestvuyet kto-to zdes'.*" There is someone here.

It wasn't the boy's words that silenced him. It was the certainty behind them that had him lifting the TAC to fit it against his shoulder, eye pressed to the scope. He caught sight of their cattle—no more than a couple hundred head—a few miles out. Their heads were hung low, big, soft jaws rolling slowly as they chewed up the meadow. They looked relaxed. Undisturbed.

"I don't see anything," he said quietly, sweeping the rifle from left to right. He lowered the TAC to look at the boy. "*YA ne vizhu nich—*"

Just then Avasa shot through the grass, ears tucked against her sleek skull, the strip of hair running down the length of her spine standing straight, even more ridged than before. She stood in front of him, lips peeled away from her teeth in a quivering, silent snarl.

Michael immediately lifted the TAC to do another sweep just as another gust of wind swept through the valley. That's when he caught the flutter of it. A spent parachute, nearly the same bright green as the grass that surrounded it, billowing gently in the breeze.

Shit.

"Do you remember what my friend Ben looks like?" he said, his tone held low. When the boy didn't answer he chanced a quick look, pulling his eye off the scope. "No more pretending, Alex. I know you speak perfect English. Now, do you remember what Ben looks like?"

Alex hesitated a moment before he nodded. "Yes."

"Good." Michael eyed the .22 rifle Alex had slung over his shoulder. "Go home. You see anyone you don't recognize, kill them," he said, pulling his gaze away from the rifle to find the boy watching the distance, eyes aimed in the same direction he'd been looking just a moment before. "Can you do that?"

Alex lifted his gaze, settling it on his face. "What about the big one?" he asked in a dispassionate tone. "Should I kill him too?"

The big one... It took Michael a second to realize he was talking about Lark. A few seconds longer to shake his head. "No. But you can shoot him in the leg if you want."

"Okay," Alex said before turning to head back the way they'd come without saying anything else.

SIXTY-ONE

Yuma, Arizona

"Alvarez?" Church craned her neck for a moment, trying to see what was inside the booth that sparked such an odd question. "No. I haven't seen him since …" The confusion on her face cleared up, replaced by skeptical comprehension. "He left the conference room to grab a cup of coffee." She shook her head. "Santos and I were buried so deep in research, I just assumed he'd grabbed some files off the stack and settled in at his desk."

"But you never actually saw him do it," Sabrina said quietly.

"No, I just …" Church shook her head. "What are you thinking, Kitten?"

Sabrina took a second look around, just to make sure, half hoping she'd spot him in some dark corner talking to an overlooked witness. No witness. No Alvarez. "Alvarez didn't duck out for coffee." Aside from the pair of crime scene techs, they were the only two in the building. "While we were all focused on finding him, he took the opportunity to leave the precinct."

319

"*Him?* You mean Alvarez?" Church narrowed her eyes for a moment. "You think he did this?"

Hearing Church say it out loud, it sounded crazy. A lot of people went to U of A. If she complied a list of people who'd attended the college during the years the killings Church and Santos found, it'd probably be as long as her leg. But how many of them moved to Yuma months before the first victim was found? How many of them were cops? How many of them had access to their investigation?

Despite the mounting evidence, Church was still having trouble buying it. "But what, that gave him a five- or ten-minute jump on you? No way he had time to get the job done that quickly."

Ten minutes at best, but once you add in her surprise visit from Phillip Song, Alvarez's lead nearly tripled. Plenty of time to get here before her. He'd left the room before she'd announced her plan to come here and confront the priest. He'd had no way of knowing she'd be here to interrupt him.

But why now? Had he meant to kill Father Francisco? Had something triggered him, or had it been an impulse? Everything she'd learned about Nulo over the past few days told her that giving into impulse wasn't how he operated. "What was he doing before he left?" She looked at Church, could feel the desperation coursing through her. "He was sitting at the conference table—was he reading something? A journal or maybe—"

"The lab report." Church narrowed her eyes for a moment—not at her but at the memories she'd been asked to recall. "On the cat you found in the prayer garden last night."

"Are you sure?"

Church nodded. "Positive."

Whatever was in that report had been damning enough to set Alvarez off. Scared him enough to push him over the edge. "Did you read it? What was in it?" Probably evidence that pointed directly at him.

"I didn't," Church said, giving her a pensive look. "I was in the middle of picking it up when you texted me." She shook her head. "I just tossed it into the file box you had me swing by and grab from the hotel."

Her cell phone rattled on her hip and she reached for it. "I need you to get a copy of it," Sabrina said, punching her finger against the screen. It was a text from a number she didn't recognize.

375 Bahia
San Felipe, Mexico
You're welcome.

Seeing it reminded her that despite evidence to the contrary, Paul Vega was involved somehow. He was hiding something. What other reason could he have for shipping Graciella Lopez off to Mexico? "Croft outside?" she said, clipping her phone back onto her waistband.

"Yeah, he's out there." Church shot a glance at the main doors to the sanctuary. "He got here before we did."

Sabrina nodded. "Good," she said, moving past the techs, couched over the spot where she'd found Father Francisco. "I've got a job for him."

She was halfway up the aisle when it hit her—what it was that had been bothering her about the pair of techs since they arrived—and she turned around to look at them, just to make sure.

Neither of them was Ellie.

SIXTY-TWO

SHE SHOULDN'T BE HERE. It was wrong—and not just because if she was caught, Paul Vega would sic his lawyer brother on her and probably sue the entire department for harassment. No, coming here was wrong because it was unhealthy. She knew that. She knew that her incessant return to the place where her childhood best friend had been tortured bordered on obsessive behavior. She knew that in doing so, she perpetuated the ridiculous fantasy that she could've done something. That she *should* do something to help Rachel, even if Rachel didn't want her to.

And yet, here she was.

Ellie switched the ignition off on her car, pulling the keys from the steering column, but she didn't get out of the car. As much as she was driven to come back to this place, over and over again, she hated it.

What happened that night ate at her. She couldn't stop thinking about it. Couldn't stop wondering. What would've happened if she'd stayed at Rachel's instead of going home? Would she have been able to talk her best friend into staying home instead of getting in that car? Would Rachel have been able to persuade Ellie to go with her, like so many times before?

Did it even matter now that she was dead?

Keys gripped in her fist, Ellie forced herself out of the car, careful to shut the door as quietly as possible. Not that anyone was around to hear her. The surrounding fields were deserted, the sweltering heat driving Vega's workers indoors for the last few hours of the day. They'd be back at it tomorrow, well before the sun rose, stooping and pulling. Tossing and packing. It was hard, grueling work that made you old before your time. She should know, she'd spent her fourteenth summer in those fields, working alongside her mother, sullen gaze dug into the dirt that surrounded her, arms and legs stiff with anger and resentment.

It'd started out as harmless fun. Running through the fields, stomping and smashing watermelons with her friends. She didn't remember when it'd turned into something more. That she was no longer laughing, hate surging through her every time she brought her foot down. That's when she realized she blamed the Vega family for her father's death.

It'd taken her months to scrub away the grime that worked its way into her hands. It had taken her only half as long to finally understand that she'd never be able to destroy enough or cost the Vegas enough lost profits to make them sorry. Because they didn't care. They didn't even know her father existed.

She never told her mother that it'd been Paul Vega himself who suggested they go into those fields in the first place. That while everyone else had been throwing chunks of melon at one another and grinding that soft, red pulp into the ground, he'd been sitting on the tailgate of his truck, watching the destruction with a smug, satisfied smile. It was obvious, to anyone who cared to pay attention, how much he hated it all.

Ellie brushed off the memory, reaching for the buzzing phone she'd jammed into her back pocket. It was her sister, Val. She called every day to check on their mother; their conversation usually ending in an argument. Val wanted to move their mother to San Francisco.

Not just mom, Ellie. We want you to come too. Devon can put in a good word for you with the police department here and you can stay with us as long—

That's about as far as she allowed Val to take it before she hung up on her. Swiping left, Ellie dumped the call into her voicemail— she'd call her sister back later. Right now, she had other things to worry about.

It was just a few steps to the pump house and she took them quickly. Reaching into her pocket, she pulled out one of the paper clips she'd tucked in there earlier. Bending it open, she worked the thin length of metal until it snapped in two. Fitting the newly separated pieces into the lock, Ellie lifted and jiggled until the tumblers gave way. Giving it a hard twist, the lock popped open.

Like any farmer, Vega rotated his crops. She'd bet the pump house and the fields that surrounded it hadn't been used in years. Stepping inside, she shut the door behind her. A row of glass block ran the perimeter of the room, set at the top of the wall. The sunlight they let in were the pump house's only source of light.

In the middle of the room was a waterwheel, as big as a car tire, attached to a complicated series of pumps and pipes that stood so tall they nearly touched the ceiling. She headed for it, drawn like a magnet to the place where Rachel had spent four days of her life.

She remembered the first time she'd come here, ignoring the large, official-looking sticker that sealed the door. The police weren't coming back. No one was investigating what happened to her friend. No one cared. The Vega family obviously used their money and influence in the community to make sure of that. They'd silenced everyone. Even Rachel.

Ellie had decided she'd be the one to find something. Some sort of clue or proof that it was Paul Vega who'd hurt Rachel. When she found it, she'd take it to the police. The newspapers. *Someone* had to listen. There had to be someone who couldn't be bought ... but when she got there, she realized how ridiculous her revenge fantasy really was.

It was the waterwheel that finally convinced her. One of its painted spokes was scraped clean. This was where Rachel must've been kept, handcuffed to the wheel. Made to do horrible things, to believe she was going to die. She looked down at the scatter of Dodger blue paint flakes in the dirt beneath her feet and felt the weight of the truth settle onto her shoulders. She was just a kid. She had no idea what she was looking for. She didn't know the first thing about evidence collection. What happened to Rachel was a puzzle she couldn't solve.

Standing in that pump house, looking at the remnants left behind by the crime scene techs, she'd envied them. They knew how to get answers. She turned around and left, promising herself she wouldn't come back here until she knew what to do. So she could find justice for her friend.

Whether she wanted it or not.

Now, looking around, all Ellie saw was evidence. Shoe prints. A man's dress shoe—size 10–12. She immediately stopped walking to pull her phone from her pocket. Snapping off a few pictures, she crouched in the dirt to get a closer look. One of the shoe prints was settled deeper into the dirt, like the foot that made it had been used to push its owner forward. Standing again, she could see it, the uneven gate, the tip of the right print turned slightly inward. The man who made it had a limp.

She had a kit in her car. She'd take casts. Print the door. Call Agent Vance. She'd seemed solid. More importantly, she was a federal agent. It wasn't likely that the Vega family could buy her like they did local law enforcement.

Hand on the door, ready to push it open, she was stopped in her tracks by the blare of her car alarm. The urgent sound of it propelled her forward, out into the heat of the day. A coyote trotted across the field, away from her. It turned its head to look back at her, something hanging out of its mouth. Probably a rabbit that got cornered under the car.

Sighing in relief, she traded her phone for her car keys. Raising them, she aimed the fob at the car to silence it. That's when she saw the white slip of paper secured to her windshield with her wiper blade, heavy black ink spilled across it. She stopped in her tacks, reading the note from where she stood, the words tightening her grip around the set of keys in her hand.

Ellie took a step back, reaching for her phone. Before she could pull it from her pocket, a strong arm snaked around her waist, pinning her arms at her sides before yanking her off her feet while the other clamped over her mouth, forcing the scream she'd built up back into her mouth.

"Well, Elena? Do you?"

She grunted, whipping her head backward, trying like hell to crack his nose with the back of her skull. He was ready for her, dodging the blow, and she connected with his shoulder instead, her head bouncing against the crook of his neck. Not ready to give up, Ellie remembered the keys in her hand and lashed out, stabbing them into his thigh. The angle was wrong, his pants too thick. The keys fumbled out of her hand, landing at her scuffling feet.

Her eyes wheeled wildly in her head, trying to get a look at him. All she caught sight of was a smooth jawline and skin only slightly darker than her own. But it was enough.

"I know you," she wheezed against the hand at her mouth, breath squeezed by the tightening of his arm around her middle. "I know—"

Her eyes took another spin before landing on the windshield of her car and the letter attached to it.

Do you believe in miracles?

SIXTY-THREE

WHAT ARE THE ODDS, darlin'?

Sabrina pushed her way out of the church, scanning the gathering mob that pushed and crowded against the yellow tape that ran its perimeter. People were worried, terrified shouts breaking through the horrified whispers.

"Is Father Francisco okay?"

"What happened?"

"Who did this?"

With every unanswered question the mob pushed harder, jostling and shouting to make themselves heard while the quartet of uniformed officers did their best to keep everything under control.

"I'll handle it." Church pointed to a lone figure standing off to the side. "There's your boy," she said before heading in the opposite direction, toward the crowd that seemed to have grown in only the few seconds they'd been standing there.

What are the odds that two sisters, a thousand miles apart, get kidnapped by two completely different serial killers within a few years of each other?

Croft shifted from one foot to the other while he watched her approach, his expression growing more apprehensive the closer she got. "I don't like that look," he said to her as she grabbed his arm and dragged him farther away from the crowd. "I like this even less."

"Yeah? You don't like being grabbed?" she said, casting a quick look over her shoulder. Church was addressing the crowd and incredibly they were all listening. "Now you know how I feel." She turned in Croft's direction to find him watching her. "Got a passport?"

"Of course." Her question sent Croft's expression from apprehensive to downright suspicious. "Why?"

They're pretty damn good. Want to know why? Want to know what the common denominator is? What makes such an incredible thing possible?

"Great." Finally, something was working in her favor. "You're going on a field trip."

"A what?" He shook his head. "No," he said, his head shake gaining speed. "Anything you could ask me—expendable, *I hope you die in a fire* me—to do that requires a passport is more than likely a suicide mission. I happen to like living. So thanks, but no thanks."

"I really don't like that word, Croft." The hand on his arm tightened for a second before letting go entirely. "But if that's how you feel, there's nothing I can do about it, *is there*?" The last of her words were heavy, the weight of them reminding him there was plenty she could do. His gaze drifted behind her and undoubtedly settled on Church. His expression changed again—half fear, half resignation. He might not be afraid of her, but he was scared shitless of Church.

You're the reason, darlin'. You. The common thread that runs through everyone's life and ruins it. No matter what you do or where you go, you're a sickness that invades and pollutes everyone around you.

"I'm a writer, Sabrina." Croft shook his head. He knew he'd end up doing what she was asking him to do, but he wasn't ready to admit it yet. Too bad for him she was running out of patience. "I'm not some badass super assassin like your dead-but-not-really-dead boyfriend. I'm a nerd with too much curiosity and a laptop. Notice the absence of a death wish. I'm a writer—I write."

"No …" Sabrina shook her head. "You invade. You push. You blackmail. You stalk. And *then* you write. And your lack of a death wish is debatable."

"That's how the job is done," he said in a sullen tone that told her he knew her description was more than a little accurate. "And I never stalked you."

"You were a war correspondent." Sabrina took another look over her shoulder. Church had the lotful of congregants holding hands, heads bowed while she led them in prayer. "You've seen plenty of action." Even the uniforms on their side of the tape were standing quietly, faces tipped downward. "Hell, you've been shot. Twice, remember?"

"Yeah, I remember." He laughed at her. "Forgive me for not being eager to repeat the experience."

No one who loves you is safe. Our boy has little Ellie, darlin', and he can't wait to get to work on her. He's gonna make her bleed and scream—

"I'm not Church. I don't have a ball gag or the time to drive you around in the trunk of my car and do God knows what to you. What I *do* have is a gun," she hissed at him, curbing the urge to bitch slap him. "The only person you need to worry about shooting you is me."

Croft's gaze traveled to the bulge at her hip before finding her face, seemingly calculating how serious she was about shooting him. "Okay," he sighed, satisfied that, despite the dispersing crowd and police officers milling around the parking lot, she was totally serious. "What do you need me to do?"

SIXTY-FOUR

Kootenai Canyon, Montana

THE PARACHUTE WAS UNMARKED. Most recreational jump schools marked their chutes because they were expensive. Run for profit, they took great care to protect their equipment, which meant that leaving a spent rig behind was practically unheard of. The Halo helmet tossed into the grass next to the tangle of nylon lines and straps confirmed that the person who landed in his canyon wasn't a weekend adrenalin junkie looking for a fix. The person walking around unchecked was a trained operator, and their landing here hadn't been an accident.

Michael looked up. As usual, the sky was clear. Because of its previous presidential owner, their canyon had long ago been removed from commercial flight paths, but a Halo jump maxed out at 35,000 feet. A small civilian aircraft could be easily missed at that altitude.

Gathering the bright green chute, he rolled it with a haphazard precision that said he'd done it a million times. Under normal circumstances, an operator would be careful to roll the chute and tuck it under a bush or rock so that it wasn't readily visible. That this one was left to drift and billow in the breeze told him one thing: Whoever had landed in his canyon wanted him to know they were here.

Or they wanted to mark their landing site.

Stuffing the chute back into its pack, Michael slung the strap of it over his shoulder. Next to the dumped helmet was the starting point of a trail, nothing more than a slight bending of the knee-high grass. It snaked eastward, parallel to the trail he and Alex had been following, hidden from view. Their uninvited guest was heading for the house.

———

The trail ended at the bridge, veering out of the grass in order to cross the river. Now he could see the impressions leading him across the water, toward the cluster of buildings that lay beyond it. He stood there for a moment, watching. Weighing his options.

The deep, shaded porch that housed a pair of wicker armchairs and a table was unoccupied. The yard that surrounded it was undisturbed. The house looked just as he'd left it an hour before. That left the barn. Whoever it was would be smart to take the barn first. It offered the best vantage point from which to watch the house while waiting for the perfect opportunity to strike.

He'd been stupid to assume that once he'd found him, Livingston Shaw would send an army. He knew better. Shaw wasn't a full-court press kind of guy. He was too sneaky to come at him head-on. Instead of looking straight ahead, Michael should have been watching for Shaw from the corner of his eye.

Dumping the pack, he crossed the bridge at a fast clip, formulating his plan on the fly. He'd clear the house first. Get Miss Ettie and the kids into the bunker and seal it. The barn was wired with explosives, just like the bridge. As soon as they were safely below ground, he'd blow it.

Mounting the porch steps, Michael put on a show, stomping the mud off his boots while he listened. He could hear his family moving around inside. The click of Avasa's toenails across the hard wood of the floor. The clank of dishes being washed in the sink. Alex and Christina talking about who was beating who at rummy.

The scrape of a fork against a plate as someone finished up a late breakfast.

He nearly kicked the door in, pulling the TAC off his shoulder in a fluid motion that brought it up into position and had it aimed at the intruder almost before Michael saw him. The face staring back at him was one he'd never expected to see again.

"Alex," he said in a casual tone, "is there a reason he's still breathing?"

"Vy skazali, chtoby strelyat', kogo ya ne uznal." You said to shoot anyone I didn't recognize. Obviously Alex wasn't ready to admit to everyone else what he already knew—he spoke better English than he was letting on. Michael wanted to ask him why. He also wanted to ask him what the hell that was supposed to mean, but instead he stored both questions away for later. There was plenty of time to ask Alex what was going on. After he got rid of their uninvited guest.

The man at the table laid his fork down carefully before lifting the napkin in his lap to wipe his mouth. "Thank you for the pancakes," he said to Miss Ettie. "They were delicious." He was wearing a jump suit, unzipped and peeled down to the waist, its sleeves tied around his waist to reveal a thin white undershirt. He appeared to be unarmed.

The old woman stood frozen in his peripheral, stunned by the sudden turn of events. "You're welcome," she said, phrasing it almost like a question before turning in Michael's direction, waiting for him to tell her what to do.

"Take the kids into the living room, please," he told her. As soon as they were hustled out of the room, Michael flipped the safety off on the TAC. "Who the fuck let you out of your box, Dunn?"

Noah Dunn placed his napkin on his plate and stood. Michael placed his finger on the trigger and waited. "Ben Shaw," Dunn said, lifting the plate before carrying it to the sink.

His finger tightened slightly. "Bullshit." He spat the word out like there was no way it could be true but he knew better. Unlike his father, who measured every move he made, Ben was an odd mixture of calculation and recklessness. Releasing one of his father's prisoners without considering the repercussions was absolutely something he would do.

"He said you'd say that," Dunn said, slipping the empty plate into the sink full of soapy water. "Pink pony."

It was an old safe word. One he'd used with Christina years ago when he'd been her bodyguard. He'd shared it with three people since then and Ben had been one of them. One of them had also been Church—who just happened to be, last time he checked, Livingston Shaw's favorite FSS operative. "What did you say?"

"Pink pony," he repeated, turning toward him as he wiped his hands on a dishtowel. "He also told me to tell you that he spoke with Sabrina a few hours ago. She's still in Yuma and, all things considered, she's safe."

The last of his message had Michael wavering. Again, as far as he knew, Ben was the only one who knew where Sabrina was. But that didn't make it so. He'd been flying blind for days now and he was getting sick and fucking tired of operating on assumptions. "Who's Sabrina?" For all he knew, Livingston sprung Dunn himself and dropped him in his backyard just to mess with him. Maybe to confirm Sabrina's whereabouts so he could send in a team to snatch her up. Either way, he wasn't telling Noah Dunn shit.

"You always were too smart for your own good, O'Shea," Dunn said, a slow grin spreading across his face as his gaze flickered to the platinum band on his finger before finally focusing on the rifle aimed at his face. "I could have killed them, you know. The kids. The old lady. The dog. That I didn't should count for something."

"It does," Michael said from behind his TAC. "It's the only reason I'm not dragging your dead body into the woods and leaving it for the wolves."

"I could've killed them and *you*, O'Shea," Dunn countered, "long before you and the boy found my chute. So how about we stop measuring dicks and get down to business."

"Business?" he said, shaking his head slightly. "You and I don't have any business, Dunn."

"Sure we do," Dunn's tone hardened slightly, telling Michael the man was a hell of a lot more pissed off than he wanted to admit. "The way I see it, you owe me."

"Seems like all that alone time has left you confused," Michael said. "The only reason you're even here is because I decided to bring you in instead of kill you like I was ordered to."

"Four years in The Box." Dunn chuckled. "Thanks for that."

"Better than a bullet."

"Guess that depends on who you ask." Dunn shrugged. "Either way, you're gonna help me now."

"Last time I *helped* you, I got myself into a bit of a pickle." Michael smirked, despite the ever-present pressure of the device Livingston Shaw had grafted to his spine—his punishment for bringing Dunn in alive instead of carrying out his kill order. "I think I'm finished helping you."

"Did you ever wonder why he sent you after me?" Dunn said as he turned, giving Michael his back. "Why he *had* to?" Lifting the shirt he wore, he revealed a neat, horizontal scar across his lower back, as thick and long as his finger.

Michael took his finger off the TAC's trigger, lowering it just enough so that he could see Dunn's back. He didn't have to ask what it was. He knew what the scar meant. Dunn had been chipped; now he wasn't. That's why Shaw had to issue the kill order instead of just making a phone call. He had to because there was no other way to get him.

Dunn had removed his own chip somehow.

"How? How did you do it?"

Dunn turned, lowering his shirt while giving him a grim smile. "Still think we don't have any business together?"

SIXTY-FIVE

Yuma, Arizona

As soon as she gave Croft the address where Vega had stashed Graciella Lopez and sent him on his way, Sabrina headed for her car. Instead of getting in and driving back to the station or going to find Santos to tell him that Alvarez was their guy and that he'd taken Ellie, she leaned in through the driver's door long enough to retrieve the red silk pouch Phillip had given her before slamming the door and resetting the lock. Church was across the lot, talking to the quartet of uniforms she'd rescued from Father Francisco's frightened flock.

Leaving her behind, Sabrina followed the path around the side of the building until she came to an unassuming door with nothing more than a shallow concrete slab to mark it as an entrance. Trying the door, she found it unlocked. Either what happened to the priest had come as a total surprise to him or he'd felt it was inevitable and taking precautions was a waste of time.

Or maybe the ol' padre felt like he deserved what was comin'.

Pushing the door open, she revealed a cramped, dimly lit studio. A twin bed pushed against the far wall. Next to it a squat, three-drawer chest served as both dresser and nightstand, books and a kerosene lamp within reach of the bed. A few feet away was the kitchen area and the building's only electricity. A minute length of counter housed a mini fridge, a bar sink, and what looked to be one of those toaster oven/coffeepot combos found in college dorm rooms. On top of it was a single-burner hot plate. Above the countertop was a shelf holding a table setting for one, stacked neatly, waiting for use next to a few sundry items. One of them was a box of loose-leaf tea.

Filling the coffeepot with water from the tap, she poured it into the tank and switched it on. A few seconds later, steam and hot water started to sputter and drip from the reservoir into the waiting pot.

What do you think you're doing, darlin'?

"I'm shutting you up," she snarled out loud, yanking the ceramic mug off the shelf. Setting it down, she jerked hard on the kitchen's lone drawer, sending the items inside scattering and rolling around its bottom.

I thought we decided that'd be a really bad idea.

Ignoring the voice inside her head, she rifled through the drawer's sparse contents. A spatula. A set of measuring spoons. Dangling from a short chain, set with a small hook at its top, was a stainless steel tea infuser. Pulling the last two items from the drawer she shut it before placing them next to the cup.

Think this through, now. You need me, remember?

Despite her shaking hands, Sabrina smiled as she reached into her pocket and pulled out the pouch. Using the tablespoon, she scooped a measure of tea from the pouch, filling the infuser before clicking it closed. She placed it in the cup, hooking the short length of chain over its lip. "Yeah, you keep saying that but you haven't told me why. Why do I need you, Wade?" It was the first time she'd addressed the voice inside her head by name and doing so tipped her over the edge. She was acknowledging that he was more than a figment of her traumatized imagination. More than a PTSD-fueled hallucination constructed out of survivor's guilt and fear.

She was admitting he was real.

The coffeepot let out a final, steamy gasp, signaling it was finished. She reached for it. "Real or not," she said, carefully pouring the carafe of hot water over the infuser, "I don't need you."

Yes, you do. You need me. You get rid of me, you'll never find him.

"I already found him." She gave the tea infuser an impatient dunk. "I know who he is and I'm going to stop him, just like I stopped you."

You don't really believe that. You want to stop him? You need me to do it.

Instead of answering him, Sabrina took her tea and carried it across the room. Reaching out, she placed it on the dresser to steep before pulling out her cell phone and the card Ellie had given her when they'd met here earlier. Dialing the number listed as her private cell, she listened to it ring and ring before her call was directed to voicemail. She hung up without leaving a message. Not ready to give up, she sent a text to Church.

Put a trace on Elena Hernandez's phone.

Don't ask. Just do it.

Settling in to wait, Sabrina studied the spines on the stack of books next to her cup. The Bible was sandwiched between *Leaves of Grass* by Walt Whitman and Hemingway's *The Old Man and the Sea.* At the bottom of the stack was a book, its spine worn and without title. Pulling it out she flipped it open. It was a journal. The realization turned her stomach and she immediately moved to close it. Setting it on her lap she looked at its smooth back cover. Seeing it, she realized that this was the book Father Francisco had been reading earlier when she'd found him in the prayer garden. That forced her to open the book again and had her flipping through its pages. Snippets of prayers jumped out at her. Scattered lines of poetry, some recognizable, some not. Random thoughts, obviously private, crowded the book's margins. Feeling like an intruder, Sabrina turned the pages fast, only half reading what was written. At the back of the book was an old photograph, taped to the inside of the back cover.

The picture was of a much younger Father Francisco. He was handsome, dark hair and eyes smiling at the camera. On either side of him were a pair of young women, arms wrapped around his waist, heads tilted, resting on his shoulders. The women were pretty, grinning widely for the camera. Behind them she could see the Vegas's sprawling ranch-style house, its front door flung wide open. People littered the background, holding plates of food and plastic cups.

Despite the fact that the photo was at least thirty years old, she recognized one of the women instantly. She pulled the picture from its mount and flipped it over. There, in a faded, ball-point scrawl, she found what she already knew.

Magda with Frank Vega and Amelia Macias
Photo taken by Gracie Lopez ~ 1979

SIXTY-SIX

VALERIE'S MOTHER STARED BACK at her from the picture in her hand. She'd been Amelia Macias then. No more than sixteen or seventeen, the photo had been taken years before marriage and children found her. She and the other girl posed happily with a young Father Francisco who, despite the obvious summer day captured on film, wore black pants and a black long-sleeved shirt that was closed at the collar. He'd already been enrolled in seminary when the photograph was taken. He was a Vega and he knew she was investigating his family. And yet he said nothing about his relation to them.

The padre's last name ain't what's important here, darlin'...

Sabrina shifted her attention to the other woman in the picture.

According to the inscription on the back of the photograph, her name was Magda. She was pretty. Long, dark hair flowing down her back, her light-colored eyes a startling contrast against her golden brown skin. She smiled for the camera, her face radiant, mouth stretched wide, flashing even, white teeth. At first glance, she looked happy but the harder Sabrina looked, the more she could see something … anxious about her.

Anxious? That girl looks downright desperate …

Magda wore a loose-fitting sundress, her bare arm wrapped around the young priest's waist. Looking at the image of Val's mother for comparison, she could see it. Where Amelia's arm casually stretched across his back, hand loose against his shoulder, Magda's arm curled tight around his waist, as if trying to pull him closer, her fingers digging into the dark fabric of Father Francisco's shirt. The young man beside her held on just as tight, the hand at Magda's waist gripped lightly, its fingers extended to gently caress the softly rounded belly she'd taken care to hide under the flowy fabric of her sundress. Magda had been pregnant, and if his body language was any indication, Father Francisco was the father.

"Coffee break?"

It took her a second to realize that the voice she was hearing wasn't inside her head. When she looked up she found Santos standing in the doorway that led out into the sanctuary, watching her. "Tea," she said picking the mug up off the dresser with her free hand. She blew gently across the rim of the cup, sending fragrant steam curling into the air. "Any luck on the canvass?"

Our boy is good. Too good to get spotted.

"A field worker noticed a dark-colored hatchback leaving the area around the time you called in the attack." Santos shrugged. "No plate number, no description of the driver."

In other words, no luck at all.

"Did you find something?" he said, eyeing the picture she held in her hand.

She set the mug down without taking a sip. "Just an old picture of Father Francisco," she said, flashing him the picture in her hand rather than try to hide it. "Who's Magda?"

Santos furrowed his brow. "Magda..." He peered at the picture in her hand, confused for a moment before recognition dawned. "Oh," he said, smiling at some memory that seeing the picture produced. "That's Magda Lopez."

The shared surname and the fact that she was the one who took the picture led Sabrina to take the leap. "Any relation to Graciella Lopez?"

"Yeah." Santos nodded his head, the recognition bleeding away, leaving a vague sort of sadness in its place. "Magda was her little sister."

Was.

Before Sabrina could ask what happened to her, Santos spoke again. "The techs are finishing up in the chapel. Dusting for prints proved to be a nightmare but they found a ball cap in the confessional. They're pretty sure they can get DNA off of it."

"Have them send it to our lab." Sabrina nodded like it was the first she'd heard of it. "We'll run it against all databases—including department personnel." It was the best she could do without coming right out and saying, *Hey, by the way, I'm pretty sure your partner is a serial killer.*

"What?" Like she knew they would, her words put the detective's back up. "You think the guy doing this a *cop*?" he said, his voice raising on the last word. "An hour ago you were convinced Paul Vega was our guy."

"And now I'm not," she said with a shrug. "You said it yourself—you've had a car sitting on Vega since he left the station and he hasn't left his house. We've got to consider the fact that he might not be our guy."

Santos scoffed at her. "And somehow that means our guy is one of *us*?"

"Wade Bauer raped and murdered nearly two dozen women— at least one of them right here in your backyard," she said, doing her level best to ignore the shame that crossed Santos's face. "And almost all of them while wearing the uniform." She stood, placing the picture on top of the book it'd been hidden in, setting both on the dresser next to her mug of tea. "No one is exempt from scrutiny."

Holy shit, darlin'. I think you made him cry.

"Whatever you say, Agent Vance." Santos nodded, rubbing a rough hand across his jaw, head angled away from her like she'd just popped him in it.

"Wait," she called out, stopping Santos in his tracks. "I didn't mean—"

"It's okay," he said to her, half turning in the doorway. "You're right. A badge doesn't make you a good guy. Matter of fact, it's a damn good place for a bad guy to hide. Doesn't make it any easier to swallow though." He jerked his chin at the steaming cup of tea next to her on the dresser. "I'll let you finish your break," he told her before disappearing through the door. As soon as he was gone, she lifted the cup.

I wouldn't if I were you. You won't find our boy on your own. Whether you want to admit it or not, you need me.

She lowered the mug slowly without taking a drink.

I'll help you. If you let me stay, I'll help you.

She stood, walking the tea to the sink to pour it down the drain. Pulling the drawstring on the pouch she'd left on the counter, she pocketed the rest of it.

You're gonna want to take that picture with you too, darlin'.

Sabrina slipped the photograph she'd found into her pocket next to the tea before following after Santos out the door.

SIXTY-SEVEN

CHURCH WAS WAITING FOR her when she exited Father Francisco's private room, sitting quietly in the back pew. And she wasn't alone. She and her companion were sitting close, knees touching, heads bent together as they spoke quietly. As intimate as the scene was, Sabrina got the distinct feeling that they were arguing.

"*On ne nasha sem'ya,*" Church hissed at the man in Russian, leaning in even closer as her hand landed on the man's knee. "*My ne obyazany yemu nichego.*"

"You gonna introduce me to your friend?" she said, walking up the center aisle toward the pair. The church was deserted now that CSU was finished and it was still considered an active crime scene. "I mean, it's only fair considering this douche bag has been following me all day."

The guy from the stairwell sat back, draping an arm over the back of the pew. "I was wondering if you saw me," he said, mouth curved in the kind of smile that made Sabrina want to choke him.

Let's hate 'im, darlin'.

347

"Shut up," she growled before jabbing a finger in the man's direction, "and *you*—who are you?" She shifted her glare to Church before he had a chance to answer. "Who is he?"

Church sighed, "Simmer down, Kitten, I—"

"I swear to God, if you call me *kitten* again, I'm going to shove my foot so far up your ass, my toes are gonna tickle your tonsils." Sabrina took a cleansing breath and let it out slowly. "Now—who the fuck is he?"

"This is Jared," Church said, holding out a hand between them like she was making a formal introduction. "Jared, this is the woman you've been so ineptly stalking—FBI Agent Claire Vance," she said carefully, gaze sharp and angled upward, silently telling her two things. Whoever he was, this man hadn't been invited and he was not someone Church trusted with the truth.

"My pleasure, Agent Vance." The man held out his hand for her to shake, his tone telling her he didn't believe for one second she was in the FBI. "You'll forgive my earlier curiosity. Korkiva has told me almost nothing about you."

"Almost nothing? Well then, you're ahead of the game because I have no idea who you are." Etiquette forced Sabrina to give his hand a few pumps with her own before immediately taking a step back. "Whenever you're finished here, I need to speak with you. Privately," she said, flicking a look in the man's direction.

"We *are* finished." Church stood. "Good-bye, Jared."

The man about to be left behind seemed to disagree. "You still haven't answered my question, *mladshaya sestra,*" he said, reaching out to grab her hand.

Church gently pulled herself free, shaking her head. "The answer is no, Jared," she told him, her tone sad but firm. "It will always be no."

"I'm sure *nasha sem'ya* will be sorry to hear that." The man smiled up at them both. "If you change your mind... you know where we are."

Sem'ya was a word Sabrina recognized. It meant family.

"I'll never change my mind," Church said, taking her by the arm to pull her toward the atrium. "My answer will always be no."

Sabrina threw a last glance over her shoulder as she and Church stepped through the door. The man was out of his seat, standing in the aisle they'd just vacated, watching them leave, that same easy smile on his face. But the light of it never reached his eyes.

———

"Did you find Alvarez?" Sabrina said as soon as they made it past the door. The uniform posted next to it was on his phone, probably trying to find out who his replacement would be.

"I found his phone," Church said, her attention divided between their conversation and the man still inside the chapel. "It pinged at the station when I ran the search. He probably dumped it in his desk drawer before he left."

There was only one reason he'd do that: Alvarez didn't want to be found. "Okay..." she said, trying to keep calm. "How about Elena Hernandez? Did you find her?"

"I had even less luck with her." Church shook her head. "Phone's shut off completely. There's nothing to ping."

"But you can triangulate the last call." Sabrina swiped a hand over her face, wiping away the thin film of sweat and grime that'd collected on her skin in the handful of seconds they'd been outside. It was past seven o'clock in the evening. They had another hour before twilight was gone. "The phone doesn't have to be on to do that. You can access her phone records and find out where she was when she made or received her last call, right?"

"What is going on, Sabrina?" Church said, reaching out to grip her arm. "What haven't you told me?"

The main door to the sanctuary swung open and the man Church introduced to her as Jared walked through it, breezing past the uniform on guard like he owned the place. In response, the cop glanced at him, brow slightly furrowed. "Agent Vance? Aimes?" he called across the lot to them, gesturing toward the man who'd just exited the building.

"It's okay," she answered, giving the uniform a reassuring smile. Jared waved good-bye to her in response. "It is okay, isn't it?" she said, addressing Church under her breath. "I don't need to worry about that guy being left alone in the middle of a crime scene, do I?"

"No." Church shook her head. "Jared doesn't care enough about you or your investigation to make trouble," she said, watching him climb into a nondescript sedan and drive away.

"Really?" she said, voice raised slightly in disbelief. "Because he cared enough about me to follow me all morning."

"He wasn't following you to *follow you*. He was following you to be a dick," Church said, waving a dismissive hand between them. "A nosey, annoying dick."

"Oh ..." Sabrina said, suddenly understanding. "He's your brother."

"What he is, is irrelevant," Church said coldly, closing the subject. "You sent Croft to find Graciella Lopez. Probably not the smartest thing you've ever done."

"What else was I supposed to do?" Sabrina said, throwing up her hands. "I need answers and I need them now. He's got Ellie and if I don't find her—"

Church's hand reached out, wrapping around Sabrina's bicep. "*Ellie?*" she said sharply. "Awfully familiar for someone you just met yesterday."

Tell her, darlin'. Maybe if she knew who her big sister is, she'd understand how serious this whole thing is.

"Elena Hernandez." Sabrina sighed. "She's Valerie's little sister," she said in a rush, answering the obvious question. "And no, she doesn't know who I am. She hasn't seen me in nearly twenty years, aside from those fuzzy newspaper pictures."

Church narrowed her eyes at her anyway. "I think you've got some explaining to do, Kitten. Start talking."

SIXTY-EIGHT

SHE RECOGNIZED HIM.

It'd been different with Rachel. She'd been terrified, just like the rest of them. And like the rest of them, she'd looked him right in the eye and seen a stranger. Even when he told her who he was, that she'd known him her whole life, all she did was cry and scream and beg him not to kill her.

But Elena didn't need to be told. She'd known who he was. After all these years, she'd recognized him. It should've brought him some measure of satisfaction, knowing she finally remembered him. It should've, but it didn't. What it did was make him angry.

Years of being all but invisible to her and her snotty clique of friends. Being ignored so completely there were times he'd begun to doubt his own existence. He'd been no one to them—less than no one. A shameful secret none of them knew. An unfortunate fact no one could deny. That she recognized him now, after all this time, told him the truth. She'd seen him. Even when she'd pretended not to, she'd *seen* him. She'd just been too much of a coward to admit it.

She was a coward then and she was a coward now—pretending to be unconscious while he stood over her. Or at least trying to. The slight, uneven hitch in her breathing gave her away and it made him smile.

She'd fought hard, not that it mattered. She ended up bound and tossed into the trunk of his car, just like the rest of them. Tasers really were one of the better inventions of the twentieth century.

Says you. Me? I prefer my girls a bit more lively...

He crouched down beside her, setting the bolt gun on the floor within easy reach. "Elena," he said her name softly, pleased to see the sound of his voice so close frightened her. "I know you're awake and that you can hear me." He reached out to touch her, gently moving the dark length of hair that fell across her cheek. The brush of his fingers against her skin made her flinch. "I'd like you to answer my question."

Her eyelashes fluttered in response, moisture gathering at the rim of them, but she kept them closed. Lifting the bolt gun he'd set down, he pulled on the knob at its top until he heard a loud *click*. She flinched again, tears slipping past the seal of her closed lids to collect against the bridge of her nose.

"You were supposed to be with her that night. Wade and I had plans for both of you. I wanted Rachel. She was a bitch and needed to be taught a lesson, but Wade... he wanted you," he said, confiding in her. "He almost took your big sister once—" He pressed the bolt gun against her temple, digging until the tip of it all but disappeared. "But she slipped through his fingers. Just like you did," he said, and her eyes popped open—whether it was from the pressure against the side of her head or his mention of her sister, he didn't know. "There she is," he said, on a soft sigh. "I need you to stop being stubborn and answer my question, please."

"I haven't heard a question yet," Elena said, her voice rough from hours of silence. "All I've heard, so far, is you postulating like a lunatic."

"Careful," he said quietly. "It's not nice to call names."

"Fuck you." Her eyes rolled in her head so she could give him a sidelong glance. "You're going to kill me anyway so how about you just get it over with."

He pushed even harder against her temple, so hard her eyelids fluttered in response.

You're the one who needs to be careful, boy. You're letting this little cooze get the best of you.

"You're right," he said, easing up. "You're right, I'm sorry." He sat back on his heels with a nod, dragging the bolt gun with him as he went.

Just ask her again so we can move on to the fun stuff.

"Don't rush me," he said quietly. "She needs to understand *why* she was chosen. *Why* I'm going to do what I'm about to do."

It's time to take the training wheels off, boy. You chose her for the same reason you chose the rest of them. Because you're—

"I understand why," Elena said from where he'd tossed her on the floor. "It's because you're a psychopathic whackjob—"

"*Shut up*," he screamed at her, lunging forward to wrap both hands around her neck. "Shut. The. Fuck. Up." He squeezed, slamming her head into the cement floor, punctuating each word. Her eyes bulged, bound hands flailing uselessly as she brought them up to try to push him away. "Say you're sorry," he hissed in her face. "Say, 'I'm a rude little bitch and I'm sorry for interrupting your conversation.'"

Silence.

"Elena…" He eased off, his hands softening around her throat. Red, angry welts glared up at him, already turning purple around their edges. "Elena?" he said again, pushing her chin with the tips of his fingers. He watched as her head flopped listlessly to the side. Something thick and dark glistened in her hair. Blood.

You're one dumb sonofabitch, you know that? This little girl just beat you at your own game. Course, she had to go and die to do it.

SIXTY-NINE

SHE TOLD CHURCH EVERYTHING.

She didn't want to. Trusting Church went against everything she knew about Livingston Shaw's former number-one operative, but she didn't see where she had much choice.

You've got a choice. You've got me, darlin'.

"Let me get this straight," Church said, turning away from the passenger window she'd been staring through while Sabrina explained everything on their way to the station. "Elena, the crime scene tech, is Valerie's little sister? Who happened to be the childhood bestie of Rachel Meeks, victim number four?"

"Yes," she said, cutting a quick glance toward the woman next to her.

Church nodded. "Who, in 2000, was kidnapped and raped by your brother and Nulo, his little pet nutjob."

"Yes," she said through clenched teeth. "And he's my half-brother."

If Church realized she'd hit a nerve, she didn't seem to care. "And Stephanie Adams, victim number two, had your DNA under

356

her nails? Elena found it but no one believed her, so they scrubbed the report. Which is why we're both here? Because Ben got hold of the scrubbed report and decided you needed to get involved."

She sighed. "Yes."

"And you think Nulo, the guy who's running around killing women now, is Mark Alvarez. A cop … who has now, according to you, kidnapped Elena Hernandez." Church swiped a hand over her face. "Jesus H. Christ, Kitten, I'm dizzy."

Church dropped her hand and looked at her. "And what, exactly, does this have to do with the priest and his pregnant girlfriend?"

"I'm not sure yet," she admitted, pulling into the station parking garage. "As soon as Croft locates Graciella Lopez, that's the first thing he's going to ask her."

Cut her loose, darlin'. We don't need her.

"Look," Sabrina said, slamming the car into park. "You don't have to get involved any further. I don't need you here."

Church laughed in her face. "You're not stupid enough to really believe that, are you?" she said, shaking her head. "If the killer *is* Alvarez then you're definitely going to need me here. Because he's a cop. You don't have the resources to find him. I do."

I'm all the resource you need. No one knows our boy like I do.

"Yeah, you've also got orders to kill anyone who might recognize me, so if it's all the same to you—"

"He's not my brother," Church said. "At least not biologically." She looked away, aiming her gaze through the windshield to stare at the concrete wall in front of their car. "My mother and father were trained by the Russian government during the Cold War. They were paired together in The Program and she was impregnated with me before being embedded in America."

"Impregnated? You mean she was forced." The thought made her sick. She knew what it was like to not have control of your own body. "They made her get pregnant?"

"We were necessary to their cover. No one suspects a family." Church shrugged but Sabrina could tell that her apparent disgust stung her. "Jared was an orphan when he was taken into The Program. He was five years old and already understood his purpose. Why they'd been sent there."

Sabrina sat, transfixed by what Church was telling her, remembering what Livingston Shaw had told her about Church. He'd called her Korkiva but mentioned she preferred Courtney. That her parents had been Russian spies, and that they'd been rooted out and killed after being abandoned by their government at the end of the Cold War. "They were killed."

Church nodded. "After the Cold War ended, we were left behind," she said, seemingly unsurprised Sabrina already knew a measure of the truth. "Given up to the CIA by another family in exchange for immunity. You asked me why I didn't kill Valerie and her baby like I'd been ordered to. That's why." Church looked at her. Her eyes were dry. "I've done things—horrible things that I never lose sleep over—but I won't kill children and I won't kill their parents while they watch." She popped the door open, stepping a foot into the dark, sweltering heat. "That's why I let Valerie and her baby live. And I won't kill her little sister either."

You can't trust her. She's been trained to lie from the day she was born.

———

She found Santos at his desk, going over the files he and Church had put together while she was gone. A quick glance in its direction told her that Alvarez's desk was still empty. "Where's your partner?" she said, not really expecting an answer. No matter what he said to her earlier, Santos was angry she was no longer focused on Paul Vega as their prime suspect. To add insult to injury, she'd opened her suspect list to include local law enforcement. As soon as the rest of the precinct caught wind of it, she and Church could all but kiss their cooperation good-bye.

Santos shot her a glance before redirecting his attention to the file in his lap. "He called in while we were at Saint Rose's. Said something about following up on a lead."

"Does he do that a lot?" she said, refusing to slink away with her tail tucked. "Take off on his own?"

"I don't know. I guess so." Santos sighed, closing the file in his lap to trade it for another. "We have different investigative styles," he said, his admission reminiscent of what Alvarez had told her earlier of their partnership. He glanced up at her again, eyes narrowed like he was catching on to her line of questioning. "He's a good kid, he just likes to take a different approach to stuff sometimes."

Funny, ain't that what the padre called Nulo? A good kid . . .

"Does that include leaving his phone in his desk so that no one can get hold of him?"

Santos sat up a bit straighter, narrowing his eyes even more. "How do you know his phone is in his desk, Agent Vance?"

Her own phone vibrated against her rib cage and she reached for it, hoping it was Croft and that he'd found Graciella Lopez. "Excuse me," she said, thumbing the touchscreen as she turned her back on a glaring Santos without checking the number. "Hello?"

"Do you know who this is?" Male voice. One she recognized.

"Yes," she said, fighting the urge to shoot Santos a look over her shoulder.

"Good," he said quietly, like he was worried about being over-heard. "I think we should meet. Alone."

Church was in the conference room. She could see her through the blinds, honey-blond head bent over a stack of files. She'd be pissed if she took off again without her, but it couldn't be helped. Elena was out there somewhere. She needed to find her, and reading through files wasn't going to get the job done.

"I thought you'd never ask."

SEVENTY

Funny he'd ask you to meet him here, don't you think, darlin'?

Funny wasn't really the word she'd used to describe it. Ignoring the voice in her head, Sabrina pulled the car into an empty slot in front of Luck's truck stop and killed the engine.

No, I think funny is exactly *the right word to use. It's funny because this is where I—*

"If you don't shut the hell up," she snarled, hands wrapped around the steering wheel so tight it felt like she was strangling it, "I'm going to *eat* the entire contents of the pouch Phillip gave me, understand?"

Her threat was met with silence and she smiled.

She popped the door to let herself out of the car. "I'll take your silence as a yes," she said, crossing the lot toward the restaurant. "Now, don't open your goddamned mouth unless I ask you a direct question."

More silence.

"Fantastic."

Pulling the heavy glass door on its hinges, Sabrina was greeted by a blessed wall of refrigerated air. A different girl this time. A pretty Native American girl, the name *Paulette* stitched across the embroidered shamrock on her uniform, came at her from behind the counter. "Is a table—"

"I'm meeting someone," she said before the waitress could pull a menu from the hostess station, pointing toward the back of the restaurant.

Following her finger, the waitress stood a little straighter. "Of course," she said with a small nod.

Sabrina wound her way through the restaurant before depositing herself in the corner booth where Paul Vega waited for her, a half-eaten Denver omelet and a side of bacon on the plate in front of him.

"Should we wait for your brother?" She offered him a cheery smile. "Sorry, I meant lawyer."

"No." Vega's smile was decidedly less friendly. He shook his head, lifting his cup of coffee off the table between them. "Arturo doesn't know I'm here."

She looked out the large plate-glass window that overlooked the parking lot. There was no squad car in sight. No unmarked either. So much for the surveillance detail that was supposed to be sitting on Vega.

He seemed to know what she was looking for, offering her a humorless chuckle in consolation while cutting into his omelet with the side of his fork. "We did an employment survey a few years ago. Hired a company to go door-to-door and ask residents questions," he told her before forking the bite into his mouth. "Two cities. Nearly six hundred thousand people. Know what we found out?" he said around his mouthful of eggs, pointing the tines of his fork in

362

her direction like he really expected her to answer. When she didn't, he smiled. "That one in three people know someone employed by Vega Farms. One in five are either directly employed or related to someone employed by us. That's over a hundred thousand people who depend on me for their livelihood, Agent Vance. Fair or not, that fact affords me certain... allowances." He gave her a look that was almost apologetic. "No one followed me here."

"Allowance. Like torture? Kidnapping?" She placed her hands flat on the table in an effort to keep herself from jerking his fork out of his hand and sticking it in his eye. "How about rape? Is that on your list of allowances?"

"Come on..." He placed his fork on his plate. "You don't really believe I did those things. If you did, you wouldn't be here," he said, wiping his mouth with the napkin in his lap. "It's okay, Claire—Santos isn't here, you can admit it. May I call you Claire?"

"Maybe you didn't *physically* have anything to do with what happened to Rachel Meeks—then or now," she said, offering him an indifferent shrug. "But I think you know who did. I think you know and just... let it happen. At best, that makes you a coward. At worst, you're an accessory to a half dozen murders. Maybe more. And *no*, you can't."

"I invited you here as a gesture of goodwill and cooperation." He frowned at her. "If you're going to be rude—"

"Cooperation? Goodwill? So far, all I've experienced is a bunch of narcissistic grandstanding," she said, refusing to give him the apology he obviously expected. "What do you want?"

He sat quiet for a few seconds, probably deciding if he was going to continue to grace her with his presence or stick her with his bill. "Father Francisco is my uncle, Isabel's brother. But I suppose you

363

already know that," he finally said, watching her with the flat, dispassionate gaze of a shark.

She nodded. "He was attacked this afternoon. But I suppose you already know *that*." It didn't matter where or how he got his information. There were plenty of people who knew what had happened and any number of them could have called Vega and told him.

He lifted his cup and took a drink. "People think that the priesthood somehow exemplifies him, but he *is* just a man. We all make mistakes. He's no different."

She wanted to ask him if one of his personal mistakes happened to be keeping his mouth shut while a murderer ran loose in his city. Instead she sat back in her seat, her hand going to the pocket where she'd slipped the picture she'd lifted from Father Francisco's room. Pulling it out, she slid it across the tabletop. "Was one of your uncle's mistakes named Magda Lopez?"

Vega's eyes watched the photograph slide toward him, his expression unreadable. "She was Arturo's nanny." His finger tapped the piece of paper between them. "That's him, with his mother."

His mother, she noted. Not *our*. Paul Vega might have been raised by Isabel and Jorge Bautista but he'd never been accepted as their son.

In the background of the picture she caught a glimpse of a dark-haired child, no more than a year old, sitting on a woman's lap. A man stood over them, his face hidden by the wide brim of a cowboy hat. "I wasn't born yet."

Sabrina studied the picture from where she sat. The slight push of Magda Lopez's stomach against the baggy fabric of her dress. The way Father Francisco's fingers rested on her hip, the tips of them pressed into the baby bump she was so obviously trying to hide. Familiar, bordering on intimate.

Something prickled along her scalp an instant before everything came into focus, so sharp and swift she was nearly blinded by it. "Father Francisco isn't your uncle, is he, Vega?" she said quietly, watching the way her words affected him. "He's your father."

Vega didn't answer her. He just lifted his mug, taking a drink before setting it down with a careful *click*. "Magda Lopez experienced complications in childbirth," he said, choosing his words carefully. "Her sons survived—a miracle, the doctors said, but there was only so much miracle to go around. The first son killed her. The second son had to be cut from her womb. After she died."

Sons.

Magda had given birth to twins. Sabrina knew without asking which son he was. She could see it on his face. Paul Vega was the firstborn, the son Magda Lopez died giving birth to. "And their father?" she said, playing along. "What happened to him?"

Vega looked away. "The father went unnamed and the brothers were separated."

"You were given to the Bautistas—raised by your aunt and uncle alongside their son." She looked at the picture, past the trio of young faces, at the mother and child in the background. "That must've pissed your uncle off."

"Arturo's grandfather was a hard man," Vega said, skirting along the edge of admission. "Francisco was the only heir to the family business. When he entered the priesthood, Arturo's father, Jorge, rightfully expected the company to pass on to him and his own son when he married into the family." He swallowed hard against the memories his words stirred. "The existence of a male Vega heir would not have been welcomed by him, let alone two."

"But he had to take you in," she said, reading between the lines. "If he wanted to remain in good standing with your family. But only *one* of you. He'd only take one of you. You were chosen while your bother was abandoned."

He didn't answer her.

"What about *him*? Where did your brother go? Who took care of him?"

Again, he didn't answer her, either because he didn't know or because he was protecting him.

"He's out there and he's *pissed*." Her statement was met with more silence but she knew she was right. "At you for killing your mother and getting the life he didn't. At your father for denying his existence. That's why he targeted Rachel Meeks. To punish you."

"And it worked," Vega told her, baring his teeth in a semblance of a smile. "Everyone believed I raped her. Even my own—" He stopped himself short. "The only one who believed I was innocent was Graciella."

She thought about the way Father Francisco refused Vega communion the night before. The way people pointed and whispered as he left. The priest believed he was guilty of what happened to Rachel Meeks and so did the rest of them.

"That's why you sent her away; because she knows the truth," she said. "That your twin brother is a murdering psychopath. You were afraid she'd tell the truth."

Vega's gaze came up, pinning her with a glare so hot and sharp she was sure he'd have hit her if he thought he could get away with it. "I love Graciella. I sent her away to *protect* her from him."

"Who is he?" She leaned toward him, her tone low and urgent. "You have to know you can't protect them both, Vega," she said, tapping the photograph between them. "Tell me his name. His *real* name."

"I don't know it." Vega shook his head. "I never knew it ... I never knew *him*. The night we were born was the last time I was ever with him. The truth is, he could be anyone."

SEVENTY-ONE

THERE WERE VOICES. PEOPLE talking, murmuring quietly. Two of them. Men, somewhere nearby. She thought maybe she'd fallen asleep at her desk again. It happened sometimes when she was working a case. She'd put her head down for a moment, waiting for results to pop up on her computer or for a uniform to deliver evidence, and end up sleeping through her lunch hour.

Nights were hard. Her mother's sleep schedule was erratic. Sometimes she'd go days without more than an occasional nap. It was exhausting.

On their last visit, the doctor prescribed her mom a sedative so she'd sleep through the night. "Fill the prescription, Ellie," he'd said, tearing the script off the pad before pressing it into her hand. "And give her the pills. You need sleep. You both do."

She'd taken the prescription and said thank you. She'd even filled it, but in the end, she let it gather dust in the back of the cabinet above the refrigerator. She never even opened the bag.

She told herself it was because she wasn't going to take the easy way. She wasn't going to drug her own mother to make her more manageable. The truth was a harder, more painful thing to admit.

The truth was that, sometimes, in the small hours before sunrise, her mother was her mother again. Not the mother who needed constant supervision. Not the mother who couldn't recognize her own daughters. She was her *real* mother. The one who took care of her. The one who told her everything was going to be okay and spent every day making sure that everything was.

The first time it'd happened, she thought it was a dream. She'd woken to the smell of tortillas toasting on the griddle, Vincente Fernandez on the living room stereo. She'd come out of her room to find her mother standing in the kitchen in her bathrobe, stretching tortilla dough and singing along to the music.

"*Mamá?*"' she'd said, looking at the microwave's digital display. It was two in the morning.

"Morning, *mija*," her mother said, leaning over to drop a kiss, a quick press of her flour-dusted cheek against her own. "Did you study for your math test?"

"It's Saturday," she said automatically. The doctor told her that it was best to go along with her mother's delusions. That it'd be less confusing for her. Less traumatic for them both.

Her mother's eyes clouded briefly before she smiled. "That's right," she said, pressing her into her chair. "Your test isn't until Monday."

She nodded, throat swollen with grief while she watched her mother butter the stack of tortillas she'd already made. It wasn't Saturday. It was Thursday and she'd have to get up for work in a few hours but she didn't care. She let her mother press her into one of the chairs that surrounded their battered breakfast table and ate buttered tortillas until her stomach hurt.

Watching her mother move around the kitchen with an easy confidence she'd always taken for granted, she listened to her chatter on about the errands she'd have to run later in the day. Taking her dress shopping for the school dance or picking Val up from work.

She never told her sister. It was the main reason she didn't want Val to come home. She told herself it was because she was afraid if Valerie saw her like that, she'd insist on upping her medication or worse, putting her in an assisted-living facility. But that wasn't it. Not really. She didn't want her sister to come home because in those brief, sporadic times, she had her mother back and she didn't want to share her. She didn't keep her sister away because she was afraid; she kept her away because she was selfish.

"Where is she now?" Val had asked the other night, her voice tight with worry. It was the Feast of Saint Rose and her mother had insisted on attending midnight mass. "You can't just let her—"

"Relax, *Mamá's* fine," she'd said, moving down the center aisle of the church, heading toward the stoup. "Believe it or not, I know what I'm doing."

"Really?" Val had said, indignation adding weight to her words. "Dr. Hayward called me. He thinks that maybe it's time—"

"Fuck him." She said it loud—too loud. Several people in the back of the communion line turned and scowled at her. She scowled back. "Dr. Hayward doesn't get to decide. He isn't her family. We are."

"I know that, Ellie." Val sighed. "I'm not saying he's right. I'm just saying we should talk about it. Make these decisions together. You and me—not just *you*."

"Fine. *You and me.* We're not putting her in a home," she said, her words heavy and final. "We can talk, but we're not talking about *that.*"

"Okay, okay..." Val sighed again, like talking to her made her tired. "Maybe I can come—"

"You can't," she said quickly. "You're pregnant, remember?"

"Can I at least *talk* to her?" her sister said, sounding sad.

"She's in line to receive communion." The fact that it was true did nothing to lessen the guilt she felt.

"Alone?"

"No," she said, guilt instantly replaced by annoyance. "She's not alone." She craned her neck to see around the line of people that stretched down the aisle. Her mother had her arm anchored through the crook of Agent Vance's elbow, her head cocked toward her while she chattered. "She's made a friend."

"A friend?" Now Val sounded torn between alarm and amusement. "Is this friend an actual person?"

"Sort of. She's an FBI agent, here to help with a case, but *Mamá* thinks..." Like she knew she was being watched, Agent Vance turned and looked at her. "*Mamá* thinks she's you," she said.

"What?"

"I know, right? It's weird," she said. "She started crying when she saw her, said, 'You came back.'"

"The FBI is there?" Val was quiet for a moment, absorbing what she'd heard. "What kind of case, Ellie?"

"A murder," she said evasively.

"*A* murder? As in one." Val sounded skeptical. As the wife of a cop, she knew the FBI wasn't usually called in unless a case met certain criteria. A single murder was too average for them to be bothered with.

"Okay, more than one." She hadn't told her sister anything. Not about Rachel being abducted. Not about finding Melissa's DNA under a victim's fingernails. Val already worried too much about her ability to take care of their mother. The last thing Ellie needed was her big sister losing her mind over her job. "It's a border-town thing," she lied. "No big deal."

Val didn't seem to be buying it. "What does she look like?" There was something strange about her sister's tone. Something that went beyond worry. But she instantly dismissed it. Val was a worrier. She also insisted on treating her like she was twelve and incapable of doing anything without her breathing down her neck.

"I don't know, Val—she looks like an FBI agent. Nothing like you," she said, a second before her cell issued a beep. "Look, my phone hasn't seen a charger all day. I'll call you tomorrow…"

———

The voices were close, the sound of them pulling her back to the present, rising and falling in what sounded like an argument. She tried to rouse herself. The attempt at movement sent a deep, nauseating pain rolling over her. That's when she remembered. She wasn't at work. She hadn't fallen asleep at her desk. She'd gone to the place where Rachel'd been held. Lured outside by her car alarm and taken. Dragged into the dark by the same man who'd killed her former best friend. He was going to do to her what he'd done to Rachel and there was nothing she could do about it.

She tried to lift her hand to her head, searching for the damage that had to be there, but her arms were heavy. Too heavy to lift. Alarm bells started to go off, faint and distant. The rolling wave of pain, sharpened by panic, pulled at her—tossing her further and dragging her closer until she was spinning inside her own skin. She was dizzy, her chest too tight to take a breath. Vomit pushed at the back of her throat, threatening to choke her. She couldn't die. Not like this. She hadn't even called Val back like she'd promised. She'd—

Stop.

Ellie tried to open her eyes again. To lift her arms so she could push herself up. She couldn't stay here. She needed to run. Fight. She didn't know which, but she knew she couldn't just lay here and wait for him to kill her. Or worse. There was always worse.

The sickness in her belly started to swell again, fed by terror and the certainty she was never going to see her mother again. She was going to die screaming, just like Rachel. Just like Melissa.

She throat threatened to release a sob.

Stop. Don't move. He already thinks you're dead. Just be still…

She remembered now. He'd bashed her head against the floor. Eyes bulging, hands wrapped around her throat while he screamed at her.

"Say you're sorry," he hissed in her face. *"Say, 'I'm a rude little bitch and I'm sorry for interrupting your conversation.'"*

But he hadn't been talking to anyone. There'd been no one there to have a conversation with. No one but him. But there was someone here now. She could hear them still arguing. About her. About how he'd messed everything up and killed her. About how he'd let the one before her get away.

"First Maggie and now Ellie."

Despite his casual tone, the man talking sounded angry.

"You're gettin' sloppy, boy. Forgettin' everything I ever taught you…"

They thought she was dead, but it wouldn't last. Any second now, they were going to stop fighting long enough to realize that he hadn't killed her—and then he was going to finish the job.

SEVENTY-TWO

It was almost nine o'clock at night and she'd heard nothing from Croft.

Let's be honest, darlin'. You sent that boy on a fool's errand to get him out of the way.

It was a four-hour drive from Yuma to the tiny beach town of San Felipe. Even if Croft did manage to make it there, there was no real guarantee he was going to be able to get her the information she needed.

We both know he ain't comin' through. At least not in time to save poor Ellie. That's why we're here.

Running a reverse trace on Ellie's phone number had taken about two minutes and provided her with the address to a neat tract home in a quiet subdivision on the other side of town. Driving there had taken less than twenty minutes. She'd been sitting in her car across the street from it for another ten, waiting for Croft to call so she wouldn't have to do what she knew had to be done.

Ellie can't hold out much longer, darlin'. Time to put on your big girl panties and get the job done.

"Who lives here?"

Sabrina cast a sidelong glance at the passenger seat. Paul Vega sat beside her, studying the house across the street with a mixture of curiosity and dread. She followed his gaze, letting hers land on the large front window. The curtains that covered it twitched quickly at their center, so fast she'd almost been able to convince herself that it'd been the air conditioner kicking on inside the house that moved them and not something else.

Almost.

She forced herself to open the car door and get out. Vega didn't move. "Do you need me to help you out of the car?" she said, leaning down to glare at him through the open door. "Because I'd be happy to."

"I'd like to see you try," he muttered as he reached for the door handle.

"I seriously doubt that," she answered, watching him pop the door and reluctantly pull himself from the car. Vega rounded the front of the car, falling into step beside her as they crossed the street and walked up the driveway.

"I've told you everything I know," he said to her, eyes glued to the front of the house. "I don't know what else I can do to help you."

"You can call Graciella and ask her to tell you what your brother's real name is," she said, raising her knuckles to knock on the front door.

"I told you," he said, irritated by her refusal to let it go, "there's no phone service."

Sabrina wasn't sure she believed him but she didn't push it. He was standing here willingly instead of threatening to call his brother and have her arrested for kidnapping him. At this point, she had to take what she could get.

"Just relax, Vega," she told him. "We're here to see an old friend of your mother's."

Almost immediately, there was a shuffling inside the house, followed by the scrape of the dead bolt being turned inside the door. It opened and Amelia Hernandez's face appeared in the crack between it and its frame. "*Mija*," she said, beaming widely at her for a second before casting her gaze toward the stoop behind her, her smile fading. "Where are my babies? You didn't bring them?"

Jason and Riley. Amelia was talking about Sabrina's siblings like they were still toddlers and not the young adults they'd become in her absence. Sabrina shook her head, forcing a smile onto her face. "They're at home with Ellie," she said, thinking fast on her feet. "She's sitting for me today, remember?"

The smile returned and she looked relieved. "That's where she is," she said, reaching out to take her hand. "I can never keep track of that girl's schedule." She tugged on her hand, pulling her inside. "Come in, come in …"

Sabrina cast Vega a look over her shoulder—*stay close*—before she allowed herself to be led into the house. Beyond the door was a tidy living room and an open archway that led into what looked like an eat-in kitchen. The warm smells of tortillas and coffee wafted toward her, opening an aching hole inside her chest. "It smells like you've been busy," she said and Amelia laughed.

"Busy is good, *mija*," Amelia said, pulling her through the open doorway. "Busy keeps us fed." She left Sabrina standing at the kitchen table, staring at its occupants while trying to remember how to breathe.

Well, hells bells, darlin'—we really walked into it this time, didn't we?

"Sit down, sit down ..." Amelia said, before looking at Vega as if seeing him for the first time. "Valerie, you didn't tell me Melissa had a boyfriend," she said, her tone teasing while she retied her apron around her waist. She'd hoped that seeing Vega would trigger a memory for Amelia, but she was looking straight at Vega with no sign of recognition. But none of that mattered. Not anymore.

Valerie sat at the kitchen table, hands wrapped around a glass of water, staring at her as if she were seeing a ghost, her face washed white with shock.

Across from her sat Mark Alvarez.

"I didn't tell you because I didn't know, *Mamá*," Val finally said, her voice sounding faint and far away. "Melissa likes her secrets, you know that."

Amelia laughed. "You both do. Secrets are what teenage girls do best," she said before turning her attention toward the stove. Humming softly, she placed a flatted round of tortilla dough on the griddle to cook. "Val, Melissa solved our mystery. Ellie is at her house, watching the twins." She shot her a relieved smile. "We've been a little worried she'd gotten into some sort of trouble."

"She's fine, Mrs. Hernandez," Sabrina lied, her attention focused on Alvarez. He was focused on Vega. He looked angry, hands pressed flat against the table, glaring up at him. "Who's your friend?"

Amelia glanced up, aimed her gaze at Alvarez for a moment. "Oh, this is Ellie's friend from school. He stopped by to visit. He's a nice boy but he's always been a bit shy," she said, giving him an encouraging smile. "It's okay, Nulo. Say hello."

SEVENTY-THREE

DESPITE AMELIA'S ENCOURAGEMENT, ALVAREZ didn't say a word. Didn't move. He was still wearing the same clothes he'd had on the last time she'd seen him—khakis and a navy blue polo with the Yuma PD insignia embroidered over his left breast, his service weapon, a Glock 22, secured in his holster. He looked like he'd simply gotten lost on his way to the station break room, not like he'd just stomped a priest's face in and kidnapped someone.

"Hey, *Nulo*," she said, careful to keep her tone pleasant. "I've been looking everywhere for you."

Her greeting went unanswered. Big surprise.

"You need to take your mom into the living room," Sabrina said to Val quietly. Instead of doing what she asked, Val seemed to dig in deeper.

Uhh, darlin'. I got something to tell you and you aren't gonna like it.

"Can someone tell me what's going on?" Vega finally said, his tone telling her he was seconds away from bolting. "Who's Melissa?"

379

"My mother has Alzheimer's," Val said quietly while shooting her mother a quick look. Amelia was too absorbed in her kitchen duties to pay attention to what she was saying. "She thinks Agent Vance is an old friend of mine." Recovered, she shifted her gaze toward Sabrina, a carefully composed expression on her face, hand extended in front of her. "You are Agent Vance, aren't you? My sister told me how taken our mother was with you."

Listen to me, darlin'…

She nodded, taking the offered hand and shaking it like the woman in front of her was a total stranger. Drawing her hand back, she settled it on the grip of the Kimber that rode her hip, flicking a glance in Alvarez's direction. "Ms. Hernandez, I need you to, *please*, take your mother into the living room and wait for me there. Do you understand?"

Val's expression went from defiant to understanding in an instant, her gaze drifting across the table to land on the man in front of her. "Okay," she said, standing slowly to reveal a large, swollen belly. Holding her hand out to her mother, she smiled. "Come on, *Mamá*, let's go see if *Wheel of Fortune* is on."

Amelia cast her gaze around the kitchen, shaking her head. "I'm in the middle of—"

"Now, *Mamá*," Val said, softening the command with a smile. "Please."

Suddenly, Amelia looked confused, like she wasn't sure what was happening. Moving the griddle off the stove, she switched it off. "Okay…" She took Val's offered hand, allowing herself to be pulled along. "Have you seen Cuervo?" Amelia said to her daughter as she walked past her on her way out of the kitchen. "Ellie will be so upset if she doesn't come home."

She watched Alvarez bristle at the question. *Cuervo* was Spanish for crow. It was also the name that'd been engraved on the ID tag belonging to the mutilated cat Father Francisco found in the prayer garden last night. That must've been what he read in the report that set him off. Knowing they were close to figuring out that Ellie was on his kill list.

As soon as they were gone, Sabrina pulled her Kimber off her hip. "Take a seat, Vega," she said, "The three of us are going to have a talk."

Vega came into view, sliding into the seat Val had just vacated. Alvarez flicked his gaze as the man sitting across from him. Something passed over his face. Distaste, bordering on disgust.

In the next room, the television clicked on.

"Where's Ellie?"

Alvarez didn't answer. Didn't look at her either. He just sat there, hands resting on the table in front of him, eyes straight ahead, hooked into Vega while his expression grew darker and darkened by the second. That's when she noticed the safety strap on his holster was unsnapped. She hadn't seen him do it.

Darlin', we gotta talk…

"There's something you need to understand about me, Alvarez," she said quietly, her tone held just above the gameshow chatter drifting in from the next room. "I'm not a patient person and I frustrate easily. Neither of those things are working in your favor right now." She thumbed the Kimber's safety off. "Where is she?"

"Why are you asking me?" Alvarez turned his head just a bit, lowering his gaze before aiming it at her face. His hands twitched on the table in front of him, inching closer to its edge.

Darlin'…

Sabrina sighed, ticking the barrel of the Kimber upward just a bit, aiming it at his knee. The movement stopped him cold. "Also, I hate repeating myself."

"Think about it," Alvarez said, tone tight with anger. "If I knew where Ellie was, do you really think I'd be here?"

"I don't know," she said, walking toward him. "You've kinda gone off the rails today, Nulo." Aiming the barrel of the Kimber center mass, Sabrina stooped slightly to lift the Glock off his hip. "Not that you're exactly a poster boy for stability under normal circumstances."

"What are you talking about?" he said, watching her as she tucked his service weapon into the small of her back. His eyes bounced up to her face. "What happened?"

"You tell me, Nulo."

"Please," he sighed, hands curling into fists. "I need you to stop calling me that."

"Why?" she said, leaning against the counter. "It's your name isn't it?"

"No, it isn't," he said, tone low and insistent. "My name is Mark Alvarez."

"But that's not who you really are, is it?" She looked at Vega. He was staring at Alvarez like he was barely grasping what was happening around him. "It's just a made-up name you gave yourself to try to restore the identity they took from you."

Melissa, I need you to listen now...

"Who's *they*?" he said, voice raised, face pale. "I don't know what or who you're talking about. I just came by to see Ellie—"

"You're lying," she said through clenched teeth. She thought of the pair of women in the living room. "You didn't come here to see Ellie because you *took* her. Just like you were going to take her mother."

"What?" He cut a look at Vega before shaking his head. "Why would I take Ellie's mother?"

"Because she's the only one left to know who you really are."

Alvarez narrowed his eyes at her. "And who is it that you think I really am, Agent Vance?"

"I think you're a kid they used to call Nulo," she said in a conversational tone that was at total odds with the tense set of her jaw. "I think you're the guy who raped Rachel Meeks." From the corner of her eye, she could see Vega stiffen in his seat and she shook her head at him, a warning to stay put. "I think you're the guy who's killed a half dozen women between here and Tucson. I think you're the guy who planted evidence on Stephanie Adams to lure me here."

"No." Despite his denial, it was obvious the name and her accusations affected him. He was shaking, gaze pinned to the table in front of him. "I'm Mark. Detective Mark Alvarez with the Yuma Police Department. I didn't hurt anyone. I didn't *take* anyone."

"Sure you did, Nulo."

He shook his head, short choppy twists of his neck like he was trying to shake her loose. "Stop calling me that."

"You did all those things," she said, chipping away at the façade he clung to. "They needed to pay for what they'd done to you. They threw you away. Pretended you never existed. I understand why you'd want to punish them. Your brother. Your father. They all abandoned you. Left you to rot … but what did any of those women ever do to you?"

Alvarez's hand curled into fists, knuckles pressing into the hard surface of the table. "Shut up."

"You know what I think?" she said, pushing at him with her words. "I think you killed those women because they got the second chance your mother never did."

Melissa …

Alvarez shot up from the table, the chair slamming into the wall with the force of it. "I don't have a brother. Or a mother and father. I don't have anyone. I never did."

"That's not entirely true, is it, Nulo?" she said, levering herself off the counter to face him down. "You had Wade."

Melissa …

"You were there. You saw him the night he left Melissa Walker in the garden at Saint Rose," she said to him, piecing it together as she went. "You saw what he did to her and you *liked* it."

"No." He shook his head, looking at Vega, trying to find someone who believed him. "*No*, I saw someone, but I—"

"You reached out to him. Wrote him letters and he wrote you back. Told you things." She tightened her grip on the butt of the Kimber, so tight she couldn't feel her fingers. "He made you feel like you belonged. Taught you how to kill."

"That *never* happened. I never wrote those letters," Alvarez said, unclenching his hands. "When I saw them, how they were signed, I knew—"

"That it was only a matter of time before you were caught. You knew we were working on finding Graciella. She was your aunt. The one who rented you the PO box. When you saw those letters, you left the station. You went to Saint Rose to kill Father Francisco—*your* father." She smiled at him, the lift of her mouth feeling predatory. "I'm sorry to have to tell you that you didn't quite get the job done."

Melissa …

384

"What?" Alvarez looked like he'd just been punched in the gut and he turned, wheeling his gaze toward Vega, who'd been sitting quietly, growing more and more pale with each word spoken. "What is she saying?"

"He protected you," she said. "When I asked him who you were, your father refused to tell me, even though he had to have known who you were. What you'd done. He protected you, and you stomped his face in."

Alvarez sank into the chair he'd just vacated, shaking his head, his gut-punched stare replaced by one that said he was seconds away from vomiting.

Sabrina!

The word—her own name, shouted within the confines of her head—stopped her cold, forcing her to listen.

It ain't him. This guy, whoever he is … he ain't him.

SEVENTY-FOUR

ELLIE OPENED HER EYES to the dark. The kind of dark that can convince you that you've gone blind. Panic edging in on her. She couldn't see. Her hands were still bound and she raised them to her face. Felt her eyes. They were open. Staring blindly.

Pushing herself against the wall, she forced herself into a sitting position, pressing her bound hands into the floor to steady herself. The movement made her dizzy and she pressed her cheek against its cool surface. Face pressed so close, she caught the scent of something she'd smelled before.

Blood—both old and new. The stench of it seeped out of the walls.

Even though she was blind, she closed her eyes, forced herself to keep breathing. To not scream. She used her other senses to ground herself. The wall beneath her cheek was rough. Made of cinderblock. Possibly concrete. Both were used often in desert construction, so wherever she was, it had to be close to home. She noticed again how quiet it was. No air conditioner's distant hum. No whirl of fan blades. It was August in Arizona. Too hot outside to be without either. Composed, she dragged her feet underneath her. Another wave of dizziness washed over her, threatening to knock her back down.

Underground. It made sense. Yuma was home to multiple military bases and boasted one of the world's largest proving grounds. Nearly fifteen hundred miles of terrain, riddled with underground bunkers built as far back as the 1950s.

She could be almost anywhere.

Using her shoulder, she pushed herself up until she was standing straight. The back of her head peeled off the wall, coming away wet and sticky. Her gut was suddenly seized by a violent nausea and she lurched over just as her stomach rebelled, pushing its contents into her throat.

She took a shuffling step forward, bound hands stretched out in front of her.

She took step after shuffling step across the room, until her outstretched hands touched against one of the walls that surrounded her. No, not the wall. This surface was smooth, not rough like the cement walls she'd been pushed against. The door. She'd found the way out. She wrapped her fingers around the door handle and jerked. Nothing happened, the handle was fixed. Unmoving.

It was locked.

Reaching down, she fumbled for a few seconds, her arms bound and jerked askew, barely able to hook her fingertips into the front pocket of her pants. Pushing her finger deeper into her pocket, she felt it. A paper clip.

She was getting out of here.

SEVENTY-FIVE

"Yes, I was there that night, at Saint Rose," Alvarez said, shaking his head, bouncing his gaze between her and Vega. "And I saw what had been done to that girl—but I never saw the guy who did it."

He was talking about her. Melissa. Alvarez was admitting to being a witness to what happened to her that night but denying he ever saw Wade. It didn't make sense.

It'd make perfect sense if you'd just listen to me, darlin'. He ain't the guy.

"*That girl* had a name."

Sabrina looked up and over to see Val standing in the doorway, hand rubbing over her protruding belly in a circular motion. She was looking at Alvarez like she wanted to deck him. He must have seen it too because he started to stutter. "I know, I just—I mean—"

Sabrina jammed the Kimber back into the holster on her hip and wiped a hand over her mouth. "Ms. Hernandez, please, if you would just go back—"

"No." Val shot her a look that said she was seconds away from blowing her cover before she wheeled around and pinned Alvarez with her dark gaze. "Her name was Melissa Walker and she was my friend."

"I know," he offered. "I remember and I'm sorry."

"Never mind that," she said, shooting Val a *stay out of it* glare. "Why were you there? What were you doing inside a church in the middle of the night?" she said. She'd gotten the story from Father Francisco but she wanted to see if Alvarez's account lined up with his.

"I . . ." He trailed off, his gaze skittering across the table, stopping when it landed on Vega. "I was hiding from my uncle," he said, his admission followed by a humorless laugh. "At least I *thought* he was my uncle. I was told he was my only family."

"Why were you hiding from your uncle?" Sabrina said, leaning her hip against the counter before crossing arms over her chest.

"Because his favorite hobby was getting drunk and beating me until I couldn't walk." Alvarez looked away. "And that was when he was feeling generous."

"Is that why you killed him?" Sabrina said, forcing her tone to remain as flat and emotionless as possible. "Because he beat you?"

He looked at her then, gazed as rigid and fixed as his jaw. "The beating I could handle. It was the other stuff I couldn't take."

It wasn't an admission of guilt but it wasn't a denial either.

"What his name?" The question came from Vega. "Your uncle —who was he?"

"Tomas Olivero." Alvarez followed his answer with a short bark of harsh laughter. "He worked for your uncle as a field foreman for years. He was the right-hand man."

Tomas Olivero was the field foreman who'd found Rachel Meeks chained up in that abandoned pump house. They'd given Magda's second son to a trusted employee. One who'd never question his origin. Santos had mentioned Olivero was dead, but he hadn't told her how.

This is all sorts of fascinating, but how the hell is any of this gonna help?

"Did you kill him, Alvarez?" she said, tuning Wade out completely. "Did you kill your uncle?"

Shame lowered Alvarez's eyes, anchoring them into the table's smooth surface. "I wanted to, but—"

"But you didn't do it," she said, shaking her head. "You didn't kill him. You couldn't."

"It was a Friday night—payday. He'd gone out drinking... I found him in his truck after midnight, my field knife sticking out of his chest." Alvarez shook his head. "I was eighteen and I already knew how it'd go—everyone knew what he did to me. No one would believe I didn't do it."

You remember what that's like, don't you? Running away ... only, the way I remember it, you really did kill the guy who got after you.

"You ran." This came from Vega, who was listening to the story with a mixture of guilt and relief planted on his face. He'd been the lucky one. The chosen son, while his brother had been discarded and abused.

Alvarez nodded. "Yeah—Father Francisco gave me money and I bought a ticket to Tucson."

"That's when you became Mark Alvarez," she said, filling in the blanks. Buying fake papers was easy enough if you knew where to look. "Why did you come back? Why not *stay* in Tucson?"

"Ellie," he said, giving her a shrug. "She was in Tucson for training and recognized me. I worked with her father in the fields. She would come see him sometimes. After he died, she kept coming to see me in the fields until I left. She believed me when I told her I didn't kill my uncle and she convinced me to come home. Said no one would remember me and she was right—no one did."

"But someone *did* remember you." She looked at Vega, directing her next question at him. "What was *your* relationship with Father Francisco like?"

"It was an open family secret that he was my father," Vega shrugged. "But we never talked about it," he said, looking at Alvarez. "We never really talked at all."

"Together, the two of you had everything our killer wanted." She pointed at Vega. "You had the money, the prestige of being a Vega," she said, before shifting her focus onto Alvarez. "And you had a father's affection. He believes he's Magda Lopez's lost son— but Father Francisco, the man he believes is his father, rejected him in favor of you. That's why he raped Rachel and killed Olivero. He was trying to take those things away from both of you."

Look at you, talking like a real-life profiler. Our daddy'd be so proud.

Something Alvarez said earlier snagged on her brain and she reached for it, prying it loose. "You said, *I saw what'd been done to that girl—but I never saw the guy who did it,*" she said carefully. "But you did see *someone,* didn't you?"

"Yeah." Alvarez shook his head. "But he'd been at Saint Rose all night, same as me. And he was just a kid—no older than I was, really."

"Wade Bauer was barely eighteen years old when he killed his first victim," she told him. "He was 'just a kid' when he took Melissa

391

Walker. He raped and tortured her for eighty-three days before he was even old enough to legally buy beer."

Aw, darlin', you say the sweetest things.

Alvarez nodded. "He was an altar boy. Always at the church. Probably more than I was, but..."

"But what?"

He shrugged. "I don't—I got the feeling Father Francisco didn't like him much."

That had to be their guy. "What was his name?"

"I can't remember his name, but it was him," Alvarez insisted. "He was the one I saw standing over Melissa Walker that morning, right before she started moving."

She pushed, tried to remember that night, but couldn't. "What was he doing?" she said quietly, not sure she wanted to hear the answer. "When you saw him standing over her?"

Alvarez looked away for a second before he met her gaze. "He was smiling."

SEVENTY-SIX

THE WIRES KEPT SLIPPING out of her fingers. It was the blood. It was everywhere, welling and dripping from where her wrists had been cut and rubbed raw by the wire that bound them together. Ellie kept trying, even though she'd given up hope.

She fit the top scrap of wire into the keyhole, working it under the tumblers while the bottom scrap worked its way past them. It was an arduous process, one she had neither the time nor the dexterity for. It'd taken her a few minutes to find the paper clip and then bend and work it into two separate pieces. Her fingers were starting to cramp, having been pinched together for so long.

Her head felt like it had been split open. It throbbed with every bump and lift she made against the lock. She worked the top wire up and down a bit, slipping it past another tumbler.

Up and down. Not jiggling. Slow and easy. That was how Nulo taught her to do it, using paper clips to pick old padlocks he'd found in the bed of his uncle's truck, but that was a long time ago. They'd been kids then ...

Mark. He wanted her to call him Mark now.

The top wire slipped under the last tumbler and she lifted, allowing the bottom wire to push forward. Holding her breath, Ellie turned the lock inside the handle.

The door swung free, opening onto a dimly lit hallway. She wasn't blind after all. She could see shapes and shadows but her vision was blurry, wavering, like she'd opened her eyes under water.

Stepping forward, Ellie looked to her right. Stretched in front of her was a long corridor, dotted haphazardly with doors. All of them were shut.

Despite the warning ringing in her head, Ellie lurched across the hall. This door was locked too. Pressing her ear against it, she listened. Nothing but silence.

She shuffled forward, shoulder dragging against the wall as she went to keep herself upright. The floor pitched and rolled under her feet, like the deck of a ship. Her head throbbed, the pulse of it slamming in her ears, keeping time with her heart. Ahead of her was another door. This one was cracked open, brighter light spilling into the hallway.

The way out.

Reaching the door, she nudged it open. Widening the crack with a bump of her shoulder, she peered inside. The room was long and narrow. Windowless, its only source of light was one of those portable shop lights hanging from a hook set in the ceiling. An extension cord fed it power, a bright orange snake that wound up the wall to disappear through a hole drilled near the ceiling. At the far end of the room was an IV pole standing sentry over an empty hospital bed. Directly in front of her was a privacy screen.

She lurched forward and reached for the screen, but it clattered over, folding in on itself before hitting the floor. She cringed at the noise. Squeezed her eyes closed, awaiting discovery, but she heard no one.

She opened her eyes. Blood. Cast-off patterns crisscrossing along the walls. Gravitational splatters surrounding the ...

"What is that?" She breathed it out loud, shaking her head, trying to find her bearings.

It took her a few seconds to understand what was in front of her. She stepped forward, drawn closer by the horror of what she was seeing. It was a breeding stand, stained with blood and ... other things.

"They shit and piss themselves sometimes while I'm doing it. Rachel did."

She froze, bound hands clasped together in what felt like prayer. The voice behind her came from the open doorway.

"She screamed and cried. Begged me to stop ..." He stepped into the room, his shadow swaying in the light that spilled across the floor in front of her. "She didn't get it—what I was trying to do for her. None of them did."

Stay calm, draw him closer, she counseled herself. *Find an opportunity.* "And what's that?" she said softly. "What were you trying to do?"

"*What was I* ..." He let out an impatient huff. "I gave them a chance to deserve what they'd been given. I gave them a chance to *become*," he said, moving closer. "The same chance I'm giving you now."

Wait...

Her fingers laced around themselves, clenched tight. "Become what?"

"A saint. Like my mother," he said, his tone hushed in reverence. "She sacrificed her life for mine. She was a miracle and she gave that miracle to me."

She shook her head, eyes fixed on the shadow that swayed around her feet. "You're sick."

"I'm sick?" He laughed at her. "You have no idea *what* I am, Elena."

"Then tell me," she said softly, pulling him closer. "Explain it to me. Make me understand."

Wait…

"I'm a miracle—just like you." He was standing over her now, close enough to touch. "It was supposed to be you that night. Rachel was going to get it too, but it was *you* he wanted," he said quietly, his breath brushing against her nape. "He had such plans for you, Elena, but God intervened. He saved you."

"Oh, yeah?" Her hands twisted, fingers clenched together. "What did he save me for?"

"He saved you for me."

Now!

She spun, exploding back, giving her arms room to swing up and out. Her fisted hands caught him under his chin, the force of them crashing his teeth together, snapping his head back even as he fell.

He went down hard, skull bouncing off the concrete floor he'd been standing on just seconds before. He was stunned but still conscious, face painted bright red with blood. "Oh, Elena," he said, laughter bubbling up behind bloody teeth. "You really shouldn't have done that."

SEVENTY-SEVEN

"Call my partner. Tell her what's going on—Santos too," she said to Alvarez before tossing a glance at Vega. "And take him home. Stick with him until I call you."

Before either of them could launch a protest, she moved, crossing the kitchen to head for the front door before any of them could stop her.

That's right, darlin'. You just keep on goin'. You don't need any of them. Not when you have me.

"Wait—" The front door slammed behind her, cutting off the person following her, but she didn't stop, kept walking at a fast clip down the driveway. She needed to get the hell out of there before she completely lost it.

The door opened and slammed again. "I'm pregnant," Val huffed behind her as she followed her across the street. "You're really gonna make me *run*?"

Goddamnit.

She stopped long enough to dig her car keys out of her pocket. Long enough for Val to land a hand on her shoulder and spin her around. "Just stop for a second," she said, her dark eyes shiny with tears. "Nothing? You've got nothing to say to me?"

She took a deep breath and let it out. "Ms. Hernandez—"

"Oh, don't you *dare*," Val hissed at her, the hand on her shoulder slipping down to clamp around her wrist. "Don't you dare do that to me, Sabrina." She whispered her name, the tail of it catching on a stifled sob. "You can't just pretend—"

I know where she is. I know where he took Ellie.

Wade's words echoed in her head. He sounded nearly as desperate as she felt. "I don't believe you," she said, fully aware she sounded crazy. "I can't trust anything you say."

"Sabrina?" Instead of pushing her away, her insane outburst drew Val closer. "What are you talking about?"

I've never lied to you. You think about that, about all the times I've helped you. Showed you the way. I'll do it again, but it's gotta be now, darlin'.

"He has Ellie," she said, twisting herself from Val's grip. "I don't have time for this. *She* doesn't have time for this."

Val's hand flew to her mouth, her head shaking. She knew what her friend was thinking. What she was remembering. Not so long ago, it'd been Val who'd been taken. David Song had taken her and it had been Sabrina's fault, just like it was her fault now.

"He almost took you once. Wade," she said, watching as her words leeched the color from her friend's face. "He wrote about it. About how you flirted with him over cherry pie and the only thing that stopped him was the fact that he had other, more *pressing matters* to attend to."

"Andy Shepard," Val breathed, her hand dropping away from her face. Shepard had been the boy Wade stabbed to death in a gas station bathroom before severing his hand. He'd done it because Shepard had hit on her. Grabbed her ass.

He shoulda kept his hands off what didn't belong to him. He'd still be alive if he'd minded his manners.

Sabrina turned again, using the key fob to unlock the car. "You should've stayed in San Francisco," she said, sliding into the driver's seat before reaching out to snag the door, slamming it closed between them.

SEVENTY-EIGHT

RUN.

The word rang in her head, pushing her forward, blind and panicked. Through the door and down the hall she'd just traveled. She realized, too late, that she was heading in the wrong direction. The way out was behind her—blocked by the man she'd just knocked down.

Ellie kept pushing forward, hands and wrists aching. Head pulsating with every footfall. She felt her knees unhinge, pitching her forward. She staggered to the side, her temple scraping against the rough block wall. It stung, the pain thin and bright compared to her head and hands, but it didn't matter. She was still standing. Still moving.

Behind her, she heard him. Hands and feet gripping and scrambling across the floor, her name an angry bellow that chased her down the corridor. She moved faster, though she wasn't sure how. Every step she took threatened to topple her over but somehow, she kept moving. Kept herself from falling.

The corridor ended in a T and invisible hands pushed her, guiding her left. She couldn't afford to stop, even for a moment. "Is there another way out?" she said, breathless with the effort of running, hands outstretched in front of her to keep her balance.

Another door. This one closed. She could hear him behind her, still talking—whether it was to her or the person who was with him, she didn't know. Throwing her shoulder against the door, she turned the knob, pushing it open, and was instantly repelled by the stench of rotting flesh. This room was just as dark, just as small as the others, but this one wasn't empty.

There were bodies. Naked and rotting. A haphazard pile of decomposing limbs and mottled flesh. She recognized the body on top, his face aimed straight at her like he was waiting for her to arrive. He was missing person case Mark was working. His name was Robert.

She started to gag, shaking her head from side to side, not wanting to take another step. "*No, no, no …*"

But necessity pushed her inside and she turned, shutting the door just before her captor reached the top of the corridor. She listened, trying to breathe silently through her mouth, sure that he'd come barreling down the hallway, throw the door open, and drag her back—but he didn't. He must have turned right instead of left, and now he was moving farther and farther away until the sound of him faded almost completely.

She reached for the doorknob. She'd sneak back out, make a run for it.

Even as she thought it, she knew she'd never make it. She might make it out to the desert, but he'd just run her down like he did Maggie Travers. She didn't stand a chance. Her head was spinning. Her vision wavering. She knew she had a severe concussion. The bones at the back of her head felt loose, and they crackled every time she moved. She nodded, leaning her forehead against the door for a moment, her eyes slipping closed. She was tired. So tired...

She knew what she had to do. Ellie turned, facing the room. Looking through the dark, she saw the tangle of foul, broken bodies shoved into the corner, revealed only by the dim light breaking through underneath the door.

She had to hide.

SEVENTY-NINE

Take the next exit.

Sabrina did, taking a soft right at the off ramp marked Castle Dome Mine Rd. She'd been driving for almost twenty minutes with no other direction other than to head north on the 95.

The two-lane blacktop wound through low-lying mountains and she followed it past a sign marked Castle Dome Airport. Past what looked like an industrial complex plunked down in the middle of nowhere.

None of this was here when I found it. I'd been here for a few days, driving around looking for a place you and I could be alone. Not sure what made me come this way. Must've been divine intervention.

She was about fifty miles outside the city. Wherever she was going, it was remote.

Still clingin' to the belief I'm not real? You still think your subconscious is coughing up suppressed memories or some kinda shit? I thought we were past that, darlin'.

Her phone rang in the seat beside her and she reached for it. Church.

"If I didn't know any better, I'd say you didn't like me, Kitten," she said as soon as she answered. "It hurts."

"I'm sorry," Sabrina said, surprised she actually meant it. "Vega called and I—"

"I know, Alvarez filled me in," Church said. "He and Vega are at the ranch house with Santos, trying to sort through twenty years' worth of telenovela bullshit."

"And Val?" She'd be foolish to think Church was unaware that Val was in Yuma. She'd probably known she was here the second her plane touched down. "And her mom?"

"I'm on my way to them now." Church gave her a long-suffering sigh. "I'll pick them up and take them back to the station. Get them settled in to wait this out."

Relief washed over her. As long as they were with Church, they were safe.

"What do you need?" Church said. "Tell me where you are and I'll—"

This is a private party, darlin'. Your little friend ain't invited.

"I can't," she said carefully. "I can't tell you where I am."

"Okay." Church sounded concerned but she didn't argue. "Call me when it's over."

Any other partner would have been screaming at her to not go in alone, demanding to know where she was. Not Church. Whether it was because she was confident in Sabrina's ability to make it out alive or because she was tired of chasing her around, she didn't know. "Courtney—"

"Ahhh, my first name again." Church laughed but the sound of it rang hollow. "This oughta be good."

"Thank you," she said. "For not doing your job."

"You're a terrible influence on me, Kitten. Be careful." And then she was gone. Sabrina held the phone for a moment before scrunching down in her seat to tuck it into the front pocket of her slacks.

Stop the car.

She pulled over, the car tires sliding into the soft shoulder of the road before coming to a stop. She killed the engine and waited.

Get out.

Popping the driver's door, Sabrina climbed out of the car. As she did, her phone rang again.

It was Croft.

"Is she there?" she said by way of greeting. "Did you find her?"

"You need to work on your people skills, you know that?"

"Croft, I—"

"I know, I know—you don't have time for my bullshit." He sighed. "Yeah, I found her."

"Well?" she said, reaching into the car to pop the trunk before slamming the door closed. "What did she say?"

"She said, 'Get off my property, I'm calling the police,'" Croft said. "And my personal favorite, 'I have a gun.'"

Bitter disappointment coated her throat. "So she wouldn't talk to you?" she said, reaching into the trunk to pull out the duffle Church had put there when they arrived in Yuma. Inside was a collection of handguns and knives. Maps and flashlights. Clothes and boots.

What does it matter, darlin'? You're gonna find out who he is soon enough.

It matters to me, she thought. Pulling out a pair of cargos, she checked the tag. Her size. Tucked inside one of its legs was a T-shirt and FSS-issue Kevlar tank. If Church were here, she'd kiss her. She started to strip, phone wedged between her ear and shoulder, hands flying over buttons and buckles.

"No. But after a few hours of threats and bullying, mostly on her part," Croft said, sounding smug, "she finally agreed to talk to *you*."

Sabrina paused for a second, listening to Croft's cell phone being transferred from one hand to another. She put the phone on speaker and set it on the edge of the trunk before yanking the cargos up her hips, fastening them quickly. "Hello?"

"You're the FBI agent? The one who was at Paul's house when . . ." Graciella let her words trail off. "I found Rachel."

"Yes, ma'am," she replied. "My name is Agent Claire Vance." The lie stuck in her throat. She yanked the tank on over her head. "I know Paul didn't hurt Rachel when he was a boy and he didn't kill her." Next came the T-shirt. Suddenly, she felt like herself again. Reaching into the pocket of her discarded slacks, she pulled out the knife she'd been carrying with her since she left Montana.

Graciella let out a heavy sigh. "It was his brother."

Sabrina slipped the knife into the front pocket of her cargos. "Who is he, Ms. Lopez?" She didn't have time to explain that Mark Alvarez, not this mysterious villain, was Paul Vega's brother. What mattered was that the old woman *believed* that the man who'd come to her, claiming to be her abandoned nephew, was telling the truth. That's why she'd helped him. Kept his secrets. Protected him all these years. "He needs help. I can't help him if I don't know who he is." Dressed, she reached into the duffle again to pull out a police-issue Maglite. Clicking it on, she aimed the beam into the desert.

"He's so angry. Hateful," Graciella said, her tone full of remorse. "When he found me, I was sure I could help him—be the family he needed, but . . ." She cleared her throat. "I don't think he can be helped anymore. I think he's damned."

Wade's laughter rang in her head.

Damned? Ain't we all, darlin'—ain't we all?

EIGHTY

Toss your phone in the trunk.

That'd been the direction as soon as she hung up with Graciella Lopez. Rental cars came equipped with GPS. It'd take about
thirty seconds to tap into the rental company's database and locate
the car. But if she ditched her phone, there'd be no way for Church
to find her beyond this point.

That's the idea, darlin'. You're wasting time Ellie don't have.

She tossed the phone on top of the duffle inside the trunk and
slammed the lid. "Now what?" she said, aiming her gaze into the
desert.

Start walkin'.

She struck out at a light jog, pushing herself deeper and deeper
into the desert terrain that hugged the base of the Tank Mountains.
About fifteen miles to the west of her, the Colorado River flowed
and churned, winding its way through the dark. She wanted to
move faster, *needed* to move faster, but the ground beneath her feet
was unpredictable and thanks to an old injury, she wasn't as nimble
as she once was.

The beam of her flashlight caught on something, the shine of it bouncing back to her, nearly blinding her. It was a reflective sign, wired to the chain-link fence that had to be at least ten feet high. She tilted the light downward, aiming it at the dirt, letting the glow of it illuminate the sign.

YUMA PROVING GROUND
AUTHORIZED PERSONNEL ONLY
TRESPASSERS WILL BE PROSECUTED

"What now?"

Up and over, darlin', and don't get caught.

She hesitated again, this time not because of her leg or the terrain that stretched in front of her. If she was caught trespassing on a military installation, she'd be arrested. Her FBI credentials wouldn't protect her here. They'd run her through facial recognition software. With his military connections, Livingston Shaw would know the second her picture was scanned into the system. And then he'd come for her.

Like I said, don't get caught.

She clicked the flashlight off, tucking it into the long pocket of her cargos before digging the toe of her boot into a diamond-shaped hole in the chain link. Cresting the top of the fence, she swung over. Letting go, she dropped to the ground, landing in a crouch, the impact pulling at her damaged thigh.

How is that leg of yours holding up, darlin'?

Her leg. Wade had been the one to shoot her, sending bullet fragments scattering through her thigh. It'd taken years to rehab it and it still ached from time to time. Her days of running a five-minute mile were long gone but she could hold her own when she had to.

"Better than your face, asshole."

He laughed at her, the sound of it ringing in her ears.

That's only because you shot me in it.

She stood slowly, half expecting a swarm of camo-painted Humvees to descend, soldiers piling out, barking orders, waving guns. Nothing happened.

"Now what?" she said quietly, still half believing she was on the verge of getting caught.

Start walkin'. And you better hurry, darlin'. Little Ellie's 'bout out of time.

EIGHTY-ONE

SNAPBANG!

The noise, whatever it was, had been repeating itself for what felt like forever. Distant at first, it grew closer and closer with each revolution. Each volley jerked at her spine. Shot tension into her legs. Urged her to scramble from her hiding place. To run.

Somehow, she knew that's what he wanted. For her to run.

She pressed her lips together to keep herself from crying. Even the slightest of movements shifted the pile of bodies she lay underneath, shifting the cold flesh that surrounded her, revealing the sickly warm pockets caused by decomposition. These people had been discarded like trash. No ceremony. No ritual. Like they'd ceased to be human the moment they served their function.

SNAPBANG!

She swallowed the tears pressing against her throat. Tried not to imagine what it'd been like to be trapped here, days stretching into months, with a monster.

"Do you know what it takes to become a saint, Elena?" he called out to her, his voice echoing down the hall. "It takes pain. Blood and sacrifice. More than you can possibly imagine. It's not easy."

SNAPBANG!

"My mother did it—she died for me." He was even closer now, the sound of his voice reaching for her from just beyond the door. "Gave her life so that I could be born. I had to be cut from her womb. If not for her sacrifice, I'd be dead."

SNAPBANG!

"I was given a miracle … Just like you …" he said it softly, his voice carrying through the door that separated them. "Just like all of them."

SNAPBANG!

The noise was deafening, reverberating around the room, and she squeezed her eyes shut, waiting for him to come for her. She listened as the door swung open, its hinges protesting slightly as it was pushed wider and wider, until it banged into the wall behind it.

He'd found her.

EIGHTY-TWO

It was dark. Too dark to see anything. It didn't matter though—she didn't need to see to know she'd been led on a wild goose chase. She scanned the terrain anyway, hoping to catch sight of whatever it was that was supposed to be here without having to resort to talking to herself again.

How many times I have to tell you? You're not talkin' to yourself, darlin'. You're talking to me.

Casting a quick look over her shoulder, Sabrina caught sight of the airbase, nestled in the basin west of the 95. It looked close, but looks were deceiving. It had to be at least ten miles away. Deciding it was worth the risk, she lifted the Maglite from her pocket and switched it on. Sweeping its beam from left to right, she caught sight of it. A concrete slab in the middle of the desert.

"What the hell?" she breathed as she approached it. Smooth and level, she recognized it as the foundation of a building that was long gone. The disappointed was crushing. "There's nothing here."

Sure there is, darlin', you just have to know where to look.

The foundation had to be several thousand square feet in diameter. The building that used to stand here would have been enormous. Gritting her teeth, she walked the slab, peering closely at the smooth cement beneath her feet, determined to find what she was looking for. While she searched, Wade talked.

The building was still here when I found this place. It was a sanitarium—one of those places they used to stick TB patients back in the day. You and me, we had the run of the place ... remember, darlin'? The fun we had?

She remembered. She remembered running blindly, bouncing and stumbling her way down hallway after hallway. She remembered the feel of his eyes on her. Watching her, giving her hope that this time—maybe this time, she'd find a way out before he caught her. Before he hurt her again.

Never did find that way out, did you? Even death couldn't save you—not yours or mine.

She wasn't searching anymore. She'd gone still, lost in the memories this place and his words called up in her, face tipped down. Hand gripping the flashlight so tight her fingers were numb. She blinked, clearing the shadows from her vision.

Something shined in the beam of her flashlight and she ticked it over just a bit so she could make out what it was. A padlock.

Staring at it for a moment, she spoke. "There's no way he brought Ellie here," she said, shaking her head. "Government property? He wouldn't be stupid enough to risk it."

Stupid? No. What he is, is obedient. She's down there, darlin'. That's a fact.

"And then he relocked the padlock behind himself—from the outside?"

There's another entrance—more of an exit, really—about fifty yards in front of you. That's how he gets in and out...and that's where he'll be waitin' for you.

She didn't move, thinking it through slowly. If he was down there, he'd have both doors locked from the inside to deter anyone who might stumble onto the place from poking around.

Unless he knew she was coming.

She clicked the Maglite off and flipped it around so she held the handle of it like a baton. Next, she hunkered down in front of the door, hooking the index finger of her free hand through the arms of the padlock, securing it in place. Choking up on the base of the flashlight, she delivered fast, hard taps to the side of the lock while pulling down on it with the hook of her finger. She had it loose in less than a minute.

There was a rumbling behind her and she turned, sure she'd see those Humvees coming for her, but it wasn't arrest she had to worry about. It was rain. Clouds had collected overhead, pushing and crowding across the night sky, mottled and swollen like a bruise.

Pulling the padlock free of the hatch, Sabrina kicked the lever open with the heel of her boot before crouching to lift it up at its edge. The door was heavy and heat drifted off of it in waves, its metal still hot from baking all day in the sun. She pulled on it and it swung open onto a gapping maw so black it instantly swallowed the beam of her Maglite.

EIGHTY-THREE

SHE'S HERE. TIME TO stop messin' around, boy, and get to work.

The warning came, loud and clear, stopping him in his tracks. He stood in the doorway, bolt gun dangling from his fingers, gaze traveling around the room. He knew Elena was in here. Where else could she be? There was no way out. Her hiding places were limited. Still, he couldn't see her. His gaze fell on the pile of bodies he'd tossed in the corner.

There'll be plenty of time to play with little sister later. Right now there's a big, fat fish headin' your way that needs fryin'.

Melissa.

"Okay," he said, nodding his head, excited for what was to come. "Okay."

He hurried across the room to the place he'd piled his discards. Peeling them off one by one, he lifted them—letting them fall to the side until he found her.

Crouching, he rolled her over, her arm flopping to the side, soft and boneless. Her hair was gnarled and dried stiff against the back of her skull by blood. He pressed a thumb against her wrist, feeling for a pulse. It was there, thready and erratic. But it was still there.

Tick tock, motherfucker. We don't have time for your little one-man show.

He ignored the harsh words. Lifting Elena into his arms, he carried her down the hall, back to his workspace. He laid her on the hospital bed in full view before heading back the way he'd come.

You really think she's gonna save her, boy?

He could hear her. The metered rapping as she broke through the padlock. The heavy clank of the lever that closed the hatch. The faint squeal of hinges as she pulled it open. She'd be down the stairs soon.

"No," he said, quietly. "But I want her to try … I want her to hope. It isn't any fun unless they have hope. Isn't that what you taught me?"

In his head, Wade laughed.

EIGHTY-FOUR

THE BEAM OF HER flashlight finally found purchase. A set of stairs. Metal treads painted a matte black. She aimed the Mag to her right and its beam reflected back to her, dulled by gray cinderblock. To the left, the beam reached a short distance before being swallowed by the black.

Whaddya waitin' for? You aren't scared are you?

Wade's words came to her—half taunt, half dare—forcing her through the hatch, onto the narrow landing that topped the stairs. Lifting the Kimber off her hip, she aimed its barrel through the open doorway, taking them slowly, panning the light in a slow sweep in front of her, assessing her surroundings before each step.

Strickland would be so proud of her.

She thought of her old partner—the way he mothered her, pestered her into prudence. He was the voice of reason she so often lacked. She'd give anything to have him here with her now.

She realized something was wrong a split second too late. Stepping on the next stair tread, she planted her heavy-soled boot in its center but it gave way, folding beneath her foot like it was made of paper. She flung her arm out, grabbing for anything that would keep her upright, but the railing had been removed. There was nothing left to stop her fall.

Her boot sank, hooking into the frame that held the bogus stair tread in place. She pitched forward, Maglite flying from her grip, its beam a bright wing beating against the dark. She heard it land on the floor, watched the light of it spin below her even as she tumbled—face, shoulder, hip—each rotation jarring bone. Battering flesh.

She landed on her back, hitting the ground so hard her lungs seized in her chest, head ringing, joints screaming. She forced out the breath that was trapped in her lungs. Pulled in another, letting it out on a soft groan.

Don't be mad at me, darlin'. You had to know trusting me was a bad idea.

Her gun hand was empty, fingers clamped around nothing but air. She turned her head, searching for it, but it was gone. Swallowed by that field of black.

Get up. Get up. Get up.

This voice did not belong to Wade. It was hers, and hearing it inside her own head was a comfort. She struggled to obey. Rolling on her shoulder, she pushed her foot against the floor, urging the two of them to work in tandem. To get moving. Get herself upright. The cool concrete bit into the bed of her foot. She'd lost her goddamn boot on the staircase.

"You don't know how happy we are that you accepted our invitation, Melissa."

She was half off the floor when she looked up, her eyes wheeling upward to catch sight of his face. Again, she was struck by how little he'd changed in the years since she'd known him. It was like he'd been suspended in time, waiting for her to come back.

"Hey, Manny. How's it going?" she said, spitting out a mouthful of blood while her hand crept slowly along the floor, searching for her gun. The wedge of sky visible through the open hatch above them opened up. A thunderous crack reverberated in her chest.

"We're better," he told her, matching her tone, "now that you're here." He smiled down at her. It was the last thing she saw before he delivered a vicious kick to her face. After that, all she saw was dark.

EIGHTY-FIVE

MANNY ROBLES. THE BUSBOY from Luck's. He'd been a foster kid back then, bouncing from placement to placement, marking time until he aged out and could start life on his own. Until he was no longer at the mercy of people who claimed to have his best interests at heart. Obviously, there'd been something broken in him, but she'd missed it, too caught up in her own nightmare to see the monster lurking in her peripheral. So many monsters…

He was dragging her down a dimly lit corridor, her arm jerked over her head, stretched painfully, his fingers clamped roughly around her wrist. She was groggy and her face felt fat. Her bare foot was numb, ankle swollen.

"… gotta tell you, I didn't think it'd work," he told her, casting a quick look at her over his shoulder. "When Wade laid out the plan to get you here, I was sure you wouldn't be stupid enough to take the bait." He smiled. "I've never been so happy to be wrong."

The DNA under Stephanie Adams fingernails. He'd planted it in an attempt to lure her out of hiding. And Wade told him to do it. He'd been talking to Manny, just like he talked to her. But it was more than just talk, apparently. Wade was driving him. Influencing him. That's when she realized Wade was gone from her head. Not just quiet, but *gone*.

But he hadn't gone far.

"Fuck off," she muttered, rolling the eye that wasn't rapidly sealing itself shut to catch glimpse of her captor while her free arm dragged and stuttered along beside her. She thought maybe her left shoulder was dislocated, which meant her dominant arm was pretty much useless.

Manny rounded the corner, pulling her along behind him, through an open doorway into a long narrow room, lit with a hanging shop light. He stopped dragging her, dropping her arm as soon as they breached the doorway. There was a bed shoved against the far wall, a small dark figure sprawled across it.

Ellie. It was Ellie. Sabrina felt her throat close, a saltwater sting in her sinuses, but she pushed it back, focusing her attention on Ellie's chest, watching for the rise and fall that would tell her there was still hope. She counted to twelve before she caught sight of her rib cage expanding, slight and slow. She was alive but barely.

Manny finally looked down at her. "Do you believe in miracles, Melissa?"

Instead of answering him she averted her gaze, focusing on trying to lift her left arm. It wouldn't budge.

"I do," he told her in a companionable tone, leaning into her field of vision. "I believe in miracles. Want to know why?"

She stared through him, refusing to play his game. The knife Michael gave her was in her left-side pocket. As soon as she got the opportunity, she was going to stab him with it.

Like he could read her mind, his expression darkened and he straightened himself with a nod. "Okay," he said, making his way over to where Ellie lay. Manny placed his hand over her nose and mouth. Within seconds she started to twitch from lack of oxygen. "*Do you want to know why?*" This time his tone was hard, his black glare drilling holes in her face.

"Yes," she said, nodding. "I want to know why."

He smiled. "Because my life has been filled with them." He lifted his cupped hand from Ellie's face. "My mother. You. Wade. I'm surrounded by the unexplainable. My very existence defies logic."

"She's not your mother—Magda Lopez." Her mouth lifted slightly, drawn tight by her cold tone. "She's not your mother, Manny. Paul Vega isn't your brother. Father Francisco isn't your father. Graciella told me how you heard the family story about the twin boys, one raised by the family and one given away. How you latched on and believed it was you. Needed to believe it was you." She shook her head. "But it's not. You're not a miracle. Graciella realized it, but you wouldn't listen. You're just another sad, sick asshole with delusions of grandeur—just like Wade."

His face went dark again. Reaching down, he fisted his hand in the hair at the top of her head and yanked her upward, jarring the ball and socket joint of her separated shoulder. The pain of it pushed in on her vision, squeezing it until all that was left was a field of white. He flung her forward, her swollen ankle as brittle as cracked glass that gives way as soon as pressure is applied.

She caught herself, fingers digging into the mattress Ellie lay on. "Do you believe in miracles, Melissa?" he said again, his words followed by a loud, sharp *SNAPBANG!* a moment before she felt the hard press of metal at the base of her skull.

EIGHTY-SIX

"Well, do you, darlin'?"

The words had been spoken out loud, the breath of them fluttering against the nape of her neck. Sabrina nodded, her right arm inching slowly toward the edge of the mattress she was pressed against. Right hand, left pocket. Tricky but not impossible.

"Yes." The knife dug into her thigh and she shifted, lifting her leg against the bed, trying to wedge its frame under the knife enough to raise it from her pocket. "I believe in miracles, Manny." Her fingers brushed against the top of the knife and she leaned forward, pushing it up until she could close them around it. She pulled it free, concealing it beneath her hand on top of the mattress.

"Good," he said, the pleasant tone at odds with the application of pressure to her skull. "That's good, Melissa. Now I want you to give her a part of what you've been given. I want you to save her."

Save her.

Again, the voice she heard was her own. This time she nodded in response before bowing her head, trying to buy herself some time. Her left arm was useless. Her ankle too. If she struck, she had to be quick and she had to be sure, because there was little chance of her getting away.

She focused on Ellie, the shallow expansion of her chest. The pale bluish tinge that stained her mouth. She was dying. Slipping away, right in front of her.

Save her.

"We both know I can't do that." She curled her fingers around the short hilt of the blade, tucking it tight against her stomach to conceal it. "Don't we, Wade."

The pressure against her skull intensified.

"I know you're in there. I know Manny isn't running the show, not anymore." She raised herself slightly onto the ball of her good foot, pushing back against the sting of metal. "Probably hasn't been for a while now. How long did it take before you realized Nulo wasn't his real name? That he lied to you in case you came after him? Manny never trusted you."

He dropped the bolt gun. Gripping her shoulder, spinning her around, his empty hand raised and fisted—already rocketing toward her face.

She spun, using the momentum he created to swing out with the blade even as she evaded the punch. It grazed her temple, catching her in the ear. The blade in her hand arced upward, separating the fabric of his shirt and the flesh beneath it.

She missed her target, slicing his chest instead of his throat. He roared, the hand on her shoulder gripping her, pulling her closer before throwing her into the wall, her hip slamming into the cinderblock. Her knife clattered to the floor, spinning out of reach.

She didn't scramble for it. She didn't assess the damage she'd caused. She didn't wait for him to attack. She just turned and fled.

EIGHTY-SEVEN

She fought to stay upright, her abused ankle wobbling and bowing with each heavy footfall. Down the corridor he'd dragged her through. Around the corner. Past closed doors.

Like Sabrina hoped, he followed her.

"Just like old times, right, darlin'?" The words chased her down the hall, spoken out loud.

She ignored what hearing Wade's tone and cadence carried by the voice of another actually meant. "You're right—Manny ain't drivin' this bus no more. I let him have his fun with all his miracle mumbo jumbo. But now that you're here, it's my turn."

Keep moving. Don't look back.

Her own voice again, urging her to focus. The sound of rain grew louder and louder until the sound of him behind her became lost in the clamor of it. The doorway came into view and the staircase beyond it. She looked past it, concentrating on the beam of her flashlight that still spilled across the floor.

Hands planted themselves on her back and he shoved her with a roar that sounded like her name. She stumbled into the wall, flinging herself to the side, through an open doorway.

She fell face first at the foot of the stairs. Her landing was followed by a bright, breathless pain she recognized instantly. Manny fell with her, the bulk of his body pressing her into the floor, the knife Michael gave her lodged in her back.

"*You're mine, Melissa,*" he screamed at her, spittle hitting the back of her neck. She felt the shift of his hand, repositioning his grip on the hilt of the blade as he readied to lift it. Drag it from her to stab her again. "*You're mine and there ain't—*"

She rolled, burying the blade even deeper, ripping it from his hand. As she rolled, she swung, crashing her right fist into his jaw, breaking teeth. Fracturing bone. The force of the blow lifted him, created space between them, and she planted her boot in that space, kicking out.

Suddenly she was free. She rolled over again and started to crawl.

Get the flashlight. Find the gun. Save Ellie.

Behind her, he laughed, jagged and gleeful.

"You know where we are, darlin'? This room is special," he said, giving her a bloody grin. "This is where I fucked you the last time."

She kept crawling, attention focused on the wash of light in front of her.

"Where I killed you." He'd found his feet. She could hear the shuffling limp of him coming after her. Moving faster than he should've been able to.

It didn't matter. She had work to do.

Get the flashlight. Find the gun. Save Ellie.

He was standing over her now and he planted his foot in the small of her back, pushing her flat against the floor. "The way you bled for me ... the way you fought me." He stooped, gripping the hilt of the knife, jerking it from the meat of her shoulder. "And now here we are again, just like the good ol' days."

She stretched, arm and hand reaching out, fingers brushing against the long handle of the flashlight. Pushing it farther out of reach. Above them, the rain fell. A torrent of water poured through the open hatch and ran down the stairs in sheets.

He hooked his foot into her armpit, flipping her over, arms flopping above her head. Kneeling, he straddled her hips, grinning down as he ran his empty hand over her torso, pushing her shirt up, exposing her belly. He bowed his head, running reverent fingertips across the collection of scars that splayed across it, reading what they said. "I gotta admit," he said, dragging the tip of the blade across her flesh, leaving a thin, red ribbon of blood in its wake. "I'm a little nervous, darlin'. It's almost like our first time all over again."

Sabrina stretched her right arm into the dark, her fingers splayed wide, the tips of them digging into the hard floor beneath her. The tip of her middle finger brushed against something round and smooth. The trigger guard of her gun.

She dragged the Kimber toward her even as she lifted it, swinging the barrel of it toward him, burying it in his chest. The smile on his face dimmed. His eyes flared. She pulled the trigger twice in rapid succession. Slugs slammed into his chest, blowing out the back of his rib cage.

Sabrina kicked him off of her and started crawling. Hands and knees, one after the other. Her shoulder had snapped back into place when Manny threw her into the wall, but it was still slow going. It still hurt like a bitch.

You think it matters, darlin'? You think you've won?

He was in her head again. Heavy with rage despite the flippant tone of his words.

You're mine, Melissa. You belong to me.

She'd made the stairs and started up, fingers gripping stair treads as she clawed her way upward, toward the open hatch.

I'll just find another pony to ride. Eventually, you and me, we'll dance again.

Rain lashed at her face and hands, harder and harder with every inch she climbed.

Until then, I'll be right here. I'm always gonna be here.

She made the landing and tucked her chin into her chest against the rain that battered her, the voice inside her head growing fainter and fainter.

Wait. Where you think you're goin'? You can't leave me here.

Wade's tone was barely a whisper, edged with something that made her smile.

Fear.

"Watch me," Sabrina said, her hands and knees sliding over the lip of the hatch. She fell forward, through the open doorway, battered face pressed against rain-cooled concrete, head blissfully silent.

She'd made it out. She was free.

EIGHTY-EIGHT

SABRINA SAT IN A blue plastic chair rather than on the bed she'd been ordered into. "Put this on," the nurse said, tossing a johnnie onto the bed beside her before rushing out, yanking the curtain closed behind her. As soon as the woman was gone, she hobbled over to the supply cabinet and jimmied the lock. Finding an ACE bandage, she used it to wrap her ankle. It was still swollen. Not broken, but the sprain was bad enough to slow her down. Afterward, she wadded up the hospital gown and used it to stop the blood weeping from her shoulder blade.

Now she waited. Truth was, she'd have left hours ago if not for the fact she'd been stabbed in a place she wasn't able to stitch up herself. So instead of making a slick getaway, she sat, pressing her shoulder into her wadded-up hospital gown wedged behind her against the wall, watching CNN with the captions on because she couldn't reach the remote.

"Wanna play doctor?"

She looked up to see Church in the space between the curtain and the wall, wagging a surgical staple gun in her direction. In her other hand was a paper bag. She was wearing scrubs—bright purple bottoms with a multicolored, tie-dyed top. Her hair was in a ponytail. The badge clipped to her shirt front was turned backwards to hide the ID photo on it. If Sabrina saw her in the hall, she'd have walked right past her without a second glance.

Beyond her, nurses and doctors buzzed around, soft-soled shoes squeezing against worn linoleum while they tangoed with an assortment of uniform officers and reporters. It was starting all over again. Santos had already called twice with interview requests from local news stations—his superiors were pushing him to hold a press conference. It was only a matter of time before the story went national.

"Yeah," she said as she repositioned herself against the wadded-up hospital gown. "The sooner I stop leaking, the sooner I can get the hell out of here."

"Amen to that, Kitten." Church slipped into the curtained room to circle behind her, snagging another chair. A moment later, Sabrina heard the snap of surgical gloves being pulled on.

"How's Ellie?" she said, hissing out a slow breath when Church peeled the johnnie away from her wound.

Church sighed. "She lost a lot of blood. Fractured skull. Severe concussion," she said like she was reading off a grocery list. "They're worried about brain damage."

Listening to the commotion in the hall, Sabrina remembered when it had been her. The bright lights and the noise. All those frantic hands fighting to keep her here. To save her, when all she wanted to do was float away. She wished it was her this time too. She wished it was her instead of Ellie. Not because she wanted to die but because if Ellie did, she'd never forgive herself.

"Hey." Church's hand landed on her good shoulder and gave it a squeeze. "If she's anything like her sister, she's going to fight her way through," she said, digging her finger into the tear the knife had made in her shirt, opening it even wider so she could assess the damage. "She's going to be okay—they both will." Church cleaned the stab wound on her shoulder, dabbing it with betadine-soaked gauze.

She nodded, smiling despite everything that'd happened over the last couple of hours. "You're getting pretty good at that."

"At what?" Church said distractedly as she gave Sabrina two quick jabs with a hypodermic needle.

"Pretending to care."

Church laughed, pulling the wound closed with one hand while straddling the stapler over the gash with the other. "I'm a fast learner," she said, right before she pulled the trigger.

Sabrina winced, her not-quite-numb flesh zinging. "How'd you find me?"

"Remember room service in Helena?" She pulled the trigger again, the staple shooting forward to anchor into the meat of her shoulder. "I ordered the entire menu and poured you a glass of orange juice?"

She remembered. She'd been sure it'd been poisoned. "I remember."

"I put a tracker in it." Church pinched. Pulled the trigger. "You're welcome. And don't worry, it'll flush out of your system in another couple days."

After a few moments, Sabrina asked another question. "Where will you go?"

"If I told you that, I'd have to kill you, Kitten," she answered, repeating the pinch-and-shoot process as she followed the line of her wound.

Sabrina thought of the man she'd called Jared. The man who was her brother, if not in blood than in shared experience. "Back to your family?"

Church paused, pressing the stapler into her shoulder. "That's where you and I differ, Kitten." She pulled the trigger again, setting the staple deep into her shoulder. "I don't have a family to go back to."

Sabrina breathed through the pain, eyes glued on the screen in front of her. The banner on the bottom of it read LIVE: SACRAMENTO, CALIFORNIA. Above it, a small group of men in expensive suits gathered around each other, shaking hands and clapping shoulders on the steps of the capitol building, pausing for the flash bulbs before disappearing inside. "You can always—"

One of those men was Ben.

Sabrina focused in on the words scrolling across the bottom of the screen, trying to make sense of what she was seeing.

Senatorial candidate Benjamin Shaw met with a committee to discuss his potential appointment to the California Senate by Governor…

The stapling had stopped but the head of the gun was still pressed into her shoulder. She didn't have to see Church's face to know she'd just seen the same thing. "Did you know?"

Church pulled the trigger a final time. "Did I know what?" she said, setting the stapler down. "That he sold his soul to his father to save everyone you've ever loved?" She wiped the wound with betadine a final time before covering it with gauze. "Yes."

"He told you not to tell me, didn't he?" Sabrina said, looking at Church over her shoulder.

"Yes." Church anchored the gauze in place with a length of surgical tape, smoothing it out with her thumbs before meeting her gaze. "There're some military types snooping around. Asking why the FBI didn't contact them before poking around in their backyard," she said, standing. She reached down, retrieving the paper bag from the floor before setting it on the bed. "Just to be safe, I think you should take the long way home."

EIGHTY-NINE

EASING HER JACKET OVER the gauze padding on her shoulder, Sabrina winced a bit as she zipped it up over the ballistics tank. Her shirt lay in a tattered mess on the floor.

Tucked into the tank was the chain Michael gave her. The key hanging from it would get her home. She cast a final look at the television. The story about Ben's pending senatorial appointment had been replaced by an image of Detective Santos standing in front of the hospital. Mark Alvarez stood next to him, hands dug into the front pockets of his Dockers, face tilted toward the sidewalk. Both of them looked uncomfortable, but Alvarez wore an expression of dazed panic that said he knew his life was about to change. When news broke about Manny Robles and his delusion of being the "lost" Vega child, someone would ferret out what really happened to Father Francisco Vega's illegitimate sons. Shine a spotlight on Paul Vega's life and the troubled childhood of Mark Alvarez, aka Nulo.

She understood exactly how poor Alvarez felt.

The phone in her pocket let out a buzz. A text from Church: **Hospital surveillance is down for the next fifteen.**

She looked inside the bag Church left behind. A baseball cap and two medication bottles. Tramadol and 800mg Ibuprofen—one for pain, the other for swelling—and what looked like a turkey sandwich with a note taped to it.

Don't worry, it's not poisoned.

C

Under the sandwich was a pair of worn journals. She lifted them out, reading the names written in neat, heavy block letters across their fronts. MELISSA. FRANKIE.

Her phone buzzed again: **Shake a leg, Kitten.**

Returning the journals to the bag, she tucked her phone away before slipping the hat over her head. Tugging the bill of it low over her brow, she left the curtained room. Formulating an escape route on the fly, she headed for the elevator. The emergency room entrance was a zoo, clogged with reporters and even more uniforms. Better to go up and over. She'd use the sky bridge, cross to a different tower and ride back down before exiting the hospital through the back. She'd catch a bus to the bank and the safety deposit box Michael—

The elevator *dinged* a split second before the doors slid open and she slipped in, keeping her face tipped down as she pressed the button for the fourth floor. The doors began to close but bounced back when someone stuck their hand into the car. She didn't have to look up to know who it was.

"The doctors are *cautiously optimistic* about Ellie's recovery," Val said quietly. "They told me the FBI agent who brought her in saved her life, so ... thank you."

"Ellie's a fighter." She nodded, eyes stuck on the button panel in front of her, remembering what Church said earlier. "Like her sister."

Val was quiet for a moment. "You're leaving," she said, her voice broken and sharp.

Sabrina nodded her head, the movement of it drawing a small sound from the back of Val's throat.

"Riley dropped out of college." Val looked at her, pleading. "She's getting ready to take the SFPD entrance exam. She feels like she's supposed to follow in your footsteps," she said, her tone laced with panic, trying to find a way to make her stay. "Like it's her job to finish what you started now that you're … gone. Maybe if she knew that you—"

"No." She shook her head, even though the thought of Riley as a cop filled her with a dizzying mix of anxiety and pride. "She can't know. No one can know," she said, finally raising her gaze to meet her friend's. "You have to forget about me. Move on. All of you."

Val nodded and looked away, rubbing a gentle hand over her belly while she let out a slow breath. "I know." When she looked back at her, there were tears in her eyes. "Are you happy?"

She thought of the house she shared with Michael. Of the kids running through the woods. Grilled cheese and pancakes. Her dog sunning herself on the front porch. "Yes," she whispered and she *was*.

The elevator *dinged*, signaling their arrival to the fourth floor.

She reached down, finding her friend's hand dangling between them. "Thank you, for saving me. For fighting for me, even when I didn't want you to," she said, giving Val's hand a gentle squeeze.

Val smiled through her tears. "Anytime."

When the elevator doors slid open, Sabrina exited alone.

NINETY

Yaak, Montana
October 2016

"Here you go, miss ..."

The truck slowed, its vintage engine easing from growl to purr while it rolled into the stop. He pulled over onto the soft shoulder of the road, mindful not to jostle the young woman who rode in the truck bed. He'd picked her up just outside of Eastport, walking along the 95 like she'd been out for a Sunday stroll instead of stranded in the middle of nowhere. She hadn't stuck out her thumb or flagged him down, but he pulled over anyway and asked where she was headed.

"South," she'd said, swinging a long leg over the back of his truck and settling into the bed of it.

"Miss ..." He hesitated before reaching for her through the truck's rear sliding window, hand hovering just above her shoulder. He didn't want to touch her. He'd made that mistake about a hundred miles back, tapping her on her shoulder when he pulled over in

Moyie Springs for gas, to tell her this was as far as he'd be willing to take her. She'd damn near snapped his hand off at the wrist for his trouble.

She'd apologized by filling both gas tanks on his Ford—the primary and the auxiliary—and offered him five hundred dollars if he'd take her as far as Yaak. He'd been on his way to Troy but he'd seen the wad of cash she had on her when she paid for his gas, so he figured she was good for it. He also figured driving a few hours out of his way'd be a hell of a lot easier than trying to take it off her.

She'd been sleeping since they passed the Golden Nugget about fifty miles back. Or at least he thought she was sleeping. She wasn't much of a talker and his offer for her to ride up front with him had been met with nothing more than a slight narrowing of her eyes, shadowed by the brim of her battered ball cap and a polite but firm *no thank you*.

He sighed, rubbing a hand over his chin, the stubble that covered it rasping with each pass of his palm. The nervous gesture sent a twinge through his abused wrist, reminding him of what she'd told him while he cradled his wrist and she pumped his gas. *I don't like being touched.*

He decided to try one more time without the touching, more willing to waste a few more minutes trying to wake her than he was willing to risk her getting hold of him again. "Miss, you're home now," he told her, leaning in just a bit so that his voice carried through the narrow opening of the window.

Like *home* was a magic word, she stirred, the movement pushing back the hem of her jacket, exposing the pistol on her hip. He'd caught sight of it when she'd first climbed into the bed of his truck. Factoring in the olive drab cargos and plain black shirt along with the heavy-soled hiking boots and mannish haircut, he figured her for another Montana Militia wannabe.

That'd changed back in Moyie Springs.

He sat back in his seat, making sure his hands were in plain view, watching her from the relative safety of the rearview. Reaching into the long pocket of her cargos, she produced a wad of cash as fat as his fist. He watched her peel off the promised five hundreds plus a few more—nearly double what she'd promised him. Reaching through the window, she tapped him on the shoulder with the offered bills.

He turned slightly, reaching over his shoulder to take the offered cash, a nervous grin on his face. "I thank you kindly." He gave the stack of bills that connected them a tug but she didn't let go, forcing him to meet her gaze.

"Did you give me a ride?" she said quietly, snagging him with a pair of hazel eyes that didn't seem to belong in the face that carried them.

He thought about the gun strapped to her hip and the fact that he believed with 100 percent certainty she knew how to use it. "No, ma'am. Picked up a drifter just over the border, but I dropped him at the Nugget so he could catch on with one of the logging camps round here. Don't believe he mentioned which one."

She finally gave him a smile, just a ghost of one really—gone in an instant as it coasted across her face. She abruptly released the money into his hand, the jerk of it sending a twinge up his wrist.

"Drive safe," she said, shouldering her backpack before swinging a leg over the side of his truck to climb out. He listened to the sound of her boots crunching in the soft gravel of the shoulder, watching as she walked away.

Disappearing into the trees, like she'd never been.

NINETY-ONE

Kootenai Canyon, Montana

SHE'D BEEN GONE FOR forty-two days and they'd settled into a comfortable rhythm without her. He made breakfast every morning before Miss Ettie took the kids upstairs. It was fall and much to their disappointment, that meant homeschool was back in session.

Lunch was usually spent in the field, mending fences or driving their small herd of cattle into the lower pastures for the coming winter. Dunn was a fast learner and even more importantly, game. He seemed as determined to stave off the boredom of isolation as Michael was.

Dinner was a quiet affair, the evening usually ending with him and Dunn doing dishes before he headed out to the barn to listen to the HAM radio spit static until he was ready to burn the whole place to the ground. He wasn't sure when he'd come to the conclusion that she wasn't coming back. He only knew that it hurt. He imagined that Phillip Song had made good on his threat to offer her a way home and she'd taken it. Still, he couldn't bring himself to take off the ring she'd put on his finger. He was pretty sure that would hurt worse than her actual leaving.

"Give me two," Dunn said, peeling a pair of cards from his hand before tossing them onto the tiny table between them. Michael dealt him the cards and watched while he tucked them into his hand, eyes narrowed, mouth quirked just a bit at the corner. They'd played enough cards for him to know it meant Dunn didn't have shit.

"We gonna ride out to 5J tomorrow, round up the last couple head?" Dunn said while rearranging his cards. Another indicator his hand was busted.

Surprisingly, he and Dunn hadn't killed each other yet. All things considered, he figured that was a good thing. Neither one of them had broached the subject of how Dunn had managed to remove his chip since the day he turned up in his kitchen. He didn't seem in a great hurry to share, beyond making sure he knew there would be a price to be paid for the how-to. For his part, Michael wasn't in any hurry to know how he did it.

Without Sabrina, it didn't really matter.

"Yeah," he said, waiting for his opponent to fold. "We've got a couple of first-year heifers out there. I don't want them—"

Across from him, Dunn went stiff a split second before Avasa picked up her head, a quiet growl rumbling in her chest. "Company," Dunn said, gaze aimed over his shoulder, cards spilled, face up, across the table.

Michael turned to see a figure standing on the bridge, watching them. It was dusk, the sun just beginning to slip behind the surrounding cliffs. All he caught in the gathering dark was a pair of cargos. Ball cap pulled low. Gun bulge under the jacket.

"Friend of yours?" Dunn said behind him, tone casual and calm.

"No," he said, even though his heart stopped and stuttered in his chest. "Go get—"

The dog shot off the porch like a bullet. Head low, legs moving so fast they became a blur, streaking across the yellowing grass. She let out a bark and the figure dropped the backpack a moment before it hunkered down to receive the dog with open arms.

They went down together, Avasa's front paws planted firmly, pinning their visitor to the bridge beneath them, her tail whipping so hard and fast her back end swung with it, nearly knocking her over with every pass.

"Well, the dog seems to be friendly with whoever it is," Dunn said behind him, the words delivered over the soft scraping of his chair along the floorboards of the porch. A few second later, Michael heard the screen door bang shut behind him.

As soon as Dunn was gone, Michael moved. Down the porch steps and across the lawn, gaining speed with each step until he was running. Stopping short, he stood at the lip of the bridge, hands moving to the front pockets of his jeans, watching Avasa greet her mistress.

The commotion with the dog knocked her hat off her head to reveal a dyed head of hair almost as short as his. She was thin again, making him wonder where she'd been. What happened to her. He wanted to ask but didn't. There was plenty of time for that, now that she was home.

———

Seeing his boots, Sabrina nudged Avasa to the side, whispering a short command that held the dog quivering but still. She ran a

442

hand over her flank, still whispering, the dull glint of her wedding band catching the dying sun with each pass. He stepped closer, until he was standing over the pair of them.

"You hungry?" His voice sounded rough, like his throat was lined with sandpaper. He cleared it. "Miss Ettie made a chicken gumbo and I think there's a few—"

"I just dragged myself to hell and gone"—Sabrina stood slowly, eyes narrowed—"and all you have to offer me is leftover gumbo?"

"It's good gumbo."

"I'm sure it is," she said. "But I don't want it."

"What do you want, Sabrina?" The words sounded heavier. What he was asking her had nothing to do with food.

"I want pancakes."

"Pancakes, huh?" He pulled a hand free, stooping to fetch her hat. She caught his smile as he bent and it bolstered her. Gave her hope.

"Yup." She nodded, taking the hat he offered her and tossing it over her shoulder. "And I want them every day, for the rest of your life."

"Every day—for the rest of my life." He reached for her, pulling her into his arms, grinning like an idiot. "I think I can help you with that."

"Promise?" she said, slipping a hand along the back of his neck, pulling him closer.

"Promise," Michael whispered, right before he kissed her.

ABOUT THE AUTHOR

Maegan Beaumont is the author of the award-winning Sabrina Vaughn thriller series. Her debut novel, *Carved in Darkness*, was awarded a gold medal by Independent Publisher in 2014, as well as being named a Foreword Book of the Year finalist and Best Debut Novel of 2013 by *Suspense Magazine*. When she isn't locked in her office, torturing her protagonists, she's busy chasing chickens (and kids), hanging laundry, and burning dinner. She is almost always in the company of her seven dogs, her truest and most faithful companions, and her almost-as-faithful husband, Joe. .

ACKNOWLEDGMENTS

Thank you to my wonderful friends and family for making allowances and for keeping me sane, even when it seemed like a lost cause. If it weren't for you, I'd be lost. Melissa—my partner in crime. My writer peeps—Susana, Mary, Linda, and Holly—who aren't afraid to tell me when it's shit. Janey Mack—one of the most talented writers I know. Les Edgerton—the most supportive and encouraging man I've ever met. You give till it hurts, Les. Don't think I don't notice.

So much love to my wonderful husband, Joe, who is more supportive than I deserve, and to my long-suffering children, who gauge my mood with the question, "How many words did you write today?" I could write a million words a day and not count myself more blessed than having you at my side has made me.

For my dad—thank you for the hot meals, the after-school pickups, the Sadie-sitting, and the way you look at me when you think I'm not looking. Knowing I make you proud is what keeps me going.

Thank you to my wonderful team at Midnight Ink—Terri Bischoff, my badass editor (with the flask to prove it!) who fights for her authors every day, and Nicole Nugent, who takes the messes I give her and makes them into real, live books! Thanks to Katie Mickschl, the best freakin' publicist on the planet, and rest of the MI crew that I've never met but who I know work hard for me.

Thank you to Miss Mary Lillie, for catching all the things I don't. (SO. MANY. THINGS.) My fantastic agent, Chip MacGregor, for being the kind of agent every writer dreams of.

And for you Annie. We're not in each other's lives every day, but we are in each other's lives forever. I'm so glad Mrs. Carter asked me to be your tour guide—hope you don't hold it against her too much and that I've been half the friend to you that you have been to me. Here's to the next thirty years …